Picasso's Errand

Picasso's Errand

Daniel Hauser

Writers Club Press
San Jose New York Lincoln Shanghai

Picasso's Errand

All Rights Reserved © 2001 by Daniel Hauser

No part of this book may be reproduced or transmitted in any form or by any means, graphic, electronic, or mechanical, including photocopying, recording, taping, or by any information storage retrieval system, without the permission in writing from the publisher.

Writers Club Press
an imprint of iUniverse.com, Inc.

For information address:
iUniverse.com, Inc.
5220 S 16th, Ste. 200
Lincoln, NE 68512
www.iuniverse.com

This is a work of fiction. All characters and events are complete creations of the author's imagination.

ISBN: 0-595-19151-7

Printed in the United States of America

For Tammy and the kids

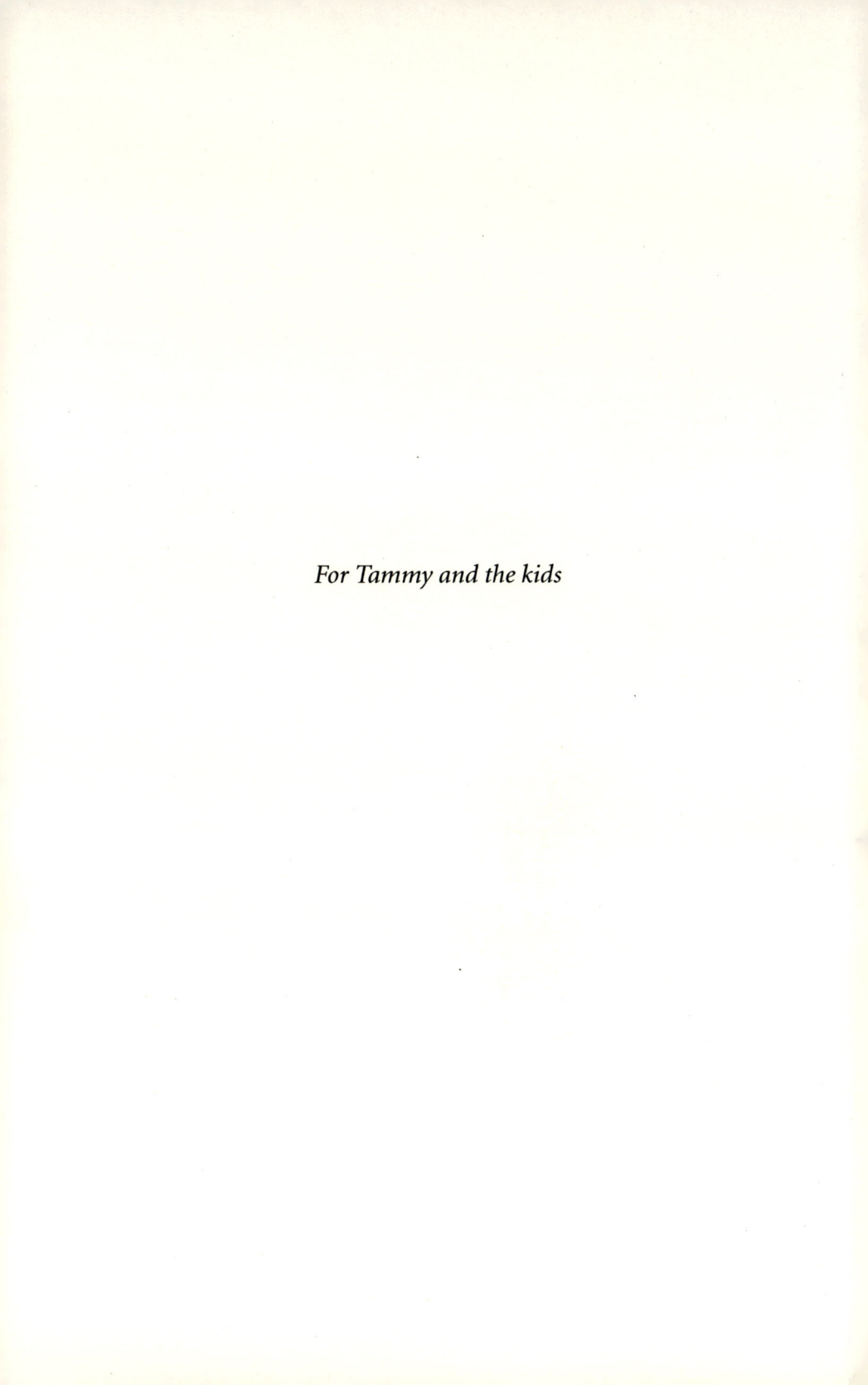

Chapter One

OK, I might as well admit it up front: I hate old people. They smell, can't hear worth a damn, are about as agile as a turtle on Valium and are likely at any moment to keel over.

My sister, Angela, says I don't like old people because I am afraid of them. She's right. I am afraid of them but not for the reasons she claims. She thinks I am afraid of them because in them I see my own mortality. No, I fear them because they are one big fucking hassle after another.

They are constantly losing things—their car keys, their way, their teeth, their hair, their control of bodily fluids. It's just not worth it to be around them.

"You could learn a thing or two from your elders," says my mother, who at 49 is not old. Yeah, I could learn how to lose stuff and be irritating as hell.

I've yet to meet one geezer that has given me reason to think otherwise. Relatives, neighbors and even complete strangers. If they can remember the Depression, they are depressing.

Take Emory Craddock as an example. I met Emory back when I first got out of college and couldn't find a good job. My brother-in-law Tony owned an aluminum siding company that did most of its sales over the phone. I was desperate for beer money so when Tony offered me a position as a telemarketer I took it.

Emory Craddock. Christ, even the name is old. Show me one person born in this century named Emory and I will personally wash your mini-van with my tongue.

"Good evening, may I speak with Emory Craddock, please?" I said turning on my sugary sweet sales voice one evening as I began yet another night chained to the telephone.

I hated being a telemarketer. It ranks up there in popularity with auto mechanics named Bubba, tabloid journalists and presidents from Arkansas.

"Yeah, you've got him," the fossilized Emory Craddock croaked.

I don't know why but I always got the freaking geezers, the smart-asses and the coked-up weirdoes. Maybe these people were just like cats and had this innate sense to cling to the one person in the room who hates them the most. I think, though, it had more to do with my shitty luck.

Meanwhile, Tony's younger brother, Myron, or Woody as his siblings called him, would always get the babes with the sultry voices or the accommodating rich old widows who were just waiting at home for some weasel to con them out of some of their money.

Woody never got cranked. Cranked was the term we made up for those occasions when you hung up the phone with so much anger after dealing with yet another moron that you had to go punch the pop machine out in the hallway. I got cranked so much my knuckles were bruised.

"Well, Mr. Craddock, my name is Matthew and I am calling you tonight on behalf of Tony Aalto's Aluminum Siding Company right here in downtown Davenport." I would always say this first part as quickly and with as much clarity as humanly possible. If I got to this point in the presentation, called "the Intro" in Tony's hand-written manual he called "The Straight Dope On Phone Sales," and they were still on the line, I would take a deep breath and launch into phase two, known as "Da Big Pitch." Unfortunately, 90 percent of the time I would be the only living soul on the line when it came time to heave "Da Big Pitch."

As far as I could tell Craddock was still there so I blazed forward. "You know there's nothing as irritating or painstakingly difficult as scraping old paint off the side of your house while the hot sun beats down on you. With aluminum siding you can kiss those days good bye." Was he still there or had Craddock dropped the receiver to go let his Cocker Spaniel out? Or had he nodded off in the middle of my scintillating sales pitch? It had certainly happened before to other guys on Tony's phone crew.

"Yeah, I'm still here," he said in a pitiful sort of tone as if he had asked himself the question "Are you still there, Emory?" a lot recently.

Suddenly, I feared that I had reached a loner. A guy who had no one to talk to except for when some dipshit like me called and tried to sell him something he couldn't afford and didn't really need. I felt the urge to hang up. Emory Craddock didn't need siding. If he were as old as he sounded he wouldn't even end up paying for the installation. His family would be stuck with the bill. Nonetheless, I pressed on. Tony must have trained me well.

"Along with making your house the envy of the neighborhood, our fabulous aluminum siding will increase the value of your home. Do you know that aluminum siding will...."

"How old are you, son?" Craddock interrupted a hint of sweetness now in his scratchy voice. "You sound fairly young." I wondered how long it had been since this guy had actually talked to a real person. I imagined most of his recent conversations had been aimed at characters on some insipid WB sitcom."

"Well, I'm 23. What difference does that make?"

"Oh, don't mind me. I'm just curious, Matthew. You must just be out of school, right? Are you married, Matt? Have a family?" With each word, his voice became sweeter, more melodic. What the hell was going on here? This was starting to spook the shit out of me.

I quickly surveyed the small room where the other phone canvassers and I worked in three-hour shifts each night. Bill and Woody, the other two guys on duty that night, were still on their 15-minute break. I started to tap my right foot methodically on the grimy linoleum floor.

As the staccato rhythm of my Reebok slapping the floor filled the room, my thoughts turned again to flight. At what point do you just give up and forget a potential sale? According to Tony's lame little manual, you don't give up until the potential aluminum siding customer terminates the conversation. In other words, slams the phone down.

Maybe Craddock was a perfect candidate for siding. Maybe he had a huge house, which meant a big commission. Maybe he was a homicidal maniac.

I looked down at the computer print out that we followed every night and saw that Craddock was in McClellan Heights, an older neighborhood— one with huge old, Victorian homes. I pushed on.

"No, Mr. Craddock. I'm not married. I'm just a working stiff, trying to make a living. Now if you're interested we could send a salesman by your house in the next couple…"

"Oh, I'm interested all right. I think it's very interesting that you used the word stiff, Matthew, because I'm very stiff right now." Jesus Christ. I slammed the phone down and pushed myself back from the table nearly falling off my chair in the process. "Jesus fucking Christ," I shouted as I jumped up from the chair and ran to the other side of the room to get as far away from the phone as possible. I turned to see who was out in the hall and saw Woody there mauling a Snickers bar and downing a can of Dr. Pepper. I was jumping up and down in the room like a squirrel on crack.

"What the hell is your problem?" Woody asked bursting into the room, flakes of chocolate coating flying out of his mouth. It was just like Woody to try and wrestle hold of a situation while bits of food flew from his bulbous lips.

"I just got off the phone with someone who was jacking off while I was trying to sell him siding. What a fucking freak," I said, trembling with rage.

"So you finally got one," Woody said calmly, taking a long drink from the Dr. Pepper. "Hey, it happens to all of us. Don't bust a nut. It was just a matter of time before it happened to you. What did this guy say? Did he want you to come over to his house to show him samples of your siding?"

"No, he just asked me personal stuff like how old I was."

"Yeah, they do that," Woody said, sounding like the old pro that he was. He was such a loser he would likely spend the next five years of his life in the phone room even though his brother ran the company. Then, and only then, would Woody work his way up to field representative, the person who actually goes to a customer's home and estimates how much Tony's company will steal from them.

"They'll ask you that innocent-sounding stuff," Woody said as he gestured with his right hand to imitate someone stroking his meat. "Meanwhile, they are throttling the old, one-eyed wonderworm. It's an occupational hazard." Woody thought this was hilarious.

He leaned over and reached into a gym bag that was sitting on the floor next to his workspace. Woody was a part-time ref at the local Y. He often brought his referee uniform into work so that he could go directly to the gym after his shift. "What was the guy's number?" he asked while rummaging through the bag.

"Why? You're not going to actually call this guy, are you?" I asked, my heart still pounding.

"Yeah. Just give me the number," he said, zipping up the bag after he had found what he had been looking for. I couldn't see what he pulled out of the bag but it was small enough for him to conceal in his porky little hand. I pointed to Craddock's name on the computer print out and Woody carefully dialed the number.

"Hello, may I speak with Mr. Emory Craddock? Oh, this is he?" Woody then produced a referee whistle in his left hand and blew it as hard as he could into the receiver. He quickly dropped the whistle and screamed into the phone: "You fucking sick cocksucking homo. You should fucking eat shit and die. You goddamn rump ranger. I hope you get fucking AIDS, goddammit." Spit flew from his mouth covering the receiver and the hand that was holding it. Without checking to see Mr. Craddock's reaction, Woody slammed the receiver down so hard I swear he nearly cracked the phone. Then, as quickly as he flew into his homo-hating rage, he started to laugh with such reckless abandon I thought he would soil his BVDs. He nearly went into convulsions he was laughing so hard. After several minutes he looked up and saw me standing there slack jawed like some shell-shocked hillbilly.

"That should teach the fucking faggot," he said, playfully punching my shoulder. "We taught him a thing or two, didn't we? He won't mess with no fucking heteros any time soon will he? The goddamn queer." He was waiting for some kind of sign of approval from me. I simply stared at him like I had just witnessed a decapitation.

After several awkward seconds I said: "Woody, I don't know who's more sick, Craddock or your sorry ass."

"Lighten up. I did you a fucking favor," he said, unzipping his gym bag to replace the whistle. "From day one you have acted like this job's beneath you. Well, fuck you. You suck at it. You don't even have the balls to do this job. You've got to be able to think on your feet on this job. But no, you just get blown away when things don't go perfectly. Waa. Waa. Waa. You're such a fucking mommy's boy. Christ, you wouldn't even be working here if it weren't for your sister. You can't even fend for yourself. You have to get your family to bail you out."

Now a lot of things came to my mind. I could have decked his chubby little ass. I could have pointed out that he had a lot of gall accusing me of nepotism. After all, if it weren't for Tony, his entire family would be on the street. But I didn't because when it got right down to it, I didn't give a shit about this job. I did not go to college for five years to spend my evenings calling up lonely old masturbators and paranoid grandmas drowning in perfume to try to con them into buying Tony's shitty aluminum siding. I had better things to do. Christ, practically anything, even watching golf on television, would be better than telemarketing.

Yeah, I could have said a lot of things to Woody but all I managed to utter was: "Bite me."

Having finished off the Snickers bar and the Dr. Pepper, Woody stood there licking his pudgy fingers, riding out his sugar buzz. "You'd like that, wouldn't you, you homo. Take a hike, Picasso. I'll tell Tony you couldn't cut it," he said, a smile creasing his punchable face. I should have decked him right then and there. Instead, I just pulled my leather jacket off the back of the chair and headed toward the door.

"You know, Woody, you don't have the authority to fire me," I said, turning to him before I left. "But it doesn't really matter because I quit. And not that it matters, but you're wrong about me. I could do phone sales if I wanted to, but basically it's for losers. Only a turd like you, who can't do anything else, would get anything out of it. See ya, tubby."

I didn't stick around to hear his reply but I'm sure it was something pithy like "fuck you." I had better things to do like going home to my room in my mom's basement and figuring what the hell I was going to do with my life.

✶   ✶   ✶

I hate being referred to as a Generation Xer. But because I'm in my 20s, older people like to use that tired phrase to explain my behavior.

I hate people who try to pigeonhole an entire population, or generation in this case, into one tidy little package. It's just stereotyping, a bullshit device for ignorant, lazy people. It's not much more logical than astrology, which my mother believes in adamantly.

This Generation X thing is just ridiculous. An entire generation sharing the same traits? Give me a break. And what's the deal with the letter X?

How fucking trendy. I am not filled with X nor have I ever been filled with X.

I am filled with A, lots and lots of A, as in anger, angst, anxiety, anticipation. I'm an asshole. Call it Generation A, you stupid geniuses. But, oh no, that would imply that we're in front, ahead, doing well, getting a passing grade. All the bastards who run this rotting planet would never go for that. Maybe it would be better to call us Generation F. Yeah, that works. F as in fucked up.

So don't call me a Generation Xer. Call me Matthew Picasso. Call me a recent college graduate who a) can't figure out what he wants to do, b) doesn't have any direction in life, c) doesn't have a calling, and d) didn't know what he wanted to do growing up except to grow up. Call me a guy who loves alcohol and who is not ashamed of it. Call me a guy who loves television and is not ashamed of it. Call me a guy whose ultimate goal is to be independently wealthy but doesn't want to work hard to get there.

Does all this make me a bad person? I don't think so. I listen to Nirvana, Pearl Jam, Jane's Addiction, Nine Inch Nails. Yet, I have never entertained one thought of suicide. I am not depressed. I am just in search of what the hell life is all about.

I went to college because I was told by my mom, who by the way never abused me, that in order to get a job today, even at McDonald's it seems, you need a bachelor's degree. So I got one. Should I go down to McDonald's and apply? That's about how much I think my degree is worth sometimes.

Getting a degree hasn't made my life any easier. It hasn't helped me one bit in my job search. It's like a diploma is a ticket to see a show. But no one told you that your seat is in row QQ and you're going to be sitting right behind some fat fuck who underarms reek like a rotting corpse and whose head is the size of Duluth.

I didn't need a degree to get a job working for Tony. Nepotism doesn't require a diploma. Tony would have hired me straight out of high school had Angela been married to the dirtbag back then. It sure would have saved me some time studying for those goddamn multiple choice tests in Geology 101. The Cenozoic Era included a) the Pliocene Epoch, b) the Paleocene Epoch, c) The Jurassic Period, d) a and b, e) all of the above, f) none of the above. By the way, the correct answer is who gives a fuck?

Tony is one of those guys who believes steadfastly in his family even if they are a bunch of morons, like Woody. Of course, Tony is a moron, too, so I guess they all have a common bond beyond the DNA and all that.

My brother-in-law, that swarthy bastard. Thanks to him I am where I am today. Nearly in jail. He's the one who smoothtalked me into taking the job as a telemarketer at his company. He promised me good wages and a chance to get a taste of the working world before I really went looking for a career.

I think he just needed some sap to help boost spring sales. What he accomplished was to sour me on the working world. Having me start out on telemarketing is about as brilliant as training someone in human relations under the tutelage of Benito Mussolini.

Plain and simple, phone sales excel in suckness. It sucks to get the phone calls and it sucks even more to make them. Sometimes, I felt like it would be actually better to work for the Internal Revenue Service. No one wanted to hear from me—not even my mother.

As a joke one night, I set out to prove this theory. I disguised my voice and called my mother.

"Hello, may I speak with a Maria Picasso, please?" I started out sounding a bit like Walter Brennan. Half old man, half crazed lunatic.

"This is she," mom answered a bit tentatively. My mother likes to give strangers a fighting chance even if she suspects that they might eventually disembowel her.

"My name is Nigel Mellish and I'm calling from Bob's Aluminum Siding Company. (Tony's competition). I'd like to talk to you briefly about the benefits of aluminum siding."

Mom was silent. I was beginning to wonder if she knew this was just a prank. "Well, I already have siding," she said after a bit. This was true. Tony had sided our house for next to nothing with a prototype siding that he wanted to test. For a week or so, our house looked brand new. Several neighbors stopped by while walking their dogs to comment on how good it looked. But soon a grotesque transformation started to take place. After a couple rainfalls, our once beautiful, American white house turned neon pink. Now, I've never been a fan of pink so to me it looked downright hideous. My mother, on the other hand, loved pink so she tried to cover up the fact that she secretly wanted to burn it down. For the most part, she kept her opinion to herself, but one afternoon I overheard her describe it to a friend of her's on the phone as "vulvaesque."

When it became obvious that it was the siding and not acid rain that was discoloring our home as Tony first maintained, he promised to replace it—eventually. Meanwhile, we tried to get used to living in our pink, vulvaesque house on Jefferson Street.

"You already have siding?" I asked and before I could say anything else mom said "Thank you" and hung up the phone.

I sat there at the phone bank in utter disbelief. My own mother, who never hangs up on anyone, hung up on me. Jesus Christ. Cranked by my own mother. Sure she didn't know it was her only son but still, I figured I would be able to at least keep her on the line for more than a minute. If one of the kindest women I know has little time for telemarketers hawking aluminum siding then what hope was there?

Woody was right. To survive in phone sales you need to have an iron will. You need to be someone who only takes the word no as incentive to keep driving, to keep pushing until that word transforms somehow into a yes. Or you need to be a spineless wonder who is so afraid to rock the boat at work that you will live the rest of your life in misery afraid to tell anyone that you really hate your job.

I was neither so it was just a matter of time before I went over the edge. Emory Craddock, the geriatric masturbator, was the straw that broke my back.

"I'm sorry, Angela. I just couldn't go on there. I had to quit. I just hated trying to sell that shit." I was venting to my favorite ventee. My sister and I talked on the phone nearly every day of our lives. Even when I was back at the University of Iowa, we'd talk so frequently that my roommates thought she was a girlfriend from back home. From girl problems to hangovers, Angela helped me through every little crisis in my life.

"Matt, that's my husband's livelihood," she said, playing the heavy. "That's what pays the bills around here. And as a matter of fact, that's what's been paying the bills for you, too. You shouldn't be putting him down. I know you have issues with Tony but he did do you a big favor by giving you that job."

"Issues, is that what you call it when you can't stand someone? He's a shithead." I said quickly before engaging my brain. Normally, I did a better job of hiding my feelings toward Tony, but this day was different.

"Matt, that's my husband you're talking about," she snapped, a bit hurt.

"I know, I know. I'm sorry. I just need to get away from that. I need to sort my life out. I never planned on selling aluminum siding over the phone especially along side someone like Woody. That guy has some serious 'issues' with everyone."

"Woody is all right. You just have to give him a chance."

I didn't bother to paint an accurate picture of Woody for Angela. After all, she thought Tony was wonderful. Her thinking was obviously skewed. Both Tony and Woody were perfect candidates for guest spots on The Jerry Springer Show.

"What are you going to do now? You need the money."

"I know I need the money but I'm not sure what I'm going to do. I just need to clear my head. I think it's time to go on one major drinking binge."

"What will that help?" My sister didn't drink and was suspecting of anyone who had more than a glass or two of anything—even soda.

"Plenty. Some of my best ideas have come from drunkenness. Look at the college years, the best years of my life. I was inebriated half the time and I was on the dean's list."

"You sound like an alcoholic," she tsked, tsked me.

"There's a big difference between drinking and being an alcoholic, Angela. Alcoholics drink to hide or escape some problem they have. I drink to have fun. See the difference?"

"Frankly, I don't. I should introduce you to my friend Sheila at AA."

"Spare me, Angela. I don't need to meet any more of your friends. They are a Rogues Gallery of depressed creeps. Name one friend of yours who's happy? Just one. Come on, I bet you can't."

The other end of the line was silent.

"I'm happy," she said finally.

"You don't count."

Angela Picasso Aalto. Saint. Altruist. Person most likely to take home a stray. In fact that's exactly what she did when she met her husband.

Angela fell for Tony Aalto, the aluminum siding sultan of Davenport, Iowa, in about three minutes. All she had to see was that Tony was a man who needed serious help. The kind of qualities that would repulse most women only made him more appealing to Angela. He is obnoxious, disrespectful, phlegmy and porcine (and for that remark I apologize to all of the real pigs in the world). Angela somehow saw an independent, rebellious man-child who would blossom into a leader with just the right amount of womanly attention.

I don't know if Tony ever fell in love with Angela. He was just looking for an attachment. Someone who would look good on his arm when he went out at night. I saw right through this superficiality, Angela only saw a knight in shining aluminum.

They met at a local meeting of the Sierra Club. Tony has tried to position himself as an environmentalist even though his business throws away about a ton of scrap aluminum every 10 minutes. He claims that he's protecting the environment by putting aluminum siding on America's homes. If you don't have aluminum siding you are painting the house and paint has to be disposed off and that's bad for the environment. This is how he sold himself to Angela and she bought it. But then Angela buys a lot of things if they are cause related.

My sister is a nurturer, a liberal, a true champion of the downtrodden. Maybe that's why we get along so well, me being downtrodden and all. Somewhere along the line, she was struck with the notion that those without any major problems should reach out to those with problems. I certainly don't share this sentiment. It's a dog-eat-dog world and you just have to be able to outrun all of the rottweilers. Angela, however, would rather cradle the pit bulls of the world in her arms and comfort them even while they are trying to gnaw her arms off.

Ever since I can remember Angela has been helping out those less fortunate. When we were young I remember her trying to take in any stray animal she ran into. Mom was constantly playing the tough cop who had to explain that we couldn't run an animal shelter in our house. Angela was also the one to make friends with all of the dweebs in school. Like Debbie Druckenmueller, for example. Debbie had this awful habit of relieving herself right in the middle of class. I never figured out whether she just had no bladder control or she was just trying to get attention but nearly once a week she would raise her hand and ask to go to the bathroom. The teachers always said yes, hurriedly, knowing that if they didn't act quickly they would be soon blotting up a wet chair. But no matter how quickly they would respond, Debbie would let the floodwaters flow. Most teachers ran over, made a big fuss and asked if Debbie was all right. However, there were a few renegade teachers, who would make Debbie clean up her mess on her own in front of the rest of the class. These were my favorite teachers but for some reason when the next school year rolled around they were always gone.

Angela made a beeline toward Debbie and tried her damnedest to befriend her. But Debbie was beyond making friends. Angela suspected abuse at home, which made her try even harder to make the poor girl her buddy.

One day Angela was able to coax Debbie to our house after school where she tried to get her to take a shower. The Urinator would have no part of it and finally had to hit my sister in the face with a social studies book to get away. Angela just couldn't understand why Debbie shunned her. After all, she was just trying to help her out.

My mom was under the deluded notion that her only daughter would someday become a nun. I guess I kind of agreed with her until my older sister turned 15 or so. Angela was a giving person in all aspects and she developed a reputation at school to that effect. It's not like she was a slut. It's just that she would only have to go out with a guy a few times and they would then go testing the springs of the local Posturpedic.

As a result I got in my fair share of scrapes with some of the lowlifes at school ~ I was constantly trying to defend her "honor." And, of course, when Angela heard that I had pounded some guy who had called her an easy lay, she would apologize to the creep for my behavior.

I'm sure that her amorous ways led to her quick marriage with Tony. After they met at the Sierra Club gathering, they started going out and soon enough I'm sure they started doing the mattress mambo and Tony figured this was the sap for him. She was attractive, caring, a good dancer. Perfect. And for Angela, Tony was a guy with a lot of problems that she could fix. He was swarthy, smelled like a sweaty sock, had bad manners, thought he was black, was mean to everyone and couldn't talk very well. Imperfect, therefore perfect.

Tony Aalto. If brains were gasoline, he wouldn't have enough to drive around the block.

When Angela first met him I was away at college at the University of Iowa in Iowa City. I heard him described over the phone first by Angela and then by my mother. So until I met him I thought of him as a Dr. Jeckyl and Mr. Hyde. Angela portrayed him as a little boy trapped in a man's body. Mom portrayed him as an ape that had been completely shaved down except for his chest and back. The two versions of this guy clashed in my mind so much that it would keep me up at nights, tossing and turning. When I headed home for Thanksgiving that year I was dying of curiosity. Who had the more accurate version? I was leaning toward mom's but she had always judged our friends harshly. She once referred to my friend Alan Gooper as "Goat-Boy" when she heard the rumor that his parents were actually distant cousins. She couldn't verify that claim but it didn't stop her from judging him as some sort of two-headed carp swimming in a very small gene pool.

When I finally came face to face with Tony I formed a third opinion. He was a swarthy bastard. Mom and Angela were both accurate in their descriptions to some extent. He was an ape but was not without charm. Being a salesman he was a smooth talker, but I just couldn't get past the fact that he thought he was black. He imitated the hand gestures and body movements of a gangsta rapper and talked like he was a player. At first it struck me as sort of comical but when he persisted in acting the role of hustler I started to retch.

"Yo, what's up moms," he said as he walked into our house without knocking on that fateful Thanksgiving Day. I looked at mom to see how she reacted to this boldness but she hid her disgust well. He handed her a bouquet of roses, complimenting her on the aroma that was wafting out of the kitchen. He then sashayed over to me and put both of hands out, palms up, in front of me.

"Yo what's up, Matty P?" he said with this 'I just got laid' grin. "You the man."

Awkwardly, I slapped his hands. What the hell was this guy's problem, I thought to myself. He was wearing baggy black jeans, brown work boots and an untucked flannel shirt buttoned all the way up to his neck. Dangling out around his fat neck was a very large gold necklace.

Because of his swagger and dress, he did look a little menacing. He was a bit taller than me at about 6 foot and weighed about 200 pounds. With a bushy black mustache, he kind of looked like Tom Selleck, if Tom Selleck had been beaten in the face one too many times and acted like he was in the Crips. I could see why Angela could be attracted to him physically but the way he was acting reconfirmed my fears that my sister had gone off the deep end with this guy.

"So college boy, you pretty smart, eh? I bet you learnin' all sorts of deep shit at school." Angela gave him a jab in the ribs when he said the "s" word. "Oops. I wish I had had the chance to go to college, man."

"Couldn't you afford to go?" I said as we made our way out of our living room into the TV room.

"No, at the time I figured college was for punks," he said laughing, looking around the room to see if anyone else thought his joke was funny. The room wasn't with him. "I know different now," he said growing somber.

"Yo, Angela, get me a 12-ouncer," he yelled over his shoulder. "And something to eat. I always like to chow on some munchies when I watch da game," he said turning to me. "What would Turkey Day be without some ball?"

And with that he plopped down into my mother's favorite recliner where he remained pretty much for the rest of afternoon drinking beer. As soon as he finished off one can he would yell for another. I'm sure if he could have managed it somehow he would have had someone else take a piss for him so he wouldn't have to miss any of his precious football game. The only other time he got up was to come into the dining room for dinner, which just happened to be at half-time.

"Back in the day, we ate the turkey on TV trays while watching ball."

"I know, Tony, but we do things a little different here," Angela said in a motherly tone. "We like to talk at the dinner table and give thanks."

"Talk? About what?"

Tony Aalto. Oldest and most corrupted of seven kids. Although I didn't meet him until that Thanksgiving Day I had made a point of finding out as much as possible about him beforehand through the grapevine. The Aaltos were notorious for being shysters, known regionally for their ability to extort money out of innocent people with the shadiest of businesses.

Tony's baby was the aluminum siding business, for which he employed Woody and his youngest brother, Rico. I never met Rico and was told by several people including Tony that I never wanted to meet him. His temper was legendary. Most people figured he had little brother syndrome, always trying to prove that he fit in, and that's what made him so angry. I figured he was just another Aalto dick. He was a foreman on the manufacturing end of the business. Rumor has it that a month didn't go by when he didn't maim one of his worker's hands by forcing it into one of the aluminum extruding machines.

The other four Aalto boys—Frankie, Marco, Bennie, and Manny—ran Aalto Bros. Auto Repair, which specialized in brake jobs. Everybody assumed that they had to be connected to the Mafia, though no hard evidence has ever been brought forward to prove this, because all four of them sure as hell couldn't make a living from the shoddy repair work they did. If you were ever stupid enough to take your car in there for a brake job the odds were at best 50-50 that your car would actually be able to stop when it was finished. Rumor had it that the Mafia forced people who owed them money to get their car work down with the Aalto Brothers. If they owed a lot of money, the brothers would do an inferior job of repairing the car, thus rendering it dangerous to drive. It was a known fact that several people died in accidents after visiting the Aalto Bros. Auto Repair Shop.

I kind of found the Mafia rumors to be a joke. The Mafia is more believable in places like Chicago or New York, but Davenport, Iowa? Well, at least it was a good story.

Although each of the sons used it, Aalto isn't really the family's name. Vincente, the boy's father, changed it from Vermicelli when he started the aluminum siding business back when he was 18. "No one is going to buy siding from someone with a name like a pasta," he had said back then. So he decided to change it to a name that was easy to remember and something that would always be at the beginning of the Yellow Pages listings.

Vincente built up the aluminum siding business through deceit and coercion. He played up his Italianess to the hilt, kissing the tips of his fingers when he liked something, eating pasta at every meal, wearing lots of jewelry, only buttoning his shirt half way so his chest hair would show. He would imply to his customers that if they didn't buy his aluminum siding that accidents would happen and we're not talking accidents like the ones caused by his four son's lack of auto repair acumen. More than once a house burned down in the neighborhood that he was targeting for sales. The cops could never prove anything but many of his older aged customers worried that if they didn't buy his siding they would get rubbed out or their house would go up in flames.

Consequently, Vincente got rich. As he got older and his sons started helping out in the business he laid off the strong-arm tactics. He was able to get business simply by marketing and doing commercials on late-night TV. At one point they even had their own show: "Vinnie Aalto's Aluminum Siding Western World" on which they featured bad, old western movies every Friday night at 11 o'clock. Vinnie, all duded up in cowboy gear, would introduce the movie and then sell siding at the commercial breaks. It was cheesy but it worked.

His fame and fortune, and television show, came to a quick end when Vincente died at age 55. He was killed in a freak accident while on vacation in the Wisconsin Northwoods. He had been driving along at a good clip when his Jaguar blew a tire on the front passenger side. The tire exploded with such force that it jerked the car off the road. He was able to wrestle the car to a stop in the ditch safely but as he got out and started to put on a spare a bear wandered out of the woods and mauled him. Now this just may be a sick rumor but a lot of people swear that Vincente, who loved to show off his wealth quite ostentatiously, was wearing a long fur coat at the time of his demise. The word is that the bear was a bit older and may have been suffering from some type of ursine glaucoma. Mistaking the stranded driver for a bear of the female persuasion the marauding bear started to mount him. Apparently when the bear realized the mistake he was so embarrassed that he tore Vincente limb from limb.

Frankie, Marco, Bennie and Manny spent the next three days scouring the forest for the murderous bear. No one had seen the mauling so they weren't even sure what kind of bear it was. Consequently, they shot at anything with fur. When state troopers finally arrested them they had killed six bears, two deer, three or four chipmunks, 17 squirrels and a hedgehog. Although invited, Tony chose not to take part in the killing spree. As the oldest of the clan he was back home putting his father's business into order. By the time the brothers had gotten out of jail and paid their fines, Tony had changed the name of the business to Tony Aalto's Aluminum Siding. He reasoned with them that they now had records and it wouldn't look good to have their name in the spotlight being animal killers and all. After they kicked Tony's ass, the four decided to open up the auto repair shop. Although they still get along there continues to be tension between the Tony camp of Aaltos and the auto repair boys.

What a sight to behold. Tony, eldest son of the Aalto clan, wolfing down turkey and mashed potatoes, food flying out of his mouth, trying his damnedest to see the television in the other room. He looked like a rabid owl.

"Tony, stop trying to watch the game," Angela snapped in between bites of stuffing. "You haven't even gotten to know Matthew."

"Who? Oh yeah, Matty, college boy," he said turning toward me during an insurance commercial. "So what you studyin', Matty?" he said repeating the one variation of my name that I refuse to answer to.

"It's Matt," I said tersely.

"What?" he said turning again to see the TV.

'I said, it's Matt not Matty."

"Ooo, chill out, man. All right, Matt. So wa,choo studyin', Matt," he said making a point to emphasize my name each time he said it.

It was obvious that Soul Brother No. 1 didn't like me. Fine, the feeling was mutual. "I'm studying English."

My answer eased the tension in the room because Tony started to laugh. "Whassup with that? Don't you know how to speak good?"

"Tony, when you study English it means…." Angela broke in.

Tony shot a "speak when you're spoken to" glance at my sister. "I know what it fuckin' means. Damn, I'm just makin' a joke. Shit, everyone should just chill out. Ain't this Thanksgiving? Ain't this the day you supposed to show good will toward you fellow man?"

I couldn't believe my ears. No one had ever used the f-word in our house before, let alone at the dinner table, let alone on Thanksgiving Day. My mom put up with a lot of crap from Angela and me growing up. She would withstand bad attitudes, temper tantrums and a few "craps, damns and hells" but never the f-ingheimer. It dropped on the Picasso household like a verbal Hiroshima. For the rest of the meal we ate in silence, the rabid owl continued to wrench his neck in order to keep up with the football game. Mother slowly chewed her food and psychically burned a hole through Tony's forehead. This was too much. She was going to lose her first born to this Cro-Magnon man.

My mother is a saint. She had raised Angela and me all by herself since our dad also named Tony, though he went by Anthony, left when we were both young. There were several versions of why he left. When we were kids we tried to come up with the one that would put him in the best light.

When I was in kindergarten, I convinced myself that he had run away to join the circus and tame ferocious lions. Then in junior high, I manufactured the story that he had been kidnapped by a religious cult. When I was in high school, I just told everybody that he was dead. I didn't really learn the real story until I was going off to college and mom and I shared a six pack one night as we sat on our front porch watching the sun set at the end of the street.

"You're a man now, Matthew," my mother said, on her second beer. I had never seen her drink more than one in the course of an evening. "I didn't want to tell you what happened to your dad because I didn't want it to affect your development. I decided that I would wait to tell you when you turned 18 or thereabouts. At first I wasn't sure if my family and Angela could keep it a secret but they did," she paused a moment to wipe her moist eyes and to take a swig of Milwaukee's Best.

"Your father and I got married real young. I really didn't even have a time to get to know him. We fell in love or maybe it was just lust. He came into the diner I was working at the time one day and we got to talking. He was from another part of town so I never knew him or of him from school or anything. He asked me out that first time he came into the diner and we went to a movie. He was quite handsome. We started dating pretty frequently after that and soon couldn't be separated. He made me laugh. He was so witty and bright. We started fooling around and soon I was pregnant with your sister. We got married and moved into an apartment down by the river. He got a job at Caterpillar and we were doing all right. Then you came along and all of sudden Anthony started to change. He was quick to anger, was having trouble with work, something was troubling him. I started to suspect that he was having an affair but I never could prove it. Then one Sunday morning he woke up really early and went downstairs by himself," she paused again and stared off silently down the street for some time. I kept silent letting her reveal the story at her own pace.

"Your sister woke me up that morning. She came in to tell me that you had woken up and needed to be taken out of the crib. I asked where dad was and Angela said he was downstairs acting weird. I went in and got you out of the crib and gave you to Angela. I walked downstairs alone to see how he was 'acting weird.'

"'Anthony,' I said to him but he did not answer. He was sitting in the middle of the room with his back turned to me. He was completely naked.

"'Anthony,' I said again. "What are you doing sitting down here without any clothes on?

"'I'm leaving you, he said calmly, considering the magnitude of his statement. "I've decided to become a nudist. I am rejecting all clothes and moving to Florida to live in a nudist colony. I will send you money but I need a change in my life, a drastic change or I am going to break and I don't want to hurt you or the children.'"

"'Don't you think your leaving is going to hurt us?' I asked him."

"'I'm sorry but if I stick around here I'm going to lose it and I don't want that to happen,' he told me. "I think it's best just to leave and start over.'"

"As you can imagine, Matthew, I was completely crushed. I immediately went upstairs, got you children dressed and called mother. She, of course, wanted all the details but I had none to give. I just begged her to pick you up so that I could deal with this on my own." She stopped her story again for several minutes and we just sat there in silence except for the constant buzz of the locusts in the trees.

So my father had gone nuts. Finally knowing the truth I longed for fiction. Running off to the circus or being dead sounded better to me than what really happened. What caused it? Was it just some bizarre chemical reaction in his brain? I couldn't believe this was hidden for so long. I couldn't believe that Angela had not confided in me.

"Dr. Klein struggled to explain it to me after Anthony left," my mom started up again. "He said that your father just couldn't handle the strain of being responsible for a family, a wife, a job and a mortgage. It was a mid-life crisis. He figured he took his starting over a little too figuratively. We come out of the womb with nothing and now your father was starting over from scratch. And yet when we're born we need others to help us survive. Your dad didn't want any help. I don't think he was completely nuts. He just wanted out and when he ran across an ad in a girlie magazine for a nudist colony down in Florida he figured it would be an adventure and definitely something different."

We sat there for a few minutes with our thoughts. Mom was reflecting back on the husband she had lost. I was trying to figure out how a man could just up and leave his family like that.

After several minutes passed she put her arm around my shoulder and gave it a squeeze. "I'm sorry I didn't tell you earlier. I just wanted to make sure that you were at an age where you could handle this."

"Uhh, thanks, mom," I muttered.

What else could I say? What are you supposed to say when your mother reveals a secret she has been hiding for some 18 years, that your father is a nudist? That he worships at the altar of a Naked God? That he doesn't believe in shirts, ties, shoes, socks, trousers, suits, underwear, belts, even hats? I'll tell you how you handle it. You get pissed off. You take it out on everyone around you. You start drinking, more than you did before. But you deal with it. Mom deals with it, Angela deals with it and I deal with it. Every day of our lives.

It has been five years since mom told me the truth about dad. I think about it every day and I often entertain the thought of finding him just to see how he's doing. Mom told me recently that dad had opened up a series of nudist colonies in several southern states calling them the Bare Necessities. She says he's very successful. I wonder how he's dealing with the goddamn pressure now.

It doesn't surprise me, though, that his nudist colonies have taken off, literally. Offer people nothing and they will want all they can get. Some of our most revered icons in society have nothing to offer and they are filthy rich. Figures.

Chapter Two

I don't like talking on the phone whether it's trying to sell aluminum siding to lonely old men who choke their chickens or just talking to a friend. Unfortunately, my sister insists on calling me everyday. I would rather just get in my car and drive over to talk to Angela in person but that might mean I would run into Tony and I wanted to limit my run-ins with him.

I don't like the phone because it is so impersonal and so damn intrusive. People can sneak up on you on the phone and I don't like being snuck up on. Consequently, I am a huge fan of voice mail. Being able to screen calls is the thin line between sanity and utter chaos.

Not surprisingly, Angela wasn't very happy with the fact that I had quit the job that her husband had so generously provided me. I could deal with that, though. I thought I was doing everyone a favor. For the two weeks I held the job I did nothing but complain about it. At least now, I would be less grouchy.

Like usual I was feeling a bit thirsty after talking with my nun-like sister, so I headed down to the Mud Flats Brewing Company, a brewpub only a stone's throw from the Mississippi River and consequently, the President, Davenport's one and only tourist attraction. Riverboat gambling.

Ever since Iowa's state Legislature approved riverboat gambling, Davenport and too many other cities along the Mighty Mississippi have depended upon gambling to boost up their sagging economies. For the most part it has worked. Several new hotels, restaurants and nightclubs have opened on the riverfront to accommodate our out-of-town guests. The fears of Davenport's more Christian politicians predicting widespread doom and gloom as the Mafia rolled into town to set up brothels and other sinful pursuits never reached fruition. The riverboats seemed to only attract geriatrics who were too afraid to fly to Las Vegas. For these old farts it was the next best thing.

Although I have never set foot on a riverboat I do appreciate the strange people it brought to town and to downtown's bar scene. I enjoy heading down to Mud Flats to drink its beer and to watch the tourists. You can always count on them for a good laugh especially the older men, all decked out in outrageous polyester. After they lose a big wad playing roulette, they either get extremely drunk and start dancing on the tables or get into fights with the locals. Consequently, my brother-in-law frequents the bar in search of a winnable fight.

On a recent visit, Tony punched out a retired water treatment engineer from Muscatine who had just dropped $200 at a poker table. Apparently the Muscatine man was up here on a date with a new lady friend. First, he tried to impress her with his gambling acumen, and when that failed, tried to wow her by showing her how strong a 65-year-old can be. He was no match for Tony, who knocked away his cane and then punched the off-balance senior in the nose.

The other Mud Flats patrons were too afraid to stand up to Tony but Trish, my bartender friend, tells me that the other bartenders spit into his drinks the rest of the night.

When Trish told me this story I was tempted to let Tony know that he drank about a pint of loogies that night but then I figured he would probably drive one of his company's semis into the side of the Mud

Flats to seek revenge. And with my luck, he would probably do it on a night when I happened to be there.

I headed into Mud Flats ready to celebrate. I was free from the Tony Aalto Aluminum Siding Company and ready to rock. I didn't know what I was going to do for money but what the hell, I didn't have many bills. I lived at home and I didn't have to start paying off my school loan until I found a real job. I could sustain a college-like lifestyle, in my best estimation, for at least three more days. So why not live a little?

Although I like to drink I don't have a drinking problem. Of course, every alcoholic says that, right? Well, I've taken those self-tests in the paper that you see from time to time. You know the ones where it has 12 questions and if you answer yes to even one then the so-called experts say you have a drinking problem. Screw them. The questions are so lame: "Have you ever missed work or school the next day after a night of drinking?" Well, sure I have. A few times in high school, I partied so hard that when my mom woke me up the next morning I couldn't get out of bed to go to my job at the Carpet Kingdom, where I lugged around 1,000-pound rolls of carpet all day long. I didn't skip work because of my drinking. I skipped because I had only gotten to bed three hours earlier, the job was shitty and I was slightly hungover. So does that mean I have a drinking problem? The way I see it I had a sleeping problem. I didn't get enough of it. So I don't have a drinking problem, nuff said.

"Hey, Trish, get me a G and T," I said ordering my favorite summertime drink even though it wasn't officially summer yet. It was late May and I was out of college for good, so to me it was summer. At the rate I was going it would be summer for quite some time.

Trish was one of my favorites at Mud Flats. She was a good listener. Of course, what bartender worth his or her weight in margarita salt isn't?

But Trish also gave decent advice. Now it could be argued that anyone looking for advice from a bartender is either a loser or has a drinking problem but I don't care. Trish had worked there for as long as I could remember. She was in her 30s and knew just about everybody in the city. Although Trish was very nice and had a pretty face she was several pounds overweight. She looked like someone who had reached a certain point in her life where she had to make a decision—either fight the weight gods everyday and be a very attractive person or say fuck it and be happy. I liked the overweight, happy Trish.

"I quit my job today," I said looking for sympathy in a place where everyone is looking for sympathy.

"Get another one," she said matter-of-factly, while washing drink glasses in the sink behind the bar.

"It's not that easy." Boy, those G and T's tasted mighty fine.

"Bullshit. There are thousands of jobs in this city. People are just too lazy to go out and find one," she said drying her hands with a rag.

"Well, I'm not talking about McDonald's or Subway. I know there are plenty of jobs out there like that. I'm talking about substantial work. Meaningful work."

"I think there are plenty of jobs like that, too. What exactly do you want to do?" She was shooting from the hip tonight.

"I wish I knew." I downed the rest of the G and T and Trish was quick to get me another.

"You studied English, right?"

"Yeah. And bars and women. Life in general, I guess."

"Great, throw on an apron and jump behind the bar. Sounds like you have what it takes to become a bartender at Mud Flats," she laughed. Another bartender brought more dirty glasses over to Trish and she shot him an evil glance. Every time she leaned over to dip the glasses in the sink I caught a glimpse of her cleavage. I couldn't help it. They were just there. I think she knew it but she didn't seem to mind at all.

What is it with guys and breasts? They are just mounds of flesh. Elbows or knees can be just as pointy but they don't get men in such a lather. I mean every woman has them. Some are big, some are small. Some are shaped like grapefruit and some are shaped like gourds. What's the big deal? I hate myself for being such a sucker for them.

"Just about everybody here has a degree," she continued. "Just because you're college-educated it doesn't mean you have to go and become a lawyer or an accountant or a doctor. A lot of people in the service industry have degrees."

"Ooo, service industry. Is that what you call it?"

"Fuck you. I'm serious."

"Yeah, I know. Sometimes I think I just went to college because it was the thing to do. Now I feel guilty because my mom paid so much for me to go and I am so directionless. I guess I could blame it on my father. Isn't that a good excuse? Our society rewards victims, right?"

Trish shot me a quizzical look. "Why would you blame it on your father?"

"My dad flew the coop when I was a baby. I thought I told you that before," I said taking a healthy drink of the gin and tonic. "I've never seen him or heard from him." I could say this now without so much as a blink of the eye. It was a cold, hard fact as indisputable as the fact that the Mississippi is one big, fucking dirty river.

"I'm sorry," Trish said looking very hurt as if it were her dad who had became a nudist. "My dad died when I was 14. It's tough having only one parent. It's tough on you and tough on the surviving parent."

Yet again, Trish the bartender and I had bonded. We were both fatherless. Before I thought our bond was more superficial—she made such good drinks and I drank them without spilling on her bar. Now we were tied at a deeper level.

"He died as he was leaving church one Sunday," she said stopping her chores behind the bar. "It was such a freak accident. He was walking out the front door with us when I ran back to our pew to retrieve something. My mother came after me. All of a sudden there was the sound of screeching metal and then a tremendous boom out front. We ran back up front to find him lying there pinned under the giant crucifix that had adorned the front of the church. It had fallen from its perch above the door. Crushed him. He died immediately."

"Oh my God," I mumbled, keeping my head down so as to avoid eye contact. The Lord does work in mysterious ways. Although her father must have gone quickly it was a horrible way to die. I think that it's further proof that if there is a God he gets a little crazy with his own power sometimes.

"Structural engineers were called in to investigate but they couldn't really find anything wrong. They just figured the supports for the cross got rusty and gave way. Man, you should have seen the lawyers and the press swoop in like vultures. It was bad enough that we lost daddy but no they had to make a federal case about it." She was now back to washing beer and wine glasses. Like me, she had gotten used to telling her "How I lost my dad" story.

The bar got more crowded but we continued to gab whenever she had a chance to come over to my corner of the bar. I was drinking a few too many gin and tonics but I figured I could always find a ride home. Around 11 o'clock a group of rowdy gamblers came in demanding that the "showgirls" come out. Apparently the balding, overweight unattached gamblers were told by some smart-ass on the street that this was a high-class strip club. As if the neon words "Brewing Company" didn't clue the world into what went on behind the front doors. "Bring out the goddamn strippers," yelled one particularly ornery and bald senior.

"I want to see some fucking tits," he bellowed, his face turning red. Nice thing about tourists, eventually they have to go home.

Speaking of which, I suddenly had the urge to do so. It had been a long day with geriatric masturbators and all. Now geriatric gamblers were threatening to raise holy hell if they didn't see some flesh.

Trish saw me making my way to the door past these cardigan-clad gamblers. "I hope you're not thinking of driving in that condition," she screamed over the din raised by the crowd.

"I'm walking. I'm walking," I yelled back as I weaved my way through the crowd. I was walking…right to my car. Yes, I had had a few but I was still fully able to drive a car. I only lived a couple miles away, so I was fine.

I shouldn't have driven the night before, I thought to myself as I scrubbed my body in the shower the next morning. With my head pounding, I went through the sorry ritual of trying to recount exactly how many drinks I had had at Mud Flats. Was it six or seven, in, umm, three hours?

A friend of mine back in college, Todd Merkle, had told me that you don't get a hangover from certain liquors. He said the lighter the color of the drink, the less of a chance you had at feeling awful the next day. Gin, vodka and light rums were a few of the drinks he had listed off. He was a chemistry student so like a dunce I believed him. I guess I had never consumed enough of any of these types of alcohols in such a short time frame to find out. Now I knew he was wrong. Of course, knowing Merkle, a world-class hairsplitter, he would probably argue that it was the addition of tonic that caused my hangover. Well, whether it was the gin or the tonic or the gin and tonic combination, my head hurt and I wanted to go back to bed. However, my mother had knocked at my door and gotten me up early (9 o'clock is early for an unemployed guy) saying that Tony wanted to talk to me. I wished he would have just called me himself but I guessed he had figured that if he went through mom he would have a better chance of forcing me to talk. He knew that mom would keep bugging me until I conceded. "Like it or not, he is your brother-in-law," she would say.

So great, I had a hangover and I had to go talk to Tony first thing in the morning. What a fabulous way to start the day.

What the hell did he want anyway? More than likely one of two things. A) he wanted to bitch at me for quitting or b) he needed me to help him patch things up with Angela for the umpteenth time. He was always calling on me to get him out of jams.

"Yo, yo, Matthew. Ange is buggin' because I got back to the crib late last night. Man, I was just hangin' with da crew."

"Ange has her undies in a bundle because I won't eat her vegetarian lasagna. I'm sorry, man, but that shit ain't down."

"Ange is freakin' because she wants me to stop chowin' da steaks twice a week. Hey, that's the real deal in the Aalto meal, man. That's how we was raised."

My all-time favorite whine however was: "Ange is ragin' because I never put the toilet seat back down? What's up with that? She got two hands. If I can put it up to take a piss, she can put it down to take a squat right? I just don't understand the ladies and the toilet seat thang. What? Did they all fall in once when they was little girls? I sat down once on a toilet without making sure the seat was down and I damn near got stuck in the motherfucker. Damn, the water got all over my ass and shit. Good thang there wasn't some big-ass turd lounging in there. I jumped out of that toilet so fast I damn near went through the roof. Shit. So don't tell me about putting down no motherfucking seat. I know better than dat. You look before you leap – every time. Don't expect the guy in front of you to do it. I don't know why women have to have us do that for them. Christ, they adults."

This is what I had to look forward to this morning. Either that or a tirade on quitting the phone bank. I had a feeling, though, that he was going to let it slide because he didn't really want me working there anyway. He just gave me the job to get Angela off his ass. I made him nervous being around. Like Caesar, Tony had surrounded himself with fools and he liked it that way. It made him look a helluva lot brighter than he was. And without me around the office he didn't have to worry about anyone honest discovering all the shady deals he had going down.

As I was driving over to the aluminum company, with the radio on extra low to keep my head from splitting in half, I wondered when Tony was going to confide in me about Angela's newest cause—ARAT or Adults Respecting Animals Today. It was her latest feel-good organization and this time she was really committed. She had been a vegetarian for some time but now she was weaning herself off of leather goods as well.

In dramatic fashion, she had thrown out her leather purses, boots, belts and shoes one day claiming: "Humans have treated animals like second-class citizens far too long. They are God's creatures. I'm sure she didn't intend for us to go around killing them."

I let the she reference to God slide. No use going there. However, I wasn't going to let every comment just sit there. "Hello, Angela, haven't you heard of free will? God gave us the ability to kill so we do, quite a bit I might add."

"It's wrong. I may not be able to do much but I am going to do my part," she said and that meant driving Tony up the wall with her nagging. Tony was pure carnivore. He ate bacon like it was licorice. If he didn't have a steak every few days he would start to snort and paw at the ground. Consequently, Angela's new ARAT kick was driving him nuts.

As I sat down in his office, though, I found that he wasn't turning to me to help him get his sister off her latest shtick. No, Tony had a completely different agenda.

"Yo, Matthew, whassup?" he asked setting down a copy of Spiderman on top of his cluttered desk. Tony's office didn't look like the den of commerce you might find in any other aluminum siding company. Sure he had samples of his siding hung on the wall plus pictures of the business taken from a helicopter, portraits of his father, his mother, the entire family, of Tony and Angela on their wedding day. But for the most part, the office looked more like a teenager's bedroom. He had posters of the Chicago Bears and Michael Jordan on one wall. There was a neon Budweiser light hanging above the door. And on the closet door where he kept his coat and boots and what-not was a perfectly preserved poster of Farrah Fawcett (Majors in those days). It was the poster that was in about 5 gazillion homes during the 1970s. The one where Farrah is sitting down on a colorful blanket smiling at the camera, wearing a red one-piece. What made this poster so risqué at the time and the scorn of many Catholic mothers is that you can see Farrah's erect nipples through the swim suit.

Although the poster must have been nearly 25 years old it was in mint condition. Tony obviously cared more for Farrah than the rest of the office.

His huge metal desk was covered with various contracts, important-looking papers and a pile of various superhero comic books. Spiderman, The Fantastic Four, The Avengers, Captain America, The Mighty Thor. There was a company coffee cup, which he used for a pencil holder, a phone and a full-size Bears helmet with a lamp sprouting out the top. Other than that it was just papers. No in basket, no out basket. Utter chaos.

"I'm doing all right," I began, taking a seat in a disgusting lime green chair that looked like it came straight from the '70s via the Goodwill. "About the job," I started. "I just couldn't stand it anymore. Nothing against you but phone sales just aren't my thing…"

"Hey, fuck it. If you ain't down with it, that's cool. The last thing I want is someone who doesn't like his job working for me." He pulled out a basketball from underneath his desk and started to bounce it. He was really carrying this black thing too far. After a few bounces, the ball squirted away and rolled across the room. He muttered "fuck it" again under his breath and turned his attention toward me. "So, Matthew, who do you think would win in a fight between Spiderman and Captain America?"

This, even for Tony, was unexpected. "What?"

"Whacho mean what? If Spiderman and Captain America fought who'd win?"

"You mean to tell me that you asked me to come all the way down here to talk about comic books?" Tony was into comic books big time. He read them to the exclusion of everything else except the sports page.

"Shit no, man I going to ask you to do something for me but I got to thinking as I was reading about old Spidey here. He taking on Dr. Octopus in this one. Shit, that Octopus is one fucked up individual with those crazy arms and shit. I thought that if a badass motherfucker like Dr. Octopus can't beat up Spidey then someone like Captain America don't stand a chance.

I mean who would win? They are both good guys but what would happen if all of a sudden Captain America got all whacked out and shit and like started fuckin' killin' everyone and Spidey had to calm his ass down." He was actually serious about this inquest, waiting there eagerly to hear my reply.

"Uh, I don't know, Tony, I guess I'd say Spiderman. He's got that web thing going and the strength of a spider, and Captain America basically just has that shield. Right?" Hell, what did I know, I gave up reading comic books as a hobby and took up masturbating when I was 14 years old—like most teen-age boys.

"Hey, can you believe that, we actually agree on something. Shit," he said smiling. When it came to Tony and his comic books you were always walking a fine line. Saying just the wrong thing could get him worked up into a lather. One time I asked him what he thought of Superman, Batman and the Flash and he about blew a gasket.

"DC Comics suck," he shouted, foam literally shooting from his mouth. He was drinking a root beer float at the time. "Don't even bring up that shit. That is strictly ABA. (As in the old American Basketball Association. It was a phrase he often used to refer to something as second class. He didn't mind that the reference was lost on nearly everyone. I only know because I asked him once what the hell he was talking about.) Shit. I only read Marvel. That's the real deal. That DC crap is lame. What the fuck can Batman do? Nothing. He's kind of strong and he has a cool car and all those gadget shit but give me a fucking break. And what's up with Superman? Kryptonite, what bullshit. The Incredible Hulk would kick his ass from here to Chicago if they ever got into a fight. And the Flash, don't get me started on the Flash. So the guy runs fast. What's up with that? Shit, Carl Lewis runs fast too but you don't seem them writing no comic book about the man."

I made a mental note at that time not to bring up the topic of comic books again. Unfortunately, he insisted on talking about them.

"Spidey would definitely kick Captain America's sorry ass. Sometimes, I think Captain America belongs with those lame DC characters. I think he's a fucking homo." Tony laughed and shook his head as he looked back down at the Spiderman comic on his desktop.

"But anyway," he said looking up again. "I asked you how you were doing, Bro, because I'm doing shitty. My back is fucked up something awful." Something was rotten in Davenport. Tony never called me "Bro" unless he definitely needed something—bad. Like the time he actually forgot Angela's birthday. He knew it was in April but not the specific date. He called me on April 2 in a frenzy begging me to tell him. After several fun-filled minutes in which he nearly promised to buy his "Bro" a car, I told him it was the seventh. It was the eighth but he somehow talked his way out of the jam. Angela was probably flattered that he was only one day off.

"What's wrong, Tony? Pick up something that was too heavy?"

He cocked his head to the side and gave me a quizzical look as if to say, "it's none of your damn business how I hurt my back."

"Uhh, man's that's exactly what happened. Angela is always nagging at me to lift with my legs. Lift with my legs. I never listen to her, though. Damn, I can't help it if I'm just a dumb guy. I lifted the grill out back to take it to the garbage to throw out the old ashes and something just ripped in my back. It's killing me." He leaned forward and rubbed the lower part of his back with both hands. By the grimace on his face I was certain that he was truly in some discomfort.

"Did you see a doctor?"

"Fuck the doctor. I'd go in there and he'd say I pulled a muscle so take it easy. I don't need him to tell me that. Shit."

"But he could prescribe you some pain pills."

"Damn, I never thought of that. Well, maybe I'll go when we're done. I just hate going to the doctor. I hate the hospital. People go there to die."

"People go there to get better, too."

"Yeah, but it usually involves a lot of pain. But anyway, you're getting me off the point. I didn't call you down here to talk about doctors and hospitals and all that shit. I wanted to make you a business proposition."

Oh, oh. Here's why he was calling me "bro." A business proposition from Tony Aalto. Was this the point when he would reveal to me that he is involved in the Iowa Mafia? Was he going to ask me to go whack someone? Collect a debt? Do some persuading of a bone-breaking nature?

"Yo, listen up. For years now, ever since I was able to motor, I've been driving down to F.L.A. in the springtime to pick up my grandparents." Fortunately, I was quick and had been around Tony long enough to know that F.L.A. was Florida. "They snowbirds, which is a stupid way to put it because they hate the fucking snow. They should say 'sunbirds' because they head toward the sun. But anyway, each June I drive down there, pick them up and haul them back. They pretty much pay for everything. Whatever you want, they will pretty much buy it for you. Want a Mr. Pibb or Squirt or Slice, they'll get it for you. Though you'll usually have to get it on account of they don't get around so good. They kind of slow, you know. This year, I can't do it with my back all fucked up and shit. I'd die if I had to stay in a car driving all day long even though it's the Caddy and it's one of the most comfortable cars on the planet. So anyway, I'd like you to do the deed and pick up Edgar and Gert." Edgar and Gert. Gert and Edgar. Their names alone sent a shiver down my spine. Old people with old names. A parent hadn't named her child Edgar and Gert since the Taft Administration. Hadn't everyone figured out by this point that I hated old people?

From behind his desk Tony just sat there smiling, working over a piece of gum. "So what you say, Bro, can you help a brother out? It would be pretty damn easy and you'll get to see America. Look at it like one big adventure."

"Why are you asking me? Why not Woody? They're his grandparents, too."

"I already thought of that," he said giving me a look as if to say his brother wasn't too adept at the thinking process. "Someone's gotta make the calls to get more business, man, and since you quit it's just Woody and that other kid, whatever his name is. Philbert or Jerome or something."

"I don't know, Tony. Why don't you just fly them up here?" My hangover was starting to center in my stomach. I felt like I was going to blow chow. I shifted in my seat and took a deep breath. Unfortunately, the air in Tony's office was about as clean as the air in the alley outside a downtown bar, which, by the way, I do know quite well.

"That shit won't work, man. I wish it were that easy but they is deathly afraid of flying. They thinks the minute they gets on a plane it will head straight up to the clouds then drop like a motherfucking rock to the ground. That's why we have to drive them down in the fall and pick them up in the spring. And besides they my peeps, my family."

Family. Yeah, good excuse. With Tony as a family member, it's a good excuse not to do something. "I don't know, Tony. I need to find a job. I need to make some money."

"Damn, what the hell's wrong with you? I have friends that would kill they own mother to do this job. Do you think I am asking you to do this for free or what? Shit. I know this ain't no easy task. Spending three days with Edgar and Gert is enough to drive me loco but it's 500 dead presidents, man. 500. They've got the cash and they can deliver it tax free," he said, smiling. Tony always enjoys sticking it to the government any chance he gets. "What job will you find in the next week that will offer you all that?"

Tony's errand did sound somewhat appealing. Hitting the road for a week. A few days on my own. That would definitely be good. But a few days with a couple of geezers sounded about as much fun as going to a Yanni concert. I guess I could bring plenty of tapes and just drown them out. That would work. But then this is Tony Aalto. White soul brother No. 1. Why should I do him a favor? He's just a swarthy bastard who happens to be married to my sister. Personally, I'd like to see him lathered down with Alpo and attacked by a pack of rabid rottweilers. Finally I said: "I'll have to get back to you, Tony. Let me sleep on it."

He had trouble hiding his displeasure. Obviously, he didn't want to have to find someone else. But whom could he get other than me? He didn't know anyone else responsible enough to get his grandparents back to Iowa safe and sound. He needed me and maybe that's the only reason I told him I would have to sleep on it. To let him dangle.

"All right," he said between clenched teeth. "$600. I'll throw in another Benjamin."

"Tony, I'm not saying I have to sleep on it to get more money," I said smiling. Man, he was desperate. "But thanks anyway. I'll get back to you tomorrow."

"You can sleep on it but they is anxious to get back to the hood. We don't want to keep them waiting." He rushed me to the door and slammed it behind me. As I walked out of the building I thought I heard something bang up against a wall in Tony's office. Tony didn't like it when things didn't go his way.

"Let him dangle," I thought to myself as I drove away.

Chapter Three

I hate indecisiveness in others so it is extremely frustrating when I am unable to come to a quick decision about something. Most of the time I can but I'm usually confronted with easy decisions like whether I wanted to go drinking or stay in and study. No contest. But here I was faced with a decision that required much thought. Should I take a week off in my job search to drive all the way down to Florida and then drive all the way back with a couple of old geezers that I didn't even know? Worse yet, they were related to my arch nemesis.

Maybe if I was older there would be no trouble deciding. The older you get, the more willing you are to sacrifice your time. A week. What the hell's a week to a 40-year-old? But when you're in your 20s every day is precious. You're young, you're in your prime. Time to get laid.

It is always time to get laid when you're in your 20s. I think about sex constantly. I'm surprised I was able to even get through college. After all, how can you remember names and dates for the French Revolution when you are thinking about French kissing the entire roster of Kappa Kappa Gamma? Thoughts of sex tangled up my mind to the point of distraction. Sex with Cindy Crawford on the beach as the waves crash against the shore. Sex with Madonna on top of a rickety card table that breaks just as you both reach climax. Sex against a brick wall in a dark alley with Sharon Stone. Sex with Michelle Pfieffer in the back of a limo. Sex with Demi Moore in a canoe in the middle of a giant lake in Montana. Sex with a Jane Pauley on her anchor desk on the set of Dateline. Sex with Pamela Lee Anderson in that little shanty they work out of on Baywatch. Sex with Suzanne Somers on the couch in Mr. Roper's apartment. Yeah, I think about sex occasionally.

But I think about other things. I think about rock music. I think about getting serious about my guitar playing and starting up a band. I have even thought up names for the group—Crap Suzette, The Grease Monkeys, The Usual Suspects, The Vivid Details. I think about packing up my stuff and heading out to Hollywood. I think I'm handsome and charming enough to find work as an actor. I have to think I would be better than half of the stiffs they have out there. Pat Sajak? Christ, he had his own talk show.

I sometimes wonder if the things I would be best suited for are the things that I should have started working on when I was 12. You can't just decide one day to be a rock star or an award-winning actor. These things take time. And I already missed the train. Someone once said (I think it was Homer Simpson) that the things you have to work hard for aren't worth having. Part of me is repulsed by this idea; Part of me thinks truer words have never been said.

"You probably don't want my two cents worth but I am going to give it to you anyway," mom said standing in the kitchen dressed in a blue business suit. An apron with cauliflower, broccoli and carrots was tied around her waist. A perfect picture of the modern-day mother.

Like usual I had wandered up from my basement room around 6 o'clock expecting my mother to have thrown something together after returning home from her job as a loan officer at a large bank downtown.

"What's for dinner, mom?" I grumbled rubbing the afternoon nap out of my eyes, ignoring her comments.

"Leftovers," she said with a certain edge of glee in her voice. She loved serving leftovers. It was her quest in life to never allow a food item to sit more than three days in the refrigerator. As a result ours was the only family in Davenport that could eat a home-cooked meal on Sunday and have leftovers the rest of the week. Sure, mom was creative. We never had the exact same thing two nights in a row but meals did get tedious. Want to know how many ways you can prepare turkey? Angela and I and our palates were knowledgeable of about 37.

"What kind of leftovers?" I questioned, contemplating eating out and then heading straight to Mud Flats.

"Ham and cheese casserole." Made sense. We had had ham on Sunday night. "Now sit down. You're eating it and you're going to like it. I want to talk to you about this errand that Tony wants you to run."

"Mom," I said whining like I used to when I was 8. "I know I have no life but I don't particularly want to do Tony any favors."

"He's your brother-in-law," she said admonishing me with a wooden spoon. "Besides it's a chance to earn some money. I've been easy on you since you've graduated but I think I'm going to start charging you rent. I love you but you need some incentive to get up and get a job."

Rent? What was this? All of sudden, she had turned on me. My own mother. If a guy can't live in his parent's basement where can he turn? Was a homeless shelter next? "You mean to tell me you're kicking me out? Christ, mom that's a little drastic, don't you think?"

"Oh, stop it," she said carrying the hot ham and cheese casserole Pyrex dish to the kitchen table. "I'm not kicking you out. I just want you to try harder to find a job. You're not sending out resumes. You're not even setting up informational interviews. I sympathize with the fact that you don't know what you want for a career but face reality, you need to make some money. You can't live in the basement all your life."

"Who plans on living in the basement all his life?" I said ignoring the casserole in front of me. "It sucks. I'm just in transition. And anyway, I wouldn't be in the basement if you hadn't transformed my room into a sweat shop."

It was true. While I was away at college, my mother had discovered physical fitness. Her latest boyfriend, Larry, a restaurant critic for the Quad City Times, which in and of itself was a contradiction in terms because there are no good restaurants in the area, had turned her on to some light weight training. She enjoyed it so much she decided to turn my room on the first floor at the back of the house into a workout room. On the one wall without any windows or door, she had installed floor-to-ceiling mirrors. Every other day she would lock herself away into the room and spend the next hour grunting and moaning. One day I barged in there during a workout to borrow some money and found her doing jumping jacks in the nude. It was quite embarrassing. She rushed to put on a robe and explained that it was a new workout video featuring TV's vamp vampiress Elvira. Although I only saw her for a fleeting moment I saw enough to know that the exercise was working. Mom had the body of a 30-year-old.

"I didn't mean that you would be in the basement all your life," she said, concerned that she had hurt my feelings. "You just need to get motivated."

She was right, to some extent. While working the telemarketing job I hadn't been sending out resumes or pursuing a real job. As long as I got a paycheck I was content to drone along.

"Do this task for Tony, then come back and get a real job," she said placing a hand on my shoulder while I still contemplated the ham and cheese concoction. "The drive down to Florida will give you time to figure out what it is you want to do. Besides your horoscope today indicates you're ready for a long trip."

Oh great, here we go again. My horoscope. Madame Maria, the horoscope-watching matron. "Mom, that is complete and utter bullshit. I can't believe that you brought that up. It's in my horoscope. Jesus." I said as I started to pick at the casserole.

"It's so true, Matthew. How many times do I have to explain it to you?"

"It's bullshit. I can't believe that you actually think that your personality is determined by the time of year you were born. How simplistic. Do you actually think that there are only 12 different personalities with all of the billions of people on Earth? Come on."

"Matthew, you know it's not that simple." We had had this conversation many times before. I didn't want to have it again. I loved my mother but when it came time to talk about horoscopes and the stars and such, I thought she was downright loony. "There are 12 distinct personalities and variations on a theme. Now you, you are a perfect Scorpio. You go to extremes. You are often diverted from your goals. You are secretive and you march to the beat of your own drummer. That's Scorpio to a T."

Mom was a Scorpio as well so I wasn't too impressed with her prognosis. She was simply describing herself.

Like the weight training, mom picked up the horoscope shtick from Larry. He was an Aquarius. Aloof, idealistic, a bit strange. As a restaurant critic, he was able to wine and dine mom to his heart's content and not go broke. The paper picked up everything no matter how extravagant. Mom loved it and she didn't mind the fact that Larry was a cheapskate. It's the thought that counts, she would say.

And I have to admit that Larry did have his charms. He was well-read and he educated my mom about the finer things in life like wines, ethnic cuisine, travel, and world politics. He also turned her on to some of his silly eccentricities like astrology and weight training. (He was deathly afraid that his work would turn him into a real-life Homer Simpson where just the mention of pork chops would cause him to drool.) And although mom didn't let on, Angela informed me that he had a penchant for pornographic literature. Angela had found several of his books in mom's bedroom once when I was away at college. She thought they were just normal books because they had such innocent-sounding titles like "Intemperate Souls" and "Martha's Secret" but when she picked up one to read it she figured out a few pages into the story. Angela is not a prude. In fact she is one of the few women I've ever known who has purchased Playgirl more than once. But she said she had never read more vile literature in her life. She said whoever wrote these books obviously had the gift of creativity but the situations were abominable. With barnyard animals. With corpses. And every one of the sex acts involved some sort of cooking utensil.

"Christ, Angela, how much did you read?"

"That was only the first chapter. It was disgusting. This Larry guy is a pervert."

Mom being mom, we figured she would bring it up to us in due time if it bothered her. She obviously cared for Larry and all of his oddities. They had been going out for four years. Fortunately, for Angela and me, there was never any talk of marriage and we certainly never had any inclination to broach the subject. In fact, I'm not sure mom really loved Larry. She just enjoyed being around him because he taught her so much. They spent many nights together but the next morning Larry would be gone when mom woke up and she never let on that it bothered her. Theirs was a relationship of convenience.

Actually, I think Larry was afraid to marry anyone. He cherished his privacy too much. A wedding would only draw unwanted attention to him and that would not be good because he was fanatical about hiding his identity as the paper's restaurant critic. If the owners of the Quad Cities' eateries knew who he was or what he looked like they could prepare for him and give him a meal that was not what a typical diner would receive. That would sully the entire process and Larry and the paper didn't want that to happen. That's why he was the only columnist without a mug shot next to his column. That's why he didn't make a lot of friends. He felt that the more people who knew him just meant that that many more people could give his identify away. He was that paranoid.

A few days after I first met him, I bumped into him again at the Dock, a trendy restaurant in downtown Davenport that overlooked the Mississippi. I was meeting an old friend for drinks in the bar section of the restaurant. I had just sat down at the bar when he came walking by in route to the bathroom.

"Larry," I said smiling, putting my hand out for him to shake.

His eyes darted left, then right. I could tell by the look on his face that he was thinking that this idiot college student was going to blow his cover. He smiled weakly. "Ah, hi, Matthew, how are you?" he asked not really caring for a response. He just wanted to be released from this obligatory salutation so he could dive back into anonymity.

"I am great," I said, feeling quite powerful at the moment. "I love this place. Don't you love this place?"

"Uh, umm, yes," he forced out. He looked as if he was going to pee his pants. Fifteen years of anonymity down the drain. What did he see in Maria Picasso? She better be worth the effort; her son was trying to ruin him.

I looked around as he stood there obediently like a servant waiting to be dismissed. There were several waiters in the area. All I would have to say is "How are you doing Larry Tudor" in a loud enough voice and he would be found out. With just one sentence, I could crush him. Crush him like the many restaurateurs he had crushed over the years with his critical pen. Put him out of business like he had done with all of those poor saps who couldn't master a red sauce or might have gone too heavy on the garlic.

"Well, I'll talk to you later at the gym, Gary," I said, letting him off the hook. He looked at me for a moment with a furrowed brow wondering why I had called him Gary, then realized that I was protecting his identity. His shoulders sank as if a great weight had been lifted and he gave me a broad smile.

"Yeah, see ya later, Matthew."

"Mom, I don't care what you say, I refuse to run my life according to one paragraph of copy in the newspaper. I don't do horoscopes." By this time I had worked my way through the ham and cheese casserole and was ready to head out to Mud Flats.

Mom set her fork down, resting her forearms on either side of her plate. "You're a grown man. I can no longer tell you what to do. Do what you please, you've always seemed to. But let me tell you this. When you get

Tony all riled up where do you think he vents his frustration? At you? No, he goes home angry and then he and your sister have a fight."

"So I'm responsible for Tony being an asshole?" I said rising from the table. "If Angela and Tony don't get a long why doesn't she just leave him?"

"It's not that simple, Matthew. I wish it were that simple," she paused a moment and I thought she was going to start crying. There was something else she wanted to say but held back. Maybe she was going to reveal an episode with dad. Or maybe she was just going chastise me for trying to live in a black and white world. We had been down that road before. For me, there was good and evil. Alive and dead. Automatic and manual transmission. Nothing in between. Mom's role in life was to get me to acknowledge the middle.

"You are a grown man, Matthew, but sometimes you're still just a little boy."

Little boy? I've got your little boy. I just shook my head and left mom in the kitchen. This little boy needed to go drinking. I had to get as far away from Maria Picasso as the Ford Escort would take me, which was about as far as Mud Flats. Trish would help me clear my head or at least get a good enough buzz.

It probably wasn't a good sign that this summer my best friends worked behind a bar but most of my long-time friends were either sticking around their respective schools for the summer or already working in their new careers. I had made it through the university in four years. Yes, I did my share of partying but I also did my fair share of class work. Now I wished I had slowed down more and smelled the roses. I didn't anticipate that my college days would be the best days of my life.

Back in high school I hung around basically with just three guys. We weren't jocks, particularly smart, band members or burnouts. And we weren't especially successful with the women. We kind of blended into the scenery and now that I look back I'm kind of glad. I think the people who are in the limelight in high school peak too early. They go off to college and can't deal with the fact that they are no longer the center of attention. Many of these high school stars were so busy getting straight As and lettering in three sports that they didn't get a chance to sow any oats. When they got away from mom and dad and went off to college they went nuts and got in all sorts of trouble.

Marshall Drew was a great example of this. Straight A student. Class president. Quarterback of the football team. We hated him. There wasn't a girl in high school he couldn't bone and in fact had scored with many of them. The adults thought he was an angel because he appeared to be doing everything right. But we knew better. He didn't drink or do drugs at parties because he was in training but a Friday night wouldn't go by where he wasn't manipulating his way into some girl's pants or beating the crap out of some freshman with his football buddies. He was a complete asshole.

Then he went off to Northwestern University with much pomp and circumstance. All the adults couldn't stop talking about how successful Marshall Drew was and how their sons and daughters should try to be more like Marshall. His freshman year he became addicted to cocaine. His sophomore year he was arrested for walking through a girl's dormitory late one night, going from door to door trying each one to see which was unlocked. When he finally found one that was open, he crawled into bed with some stranger and when the girl started struggling he punched her unconscious and raped her. Daddy Drew, a very powerful lawyer downtown, was able to get him off arguing that the sex was consensual. I'm not quite sure how he explained the bruises on the girl's face but the jury bought it. Daddy Drew should have let him go to jail. Marshall proved that he did have at least the semblance of a heart two months later when he wrapped his lips around a handgun and pulled the trigger.

As much as my friends and I hated him we couldn't help but feel sad. What a pathetic path he had walked down after graduating from high school. From hero to zero. He couldn't adjust to being yet another peon freshman.

So I am kind of glad that I never was Mr. Popular in high school. Of course, I wasn't necessarily Mr. Big Man on Campus in college either. But at least in college you're dealing with so many people who are on their own for the first time it's much easier to get accepted. It wasn't long before I was going on dates a couple times a month if not more.

Whenever I talked to my friends from high school I found that they were experiencing the same phenomenon. We were no longer a bunch of geeky kids who faded into the woodwork. We were individuals with interests and ordinary libidos.

After a couple years at school, our high school clique drifted apart. David Steinmetz stayed at the University of Missouri in Columbia, Missouri, to work on his law degree; Steve Cash moved out to San Francisco and set up his own studio where he worked on his sculptures made of Play-Doh, Lincoln Logs and tinker toys; and Rob Cantucci moved to Minneapolis to open up Cantucci's Canteen a fast-food restaurant where the employees dressed in fatigues and served up such delicacies as creamed chip beef on toast and Hungarian goulash.

And then there's me, who was walking through the door of Mud Flats for the second night in a row.

Trish greeted me with a smile. "Welcome to Mud Flats, sir. New in town?" she said as she filled a pint glass with beer.

"Hi ya, toots. Did you have to call in the riot squad to clear out those drunken tourists last night?" I said taking my place at the bar. Trish was looking as chipper as ever ready to dole out droll advice.

"No, fortunately Officer Cox came in and threatened to bust some heads if they didn't come to order. They settled down quicker than shit and left a few minutes later with their tails between their legs. I appreciate you sticking around to help. I take it you got home all right?"

"Yes, I was fine but if it makes you feel any better I plan to drink less tonight." She slid a gin and tonic in front of me. I stared at it for a moment then mumbled, "No, let's stick to beer tonight." She took the drink away and replaced it with a draw of Mud Flat Amber, one of several of the brewpub's delicious offerings.

As I nursed that first beer I filled her in about Tony's Florida proposition. She had heard countless stories about Tony before and knew that I hated his guts so I was surprised to hear her say, "I would do it."

"You would? But Tony's an asshole."

"You're not going down there with him are you? You'll be alone for half the trip. Have you ever been to Florida?"

"No. I figure it's full of retired Jews, Cubans, drug dealers and families heading to Disney World. Nice mix, huh?"

"I can't figure you out," Trish said taking on an indignant tone. "You're not sure what kind of career you want to pursue. You're bright, you're funny, and you're attractive. You could take over the world and yet you're not willing to lift a finger to do it. You want other people to tell you what to do and when to do it. Are you waiting for someone to tell you what career to follow? Are you waiting for some CEO to call you at home and say Matthew we want to pay you $100,000 to sit in an office with a window and do nothing? Well, it ain't going to happen. Not in this lifetime."

Trish walked away to take an order. She came back with as much vigor as when she left. "You need to take chances. Just take the trip and shut up about it. It's not that big of deal, OK?"

The noisy bar grew silent inside my head. Trish marched off to fill several pint glasses with beer, looking at me occasionally from the corner of the bar. Obviously, she expected me to come to a decision right then and there. She wanted to see if she could take on a convincing tone. She couldn't. I valued her opinion but the final decision was up to me and I would come to it in time not because some overweight, yet attractive bartender told me what to do. "What was that part about me being attractive?" I said with a smile when she finally made her way back to me.

Trish's frown slowly disappeared. "You shithead," she said, laughing and tilting her head back to reveal a very sexy neck.

I must have been a vampire in another life because I notice women's necks more than most men. I start with the face first, then go to the breasts. What man doesn't? Small breasts have never kept me from going out with an attractive woman. On the other hand, large breasts can compensate for a more homely face. But I digress. Again, it's that breast thing. I can't explain it. But anyway, after checking out the breasts, I will try to get a good look at the neck, which is hard to do. To get a really good, representative view of the neck, the woman must be looking up at something. The rest of the body is inconsequential to me. As long as they are not too heavy.

"You're funny," Trish said as she poured me another beer. "This one is on the house, for making me laugh."

The bar got more crowded as beer three, four and five came around but Trish still stopped by enough to keep our conversation going. We talked more of our histories: how she grew up in farming community just west of Davenport and dreamed about moving to a big city like Chicago or Minneapolis; how she spent one year at St. Ambrose University studying business and ran out of money; how she went through a two-year period of trying every diet known to mankind. She even spent three days on the Popeye Diet, eating nothing by spinach. She told me that when she was a kid she thought that if you flew over the United States in a plane you'd be able to see the names of each state etched into the earth just like on a map. I was happy to hear that I wasn't the only one who thought this.

I told her a little bit more of how my dad left us; about Angela's latest crusade with ARAT; about Tony's wonderment over who was indeed the most powerful superhero; about the guy I lived with in college who got hit by a Campus Bus and actually had died for a few minutes but then snapped back to life. His name was Warren Supple and his diet consisted of nothing but Tombstone pepperoni pizzas and Coca-Cola. That's all he ate two meals a day, every day of his life. He got hit by the bus after a football game our freshmen year. The Hawkeyes had just upset Michigan. We were all walking home from the stadium and Warren, a little too cocky for his own good, ventured right in front of a bus thinking that it would stop. It didn't. Afterwards in the hospital I asked Warren if while he was dead he had an out-of-body experience like many people who die then come back to life do. Did he see God? Did he see a bright white light?

"No," he coughed. "I just saw black."

"That is so bizarre," Trish said, leaning over in the sink to dunk and rinse the seemingly endless string of glasses that were cleaned, filled and passed out to thirsty patrons. I couldn't help but look down her shirt whenever she bent over. I had a pretty good buzz going and that usually gets my lower regions going.

"It scares the shit out of me," she said pausing to wipe her brow with the sleeve of her white jersey.

"Buses?"

"No, death. I mean what happens when you die? Our minds can't fathom not existing. Even when we're sleeping our subconscious is still going in dreams. And yet, if there is an afterlife, can you imagine living forever? I can't. What would you do all the time? It's just so freaky. Maybe when you die you do go to heaven but only for a while. Maybe you resolve all the questions you had while on earth, kind of tie up all the loose strings and when that is done, you cease to exist. Maybe heaven is more like purgatory."

"I see you've spent a lot of time thinking about this, Trish. Is that what you do all night while all of those around you get smashed?"

"Actually, yes," she said smiling.

"Well, I think that when you die, you die. And maybe, just maybe, you get reincarnated. I think God is a recycler. Maybe after 10 life times you are done and either stay in heaven or get thrown on some huge, giant scrap heap."

We continued talking until the bar closed. It was the most engaging conversation I had had in a long time. I usually saved these deep, intellectual talks until I was on a date but for some reason I just felt so comfortable around Trish. Many of my best dates have involved dinner and talking until about 3 a.m. No sex. I have found that a good conversation is more rare than sex. Not a replacement for it, just rare.

As the bar patrons filed out the door en route to their drunken drives back home, Trish announced that she was going to give me a ride home because she was worried about me.

"Oh, I can drive," I said, standing up quickly and then feeling a little lightheaded.

"You probably could, God knows you've done it before," she said as she untied her apron, folded it and placed it behind the bar. "I just don't want you on the road with all those other drunks that are going home right now." As she guided me out the door she told another bartender to close up for her.

I flopped into her Toyota pickup like a sack of wet cement. Not having to drive home myself I suddenly became more drunk. I didn't have to psyche myself mentally for any obstacle course so I kind of just let loose.

"You're not going to fall asleep on me, are you?" she moaned as we pulled out of the bar's parking lot.

"No, I'm just going to pass out for a few minutes."

As we pulled up to my mom's house a strange feeling came over me. I had thought Trish was just being a good friend giving a drunken guy a ride home but I was beginning to think she had an ulterior motive. Was she trying to seduce me? If I had been sober, like she was, I wouldn't have lingered in her truck at all. I would have waved thanks and jogged inside. But I wasn't sober. My brain was floating in about 96 ounces of beer. "Uh, well, thanks, Trish, for the ride."

"I had a good time," she said turning toward me. She tried to stare into my eyes but I couldn't bring myself to look at her. I know that if I did we would be mashing in that front seat right away. "Did you?" she asked quietly.

"Did I what?

"Did you have a good time tonight?"

"Hey, this is sounding strangely like the end of a date," I slurred.

"I'm just asking if you enjoyed our talk."

"Yeah, I enjoyed our talk. I haven't had a discussion like that in some time. We have a lot in common."

Before I could react, she had moved over on the bench seat, placed her left hand on my left thigh and was kissing me gently on the lips. And I was kissing her back. What was going on here? I hadn't planned on this. Although Trish was a friend, pretty and had a great personality I wasn't attracted to her in a physical way. It was the beer. It was shifting my reasoning power down to my Johnson.

My mind was saying no or at least was leaning toward no yet I didn't resist. I found myself groping her, she groping me, becoming one tangled feverish mess in the front seat of her truck. "Oh, Matthew," she moaned as we wrestled, lip locked. That was it. Blood had definitely vacated the brain and headed south. All she had to do was moan desirously and I went on autopilot. I asked her if she would like to come in already knowing the answer.

We headed straight to the basement. We paused only briefly outside as Trish sized up the exterior of our pink and white house. If she had not had sex on the mind she might have made a snide remark about our fabulous siding.

It was late and I didn't want to wake mom so we tried to be as quiet as possible. I didn't think she would mind, anyway. I was an adult. Trish was an adult. Just two consenting adults ready to do some nude wrestling in the basement.

No sooner had we got into the basement and we were into bed struggling with each other's clothes. My reasoning abilities had completely left me. I was going to get laid and I was going to do it as quickly as possible. It was as if all of sudden I was a virgin again and my sole mission in life was to lose that burden, that badge of shame and immaturity. Trish was no longer my friend at Mud Flats. She was a target.

She was moving at just a great of speed. Someone had lit a fire in her loins as well. She didn't seem to mind that we were about ready to fuck in great squalor. My room looked as if it was ground zero for some kind of clothes bomb. I actually had a week's worth of dirty underwear piled in one corner. Two or three piles of clean shirts and pants haphazardly folded on top of my oak dresser. Issues of Sports Illustrated that went back three months were intermixed with pairs of Levi's strewn on the circa-1970s orange, yellow and brown shag carpet which had been walked on and vacuumed so many times that the shag had been beaten out of it. And then there were the dirty dishes. Bits of half gnawed-on Pop Tarts, a half-full glass of milk, five or six empty cans of Coke littered the top of my desk. My mom had called it a pigsty and I couldn't argue with her. It was a mess.

Well, fuck it, this pig was about to get laid.

Chapter Four

I have put myself in some pretty embarrassing situations in my life but never one so humiliating as having your mom enter your room all dressed prim and proper for work and finding you as naked as the day she vacated you from her womb lying next to some completely nude 150-pound, tattooed woman who she had never met before.

Without so much as a knock or a "yoo-hoo" she just walked in. Woah. Back up one second. Tattooed? In our passion the night before, I had not even looked at Trish's body. She was fat, fatter than I recalled, and on her left thigh she had a tattoo of a Cobra with blood dripping from its fangs. I hate fucking tattoos. If I would have seen that last night I very well might have stopped our little tango right in progress even if I was wearing beer goggles.

"Ah, excuse me," my mother said quickly backing out of the room, slamming the door. It happened so quickly that I couldn't tell whether mom was embarrassed or pissed off. She certainly had something to be pissed about. She had never met Trish before so it certainly looked like I was waking up from a one-night stand. And as any single person out there knows, one-night stands are a thing of the past.

"What just happened?" Trish said groggily pulling the bed sheet over her flabby body. "Was that your mom?"

"Yes. Usually she knocks," I said quickly pulling on my underwear. I figured I better get covered up as soon as possible in case my penis got the wrong idea.

"Oh my God, I'm so embarrassed."

"Don't sweat it, Trish. She won't do anything. She's more embarrassed than either of us," I said rubbing my throbbing temples with both hands. For the second day in a row, I had a hangover. Shit. I had to stop doing this to myself. My liver was going to go on strike.

Visions of Mr. Milland flooded my mind. Every time I woke up feeling this way I thought of a teacher I once had back in high school, who once chastised our class for our drinking binges. It was a humanities class and we were very open with Mr. Milland, who reminded me of a meatier, gentile Woody Allen. Each Monday, we would tell Mr. Milland about all the partying we did the weekend before. He just shook his head and said: "I had a hangover once and that's all it took to convince me that drinking to excess isn't something you ought to do." He was absolutely right but since when did high school students ever listen to someone wiser than them?

I felt like puking. Partly because of the leftover alcohol in my system and partly because Trish was really kind of repulsive. I had made love to a slightly prettier version of Roseanne. And what was with the tattoo? Tattoos were for Marines, truckers and criminals and as far as I could tell, Trish was none of these. I hate tattoos. They're evil. I think that if you surveyed all of the inmates in state penitentiaries across the nation you would find that 97 percent of the men and many of the women have tattoos. It's a natural progression. Get a tattoo, commit a crime. I would go so far to say that if you were to tattoo the Pope within a few days he would start shoplifting crucifixes in the Vatican gift store.

I just don't understand how someone could, with rational forethought decide to desecrate his or her own body. And for what? The damn things are ugly. Nonetheless, I found myself mesmerized by Trish's snake as we lay there awkwardly on my bed. Like someone looking at a ghastly car wreck, I couldn't turn away.

"When did you get that?" I said trying to disguise my disgust.

"Oh, that was an idea of an old boyfriend. I went through a brief biker chick phase. I think I only keep it because no one but people I'm intimate with can see it."

"It's, it's...."

"Hideous," she answered laughing. "I know. I know. I guess you live and learn." She leaned over and gently kissed my lips. The blood, involuntarily, started to rush out of my brain and headed to my groin but I detoured it by conjuring up thoughts of Mike Tyson pummeling some skinny white contender. All of sudden the thought of any kind of intimacy with Trish repulsed me, though my dick would have been ready for action in a flash.

"I'd love to stay and meet your mom and all that but I should get going," Trish said sitting up in bed with her back to me. I watched her curiously as she put her clothes on. She struggled to clasp her bra on and for a moment I almost tried to help but what the hell could I do? Bra technology was out of my league. I had trouble enough getting them off, let alone on.

Like the rest of her body, her breasts were a little larger than they should be. Many creeps I have known would say that it's impossible for a woman to have too large of breasts but I don't subscribe to that. A woman ought to be proportional. I like large breasts but if they are too large for the frame then they look wrong. That's why I don't understand all of these women who have breast implants. And who are the doctors giving consultations? Is the size simply up to the patient: "Give me the largest you possibly can, doctor?" "How 'bout this big?" the doctor says holding up a large orange. "No, bigger." "How 'bout this big?" he says with a grapefruit. "No, bigger." "How 'bout this big?" he says holding up a melon. "That's it." "Well, I must warn you that breast implants of this size will lead to curvature of the spine and if they for some reason explode, they will go off with the force of a small nuclear warhead that will not only kill you but everyone in the room." "Will men like me with boobs this big?" "I certainly would." "Then let's do it."

If you ask me, implants should be outlawed along with the cosmetic surgeons who are so willing to disfigure these women.

Standing up to put on her panties and then her pants I really got a good view of how wide she was down there. Most of the time, I had seen Trish from the waist up because the bar always hid her lower half. She really was a large woman. I shouldn't have had such a big problem with this but I did.

I closed my eyes and cursed myself for having reduced this sweet, kind woman into nothing more than a slab of meat. I really liked Trish but I couldn't set my superficiality aside and accept her for who she was. She was beautiful on the inside but on the outside she was, well, fat.

She, on the other hand, seemed to have no problem with her appearance. "Last night was fun," she said smiling after she had finished dressing. She leaned over the bed and touched my cheek.

"Yeah, I enjoyed it," I said truthfully. I had enjoyed it but I wasn't enjoying the morning after. Not at all.

"Call me," she said quietly and headed toward the door of my bedroom. As she opened it, she turned again to leave me with one more soft smile.

Oh my fucking God, what have I done? I had a few beers and wound up sleeping with the bartender, the fat bartender, and now she thinks we are an item. This was not like me. No matter how drunk I had gotten in college or high school for that matter I had maintained a certain standard for the women I pursued. They could not smoke, smack their gum, twirl their hair in their finger, be dumber than your average fence post, have gone out with anyone on any football team, been a cheerleader, listened to country and/or western, have a tattoo, or weigh more than me. Here I was breaking at least two taboos at the same time.

Lying there alone in my bedroom, half-naked, disgusted with myself I had an epiphany.

"Angela, tell Tony I will do it," I said moments later, dressed and standing in the kitchen while my mom gave me dirty looks from the dining room. She poked at her raisin bran like she was jabbing me in the back with a stiletto. I turned so I didn't have to see her. I must have looked like shit. My eyes were narrow slits and my hair looked like a cheap imitation of Don King. I had gas, beer always effected me in this way, and my breath probably smelled about as good as a sock worn by a marathoner.

"That's great but I think you should tell him yourself. I'm out the door here and he already went into the office."

"Aww cripes," I protested. It was hard enough deciding to do this favor for Tony but now I had to communicate it to him. "Where are you going in such a hurry? Can't you just call him and tell him?"

"No, you need to do it yourself. Some of us from ARAT are going over to the zoo this morning to stage a protest."

My hangover suddenly kicked into overdrive. "What? Why?" I whined, rubbing my forehead, which felt like someone had skewered with a shish-ka-bob spear.

"One of our sources has informed us that they are shipping in a rare breed of sloth today. One that now exists almost exclusively in captivity. We want to let the zoological society of the Quad Cities know that we don't appreciate this enslavement. The four-toed sloth will not reproduce in a zoo setting. They are going to force the extinction of this species."

Jesus fucking Christ. "The people at the zoo are experts," I said calmly, deserving a gold medal for my restraint. "Don't you think they know what they are doing? Do you think they would actually cause a species to become extinct? Do you? Come on, you've got in with a group of nuts who are disregarding any kind of logic. They are a bunch of paranoid Bob Barkers and Brigitte Bardots who think they are doing something right when they are completely wrong." OK, so I won't get that medal.

"This is so like you," she said in a strident tone. "You are instantly against any group that stands up for its beliefs. Do you stand up for anything or anyone? If we don't protect animals who will? Do you know what kind of horrible things are done to animals every day in the name of science? Little bunnies' eyelids are forced open while lab technicians drop different formulas of shampoo in their eyes. Rats are forced to diet on all types of medicines that kill them slowly and painfully. Someone has to stand up for the innocent animals. They are God's creatures, too."

Why was I even having this argument with Angela? It was a no-win situation. I was not going to convince her that ARAT was populated with a bunch of losers that drift from one cause to the next like so many retarded lemmings. Of course, this was pure Angela. Who can she save today? "All right, Angela," I said throwing some cold water on the conversation. "I'm sure there are a lot of good reasons to be in this group. I understand that a lot of animals are tortured in laboratories. I just don't understand why you need to take on the zoo. Just think of all the little kid's days you'll ruin with your protest. Families will be out there to bond and they will come face to face with a group of militant Birkenstock-wearing, granola-crunching, backpack-toting, neo-hippies."

She was silent for a moment. "Is that how you see me?"

"No, you know that," I said rubbing my temples while I propped the phone between my shoulder and ear. "I'm just saying that you have good reasons to be in that group. Your heart is in it. But these other people go too far. They are into it because they are bored with their lives. They need some kind of pursuit outside the home. Do you think they are all vegetarians? Do you think they have sworn off leather? It's pretty easy to say you're opposed to the haircare companies that subject animals to torture. Just get a different kind of shampoo. But look at their shoes, look at the purses, look at their belts."

"I'm not in this for them," she said. "I'm in this for me." This wasn't the first time she had uttered these words. I'm sure she had gone through this little speech with fathead Tony as well. Not wanting to sound like him, I backed off. I wished her good luck and said I'd be watching for her in the paper and on the nightly news.

As we finished up the conversation she said that she would go and tell Tony that I had accepted his offer to pick up his grandparents. "No, it sounds like you have enough to do today what with saving the four-toed sloth and all. I will talk to Tony myself. I have to get details for the trip anyway." I hung up and once again felt like shit. My sister was a saint. Why was she married to such a schmuck and have such an asshole for a brother?

"Is that your new girlfriend?" my mother asked after I had showered, shaved and devoured a few bowls of Cap'n Crunch, breakfast food of all junkfood junkies. (And I'm talking the plain kind not that stupid crap with the crunchberries.)

"Well, she's a girl and she's a friend but I wouldn't necessarily put those two words together," I replied fearing where this conversation was headed. Ever since I got home from college mom had been super critical of my actions. I think she figured that if she rode me hard enough I'd get my life in order more quickly.

"You're an adult, so I won't lecture you. But I can't help but comment on your irresponsible behavior. One night stands are dangerous nowadays. I hope you are being careful."

"Yes, I am, mom. I am not stupid." But was I? I was a bit hazy as to whether I had slipped on a condom the night before. Hell, Trish and I were moving so fast once we got into the bed that I didn't even notice her tattoo. Did I take precautions? My stomach started to constrict and my balls shrank. My body was going into panic mode. Christ, did I put on a rubber? Why couldn't I remember? It would be just my luck that my sperm would impregnate a bartender the first chance they got. They were conspiring with my liver.

"Who is this woman anyway?"

"Aww mom, I would love to sit her and chat but I've got to talk with Tony," I rose from the table.

"Does that mean you are going to Florida?" she said apparently happy herself to change gears from Trish to Tony.

"Yes, that's what it means," I said slamming the door on the way out into a brisk wind. That's one thing I hate about Davenport in the springtime—the weather can never make up its mind whether it wants to hold onto winter a few more weeks or head straight into summer.

I hopped into my mom's Ford Escort and wondered what kind of car I would drive down to Florida. "I sure wouldn't want to drive all that way with this thing," I thought to myself. "Christ, this piece of shit would probably die outside Peoria." The engine wheezed and my mind shifted gears back to the night before.

I really liked Trish but I shouldn't have slept with her. My mind and penis were still in college mode where quantity meant more than quality. I'm not quite sure what it was but in college I just wanted more, more, more women. The longest I ever went out with someone was for three dates. I wasn't looking for any kind of meaningful relationship. I just wanted to sleep with as many different women as possible. Sorority girls, girls who hated sororities, rich girls, poor girls, white girls, Indian girls, Hispanic girls, black girls, tall girls, short girls. But never fat girls. I didn't sleep with all of them but I did go out with a representative sample of each.

Maybe I was trying to make up for high school. It wasn't that I was necessarily a loser in high school. I just didn't date many women and especially from my own school. In four years of high school, I may have had three dates with girls from my high school. And it wasn't for lack of trying. They just weren't interested and I'm not sure why. It's not like I had a horn growing out of my forehead or that I had hair on my palms. Maybe it was just because these girls grew up with me and remembered me from my pre-pubescent days as the ultimate spazoid, when I was known to eat the occasional crayon.

Tony's was just a few blocks away and here I was thinking about women and not the task at hand. What was I going to say to him? I didn't want to make it sound like I was doing him a favor. I wanted to make it sound like it was simply an economic opportunity, that I was only doing it for the money. Or did I want to make it sound like I was simply doing it for my sister? Yeah, maybe that was the ticket. "Tony, I hate your guts but because you're married to my sister, I'll do this for you." That would sound nice.

His secretary, Irene, wasn't surprised to see me. In fact, she said in between lip smacks, "He's inside waiting for 'ya." This lip-smacking habit was so annoying I figured Tony would have canned her a long time ago but all I had to do was look several inches below her mouth to see why the swarthy bastard kept her on. Irene had breasts the size of corn silos. They were only surpassed in sheer magnitude by the stack of hair that balanced on her head like the Leaning Tower of Pisa. She fancied herself as eastern Iowa's version of Dolly Parton. She was even known on occasion, whenever there was a Karoke machine within spitting distance, to sing "9 to 5." She couldn't sing worth a damn but come to think of it, neither can Dolly.

Irene looked a bit different this day. Her breasts were still gargantuan and her hair lofty but she was glowing, proud of something she had accomplished. Had she finally figured out how to turn on her computer?

Simply put, Irene was a fucking moron. Although she had been working for the company for 15 years, she was always asking Tony or anyone else around how to do her job. The rumor was that she had been mounting Tony's dad for years up until his death and that's the only reason she was employed. Company pin cushion. Looking at her Barbiesque features, it wasn't hard to imagine.

"You seem to be in a good mood today, Irene," I said walking past her desk.

"Yeah," she said a bit dreamily trying nonchalantly to fit her stocking feet back into her black pumps.

Tony opened his office door just as I was about to enter. "Yo, Matthew, whassup? Have a seat," Tony said guiding me through his office with his arm around my shoulder. I couldn't help but notice that his fly was unzipped. Normally, this would not bother me because Tony was always walking around in some state of undress be it with his shirt untucked or with only one shoe on but coupled with Irene's dreamy expression I got the distinct impression that Irene had just got done "earning her keep."

"So, what it is, my man. Lay the good news on me." He pushed his Chicago Bears helmet lamp out of the way and sat down on the end of his desk so that his legs could swing freely. With the comic books by his side, he looked like a deviant Beaver Cleaver.

"How's the back, Tony?" I said trying to shift gears. I wanted to delay the agony of telling this trained chimpanzee that I would do him his favor.

"Oh, it's all right. I just can't do no exercise or lift nothing. So I guess I won't join the Bears this year," he said laughing, motioning toward the helmet light. He leaned forward and smiled trying his best to get the words he wanted to hear out of me. Just then he glanced down and noticed his fly. "Jesus Christ, what a fucking slob. Left the barn door open. The stallion could have burst free." He not so deftly fumbled the zipper back up. "Man, I'm such a pig. Damn, I've got so much shit on my mind that I forget things. I hope I don't have no pee stains on my trousers." He stood up with his arms outstretched to the side. He turned a few times looking down then hopped up back on the desk. "I'm clean. Damn, having a dick sucks sometime. I mean the sex thing and all is dope. But going the bathroom sucks. Don't you hate those trough things like they have at the stadium? Damn, I may be a stallion but I am not any horse. I shouldn't have to piss in a motherfucking trough. They expect you to whip your dick out while you're standing next to some big oaf with a huge schlong on one side and a little kid with barely nothing on the other. And then you stand there and if you get shy you get the feeling that everyone is looking at you and laughing. 'Look at Holmes. He can't even take a piss.' It sucks. It's almost enough to make you want to stop watching football games. But anyway," his expression turned serious again, "whassup?"

Well, let me see, I could stall him some more and allow him to move onto another delightful subject likes his bowel movements or I could just tell him and get the hell out of there. Tough decision. "I've decided to pick up your grandparents as a favor to Angela."

"Damn, that is dope. You all know I would do this myself if it wasn't for my back," he said rubbing his lower back as he slid off the desktop. "And you know it could really be kind of cool." He patted my shoulder as he walked by toward the door. "Seeing the states. The freedom of the open road. Cranking up the tunes. I've always thought it was down. It's kind of like a therapy thing. Out there alone, away from all that shit you have to put up with every day. It's cool. You should dig it and Edgar and Gert are cool. They old but they be pretty hip. Come on, I'll show you the Caddy." I followed him as he swaggered past Irene and past the telemarketing room where I used to work. As we passed by the vending area outside the telephone room we ran into Woody who was ripping through another Snickers bar.

"Talked to any spankers lately," he said derisively in between bites of chocolate, peanuts and nougat. With the non-Snickered hand, he pantomimed someone masturbating.

"Hey, you're pretty good at that. You must get a lot of practice," I said laughing as we stopped at the candy machine. Tony dug into his pocket and pulled out his keychain to find the key that would give him free access to the candy machine.

Inside was his supply of Marathon bars, a long, thin, chocolate and caramel braided candy bar, that I had thought went out of production sometime in the 70s. Apparently not, though, because there they were in the vending machine. Either those candy bars that Tony ate like, well, candy, were 20 years old or Tony had a special contract with whatever candy company that made them to send him a crate each month. He loved those bars as much as his dip-wad brother enjoyed Snickers.

It was pretty much an unwritten rule that no one tried to buy a Marathon bar, less they diminish Tony's precious supply. I am not sure the oversize bar would have come out anyway. The only time I saw them come out of the machine was when Tony went in after them, with gusto, I might add.

"You cocksucker. If Tony weren't here right now I would kick you fucking ass," Woody said finishing off the Snickers and rubbing his hands free of chocolate. This outburst was typical of Tony's younger brother. Woody would often take potshots at people and when they would come back with a zinger and outwit him, which was about as easy as confusing a Cocker Spaniel, he would resort to unenforceable threats.

Tony closed up the candy machine door and stared at his younger, even more stupid than he was, brother, and shook his head. "Do I pay you to eat candy?"

"No," Woody replied slackjawed.

"Do I pay you to stand out in the hallway?"

"No."

"Do I pay you to insult my brother-in-law?"

"No."

"Then shut the fuck up and get back to work, punk," he shouted with such intensity that he startled both Woody and me. The Snickers mauler bowed his head and quietly shuffled back into the phone room.

"I have to apologize for my fucking brother," Tony said as we made our way through a catacomb of hallways back to the warehouse section of Tony's property. "He's just buggin' coz I am asking you to do this errand. They his grandparents, too, but I need all of my telephone people here. And shit, he don't know squat about directions. He couldn't find Florida if he were standing in the middle of fucking Disney World. You know how some guys you can give the most detailed instructions to and they still fuck it up. That's Woody. He just ain't too bright about shit." And this coming from Tony, the brain surgeon. Ouch.

"Say, Tony, there's something I've always wanted to ask you," I said trying to keep up with his pace. He sure didn't look like a man suffering from serious back pain. I was beginning to suspect that Tony just didn't want to drive down and back to Florida again.

"Yo, whassup?"

"Why do they call him Woody? Isn't his given name Myron?"

"Damn, I thought you knew that story. Shit, I gave him that name. When he was just a little shit moms used to make me change his diaper and all that. One time when I was wiping his ass I seen he had a woody so I told my dad about it. Damn it was the funniest thing. I mean, shit, what was a baby getting a woody about? It's not like he knew what to do with it or nothing. So we started calling him Boner but moms wouldn't have none of that shit. She said, 'You're not calling my baby Boner. That's terrible.' So then dad said, 'Let's call him Woody coz mom doesn't know it means the same thing.' So it kind of stuck."

This explained why Woody had so much rage.

Finally, we reached the warehouse at the back of Tony's property. At the far end of the room, surrounded by empty palettes, was a car beneath a dirty, white tarp. With my help, Tony pulled the tarp back to reveal a mint condition gold-colored 1972 Cadillac Fleetwood. I'm not into cars but I could tell that this was something special. Someone had taken very good car of it. I guess that made sense, though, considering the fact that it was a snowbird's car so it was never driven in winter.

"Go ahead climb in, Captain, and check this shit out," Tony said opening the driver's door for me. I sat down and gripped the wheel. Yes,

I could see myself cruising the interstates with this. Too bad it wasn't a convertible. Then I would really be styling.

"Dope ain't it?" Tony smiled popping his head inside.

"Yeah, I'd say."

"You don't think I'd send you down to Florida in some kind of garbage truck, do you? Fuck no. When I roll, I roll legit and so should you." He put a hand on my shoulder. Tony and I had never showed any affection toward each other. No hugs, barely even handshakes so I was a little bit leery of his gesture. He gripped my shoulder and slowly began to squeeze. "Yo this car means a lot to my Gs and to me. It would be a shame if anything happened to it. Understand?"

"Yes," I said still playing with the wheel as if I was racing the car. "Don't you trust me?"

"Oh, I trust you all right. I know you been taught to do the right thing. Your moms has done a good job raising you and Angela all by herself." He pulled his hand off my shoulder and started to walk around to the other side of the car. "I just want you to be down with the rules of this little errand. Coz if you ain't down, you don't get yo money. You want yo money, right?"

Enough already, you swarthy bastard. What the hell are you getting at? Didn't I say I would do this already? All of a sudden, he was getting creepy on me. I figured I was doing him a huge favor and now he was becoming Milton Bradley with the rules. "Yes, Tony, what are you driving at? Am I supposed to drive exactly at 53.7 miles per hour and never touch the radio? Am I only to fill it with Texaco premium or am I supposed to throw it into reverse and drive backwards all the way down to Florida?"

"Hey shut the fuck up, you smartass," he snapped. "I know you think you got my ass behind the motherfucking 8-ball and that you are all doing me a big-ass favor and shit but this a motherfucking job all right and I got some rules." He paused a moment to see if I had a smart-ass reply. I didn't.

"First, do not speed. If Johnny Law gives your ass a ticket, you pay for it. Second, no hitchhikers. I shouldn't have to tell you all this but I will anyway. And this includes any Bettys you meet along the way. If you get lucky one night in some town you cannot take your date along with you. I only want people who respect this car in the car and that includes you and Gramps and Grams. Third, no drinking and driving. Not one beer, not one joint, understand?"

"Tony, I don't do the reefer." I lied. Actually, it was only a half-lie. I didn't smoke at the time but I certainly had in the past and felt like taking a big hit off a bong whenever I had to deal with this turd.

"Yeah, right," he said making a face. "Fourth, no driving after 10 o'clock at night. More drunks are on the road after 10 and you will be tired that late at night. It's just not safe."

"Tony, I appreciate your concern for my safety," I said, my voice ripe with sarcasm as I climbed out of the car.

"Yo, I'm worried about the fucking Caddy not you, shithead. Rule No. 5," he pushed on. "Stay at cheap hotels, say like $70 a night. I ain't made of money. Don't give me that look. I don't want you staying at no fucking Ritz and ordering room service. You can find plenty of good, cheap hotels along the way. I know. I've done this plenty of times. Six, and this is the most important, respect my grandparents. They old, they set in their ways. Don't try and rock their world. They've been very good to me and I don't want to send them some punk who fucks up their minds. They the ones who are paying you so you're really working for them. I want you to be polite and all that shit. You know, like yes, sir, no, sir. They will want to talk because it's a long drive so don't give them the fucking silent treatment.

"Just so you knows, Edgar used to own a bakery in downtown Cleveland back in the day. He loves to tell stories and shit of how the mob was always trying to get him to pay him extortion money. And Gert will probably tell you how she used to be a showgirl in Las Vegas. It's just a bunch of shit but she likes to think it's true. She actually grew up in Cleveland and never traveled outside the city limits until she met Edgar. They moved to Davenport when they were in their 30s. A fire burned down their bakery and they moved in with Edgar's brother, Harold, who owned a company downtown that made athletic supporters and shit.

"Don't be surprised if Edgar tries to tell you the story about how he how swam across the Mississippi every day for three months to get ready for a fight with Joe Louis. It's all bullshit but Grampa likes to tell that one, too. Especially, when he tells you how he was disqualified because the referee was a nigger lover and that he really beat Louis fair and square." Tony started laughing. "Gramps is da bomb."

I was beginning to think that it would be a very long trip back from Florida. Tony's grandparents, not surprisingly, sounded like a couple of fruitcakes. I appreciate a good story but not when it is so obviously false. During my freshman year at college, I lived across the hall from a guy, Howie Rankelwitz, who told similar stories. How he once dialed a wrong number in New York and ended up talking to Madonna. That was ludicrous enough but then he had to make it even more unbelievable by saying that after talking to her for 15 minutes she told him she was getting incredibly horny and wanted him to talk dirty to her. By the end of the conversation, 45 minutes later, he said she was masturbating while he told her that he was going to tie her down to the subway track and fuck her while a train was coming. Good story but totally unbelievable.

"So pay attention to them," Tony continued. "They are not nuts just a little, uh, what's the word. Eccentric. They just a little eccentric, man. Now do you understand all da rules?"

I nodded.

"You gonna have to say, 'Yo, Tony, I fully understand da rules' because this is very important to me. I can't have you raising hell all the way down to Florida and back."

"Yo, Tony, I fully understand da rules," I said mocking his I-want-to-be-black delivery. "You know, this isn't exactly going to be a picnic for me, Tony. I'd rather be doing other things. I mean this is a job so I'm going to treat it like a job. Wasn't I a good employee? Didn't I show up on time and fill out my log sheets completely? You know your brother can't say the same."

"Yeah, you was a good employee for all of two weeks," he conceded.

"I believe in quality not quantity, Tony. I was an *excellent* employee for two weeks." I didn't need this moron questioning my work ethic. This guy who reads comic books, snacks on 20-year-old Marathons candy bars and drinks Sprite all day long.

"All right, all right. Shit. I'm axing you to do this one trip and I'm axing you not to fuck it up, understand?" He produced and then dangled two sets of keys to the Caddy in my face.

"Fair enough," I said reaching for the keys. "Why is there two sets of keys?" I said letting them slide into my pocket. They created quite a bulge. Hey, I'd be popular with teenage hitchhikers.

"Because if you lose one pair then you ain't fucked. I truss you but I don't truss you that much. Now good luck and remember da rules," he said as he patted me on the back. "Here's a Visa card for you to use for gas, hotels and emergencies. And here's 200 dead presidents for food on the way down and back for you and Edgar and Gert. That's not much so you'll have to go to Mickey D's and places like dat. Want someplace fancy, you can pay for it yourself."

That Tony—quite the big spender. I figured after one or two meals of Big Macs and fries, his grandparents would be springing for something nicer. I know old folks like McDonald's but even they can only consume so much MSG. On the other hand, being related to Tony they might be able to subsist on crap food alone. Neither Tony nor Woody had much of a discerning palette. When they wanted to treat themselves they drove right past McDonald's and Burger King and headed to Denny's. Ahh, high living. This was strictly a drink-beer-from-the-can type family. Drinking from a glass was for fags, Woody once told me. With this kind of attitude running rampant in the Aalto family, maybe the old geezers would consider Big Macs a treat.

"All right, big guy, I'll starve myself down and back. And I'll follow all of the rules. You want me to be responsible and I will be. Enough with all of the instructions. You sound like someone's dad."

"Thanks, man. Angela said I wouldn't make a good father. I guess she is wrong, ain't she. I would make a great father, straight up." He opened up the driver's side door for me. "It ain't got much gas so head straight for a gas station. Head home, pick up your stuff and then leave today. I'll call down to Edgar and Gert's and tell them you'll be down in three days. There's a map in the glove compartment that is highlighted with the exact route I take every year. It's the best route. There's also a sheet in there that gives instructions on how to get to their place. Now get the fuck out of here and don't wreck the fucking Caddy or I'll mess you up."

It took a few tries but the Caddy eventually started up. It must have been sitting in the warehouse since the fall when Tony had driven his grandparents down to the Sunshine State. It roared to life, happy to once again be running. I checked all of the turn signals and lights. Everything was working including me. For the next week I had a job. Open road, here I come.

Chapter Five

After filling the Caddy up with gas I headed back home thankful that mom would be at work. I didn't want to see her looks of recrimination. So I had slept with a fat chick who I really didn't know all that well. Big deal. So I was acting like an idiot. Done that before.

She was thinking, I'm sure, but would never say it—that I was acting like I was still in college. And I was. I'm sure she wanted to tell me that it was time to enter the adult world as much as I didn't want to. And I say why can't you be a kid longer? You get 18 years to have fun and then it's all work the rest of the way. Back in the Middle Ages it was different. Back then you died when you were 36 so it was more evenly distributed, 18 years of fun, 18 years of work. Because of modern medicine, we are being kept alive too long, far outliving our usefulness. Just look at Bob Hope.

I think society should at least give you until 30. Don't get me wrong, I'm certainly not advocating any more time in school. Rather I am suggesting a period of free time from say age 24 to 30. Call it the Big Recess. Offer it as a reward for getting educated, for putting in all of those years learning worthless topics like trigonometry and Shakespeare.

Before I go on further, I have to ask: What is the big, fucking deal with Shakespeare and why is he required reading? What makes him so great? I've read his stuff before and let me tell you it's nothing to write home about. It practically takes you 10 pages before you understand what the hell he is trying to say?

What about authors like Dickens or Twain? Why don't they get more recognition? I'm sure some schools somewhere teach them but every school I went to force-fed me Shakespeare, Shakespeare, Shakespeare. Enough already. Somewhere along the line someone with the Secret Shakespeare Society must have bought someone off. Some book publisher had to unload a warehouse of Shakespeare plays because he had printed too many so he bought off the board of education. That's what happened.

Anyway, back to the Big Recess. The government would subsidize the Big Recess and you could use it as you wish either traveling the globe or simply sitting in your living room in your pajamas watching talk shows that explore such topics as aliens and how they are capturing and enslaving the world's supply of heterosexual figure skaters.

Each month you would receive a check from the government to help subsidize the Big Recess. It would be like social security except you'd actually get to use the money for something worthwhile. Rich people wouldn't qualify for this stipend, however. And dropouts wouldn't either. I think Congress should seriously consider the idea.

The house was quiet as I packed a duffel for the trip. I threw in some jeans, a few T-shirts, some shorts and my swim trunks. I take my swim trunks wherever I go though I rarely use them. I guess I just want to be prepared if the mood strikes me to jump in a pool.

I'm not a wet kind of guy. Except for showers, I rarely get my head under water. This reluctance to imitate a fish is probably due to the fact that I was nearly drowned when I was seven. Hugh Blankenship, a highly spirited 10-year-old as his mother put it, tried to drown me at the community pool one day. We were playing in the shallow end, splashing the littler kids when Hughie either grew tired of simply making the kindergartners scream or was suddenly possessed by the devil. He came up with the brilliant idea to dunk me. Once, twice, three times he shoved my head under. On the fourth dunk, he held my head underwater. He must have been pretty damn strong for a highly spirited 10-year-old because I was writhing around like a garter snake. I was struggling with all of my might to get just one gasp of air but I couldn't overpower him. I don't know why Hugh decided to pick me as his victim; I hardly knew him. He had just decided to murder someone that day and I happened to be conveniently placed within arm's reach.

As I was about to pass out, a lifeguard sauntered his well-tanned hide over to the shallow end and yelled at Hugh to stop drowning me. Hugh ignored him. He was intent on killing someone this sweltering July afternoon. Finally, much to the lifeguard's chagrin, he jumped into the pool, pulled Hugh aside and yanked my head out of the water. In between gasps of air, I started to ball. I don't remember much more after that except for the weird look on Hugh's face. He wasn't laughing or frowning. It was a look of disbelief. I have never figured out what it was that he couldn't believe—that he had nearly killed me or that I was crying.

Hugh is in medical school at the University of Wisconsin at Madison now.

After packing the duffel, I filled my backpack with tapes that I would listen to during the trip. I picked some particularly obnoxious ones—Carnage Camp, the Butt Uglys, the Morticians, Spatterdash, the Blah, the Virile Monks—for the ride back up with Tony's grandparents. I threw in some music magazines and a copy of Ayn Rand's *Atlas Shrugged*. At more than 1,000 pages, I figured I would be reading it for the next decade. Like the swim trunks, I always packed the book though I had yet to read one chapter.

As I headed out the door, the phone rang. I made a move toward the phone but then thought otherwise. Whoever it was would have to wait a week for whatever it was they wanted, so why bother.

"Hey, it's Trish," I heard through the answering machine. "I just wanted to see if you had plans to stop by Mud Flats tonight. I'd love to talk some more. See ya. Good-bye." Her sweet voice was full of commitment. Fuck. Reason No. 57 why I had to get the hell out of town. You sleep with someone once and all of a sudden they think you're married.

I tossed my duffel in the back seat and leaned across the expansive front seat to open up the glove compartment. Deep from the bowels of the front seat a stench of stale cigarettes began to rise. It was a really old smell as if someone had smoked in this car a lot, a long time ago. Maybe Edgar or Gert had conquered cancer sticks and never bothered to fumigate the Caddy. I looked in the ashtray and sure enough there were a couple cigarette butts crushed in there. Both had a hint of red lipstick so I figured it must have been the old woman, though I guess it could have been Edgar. As far as I knew he liked to smoke and cross-dress.

From the glove compartment, I retrieved Tony's route map. There wasn't much else in there. A book of matches from a Super 8 in Nashville. A couple of Band-Aids. A golf tee. The Caddy's Owner Manual. A pencil. A few pieces of small blank paper. And a packet of E-Z-Wider cigarette papers. Now this could have meant a couple of things. Either Gert used to roll her own cigarettes or someone had been rolling joints in the Caddy. Something didn't make sense here. The cigarette butts in the ashtray were definitely from a factory, not hand rolled. I tried to remember if Angela had ever mentioned anything about Tony smoking pot. Not that there's anything wrong with it. In fact, it would explain some of his weird behavior and his penchant to crank Pink Floyd music at home whenever Angela tried to talk to me on the phone. Well, whatever, it was a mystery that would remain just that.

Tony's map was well worn and I had to be careful not to rip it as I unfolded it. I didn't doubt that this was the best route—I was just curious where this errand was taking me. His grandparents were in Bal Harbour, just north of Miami. I probably could have driven there in two long days but what would be the point because they weren't expecting me until Sunday afternoon. It was Friday morning now. I could take it easy and enjoy the scenery.

The route took Interstate 74 down through Peoria and Champaign to Indianapolis. From there it took Interstate 65 down through Louisville to Nashville. It then headed to Chattanooga on Interstate 24, then jumped to Interstate 75 through Atlanta to Lake City, Florida. In Lake City, it took Interstate 10 to Interstate 95 to the Coastal Interstate down to Miami. There was nothing but interstate ahead of me, which made driving easy but extremely boring. If I had my way I would drive two-lane highways all the way down and back but then the old geezers would probably be dead from old age by the time I got back home.

The problem with interstates is that you really don't get to see America. You just pass it by quickly, which is fine if you are a speed-crazed trucker. I'd rather see the behind-the-scenes America, where a two-lane highway becomes Main Street in every small town. I was amazed to find out in the college that the interstate system was designed by the Eisenhower Administration in the 1950s as a means to mobilize troops for war. Up until that time I thought it was made to allow Americans the ability to get where they are going faster on their vacation. That's how naive I was. That's like thinking that guns were invented to defend ourselves or to use hunting when the real reason is to kill people you don't like.

I folded the map back up and put it back into the glove compartment. As long as I remembered the next major city on the route I figured I would remember which interstate to take. It certainly didn't require me constantly checking the map.

Before I started the Caddy again, I decided to check out the entire car. Having found the E-Z-Wider papers made me wonder what else might be hidden inside. I started with the trunk but found nothing except a wool, navy and orange Chicago Bears stadium blanket, jumper cables and all of the tools necessary to change a flat tire.

I jumped into the back seat and was amazed at the amount of room back there. You could hold a football game back here, I thought to myself sliding back and forth on the smooth seat. The old farts will be very comfortable back here, I said as I then bounced up and down on the seat. I wondered whether they would both sit back here or whether Edgar, being the man, would insist on riding shotgun. I hoped they would want to stick together. I didn't want some old geezer in the next seat over telling me to slow down or do this or do that. Of course, being in the back seat would not stop him either, probably.

Beneath the front seat I found a few more items. A small butane cigarette lighter, half a pack of rock hard Big Red chewing gum, and issue #274 of the Fantastic Four. Believe it or not, they were saving the world from evil. Don't superheroes ever get a day off? I'd love to see an issue where they just go to the Ice Capades or on a picnic.

I figured Tony would be happy to know I had found it. Knowing him, he had probably been tearing his hair out trying to find it. He keeps all of his comic books in a windowless room in his basement. I snuck in there once, expecting to find Tony's stash of pornography. Instead, I find a shrine to Stan Lee and the Marvel Comic kingdom. Tony stores them on shelves he built himself. They are arranged alphabetically and covered with plastic so that they don't get mildewy. In the middle of each shelf he has a favorite copy displayed standing upright. In the middle of the room on the concrete floor is a humidifier that keeps the comic books from drying out. Heaven forbid that Tony's basement ever floods.

I threw the Fantastic Four comic book on the ledge between the back seat and the rear window and crawled out of the back. My inspection of the car was now complete.

The car started right away showing no sign of the hesitation it had in Tony's warehouse. With a full tank of gas, I was ready to roll. I checked the rear view mirror, the side mirrors and all the gauges. I pulled a Nirvana tape out of my bag and pushed it into the tape player, holding my breath as I waited for the music to come on. It would have been a disaster if the tape player hadn't worked. In fact, I probably would have told Tony I couldn't go but soon enough Kurt Cobain was complaining about something or other I couldn't make out and I was off.

It was getting close to noon so I had missed several hours of good driving time. I would have to drive into the night to get as far as I wanted for the first day. That was all right. I was looking forward to the freedom of the open road. No Tony, no mom, no Trish, no searching for a job, no laying on the couch all day trying to find something good to watch on TV. Just driving and cranking the tunes.

I was beginning to wonder if all the resistance to the assignment was really necessary. I don't like Tony but it wasn't like I was driving all the way down to Florida with him. So what if it was a favor for him? He was my sister's husband and whether he was a goon or a genius I was beholden to him. That's just life. You don't have to love your in-laws just tolerate them.

This trip was a great opportunity to get out and see the country. I was going to go through states I'd never visited before. Christ, states I had never even thought about. I would hear people talk slowly with a southern accent. I would see palm trees. I would eat grits. I would hear people say stuff like "Yup," "Y'all" and "I tell you what." I would see America.

There's something intoxicating about being behind the wheel of a large automobile, especially a smooth-riding, luxurious Caddy. It's like I was escaping time. As long as I didn't stand still, all of life's problems would not catch up with me. Fuck Davenport. It can do without me for a while. See ya in a week, I'm hitting the open road. Just me and my golden Caddy.

By the time I reached the interstate I was flying. I didn't have a care in the world. I really did leave all of my troubles back at the house. This was going to be like a vacation for me and the best thing was I was getting paid for it.

Awesome.

* * *

"This sucks," I yelled at the top of my lungs as traffic came to a standstill on Interstate 74 just outside of Peoria. The trip up to this point had gone smoothly in just a couple of hours. Traffic was heavy but moving along at a good clip but then I ran into every driver's worst nightmare, road construction. I don't know why the morons in the Department of Transportation needed to work on major thoroughfares during the middle of the day. Couldn't they work on the weekends or at night?

And who would have anticipated traffic problems in Peoria of all places? Christ, it's not like it's Chicago.

The geniuses at the DOT had traffic down to one lane in both directions and even then were only allowing a few cars through at a time because they were hauling rock or some other shit back and forth over the road. Two o'clock became 2:30 then 3 o'clock before I finally got away from Peoria. An hour of traffic in freaking Peoria. I made a mental note to send a scathing letter to the governor. Dear Governor, drive your own fucking car through one of these construction zones and get a clue.

I was always fantasizing about writing letters to people who pissed me off. I never did it but it felt good to imagine conjuring up some sort of pithy missive filled with razor sharp wit that cut some asshole to the core.

Having spent so much time in Peoria I felt the urge to air out the Caddy, to catch up on some lost time. I knew one of Tony's main rules was no speeding but I didn't want to fall any further behind in my schedule so Rule No. 1 be damned. I floored it to make up for lost time.

After two or three miles I was back down to the speed limit. I'm just not one of those screw-the-consequences kind of guys. I can't help but envision the result of my every action. I figured that if I were to speed for too long, Johnny Law would materialize from behind some kind of anti-abortion billboard where the fetus is pleading to unwed mothers and I would get a ticket, which I certainly could not afford to pay. And, besides, getting pulled over would further slow me down because the cop would have to make sure that the Caddy wasn't stolen. No, 65 was fast enough to get me where I was going.

As Illinois turned into Indiana, I couldn't help but think of John Cougar Mellencamp. As I drove along through his home state I couldn't really figure out what it was about it that had inspired the rock and roll pop star. It wasn't as boring as driving through Nebraska but it wasn't exactly take-your-breath-away beautiful. It was rural. Farm fields, pigs, cows. I guess it's all a matter of perspective. This was his home, not mine. I was just passing through. He would probably think Iowa was boring to drive through, which for the most part it is.

The boringness of a state's scenery is the kind of shit that runs through your mind when you're driving alone across the country. On one hand I was happy to be away from the congestion of city driving but on the other city driving keeps your mind busy. You had to be alert at all time. You can't blink for a second less you get run off the road by some tie-wearing go-getter blathering to his stockbroker on his cell phone.

Out here in the country there is nothing to keep your attention except for the occasional billboard for Shoney's or the World's Largest Truckwash or the Pro-Life movement. I guess there's also the livestock to keep you entertained though that gets old after about three minutes. If you're real fortunate, you may be lucky enough to come across a couple bovines humping. Now that's entertaining. I don't know why it is but I've caught a lot of different types of animals in the act. As a kid, I stumbled across cats and dogs and even squirrels doing it. Then as I grew older I witnessed ducks, horses, pigs and even raccoons do it. Maybe it was God's way of telling me that I should become a veterinarian, or at least a voyeur.

As I thought about animals in various positions of coitus my mind wandered back to Angela and her pals with ARAT. Did they save the four-toed sloth at the Quad Cities Zoo or did they just all end up thrown in the slammer? I was beginning to get bored of the countryside so I decided to take a break and call Angela.

"Hi, Angela. So you're not in the slammer," I said when she answered on the fifth or sixth ring. I knew how these protests went. I never really protested in college but I knew several people who would hang out on the fringe at protests and they were the ones who ended up getting arrested. I guess it was easier for the police to nab those on the outer edges of the crowd than work their way into the middle. They didn't want to go too deep into enemy territory.

"Yeah, I'm here but seven people were arrested," she said her voice quiet, tired as if she had just gotten herself calmed down after a traumatic experience. "I'm surprised I wasn't arrested. It seemed for a minute that they were going to arrest all of us. Those cops were scary. Someone at the zoo must have a lot of pull because the minute we started to chant and hold up our signs at the front gate they pounced on us. We didn't even get a chance to get near the sloth's cage where most of the TV cameras were waiting."

"So you won't be on the news tonight?" I said standing at a payphone at a state-run rest stop. Next to me families were coming in and out from their vans and sedans to visit the restrooms or shove quarters into the vending machines for bags of Doritos or Ruffles that contained about four chips.

"Oh yeah we will, except they mostly just got footage of the cops escorting the people who got arrested into a school bus. We'll have to wait and see how they spin it. We told the reporters that we weren't breaking any laws, just having a peaceful demonstration in a public place. We told them about the plight of the four-toed sloth and hopefully they will use some of that."

"If you were just having a peaceful demonstration why did seven people get arrested, Angela? The police know that's what you want. They wouldn't arrest you and give you the publicity if you weren't doing anything wrong," I said scanning the lobby of the rest station. The place reminded me of an airport. People from all over the country gathered in one common spot—urinating, eating, looking dazed and confused.

"Well, there were a few of the members who dressed up in animal outfits and..." her voice trailed off.

"What? What did they do?"

"A couple other women were dressed in white lab coats and they did this little, kind of, play."

"A play? What kind of play?" I said pushing her to reveal more.

"The woman in the lab coats had these fake hypodermic needles that shot out a pseudo blood mixture and well they were only supposed to shoot it on the members dressed up in the animal costumes but they got a little wild and started shooting it on innocent bystanders. They just wanted to get everyone's attention."

"Yeah. Well, it sounds like they certainly got the attention of the Davenport Police Department. Are you all right after all of this?" It was difficult for me to be sympathetic toward Angela. I loved her but I just didn't agree with her on about half of her actions. She really tried my patience.

"Yeah, I'm all right," she sighed. "Actually, I'm kind of glad that those women were arrested. Maybe that will settle them down. We had a meeting after the demonstration at the zoo and voted to let them stay in jail overnight. We won't post bail until tomorrow morning. We need to send a signal to all of the members that we need to be organized, that we can't go off half-cocked because we will just end up looking bad. And we can't look bad if we are to continue with this cause. I really believe this is right, Matthew. I know you don't agree with us or our principals but humans have been too cruel to animals for too long. We can't be bullies just because we are stronger and smarter."

"But Angela…" Damn it, I can't just let things go. I hate that about me. I'm a perfect example of someone who doesn't understand the adage: It's better to be silent and be thought a fool than to speak and remove all doubt. "It's human nature to eat meat. We're carnivores. Just like dogs and cats and lions and tigers and bears. That's why we have teeth that can cut meat. It's natural."

"We have evolved into meat eaters. Our bodies have adapted over the centuries to eat meat. The first humans ate berries and nuts."

"That's not true. And even if it was true they only ate berries and nuts because they didn't have any tools to capture the meat. Once they figured that out they went to town."

"Well, I think it's wrong and I'm going to continue to demonstrate. You are entitled to your opinion and I have mine."

"Yeah, you're right," I said. "It's just that you are fighting a battle you cannot win. Man is always going to eat meat, wear furs and buy leather jackets."

As Angela and I argued over the phone a rather large women in a purple and orange dress set camp a few feet away from me. Apparently, she was either waiting for a chance to discuss animal rights with me or call her connection at Overeaters Anonymous. "Hey, I gotta go. There's someone here who wants to use the phone." I didn't really feel a pressing need to yield the phone to this fat purple and orange blob but I was tired of going back and forth with Angela.

"So you don' t want to hear about what's next for ARAT," she teased. She knew what kind of bait to toss this fish. The fat woman would have to wait.

"Oh come on. Haven't you guys done enough for one week? The news channels aren't going to follow you to every single protest. You're going to dilute your marquee power."

"We're not worried about the press for this one. If they come, they come. This protest is personal," she said very seriously. "Remember Clayton Dale Tuleen III, the reputed white supremacist who lives down by Galesburg? Well, it's no rumor. We have proof that he is indeed a bigot and we're taking action.

"Hold on a second, what's some white supremacist have to do with animal rights? Aren't you guys getting your causes confused?"

"He's a cattle farmer," she said matter-of-factly. "We're going to set free the cows he has imprisoned and if we do a little damage to his property, so be it."

I couldn't believe what I was hearing. I glanced over at the orange and purple blob to see if she was still eavesdropping on our conversation. In one hand, she held a king-size bag of nacho cheese chips, in the other a Diet Coke. As long as she had something to consume I would be all right.

"I have disagreed with you in the past on just about on everything, Sis, but mark my words you are way out of your league here. This is utterly, totally wrong. Clayton Dale Tuleen is not a man to reckon with. He has rifles and knows how to use them. This is a man who is consumed with hatred toward blacks, Jews, homosexuals, fingernail chewers, exercise video producers, soccer goalies and any one else who doesn't share his views, which is basically everyone who is sane. He won't take kindly to a group of left-wing animal rights activists. Someone could get killed."

"No one is going to get killed. We need to send a message. Demonstrating at the zoo is small time. We need to do something big to get the attention of the world. We need to make some sacrifices so that animals will be freed from their years of slavery."

I felt a tap on my shoulder. It was purple and orange. She had emptied the bag of chips.

"Hey, buddy," she gurgled in the type of voice you'd expect to come out of a hippo if it could talk. "You 'bout done? It's a public phone you know."

"Yeah, I'm just finishing up," I said shooing her away. "Angela, please don't do this. Call in sick. Say you have another protest to go to. Make up an excuse but don't go."

"I've already put it on my schedule. I'm going. We need to send a message."

"This is so wrong," I said as I motioned to purple and orange that I was wrapping up the conversation. She was beginning to snort and pace like an amorous rhino.

"How's the driving?" Angela said switching gears suddenly.

So, it was done. Even if I had returned to the ARAT conversation there would be no convincing her to stay away from Tuleen's farm. She had made up her mind and no one could change it. She actually thought she was doing the animal world a favor. As if animals gave a shit.

And for those others in ARAT, it was a chance for them to do themselves a favor by getting involved in a political cause. The assault on Tuleen's farm would help them justify something they did in the past. Angela was strictly doing it out of altruism. Now I would have to worry about her until this Tuleen assault was over and she was safe back in Davenport. Sometimes I wish Tony had more of a spine so that he would stand up to Angela and say, "No, you're not going." But, then, she would go anyway because no one tells my sister what to do.

"How's the driving?" Angela repeated.

"Uh, it's boring as hell," I said honestly. "Driving alone sucks. I don't know how truck drivers do it. I am almost to the point where I will resort to listening to talk radio."

"My, it must be bad," she said, laughing. She knew I hated talk radio. I am of the belief that the only time there should be any talking on the radio is to introduce the next song, give the weather report or to tell us that we've been invaded by aliens. Otherwise it should be all music.

"Well, I gotta go, there's someone here who needs to use the phone. Please be careful. Use your head." I hung up and turned to face purple and orange. She was not happy. She stood there leaning against the wall with her flabby arms crossed. "Hey, I'm sorry. My sister is going through a crisis," I told her.

"Save it, pal, I've gotta call my support group," she said rushing by to grab the receiver. As she started to dial the number, she turned to me. "I had been very good about junk food until now. But all of this driving has gotten to me and now when I want to call my sponsor, someone's on the goddamn phone for hours. So what do I do? I internalize my anger and wolf down a bag of chips. I've fallen off the wagon and it's all your fault, you and your fruitcake sister."

I walked away as she continued to blather on. I've got my own problems, I don't need those of some Jenny Craig reject.

I was bored and I was angry as I made my way back to the Caddy. I didn't relish the fact that I had to climb back into the golden cruiser and drive for another three hours. God damn those ARAT bastards, they were going to get Angela hurt or killed. My sister was destined to die a martyr for some lame-ass cause and there was nothing my mom or I or Tony could do about it.

I unlocked the Caddy and sat there motionless with the door open for several minutes trying to calm down. I needed to get my mind off ARAT, their stupid ways and Clayton Dale Tuleen. At this point, I was just too irritated to drive. I would probably have taken someone out if I got onto the highway now. I had to mellow out. Chill.

I needed a diversion to get my mind off of Angela and her immediate future. I needed a diversion to keep my mind off my immediate future. Surely I would die from boredom driving through rural Indiana.

That diversion came to me on two legs in a second-hand powder blue suit.

Chapter Six

"I hate to be a bother, young man, but could I trouble you for a ride?"

It was as if he appeared out of nowhere. I was sitting there in the front seat of the Caddy, door ajar when this man materialized two feet away from me. The voice was calm but the eyes, leathery skin and deeply cut wrinkles were those of a drifter. His jet-black hair was greased back and looked out of place given the lines in his face. There was not a touch of gray in it and it looked like it belonged to a much younger man.

The suit was well worn as if it had been through years of job interviews, weddings and funerals. The pants were flared a bit too much to be fashionable and the lapels were too wide as well. That suit was probably 20 years old. Beneath the jacket he had a white shirt that had been worn thin by being laundered too many times. He also wore a thin, solid red tie that was probably newer than the suit by five years or so.

Around his neck, dangled a cobalt blue plastic kaleidoscope that hung half way down his chest. It wasn't one of those fancy kaleidoscopes that can be turned to show different designs, rather it was one of those cheap ones that simply multiplied the image you looked at, like you were looking at something through a fly's eye.

"I carry this wherever I go," he said noticing that I was intrigued by the toy around his neck. "It lets me see things I like—many times. You see one cigarette. I see 64." His thin smile added another crease to his face.

He looked physically fit but tired as if he had walked too many miles in the sun along dusty, two-lane highways. He wasn't much taller than me and probably weighed a little less. He was wiry—thin nose, close-set eyes, small mouth—but appeared strong. He had the hands of a day laborer—thin, sinewy, capable.

"Where you headed?" I asked quietly, really only giving him the time of day because of the suit. That suit told me he was trying. He may have had some tough luck in life but at least the suit and his kind voice showed that he was at least trying.

"New Orleans. Vieux Carre. The French Quarter," he said his smile expanding showing a mouth full of good-looking teeth stained by years of cigarette smoking.

"Sorry, I'm not headed to Louisiana," I said.

"But you're headed south, correct?" He leaned in close enough for me to smell his breath. No trace of alcohol, at least that I could detect. Actually, his breath smelled like dust.

"Well, I'm headed to Florida but that's pretty far from where you're going."

"Then maybe," he said smooth and cool like ice cream, wrapping his long fingers around my left forearm, "you can take me as far as Nashville." I started a bit when I felt his grip. It was firm, reassuring yet menacing at the same time. It was like how a father would grip his young child when the child had wandered too close to a busy street. "It would be a great favor if you could," he said still smiling. What was up with all of the smiling? The only people I had seen smile this much were preaching on Sunday morning cable broadcasts.

At first, I was tempted to inform him that picking up hitchhikers was strictly in violation of Rule No. 2 but then I thought I have no intention of following Tony's stupid ass rules. I know it's wrong to pick up hitchhikers but this guy didn't look bad. Sure, he was rough around the edges but he probably had a lot of great stories to tell. It might be nice to have someone to talk to for a few hours. Maybe he worked for the circus for a while in his youth. I have always had a fascination of the circus life. It is such a close knit society. They all probably sleep around with each other. Maybe he had done it with the Bearded Lady.

Or maybe he was a recovering alcoholic. I could quiz him on it and prove to myself that I had no drinking problem. Maybe this stranger could give me the kind of advice I needed to figure out what I wanted to do with my life. Or maybe he would just slit my throat and steal the Caddy. Oh, that's bullshit. He wasn't going to hurt me. He had a suit on for crying out loud. This guy wasn't your average run-of-the-mill hitchhiker, the kind that stand by the side of the road wearing a black Metallica T-shirt with the sleeves cut off, ripped up blue jeans and one of those wallets with a chain attached to prevent anyone from stealing it although it's completely empty. Those kinds of people give hitchhiking a bad name. Christ, if they would just clean up their act they would get more rides. Who would be stupid enough to pick up someone like that? Hell, they might as well be holding a cardboard sign that says "Pick me up and I will fuck you up the ass" on it, scrawled in pig's blood.

"All right, I could give you a ride for a few miles, but not all the way to New Orleans. I have to keep on schedule. Throw your stuff in the back seat."

Slowly he loosened his grip on my arm. He straightened his back and nodded. "I am much obliged, young man." He walked slowly around to the other side of the Caddy and opened the front door. He had nothing to put in the back seat. He eased his long, lean body into the passenger seat and placed his palms on his knees. "I am ready," he said staring forward.

And with that I started up the Caddy and headed out onto the highway. "Hey, mister, you better fasten the seat buckle." I said noticing that he had not moved since sitting down, his palms resting perfectly still on his kneecaps.

"Ah, yes, the seat buckle. We are all in need of a bit of restraint. Thank you for thinking of my welfare, young man." He buckled himself in and then pulled a stick of lip balm from his pants pocket. Like a woman applying lipstick, he applied it directly on his lips, first with the upper lip then down on the bottom. Most men I know are afraid to apply lip balm this way. They will dab some on their finger and then wipe it on their lips. When he had finished applying the balm he smacked his lips together twice, continuing to stare forward.

Well, this was certainly going to be interesting, I said to myself. This guy sure was eccentric. His voice sounded a bit like that old actor James Mason but he wasn't British. No, it sounded like he was from the south, or at least was a long time ago.

After driving in silence for five minutes or so I asked him: "What's your name, mister? I'm Matthew."

"Well, nice to make your acquaintance, Matt," he said emphasizing the T's in my name. He leaned over toward me to shake my hand. Once again he had a firm, reassuring grip that was almost painful. "My friends called me Diablo last month," he said slowly, as if he were thawing out after taking a long walk on a bitter January afternoon. Diablo? What the fuck?

"However, to be honest with you, I'm growing rather tired of it," he continued as he slowly warmed up to the conversation. "I need a new name. What should I be called this month?" he asked himself.

What should I be called? Five minutes into it and I was already rethinking my choice to give this guy a ride. There's a good reason why hitchhiking is illegal—because the people who do it are freaking nuts.

"Nosferatu," he said, turning toward me. He raised the fly's eye toy to his eye and sized me up through it.

"Nosferatu," I said slowly. "Like that old-time vampire?" Christ, now I know I had made a mistake. This guy's elevator not only didn't reach the top floor it was fucking broken down in the basement.

"Kind of melodic, don't you think? Nosferatu."

"Yeah, it's melodic," I managed to get out trying my best to sound sincere.

"Well, that decides it then. Call me Nosferatu." He let the toy kaleidoscope drop so that it dangled on his chest again.

Several minutes passed by again.

"But what's your real name?" I finally asked hoping to turn this nut case back into a real man.

"What's in a name, Shakespeare once wrote, if it was he who indeed wrote it. One never knows. My real name is Harry Jones but it is so nondescript that I rarely use it. It's harder to remember a name like Harry Jones than it is to remember something like the Crusher or the Impaler or Diablo or Nosferatu. Wouldn't you agree? Harry Jones is not a name that gets men to do things for you. Harry Jones might as well be a number. It doesn't demand attention."

The proverbial ice had been broken. Harry Jones/Nosferatu was completely at ease in the front seat of Tony's grandparent's Caddy. I, on the other hand, was not. Rule No. 2. Rule No. 2. Why couldn't I follow instructions? It was obvious to me now that I should have left Nosferatu Jones at the rest stop. But, as I thought about it barreling down Interstate 65 heading south to Louisville, did I have any choice? He had appeared out of nowhere and the way he grabbed my arm was menacing, like I had to do whatever he asked. I could have told him to get lost but the way he held my arm, I doubt he would have gone. So here I was stuck with "Nosferatu," the eloquent, but whacked-out hitchhiker. Might as well make the most of it.

"The Crusher and Impaler. Those are all names you've gone by?" I said.

"Absolutely. Kind of fun, isn't it?" he said playfully. "It's so boring being called the same thing all your life. I got tired of everyone calling me Harry all the time. 'Don't pick you nails with that switchblade, Harry. Don't cut your sister, Harry. Here's your cell, Harry.' It's enough to make you crazy. I don't know about you, Matt," he said, emphasizing the Ts again. "But I hate to be bored. I really, really hate to be bored." He looked at me again through his fly's eye toy.

Gulp.

"Why don't we come up with a new name for you, Matt? It could be a name that only I call you, a pet name, something that has special meaning to me and to you.

"Matthew is fine with me," I said quietly.

"Let me see," he said bringing his forefingers together under his chin. "How about something like Matthew the Apostle or the Cadillac Kid…"

"How about just Matthew?" I chimed in more loudly.

"You're right, those names are no good. How about…"

"You know, Harry, it would be easier for me to remember if you just called me by my given name."

He was silent for several miles and I wondered if I had offended him. I didn't want him to keep up his creepy talk but I didn't want to piss him off either. "I've got it, " he spurted out suddenly, snapping his fingers simultaneously. "Faust. That's perfect. You shall be called Faust, the man who sold his soul to the devil." He laughed.

Jesus, this guy was freaking me out.

"So, Faust, do you have any thing to eat in this vehicle?" He said removing his suit jacket, jerking his head around like he was some squirrel foraging for food on the forest floor.

"This isn't a convenience store," I snapped, angry that I had put myself in this situation, picking up a complete stranger who was more that likely going to make my life more difficult than it already was. What the hell was I thinking?

"My, you're a bit punchy, aren't you?"

"Well, what do you expect? You're a hitchhiker," I said, figuring that it didn't really matter how I acted. This nut was going to do whatever he chose to do. Why be cordial? "You're supposed to sit there and behave. Maybe tell a few stories about your life, tell me about the scrapes you've had with the law and then talk about how you're heading somewhere to turn your life around. That's how hitchhikers act. They don't sit down and give the driver of the car a new name and ask if they have anything to eat. Jesus."

"I'm sorry I don't fit the mold, Faust," he said sounding a bit hurt. " I'm just asking you to be hospitable. After all, I am your guest. You don't invite someone into your home and then not offer them a bite to eat. It would be rude." He folded his suit jacket in half and gently lay it in the back seat. As he leaned back I noticed a whole new dimension to Nosferatu. His white dress shirt had no sleeves. They had been haphazardly cut off at the shoulder. And worse yet, he had tattoos up and down both arms. When I say tattoos in the plural, I really mean plural. They were solid from his armpit to just above his wrist. Nothing but tattoos. And we're not talking hearts and cupids. We're talking dragons, skulls with snakes slithering through eye sockets, gargantuan-breasted nude women straddling rockets, motorcycles, knives, guns.

Tattoos. My God. Tattoos. What was I going to do? Tattoos, the calling card of the homicidal maniac. The passwords to the gates of hell. Tattoos. Skin graffiti. One way tickets to the big slammer. All of a sudden he turned from an eccentric drifter down on his luck to one fucking scary individual.

"You like them?" he said with a grin on his face.

I didn't reply. I just kept my eyes on the road.

"A story goes with each and every one of them," he continued. "I love tattoos. They define a man. They say, 'I'm interesting.' They say, 'I'm an individual.' A lot of people despise them, think that whoever has one is a criminal. How small-minded. That's why I wear my suit coat when I'm hitchhiking. People tend to drive right by a man with tattoos. On the other hand, if you look a little dressed up like you're a businessman who just happened to get a flat tire or have some other kind of car trouble, you're much more likely to get a ride. It's sort of my little trick. And I have found it works quite well."

I'll say it works. I never, in a million years, would have picked up this freak if he looked like he looked now in the front seat of the Caddy. Christ, I would go so far to say that if a man was drowning and I swam out to him and saw he had tattoos, I would not only not save him, I'd probably shove his head under water. Frankly, tattoos scare the shit out of me. I can't understand why someone would purposely disfigure themselves with something so God-awful ugly. Nosferatu had tricked me all right.

"So, Faust, since you don't have any treats to offer me, we'll just talk. I have found that a good conversation can make a long drive seem like a short one. I once traveled the length of the Mississippi with a former Nazi who had been able to escape the Allied Forces, changed his identity and moved to America. It was most interesting. So, why don't you begin? What's your story? Why are you driving to Florida?" he said, rubbing his arms vigorously. Without asking permission he leaned forward and turned off the air-conditioner. Obviously, he felt at home in the Caddy. There was no tentativeness of unfamiliarity on his part.

This stranger had forced himself into my car and now was demanding entrance into my private life. I didn't feel like telling this guy jack shit. "Well, there's not much to say," I mumbled as I kept my eyes on the road.

"Oh come now. You may be young but I'm sure you have some interesting stories to tell. That's what the open road is all about, right? Where are you going? How did you get this wonderful car? Come on, open up. It would make for such pleasant conversation."

"I don't really feel like talking right now."

"Running away from something? Did you knock up Sally the cheerleader?"

"Yeah, right."

"Or perhaps no one is treating Faust with any respect so he just took off to clear his mind and Florida sounded like a good place to go?"

"Nope," I said, wishing he would just shut the hell up.

He sat there silently for several minutes. Had he figured out that I didn't want to talk or was he trying to come up with another guess on why I was in this Caddy driving cross the country?

Suddenly, he pounded the dashboard with both hands. "Dammit, Faust, open up. What's your story?" he shouted.

I just about drove off the road.

"Jesus Christ, dude, fucking mellow out, will you?" I shouted as I pulled the Caddy from the shoulder back into the right lane.

"There is no need to shout," he said calmly. "And there is certainly no need for profanity. If you don't want to tell me about yourself, fine. But that will make our trip down to New Orleans exceedingly mundane. Two people simply staring at the countryside, simply killing time."

"Listen, man," I said, cursing myself for getting into this situation. "I am not driving you all the way to New Orleans. That is completely out of my way. If you want me to open up, I'll tell you about my boring life but I am not driving down to freaking Louisiana."

A smile creased his face. "OK, go ahead, Faust," he prompted.

I summed up my life story as briefly as possible while we headed down Interstate 65. Born in Davenport, father left family when I was a baby, mother raised us on her own, she never re-married though she has gone through several long-term boyfriends, my sister is a saint married to a moron, Tony's family is a bunch of crooks, I was heading down to Florida to pick up Tony's grandparents, blah, blah, blah.

Nosferatu was a good listener, soaking up every word as if my story was actually interesting. When I was done, he reached into his pocket to pull out the lip balm. He applied it daintily while asking: "OK, but what about you? You've told me about what brings you to today but what about you? What about the real Faust?"

"Hey, you can cut it with the Faust crap," I said. "My name's Matthew, not Faust."

"All right then, Matthew," he said, placing the lip balm back into his front pant pocket. "You've told me about your family but nothing about you. What are your feelings about your dad? About your mother? The way we feel about our parents reveals a lot about how we feel about ourselves. You gave me nothing but cold, sterile facts, what about your feelings?"

Christ, who did this guy think he was? The hitchhiking Joyce Brothers? Despite a burning desire to slam on the brakes and kick him out of the car, I answered him. The way he looked at me was almost hypnotic. "I love my mother very much and I don't really have a dad so I am ambivalent toward him."

"Wait a second," he said, laughing. "You can't sit there and tell me you have no feelings toward your father. Whether or not he was there for you as a child, he is still a central part of your being."

"I've never known the guy. He might as well have been a sperm donor for all I care. He knocked my mother up, stayed around long enough for me to be born and then took off. He's a non-entity."

"Nonsense," he snapped, slapping the dashboard with both hands again. "I don't believe it. I don't believe it for one minute."

"Hey," I shouted. "Take it easy on the car, buddy."

Dammit, this nut was getting on my nerves.

"Your connected to your father whether you want to admit or not. You are part of him and he's a part of you," he said leaning over to grab my right arm.

"All right, all right," I conceded, yanking my arm free. "I'm pissed off at him, for Christ's sake. Of course I am. Why wouldn't I be? He fucking left us. He was a goddamn coward. He couldn't handle the responsibility of a family and just took off, worthless piece of shit."

"And you're afraid you're just like him," he said slowly, menacingly.

"I am nothing like my dad," I said spitting out each word. "Next subject," I barked after a few moments of silence. "We are officially done talking about me."

* * *

"I used to have red hair," Nosferatu said quietly, almost to himself.

"What?" I mumbled, my attention returning back to the car. We had been driving in silence for that past few minutes. I had spent the time thinking about dad and where he was now, whether he had re-married and had other kids. I had a lot of questions about dad. It's not as if I didn't think of these questions all the time. I did. It was just that in the Caddy with nothing to do but think, the questions seemed more weighty.

I also wondered what my family would have said if they had seen me in this situation. Mom would have had a cow. ("Matthew, you know better than to pick up hitchhikers.") Tony would have had a cow. ("You motherfucking idiot, I says no hitchhikers. Stick to da rules.") Angela would have saved a cow but otherwise would have been fine with me picking up a person in need.

"I used to have red hair," he repeated. "In my younger, care free days, I had hair the color of a carrot. Some people would say it was orange. I hated it. My parents thought it was cute. The kids at school would tease me, 'Carrot top, carrot top,'" he said in a sing-song voice. "I'd get into fights at least once a week just because the color of my hair. One kid, Everett Kimbrough, was particularly cruel. He used to say that only homosexuals have red hair, that my hair turned red when my dad buggered me as a baby. He said his father told him that that's why people have red hair. They're parents had molested them at an early age and their hair turned red with rage. I was such a dumb little kid that I believed Everett. He used to hold me down and dunk my head into puddles after it rained. 'Red Faggot, Red Faggot,' he would spit into my face as he forced my head down into the muddy water.

"I wanted to cut it all off. I would rather have been bald than have that damn red hair. My father told me to grow up and be a man. 'If someone doesn't like the color of your hair, punch him in the stomach. If they punch you back, kick them in the nuts, again and again,' he told me. But I couldn't fight back with everyone who made fun of me. There were too many of them. I would be fighting every day. My father called me a pussy and said he would start referring to me as his daughter. He told me if I didn't stand up for myself he was going to beat the tar out of me. He was going to make a man out of me yet. So one day I fought back when Everett came after me. I felt as if I didn't have a choice. I couldn't go against the old man. So when Everett called me the Red Faggot in front of my classmates, I punched him in the stomach. He staggered back a bit, stunned that I was actually defending myself for once. I must admit it felt pretty good punching him in the gut. He walked away and I thought I had won but then he returned carrying a piece of wood he found behind the school. He then beat me in the head until I was bleeding and practically unconscious. 'Now, there's some red blood to go with your red hair, Jones, you faggot,' he said dropping the piece of wood. He then walked away laughing."

Harry "Nosferatu" Jones was silent for a moment. I kept my eyes on the road.

"I mean have you ever seen a movie star with red hair that you liked?"

I thought for a moment and couldn't think of anyone. There was David Caruso from "NYPD Blue" but his star flared out quickly. And Donny Most, the guy who played Ralph Malph on "Happy Days" had red hair. He certainly was no chick magnet. He was right, I couldn't think of one leading man with red hair.

"Lucy," I exclaimed after a few minutes of thought. "Lucy had red hair and she was a huge star."

"She was a woman. I'm talking about men."

I thought for a few more seconds. "Woody Allen. Doesn't Woody Allen have red hair? Or at least used to."

"I'm talking about real men, not some pint-sized New York Jew boy. You don't see Woody Allen busting some door down and plastering the room full of bad guys with a sawed-off shotgun. I'm talking about heroes. You can't think of even one because there isn't any. People don't like men with red hair. It's a simple fact."

All of a sudden Nosferatu turned to me and started to laugh—a really hearty laugh as if God had flicked on the insane switch in his brain. He laughed like this for several awkward minutes. I kind of laughed and smiled half-heartedly because I had no idea what the joke was about.

Finally he settled down and calmly said: "So that's why I started dying my hair in high school. At first people thought I was strange for doing it but after they got used to it they started to accept me more. I was no longer the red-headed freak. I no longer belonged on the circus midway. And the girls, those lovely high school tarts, started to notice me. It's amazing how a little black hair can turn your life around. First I'm getting beat up by Everett Kimbrough, next thing you know I'm sleeping with his younger sister."

He paused a moment to shake his head slowly as if his own story was hard for him to believe.

"Yeah, that's right. I dated Kim Kimbrough, my arch-enemy's only sister. I called her Kim-Bro. We were pretty hot and heavy, too. One time we even fornicated on his bed. He was out of town for the weekend and we started to mess around and Kim-Bro knew how Everett and I didn't see eye to eye and so she suggested messing around on top of his bed. I wouldn't say that the relationship was based solely on passion but it sure wasn't for her brains. After all, she and Everett shared the same parents and Everett was as dumb as a post. Kim-Bro and I broke up soon after Everett found out about us. First he pounded on her then he came after me. He was a strong kid, put me in the hospital with a concussion."

He rubbed his temples and stared at the flat countryside out the passenger window. I wanted to ask him why he thought Everett had so much hatred for him. It couldn't be just because he had red hair or because he had fought back once or even that he had been sleeping with his younger sister. But then Nosferatu never did say how young Kim was. Maybe she was only 12 or 13 and if that was the case I could see why Everett would hate him. Maybe Everett was jealous of him because Everett had been sleeping with Kim before. I envisioned an entire white trash soap opera and just didn't want to go further.

"I hope you have an enemy, Matthew," he said turning back toward me. "Because, Lord knows, we all need one."

"What?" I asked, thinking immediately of Tony, public enemy No. 1, Al Capone, Charles Manson, Adolf Hitler in the world of Matthew Picasso.

"I said I believe that everyone needs an enemy. It keeps us healthy. Mentally. We need someone to vent our anger at, someone to hate when things do not go our way."

"That's ridiculous," I said still thinking of Tony sitting there at his desk reading the latest issue of The Incredible Hulk with all the intensity of Garry Kasparov concentrating on his next move. "You and I may have enemies but not everyone has or needs one. What about someone like Mother Theresa?"

"Wasn't Satan her enemy?" he said quickly. "I've put a lot of thought into this, Faus…Matthew. It's not ridiculous. We have to put up with a lot of difficulty, a lot of resistance in this world. You can't do this, you can't do that. We're all like tea kettles on the stove. As the world turns up the heat, we need to vent off a little steam here and there. Look at America. We've always needed an enemy. We had the Indians, the British, the Germans, and then more specifically Hitler, then the Japs, then the Russians."

"Yeah, well the Cold War is over," I interrupted.

"Yes, but now we have spread our hate around. Some people hate Khaddafi or any Middle Easteners for that matter. And what about race relations? There is a lot of hate in this country. Niggers. Jews. Wops. And then there's everybody's favorite target, homosexuals. Faggots. Dykes. And what about fat people. We hate fat people."

A picture of that orange and purple junk food swilling mama at the rest stop popped into my mind.

"We have a lot of anger in America. It's all a product of capitalism, Matthew. We are taught to strive. To crush the opponent. To succeed at all costs. But not everyone can win so when we can't get our way, we hate. It's easy.

"I've always had an enemy. When I was young it was my father. Then it was Everett. Now Everett is no longer of this Earth and so I have found a new enemy—Jerome Paul."

For a millisecond there, I thought he was going to say me. A shiver made its way down my spine as I asked: "The talk show host?"

"That's the one. In fact, he should be coming on in a few minutes," he said, looking down at his watch. It was 6:45.

Jerome Paul hosted a syndicated radio talk show from 7 to 9 Monday through Friday. He was the liberal version of Rush Limbaugh. Obese, dapper, balding, rich, inflammatory. He didn't really believe in every thing he said, he just said it to incite people. No cow was too sacred for Paul. Often times, he went after the callers who disagreed with his viewpoints with a vengeance. As a result, callers threatened his life right on the show on practically a daily basis.

Jerome Paul was based out of a not-so-popular Creole restaurant in New Orleans' French Quarter called the Blackened Crawdaddy. Most of the show he spent sucking down shellfish or jambalaya. There were many reasons why I didn't bother to listen to the fat pig feign intelligence but the main reason was because I couldn't stand to hear him talk and chew food at the same time. He was disgusting. And I hate talk radio.

Although the Big Easy is known for tolerating a lot of weirdness, the city certainly did not embrace Paul. He sat back in the restaurant and ranted and raved about same-sex marriages, abortion, welfare and affirmative action and all around him the town and the state of Louisiana were seething. He once said off the air that to save America the government should start killing off everyone with an IQ of less than 90, which he added insult to injury by saying Louisiana would be a lot less crowded. He denied saying the remark but whether he really said it or not was not the point—he had infuriated the entire state while raising his ratings at the same time.

His show was an odd two-hour mix of conservative bashing and self-gratification for the Southern Bell of Truth, as he referred to himself.

He surrounded himself with bodyguards, who were rumored to be members of The Pink Patrol, a gay militant group based right in the Quarter. He could hardly walk the streets alone for fear of getting his head blown off by some NRA card-toting conservative. He was the most hated man in all of Louisiana history, making Huey Long look like a Boy Scout.

If the vile things he said on the radio weren't enough to make you dislike him, there were rumors as well—that he was a transsexual, a transvestite, a child molester, that he married his mother and continued to have sex with her 5 years after her death. These vile comments were spread by conservative journalists who begged for him to be censored, or better yet, pulled off the air. Secretly, these writers wished he would always have a job because he made for such interesting copy.

"So I suppose you want to listen to his show?" I asked reaching for the radio.

"Want to. I must," he said rubbing his hands together.

"If you hate him so much why do you listen?" I said clicking on the radio. "That's exactly what he would want you to do."

"It is not only good to have enemies, it is good to know them and engage them in battles frequently. Tonight is just another battle," he said while applying yet another coat of lip balm.

"Another battle that he is going to win because you'll listen to him, get pissed off and get your blood pressure up. Meanwhile, he'll sit back and get fat on jumbo shrimp," I said laughing, happy that the subject of conversation had veered off me.

"He may win his share of battles but I will win the war. Every dog has his day." I glanced over at him as I fiddled with the radio to find a station that carried him. Nosferatu was entranced. His hatred for Jerome Paul was obvious. So much that I thought he might start frothing at the mouth. I didn't fully disagree with his 'you had to have enemies' theory but he was taking it a bit too far.

"Bonsoir, my friendly liberal Americans," Jerome Paul crackled over the AM dial. I had found him just in time. "And to those conservatives who tuned in again to listen to the man you love to hate I have this advice for you. Turn off the radio and go polish your gun because if you listen tonight I'm sure you'll want to go postal and kill some innocent bystanders as you exercise your inalienable God-given Second Amendment right. That's right. You guessed it. The topic tonight is gun control."

The hitchhiker let out an audible moan as he fidgeted in his seat. "You fat bastard."

I wasn't sure how to respond to him. If he hated him so much why did he bother to listen. I could care less what some obese shithead in New Orleans had to say about anything unless he was going to tell me where to eat.

"Before we get to some phone calls it's time to read a little hate mail," Jerome Paul continued. "As those of you who tune in every night know, yours truly gets besieged with hundreds, nay, thousands of letters each day from hateful people who think I deserve to be in jail simply for speaking my mind. Don't we still live in America? The people who so rabidly defend the Second Amendment are the very ones who want to destroy the First. Rather than burn these maligned missives of mischief I pick a few to read each night. The first comes from Decatur, Alabama: 'Dear Jerome Paul, I hate your f-ing guts.' Well, listeners, yet another letter from someone who failed to complete the second grade. I continue: 'The only reason I can imagine you're still on the air is because you're buttf-ing all of the FCC board of directors.' No, Mr. Decatur, I'm on the air because of ratings. If you'd stop listening to me then my ratings would go down and my show would be canceled but you're too stupid to understand that, aren't you? Now run along and join your local KKK rally in progress.

"The next letter comes from Lebanon, Indiana: 'Dear Mr. Paul, I hope you are enjoying your time on the air waves because you won't be there much longer. I'm coming to get you. I'm going to hunt you down like the wild animal you are and do the world a favor. And then I'm going to be a national hero.' Just like a conservative to threaten me with violence. Why don't you inbred, cloven-hoofed jackasses take care of me the liberal way and boycott my show? Put pressure on my bosses to get me fired. Don't threaten me. Don't you know that that only makes my bosses happy?"

My psychotic guest was smiling as he sat silently rocked back and forth in his seat. He was definitely enjoying the Hate Mail segment of the show. "Do you think he's getting the message?" he said, turning to me, smiling as he peered at me through the Fly's Eye.

"What message? That there are a lot of sick people out there who hate him? Yeah, I think he's got an inkling." He got the message all right and he was riding it all the way to the bank. As long as the people who listened to his show were anything but indifferent, he would be rich and happy.

Jerome Paul wasn't kidding when he told his listeners how to get him kicked off the air. He was absolutely right. Don't listen and he'll fade away. But his enemies kept listening. Maybe they used him as a stress reliever. Instead of beating their wives or kids, they would focus their hatred on Jerome Paul. Or more likely, they would listen to him, get outraged, and then beat their family after the show or head out onto the street and hurt innocent strangers.

"He must be stopped. He must be stopped. He must be stopped," Nosferatu repeated quietly as he hung unto Paul's every word. I leaned over and turned off the radio. His trance was given me the creeps.

"There I just stopped him," I said glibly. "That's all you have to do—turn off the radio."

"Oh, now why didn't I think of that? It's such an easy solution," he said sarcastically as he leaned over and turned the radio back on. "Good idea, quitter."

"Quitter? I'm no quitter," I said, tempted to turn the radio off but figured we could play turn it on, turn it off for miles before one of us gave in. So I gave in.

"Look, you won't even turn the radio off again," he said. "You want to but it's not worth the struggle to assert yourself, is it? Our country is going to turn to mush because of you and your kind, Faust," he said angrily. "You don't care about anything. The TV has ruined you. Don't like something? Turn it off, change the channel. Don't endure anything. Don't like Jerome Paul? You simply turn off the car radio as if that will make him go away. Oh sure, it may make him go away in this car, this tiny universe, but what about everywhere else? He's still out there, corrupting the world with his filth. He's a menace and he must be stopped but he won't be stopped by anyone from your generation. You don't care. You would not lift a finger to protect anything you believe in. You want everything handed to you. That's why you don't have a job, Faust. That's why you live in your mother's basement. That's why you don't have a girlfriend. You figure that if you don't commit to anything you won't have to quit it like your father did."

"That's not it," I interrupted.

"You're taking the easy route," he continued. "Never take on responsibility and you'll never be held responsible."

"All right."

"Just coast through life. Let everyone else make the tough decisions."

"That's enough, Jones."

"Let mommy take care of everything."

"Shut the fuck up," I yelled closing my eyes even though the interstate was crawling with cars. "Do you want a ride or not cause if you keep this bullshit up I'll just pull over and you can walk to fucking New Orleans."

"Aww, I've struck a chord," he said stretching his legs out in front of him, as if making me uncomfortable made him more comfortable.

"No you haven't struck a chord," I spat back. "It's just that you're wrong. I've had responsibility all my life. I was the man of the house. I've held jobs. I got my degree…"

"Man of the house," he said harumphing. "Boy of the house, you mean. Did you ever have to fight off an intruder or put out a fire as 'Man of the House?'"

"No."

"Well, then you were no more man of the house than woman of the house. You're living in a state of denial, Faust. You are not even responsible to your own feelings. You're typical of your generation. A legion of slackers. 'Our parents have ruined the country. There's nothing we can do about so why try.' That's your rallying sigh. So you sit around and watch your 68 channels on your 27-inch Sonys, dreaming about ways to get rich without having to earn it. You sit there and watch you talk shows that feature miscreants living in trailer courts because their pathetic lives make you look like a king. You sit there and pass judgment when you're no better than they are. Your life is just another Springer show waiting to be broadcast."

Obviously, Nosferatu had been spending a lot of time thinking about this. Where was an ejector seat when you needed one?

"Lights, camera, action," he shouted at the top of his lungs, nearly causing me to lose control of the Caddy. "This is your life, Faust. I'm Jerry," he said holding his lip balm up to his lips as if it was a microphone. "The topic today is 'Slackers who live in their parent's basements.'"

"Will you shut the fuck up?" I screamed trying to conquer the chaos that had taken over the moment. "Jesus fucking Christ. If you don't shut up I'm going to pull over and kick you out.

"Didn't you already say that? You wouldn't do it. You couldn't do it. You're not man enough," he said, laughing.

"Do you think I would have allowed you into this car if I had known you would be hassling me from here to fucking Timbuktu about my goddamn personal life," I said trying my best to calm down. "Enough is enough already. I don't want to talk about it."

So we didn't. We drove in silence for 10 miles. My heart was pounding. My head was throbbing. I wanted to get off this ride but I was stuck with Harry the clown. We were both strapped into one very scary rollercoaster ride that wasn't ending. I was tired. I was hungry. I just wanted the day to be over. I just wanted to be rid of this freak.

What was I thinking? Why did I ever accept this assignment? How did I allow myself to be put into this situation? Why wasn't I back at Mud Flats having a beer, trying to look down Trish's shirt? Better yet, why didn't I go into grad school so I could still be back in college? A life I understood. A life I enjoyed.

"You're not thinking about dropping me off, are you?" he said, breaking the silence. He turned to me and grabbed my right arm tightly. "That would not be good," he said slowly, evenly. "It would take me a long time to walk to the next town. And I don't like walking."

I said nothing as I yanked my arm free from his grasp and looked for a truck stop to pull over.

"I said you're not going to drop me off," he repeated slowly through clenched teeth. "It would not be in your best interest to drop me off. Are you listening, Faust? Can you hear me?"

Oh, I could hear him all right.

Chapter Seven

His eyes narrowed to slits, his sinewy fingers dug into the padded dashboard. He breathed through his nose as if he was lifting a great weight over his head. Despite all of these signs that I was sitting next to a crazy man just about to go over the edge, I was determined to pull over. I had to stop and think. I had to take a leak, too.

"Hey, settle down, man. I heard you. I'm not going to drop you off," I lied. "I just need to take a piss and get some gas. All right. Is that all right? If I don't get some gas then we'll both be walking and I don't like walking any more than you do."

We were just outside of Louisville at this point. Nosferatu looked at me skeptically. The doubt I had placed in his mind was going to be hard to remove. "Just sit in the car if you don't believe me. I can't leave without the car," I said while thinking: "How am I going to ditch this son of a bitch." I would have to be smooth. One fuck up and I would be stuck with him for who knows how long.

"I think it's time I tell you the rest of the story of Everett Kimbrough," he said, sinisterly.

What was this? Was he trying to throw me another curve? Throw me off balance? I was trying to figure out a way to get rid of him. Not too far ahead I saw the red, white and blue sign of an Amoco station. I pulled into the right lane to exit the interstate. He was blathering away about the last time he saw Everett. I was only half-listening.

Just as I was about to pull off the interstate he shouted "Faust" at the top of his lungs. It was so loud I nearly wet my pants. I veered back onto the highway, narrowly missing a sport utility vehicle the size of Connecticut. The bastard honked as he blasted by.

"Listen to me," he yelled. "I am telling you a story that is of great interest to you," he said grabbing my right forearm again.

"Jesus fucking Christ, are you trying to cause an accident or what?" I yelled keeping my eyes on the road, while I tried to wrench my arm away from his grip.

"I realize you are looking for a gas station, Faust, but it is not that difficult. Just pull off at the next exit and I'm sure you will find one. It is not half as important as what I am telling you."

"What the hell are you telling me?" I said tersely not really giving a shit about what he was talking about.

"I killed Everett."

Did he just say killed? OK, now I gave a shit.

"It's really kind of ironic how it happened," he said while calmly applying more lip balm. Jesus Christ, this guy had antifreeze running through his veins. After nearly getting squashed by that SUV, I was a physical wreck. I could barely grip the wheel my palms were so sweaty and my heart was chugging like a frat boy at a house keggar.

"Several years after my last run-in with him," he continued calmly, apparently not concerned that the driver of the vehicle he was traveling in at 65 mph was having a heart attack.

"I was hitchhiking outside of Muncie, Indiana. I had just quit working as a landscaper at Ball State University and was heading home to Lebanon. Well who should pull over to pick me up but old Everett? Having hitchhiked as much as I have I didn't stop to scrutinize the driver of the car as I threw my stuff in back. I just jumped right in thankful not to have to walk anymore. I didn't realize who was behind the wheel until we were already going. At first he didn't recognize me. We hadn't seen each other in quite some time and I was still dying my hair black. But when he asked where I was headed he put two and two together. 'Well, if ain't the old Red Faggot,' he said laughing. Well, relations went down hill from there. I told him I wanted to get out. I'd rather walk across the country than drive across town with him. Instead he pulled off the road and drove rather quickly to the middle of a field. I would have jumped out the door but he was going too fast. As soon as he stopped that car, though, I was out the door and across the field like a jackrabbit. I must have been 50 feet away before I heard the rifle blast. The bullet flew over my head and I stopped in my tracks. 'Get back here, you Red Faggot' he called to me. I turned around. He was grinning from ear to ear, standing there with a deer rifle pointed right at me. I slowly walked back to the car, knowing that I was damned if I tried to run and damned if I stayed. As soon as I was close enough he swung the butt of the rifle across my face. I fell to my knees, writhing in pain. He then proceeded to give me the worse beating of my life. Worse than anything my father had ever done. Worse than anything Everett had ever done before.

"After he had knocked me unconscious he must have just strolled back to the car and drove away. A farmer who was planting soybean in the field found me the next morning. He nearly ran me over with his tractor.

I figured I had used up about all of my lucky breaks in life. But then one day a couple of years later I was driving to the state hospital in Indianapolis to see my mother. She had been living there for years. I wasn't too far out of the city when I saw a hitchhiker that looked awfully familiar. It was Everett thumbing his way into town. He must have fallen upon some pretty hard times because he looked as if he hadn't taken a shower in days. He smelled something awful, too. I had a beard then and dark sunglasses. I remember it was a beautiful sunny day in July. When he climbed into the car he didn't recognize me at all. I told him I was from Seattle and that they called me Sparky. I told him all sorts of lies and we sort of hit it off. When we got into Indianapolis I forgot all about my mother and spent the afternoon drinking in some dive with Everett. I told him how I used to pick on kids when I was in school and he told me how he particularly like to beat up on a guy he called the Red Faggot. By the time we left the bar we were both pretty liquored up and it was dark. We were walking through an alley on the way to the car when I told him I was whom he called the Red Faggot. He couldn't believe it but then I told him how I used to screw his sister. He tried to take a swing at me but he was so inebriated that he missed. I threw him up against a brick wall. Five, six, seven times until I had knocked him unconscious. I then pulled him into the middle of the alley, got into the car and drove over his head. I can still hear that sound of his skull cracking under the weight of the car. It was the sweetest sound I have ever heard. That's what I plan to do to Jerome Paul. Like Everett, he must be squashed like the cockroach he is. I've taken all I can stand. It's time I fight back. So," he paused to bring the Fly's Eye up to his right eye, "when I tell you it wouldn't be wise to try to drop me off now, I mean it because I am on a mission, a mission that I must complete at any cost."

I had missed the past several exits while he had been talking. Another one was coming up. I couldn't afford to miss it or we would be stranded on the interstate. At this point I thought it was best to get near other people, as many people as possible and preferably ones with badges and guns. The information that Nosferatu so kindly shared with me was just too much. I'm cynical and doubt a lot of things but there was no way I could not believe this. He was too convincing. I'm sure he had killed this Kimbrough character and was on his way to kill Jerome Paul. I had no doubts whatsoever that he would kill me too if I didn't do what he said. I was so scared I thought I was going to soil myself.

I just had to trick him. But how? He already knew I wanted to ditch him. I couldn't talk my way out of this jam. He was too smart. He wanted to go to New Orleans and he wanted me to take him there.

Jesus H. Christ, I was sitting next to a cold-blooded murderer. An honest-to-God killer. Like every kid born in America after the invention of television, I had grown up soaking in violence on a daily basis. From Wile E. Coyote to Clint Eastwood to Starsky and Hutch. I had been spoon-fed death and dying through the boob tube since I was old enough to see straight. By now you would have figured I was pretty desensitized to violence but no, I was scared shitless. I wanted to be back in Davenport. I wanted to be safe in my bed at home. I wanted my mommy.

I pulled the Caddy off the highway and headed up the exit toward an Amoco. I glanced over at Nosferatu who now was strangely silent. He was simply staring forward with a slight smile on his face, his mind swimming in its own pool of dementia. This guy scared me more with each passing second.

"I'm just going to pull into this Amoco station for some gas and to go to the bathroom," I said in a shaky voice I couldn't hide.

"Don't try anything," he said softly as he dug into his pocket to retrieve his lip balm once again. Playfully, he turned toward me and looked at me through the Fly's Eye. "I can see 64 Fausts. And they all look like they are about to crap their pants. We're talking about a lot of soiled underwear." He chuckled softly.

I don't know anything about schizophrenia but I was sure he had a big house there. After a few hours with him he had gone from southern gentlemen to raving lunatic. What was next?

"I'll stay here in the car but I will watch you," my nutty companion said evenly. "If I feel you have been gone too long I will come and get you. You will leave the keys in the ignition."

"Is this anyway to start a relationship?" I said trying to lighten the mood a bit, thinking that the last thing I wanted to do was to leave the keys in the car.

"Just make it quick, Faust," he replied curtly.

Resigned to my fate, I got out of the car to pump gas. I desperately wracked my brain for some kind of escape plan but in my mind's eye I just kept picturing him in that dark alley with Everett. This man's dangerous. He's a raving lunatic. Maybe I should just yell for help? What would he do? Probably get out of the car and slap me to the ground. Maybe I should just explain the situation to the gas station attendant and tell them to call the cops. The cops could track us down on the highway and pull us over. But that might not work either. What if the gas station attendant is a moron who doesn't know the number for 911? He could panic and make a scene and then I would end up with a broken head.

I just wasn't good in these think-fast-or-some-madman-is-going-to-kill-you situations. I finished pumping gas and started to walk to the cashier. Did he have a gun or a knife? Or how did he plan to kill me? He had only threatened me verbally. He hadn't shown any weapon. Maybe he was simply bluffing. Maybe he was unarmed. Maybe he wasn't that strong. Maybe he only killed Everett in his mind. Yeah, maybe all my friends would come to my funeral.

As I paid for my gas I gave up the idea about asking the station attendant for help. "Tate," as his nametag stated, had trouble operating the machine that made an imprint of Tony's credit card. Surely he would have a brain aneurysm if someone asked him to complete a complex task like call for the police. He'd be better off going back to his Hustler magazine which I saw spread open on the back counter like one of its model's legs.

I paused at the front door of the station as I walked back to the restroom on the side. I looked at Nosferatu and pointed to the restroom key I was struggling to carry. The key was attached to a chain that was attached to a rather heavy hubcap. No, I was not going to steal the key, folks. The madman gave me a grim look and pointed to his wrist indicating that I was taking too much time.

In the bathroom I quickly unzipped my fly and relieved myself. At first, I thought I was going to come up shy I was so nervous but it came out eventually. Time. I had to hurry.

I was almost done with my tasks and I had not come up with one possible escape plan. Was I resigned to just get back into the car and drive Adolf Hitler to New Orleans so he could kill some fat slob of a radio personality? And when I had driven him to New Orleans, what then?

Like he would just shake my hand and say, "Thanks, my boy. See you around." More likely he would lead me into the nearest alley and play handball with my head. I had to come up with a plan.

After pissing, I splashed cold water on my face. Not because it was the cliche thing to do in moments like these but because that's all the tap would give me. These gas stations never have hot water in the bathroom, which is especially pleasant when you have to wash your hands in the middle of January.

When I returned the bathroom key/hubcap, I accidentally dropped it onto the glass counter with a loud crash nearly breaking it. Tate barely blinked an eye as he continued perusing Miss June. I, on the other hand, nearly had a heart attack. If I were going to come up with a plan to escape it had to be quick.

Between the cash register and the car I needed to disappear, I thought as I walked out of the front of the gas station. No, that wouldn't work. I needed to get him out of the car. I needed to drive away alone. I couldn't force him out. I would need to trick him out. I needed to outsmart him. Unfortunately, I was feeling pretty dumb.

I got into the driver's seat and fired up the car. Nosferatu was either sleeping or resting his eyes. He looked so peaceful over there in the passenger's seat like he was my dad and we were on a trip to grandma's house. The Caddy and all eight of its cylinders purred contentedly oblivious to the nervous wreck behind the wheel.

"It is all right if I get some tapes out of the trunk?" I managed to squeak out. I had come upon a plan. I'm not sure where it came from but all of a sudden there was hope. Hope that I would live to see another Police Academy movie. Hope that in a few minutes I would be driving away from this gas station by myself. Hope that I would still be completely intact, without any body parts missing.

"Aren't they in your bag in the back seat?" He opened his bloodshot eyes.

"Not all of them. I threw a box of tapes in the trunk as well. Is it all right if I get some? I figure we're probably done talking for a while."

"I'm not done talking to you… but yes you may go back and get them as long as you hurry up. We need to get moving along," he said and once again closed his eyes.

I left the car running and the front door open. I took a deep breath as I made that long walk back to the trunk. This was going to have to go off perfectly or I was dead. I took out the spare set of keys and unlocked the trunk, opening it and then waited. There was nothing there except for a jack, a crow bar and a crumpled up Marathon candy bar wrapper. About half a minute passed and he didn't move. Had he fallen asleep? Was he too busy seething at the words of Jerome Paul? A few more seconds passed and then he yelled, "What the hell is taking so long? Just pick one and get in here." I didn't say a word. My heart was pounding so hard I was afraid it was going to crack a rib.

Fortunately, we had picked an obscure Amoco station. Very few people were stopping for gas so there was no pressure on me to free up the space in front of the pumps. My plan would not work if some wisenheimer was honking his Toyota at me waiting for me to move. No, I only needed him to get impatient.

And he was. "Hurry up, Faust. If you're not in here in 10 seconds there's going to be trouble." He shouted from the front seat. My chance was coming. Leaving the trunk open, I crouched down and slithered up the driver's side of the car just behind the open front door. Come on, Nosferatu, you fucking psycho, take the bait. Take the bait.

I had to do this all by sound or I would be caught for sure. I was no hero but I had to be hero-like. I had to do this just right. I had to be fucking Indiana Jones, James Bond and Batman all rolled up into one. I can do this, I can do this, I thought to myself just like the little train that could.

A few more long seconds passed, then I heard the passenger door open and shut. I'd give him two more seconds to start walking to the back of the car, look behind the open trunk and find I was not there still looking for a tape. When I had envisioned him near the back of the car, I jumped into the driver's seat, leaving my door open and jamming the car into drive and was off. Alone. In the right side mirror I could see that fucker standing underneath the station's canopy near the gas pumps, a look of total disbelief on his face. I had tricked him. My plan had worked. But wait, what was that next to him? He had pulled my duffel bag out of the backseat as insurance. I slammed on the brakes. My door slammed shut, nearly crushing my left foot in its path. I looked into the side mirror again (the rearview mirror was blocked by the trunk door) and saw him moving in my direction. He figured he had me because of that duffel bag and he did, almost. It contained all my clothes, my music, my extra money. Basically everything except the clothes on my back and my wallet. But I wasn't stupid. If it meant trading off my clothes, et al. for my freedom there was no question of which I would chose. But why not have both?

He was now running full-blast toward the Caddy. I took my foot off the brake and took off again. Did he think he could catch me? I couldn't quite make out the look on his face but I'm sure it was no longer disbelief.

I turned right toward the gas station office, squealing tires just like the movies. He was still running after me. I circled around to the other side of the pumps. How long could I go before he figured that I was circling around to pick up my duffel? I lost track off him when I was half way round the central building where Tate no doubt was oblivious to this one-car race around the Amoco speedway.

I was going to get that fucking duffel and lose him, damn it. Still no sign of the psychopath as I circled right again and saw the duffel sitting next to the pump. Unfortunately he had left it right next to the pump so I couldn't just zip by and pick it up outside my side of the car. I would have turn around so the car was facing the other direction. I zoomed past my bag and made another big loop in the gas station lot. Still no sign of him. Was he lying in wait for me or had he had a heart attack on the other side of the lot after all that running?

I made another approach at the bag with my side of the car closest to the pumps. As I neared the bag I saw him out of the corner of my eye. He was running toward the Caddy but he was lagging behind. There would be enough time for me to stop grab the bag and get out of there as long as I didn't dawdle. As if.

I brought the Caddy to a halt next to the bag, opened the door, grabbed the bag and was off again but apparently had slowed long enough to allow Nosferatu to catch up. He must have gotten an extra burst of energy somehow or else learned how to fly. I heard a loud clunk on the back of the Caddy. He had dived into the open trunk. Jesus fucking Christ. This guy wasn't giving up easily.

I took off out of the gas station and headed toward the highway swerving back and forth trying to knock him senseless back in the trunk. How was I going to get rid of him now? I couldn't very well stop the car and ask him nicely to vacate the trunk. Did he figure that I would just keep driving? Or did he think that I didn't know that he had jumped into the trunk? Maybe I should just keep driving until I found a state trooper then have him arrest the freak. Or maybe I should just try and bounce him out of the trunk. It was still open.

His shouting interrupted my scheming. "Faust, stop the goddamn car. You're going to kill me."

"Fuck you," I shouted at the back seat. "You're the only killer around here and I'm not going to let you get me."

"Oh, I'll get you all right. Jerome Paul can wait. You are my new enemy and you know what happens to my enemies. I know where you live and I have friends there. They will help me. I will get you."

He was bluffing. He didn't have any friends in Davenport. This guy probably had very few friends except for the ones he manufactured in his own mind.

"Fuck off. You ain't getting me. Davenport is a big city and you don't even know my last name," I shouted back as I headed down the ramp to the highway. I was trying my best to find anything on the shoulder of the road that would jar him out of the trunk. Rocks, roadkill, beer cans. Anything. After a few good bounces he was silent. I had either stunned him or he had fallen out. I looked out the side mirrors and saw nothing but it was dark now and a light rain was falling so visibility was pretty shitty.

I soon found out that the resourceful maniac had not fallen out. He was simply resting, gathering some energy for his last assault. Like a battering ram he started kicking the back seat from inside the trunk. I don't know a lot about how cars are built but I was sure that if there was a way, he was going to get back into the cab of the car through the backseat. Now my panic of fighting off a homicidal maniac was compounded by the vision I had inside my head of Tony and his grandparents strangling me for ruining their car.

Rule No. 2 came back into my mind. No Hitchhikers. For once I wished I had listened to that swarthy bastard.

"I'm coming to get you, Faust," he said between kicks. "Better start praying." The entire back seat was shaking. I could only imagine how many more times he had to kick it before he would be literally breathing down my neck.

Up until this point, I had not been a religious person. Our family was made up of recreational Lutherans. We went to church only on Easter and Christmas. We would arrive early so that we got a seat and made the regulars who waltzed in at the last minute resentful because they then had to stand through the service at the back. I believe in a higher spirit, a God, if you will, but I didn't plan on really getting to know him until I was well past 30 or 40. So it was a little odd for me to start praying as I drove down a rain-soaked Interstate 65 while a raving lunatic was adding a fifth door to my brother-in-law's grandparents' Cadillac. But I did.

I'm sure there is an appropriate psalm or prayer for this exact situation somewhere in the Bible but damned if I knew it so I tried the Lord's Prayer, the only one I really remembered. After I was done fumbling through it, I ran through it again, more smoothly this time. He was still pounding away at the backseat, shouting one obscenity after the other. He definitely had a problem managing his anger.

After the third or fourth run through to the Lord's Prayer I finally got it right. I must have because God or one of his minions answered.

Nosferatu's frantic kicking had knocked off everything from the backseat including the suit jacket he had placed there when he first entered the Caddy. It was the last thing to fall off the seat and it made some noise doing it. There was something heavy inside that out-of-date coat because it landed with a clunk on the back floor. With my right arm I reached back to feel what it was and when my digits had discerned the object a huge smiled bloomed on my worried face. It was a gun. Thank you, Lord.

I really don't think God rallies behind the Second Amendment. Guns scare the shit out of me but in this case I could put aside my political beliefs. This gun was going to save me. I used the electric window opener to roll down the back passenger side window and fired the small handgun out the window not really thinking of whether the bullet might hit something on the side of the road. (I think I might have wounded a speed limit sign.)

He stopped kicking. My having his gun suddenly changed his attitude. Funny how that happens. He knew now that it was I who was calling the shots, literally.

"OK, Harry. I found your gun and I'll be keeping it," I shouted at the backseat. This discovery had unleashed the floodgates on my adrenaline. The feeling that came over me was better than any drug I had experimented with at college. It was better than any orgasm I had ever achieved. "I'm going to slow down and when I do you're going to get out of the trunk. Close the trunk door nicely and then wave bye-bye. I will then drive off with your gun and alert the authorities. You will then go to jail for the rest of your life. Understand?"

He was silent for a few minutes, probably weighing his options, which in my mind were nil.

"You better pray that I never see you again because if I do I will be the last thing you ever see. You've out-tricked me this time. But every dog has his day." And with that he was silent again.

"I will assume that your little speech means that we are in agreement." I slowed the Caddy down and waited. He complied, even shutting the trunk with a gentle ease. As soon as I could see him in the rear-view mirror I gunned the accelerator and showered him with wet gravel from the side of the road.

I had escaped—alive. The enemy had been left on the side of a major interstate defenseless. No coat to hide his tattoos. No gun to kill Jerome Paul or anyone else for that matter. I pulled his suit coat up front to see what else I had taken with me. The gun must have been the only thing on the inside of the jacket. A couple stray bullets rolled around in one of the front pockets. Other than a few folded up tissues in the other pocket, the jacket was empty. Part of me wished I had gotten his wallet, just so his life would be even more difficult. The other part of me figured I had done enough damage. I tossed the coat into the backseat making a mental note to toss it in the next Dumpster I came across.

"Try and pick up a ride now," I yelled to myself. "Only a fucking idiot would pick up you and your tattoos now. You and your lip balm can kiss my motherfucking ass." Shouting made me feel good. I had to spend the rest of that adrenaline that had me flying.

Full of a sense of pride, accomplishment and relief, I let loose the longest, loudest, most vile stretch of obscenities this side of an Eddie Murphy concert. I must have spent five minutes swearing: Fuck.

Fuck. Fuck. Fuck. Fuck. Fuck. Fuck. Fuck. Fuck. Fuck. Fuck. Fuck. Fuck. Fuck. Fuck. Fuck. Fuck.

With that out of my system, I laughed then grew silent for several miles. To tell you the truth, this range of emotions I was going through freaked me out. I kept glancing at the gun, which was resting on the seat beside me, and Nosferatu's coat, which was crumpled into a heap in the back seat. This really happened. I was almost killed. I had escaped death.

As I continued down the interstate, my adrenaline high slowly began to ebb. I looked down at the accelerator and noticed that I was going 80. I slowed down to the speed limit and swallowed hard. I needed a drink but I was afraid to stop. I needed to put some distance between Nosferatu and me. It was after 8 and I hadn't eaten for hours. Yet, I wasn't hungry.

I looked over at the gun sitting beside me. I never thought that something so dangerous and evil could make me feel so comfortable but that pistol was my best friend right now. It had saved my life. "Thank you, Mr. Gun," I said as I touched in gently.

Angela had once said that a gun is simply an extension of a man's penis. That it was nothing more than an extremely violent phallic symbol. Whatever. This gray schwantz with the shiny bullets let me live to see another day. I picked it up and slid it under the front seat. I'd keep it for the time being and maybe turn it over to the cops later. The cops. Should I try to contact them about Nosferatu? Christ, I don't remember where he got out. And what would they charge him with? It was simply his word against mine. I guess I could tell them that some homicidal maniac planned on assassinating Jerome Paul. But what was unique about that? The number of people who wanted to do that could fill the entire French Quarter.

I decided the best thing for me to do at this time was to just drive.

Chapter Eight

I drove on for quite some time after escaping from Nosferatu. I was somewhere near Bowling Green when I decided it would be safe enough to pull off and get something to eat. Despite being miles away from the monster I still felt so paranoid that I parked the Caddy behind a cafe, where it would not be seen from the Interstate.

For a moment I entertained the thought of calling Angela to unload on her but then figured it wouldn't help to dump on her when she had enough problems of her own dealing with her ARAT cronies. And what if she happened to tell Tony that I had picked up a hitchhiker and was nearly killed? Knowing Tony he would probably reduce my payment or come after me. No, I decided it was best to keep the story of my narrow escape from death to myself for now. I could barely believe it myself, let alone expect others to.

Melba's Cafe, which advertised "good grub like you get at grandma's," awaited. Announced by a tinkling bell, I entered Melba's greasy spoon, exhausted after taking on Satan himself. The patrons sized me up much like neighborhood dogs will size up a new mutt, except for the part where they sniffed your ass. A waitress, who looked amazingly like Linda Lavin from that crappy '70s sitcom Alice, forced out a "Howdy" and motioned me to sit down at the counter. I hoped Linda/Alice, whose nametag said Marva, wouldn't continue with this perky charade. I didn't think I would be able to eat if she did. It was obvious that strangers weren't welcome here but tough shit; I was tired and hungry. Melba's would have to put up with me for 30 minutes.

"Hi," I said quietly taking a seat. I didn't look around but I could feel the hot gaze of everyone in the cafe except for the guy sitting next to me. He had his head buried in the middle of the Weekly World News. "FBI Discovers Underground World Populated By Mole People Who Feast on Human Flesh," screamed the cover of the paper. I chuckled to myself as I picked up a menu to figure out dinner.

After driving for so long my body was taking a while to adjust to my new surroundings. It was extremely bright in the cafe. Nothing was subtle about the place. The chrome was highly polished. Signs advertising everything from food items to county auctions were all written in garish, neon colors. Various mobiles with Easter eggs dangling down were hanging from the ceiling. The menus were printed on pink paper and featured items with goofy nicknames. Hamburgers were called Beautiful Bovine Burgers. Meatloaf was Mouthwatering Mountains of Meat. Pork Chops, Plentiful Porcine Planks.

It struck me that Melba must be a divorcee with no life other than her cafe. She poured her whole being into this place and she apparently had a thing for the color pink and alliteration including her waitresses, who I could see by the nametags were named Marva, Mary and Margaret. Was this some kind of joke?

Marva appeared before me with a crappy fake smile pasted on her face. Maybe it was my current condition—worn and frazzled and starving—but this place was straight out of the Twilight Zone. A paranoid thought zoomed through my head—If Nosferatu were to pick one cafe in all of America to visit wouldn't it be Melba's?

"What'cha going have, son?" Marva said, chewing a white soda-pop straw. She was wrapped tightly in a pink dress with white highlights.

Her red hair was piled up high on her head and held steady by a pink and white bellhop-like hat. She looked like a giant valentine from hell.

"I'll just have a hamburger and fries. Thanks." I turned away to look at the Weekly World News cover again. Marva didn't move a muscle.

"I'm sorry, son, but I'm not sure I follow you. Are you saying you want a beautiful bovine burger and the fantastic fries from France? Is that what you are saying you want?" she continued working on that straw, pointing a pencil in my face.

I turned to size up the giant valentine. What the hell is this, I thought to myself. "Yes, please, Marva," I said trying my best to keep my irritation in check. "And a..." I said looking through the menu to see what these morons called a coke.

"A coke?" she suggested.

"Yes, thank you."

"You know, son, we'd take more kindly to strangers round here if they weren't so rude," she said snootily and turned to hand my order to the cook. I let her comment slide and turned once again to my right to see if there were any other newspapers to read on the counter. The Weekly World News reader was waiting for me, though.

"I see you done interested in this here newspaper," said a squeaky voice full of Kentucky twang from behind the Mole People headline.

"Actually I was looking for a real newspaper," I replied looking up and down the counter.

"Well, you can't get no more real than this 'n, ri'chere," he said revealing himself as he closed up his copy of the Weekly World News and placed it down on the countertop. On the back was an ad for a yearly subscription to the paper. The ad featured highlights from other recent issues: "Elvis Alive, Doing Two Shows Nightly At Mars' Casino," "Jackie O.'s Ghost Reveals Hubby's Killer From Grave," "Unabomber Had Sexual Relationship With Bigfoot." Mr. Weekly World News looked like he spent more time reading slop than cleaning. His teeth were yellow, his hair, or should I say his pseudo hair because he had one of the worse toupees I have ever seen, was shaped like a Frisbee, and his eyes were perfect for a Visine case study. Actually, if I hadn't been so damn tired this little troll would have frightened me.

"Real fake, you mean," I said chuckling, wishing my dinner would come sooner.

"Well, I beg ta differ, mistah. You must be one of those uppity folks who don't believe in the Weekly World News, say it's full of the made-up stuff. Now I reckon that on occasion they will throw in a story or two about sumtin ridiculous but that's just to keep things interestin'. Other than that it's more believable than the crap you read in those daily newspapers. All that talk of wars and stuff in Europe. And what's all this here business about O.J. Simpson killing people? He's a football player, not a damn gangsta. It's all a bunch of stuff to rot your mind. Now this stuff ri'chere," he said pointing at his paper, "this here is the real news.

"I tell ya what," he continued. "Why don't those daily newspapers ever tell us about visitors from outta space? Damn straight, they is visiting us on a nightly basis, kidnappin' our women and chillren and using them for their experiments. You never read about that stuff in your daily newspapers, now do ya?"

What was the deal? I thought to myself as Bubba sang the praises of the most insipid collection of lies ever to be gathered in one place. Apparently, I had turned into a nut magnet. First Nosferatu, now Bubba the troll and part-time UFO expert. "No, I don't," I answered him figuring that it didn't make any sense to argue.

"Damn straight. It never ceases to amaze me how few folks know about them aliens when they is everywhere. A feller can't even turn around with knocking one of them there aliens down. They all over the place nowadays and they is getting bolder by the minute. They know that the govment is lying to us. They know that the govment is telling folks that aliens don't exist. So the aliens figure they don't have to hide no more because we will just think we is going crazy if we see them and tell someone about it."

"Jerry," Marva snapped at my new friend from behind the counter. "Are you bothering this young man with all of your UFO talk?" she admonished him as she poured him some more coffee.

"Damn straight, woman," Jerry barked right back. "Those daily newspapers won't do it so I gotta go round edjucatin' folks like this one ri'chere."

"Jerry is downright friendly with those aliens," the waitress said as she turned to me smiling. "He sees them all the time." She gave me a look like she thought old Jerry should be locked in a very small windowless room with padded walls.

"Damn straight, woman, I do see them all the time, but I sure as hell ain't friendly with 'em. They the enemy. The way I look at it they is invadin' our space with their flying machines and what not. We didn't invite them, they're not announcin' themselves, so I say they spyin'. And if they spyin', they the enemy. So I'm engagin' them in battle."

"Your meal will be right up," Marva said patting my right hand softly as she walked away.

"Engaging them," I mouthed to myself but apparently loud enough for Jerry to pick it up.

"Damn straight, man. We gone toe to toe with them on a number of occasions. Huey and me, that is," he stopped and turned to scan the contents of the cafe. As far as I could see it was filled with a bunch of trailer trash. Women with too much lace attached to cotton and men with a lot of camo. Focusing in on one corner, Jerry the Mole Man sat straight up on his stool and barked: "Huey, ri' chere, right now."

A skinny man, not much older than me, with a dirt mustache and a crew cut popped his head up from a group of four other bubbas. Huey nodded and waded his way through the group not taking an eye off of Jerry. Huey was wearing dirty, torn Levis and a white wifebeater that carried two or three strands of sauce-soaked spaghetti. His tall, beanpole body was cut in half by an extremely wide black belt that looked as if it was wrapped around him twice. He must have weighed all of 97 pounds. His most distinguishing feature, though, was the tremendous purplish-red bags under his eyes. It looked as if Huey was a creature who operated on only 20 minutes of sleep a day.

"Hey, Jerry," Huey said, actually saluting my dinner companion. "How y'all doing tonight?" he said slowly like some of the stoners I knew back in high school. The young man appeared to have the IQ of a torn grocery bag.

"All right, cut the pleasantries, boy. I didn't call you over here to chew the fat. I wanted you over here so we could tell, tell, say I never caught your name?"

"Graham. Graham Chapman," I said pulling a name out of the blue. These guys didn't need to know my real name. I now regretted even telling Nosferatu my real first name. For the rest of this trip I was going to be Graham Chapman or John Cleese or Eric Idle. Anyone but Matthew Picasso.

"Well anyway, I was explaining to Graham…" Jerry continued.

"Like a graham cracker," Huey said slowly, laughing.

"Damn straight. Now shut up, will ya? Anyway I was explaining to Graham about our encounters with the spacemen," Jerry said then turned to me. "He likes to call them spacemen. I don't think he knows what aliens are."

"I know what aliens is. They illegal," The rocket scientist said with a straight face.

Where is a baseball bat when you need one? It was time to put me, Jerry and the rest of the world out of its misery. This Huey character was dragging the entire Homo Sapiens species down.

"Huey," Jerry barked. "Shudup. Now where was I? Oh here comes your dinner," he said spying Marva walking our way with my ticket out of here. Now I could concentrate on my food, and these hicks could go back to their space fantasies.

"You go ahead and eat, buddy," Jerry said, putting a hand on my shoulder. "We will just fill you in on the details here."

I swallowed hard on my first bite of the beautiful bovine burger. I had indeed become a nut magnet.

"Anyway, we been engaging the enemy, or spacemen, for some time now. It all started three years ago when one night me, this one here, Stu Fripps and Guy Larry Carboneau were playing poker at Huey's trailer. Stu got up to have a cigarette outside account of G.L.'s aversion to smoke. G.L. is what we call Guy Larry coz Guy Larry sounds kind of faggy. Anyway, Stu was out there for all of 10 seconds when he's making a bee line back inside huffing and puffing and looking all bug eyed like he had just accidentally swallowed his Winston. 'What the hell is your problem,' I said and at first he wouldn't say. Something had done spooked him real good. But we kept on him and finally after a few minutes he told us he had seen one of them, there UFOs. Now most times we would have busted out laughing because Stu is kind of a joker. He's the one over there with the seed cap on kind of sideways. You should see him do his Elvis the Catfish imitation. Funniest thing you ever seen. But anyway, that night, Stu's face was white as a ghost and we had heard quite a few of the neighbors talking about UFO sightings outside of town. Well, we had been drinking quite a few beers as we played poker that night but we sobered up real quick. Huey grabbed his Remington and the rest of us headed outside. Stu had planned on staying at the table but when we all got up he followed us out probably too scared to be by his lonesome. Now the area outside the trailer was glowing as if someone had installed a street light overhead while we were inside playing poker. Normally, the whole trailer park is pitch black. We looked up all at the same time and, damn straight, if they wasn't one of them, there flying saucers hovering about 100 feet off the ground. Stu had already seen this so he couldn't bring himself to look at the machine, which was silvery and full of lights that gave off an unearthly glow. I swallowed hard not sure what to do. Shit, I thought I might just about crap my drawers. Well, G.L. and Stu ran back into the trailer like a couple of pussies. Huey, good old Huey, raised his rifle and shot out one of the saucer's lights." Jerry paused to chuckle. I looked over at his buddy, who was mesmerized as if he was hearing the story for the first time.

"Shoot, Jerry, you sure know how to spin a yarn," Huey said in awe.

Throughout this tale I had continued to eat my dinner. I wasn't sure how to react. Should I congratulate Jerry on his abilities to tell a good story or should I pretend to believe him and ask him more about the aliens? Or should I just finish my meal, pay the bill and get the hell out of there? Then a thought crossed my mind—what if it was Melba's food that drove these people to lunacy. Here I was, wolfing it down.

"Well, those spacemen didn't like this one bit. Damn straight, I bet it was the first time they had been shot at by Earthlings. They landed the flying saucer in a nearby meadow and we followed it but not before I ran to my pickup and pulled out my own rifle. I stuffed my pocket full of cartridges. If we was gonna engage the enemy we was gonna need plenty of ammo.

"Under the cover of darkness we made our way to the spaceship, which had three small legs that propped it up off of the ground. As soon as we got within shooting distance we took our position behind a small hill. It must have been 10 minutes before the door of the spaceship opened and when it did it made a hissing noise. Hssssssss."

Huey especially liked this special effect and started to smile.

"And with the Lord as our witness, aliens started coming out. One, two, three, four of those little bastards. They were all gray with big, old bald heads and dark egg-shaped eyes. They arms were skinny as bean poles and long, nearly hanging to the ground. They legs were skinny, too, but pretty damn short, too short to run very fast. These space creatures are no athletes, I can tell you that. In fact, if you ask me, I think they do a little too much thinking and not enough exercise. Maybe that's why I wasn't scared. I can't speak for him but seeing how puny these bastards was, I weren't scared at all."

"I weren't scared of no spacemen either," Huey said, punching Jerry's arm lightly.

"I didn't say you was, I just said I couldn't speak for 'ya."

"You speakin' just fine. Go on now with that story, will 'ya?"

"So anyway, we lay on the ground behind that berm, motionless. This guy here was waiting for me to take the lead. I was waiting to see what the hell these aliens was going to do. While three of them continued to look around, the fourth walked over to the busted light and checked it out. He pointed something at it and, zap, the light was fixed. Just like that. Damn straight. We couldn't believe our eyes. It was really sumptin'. That certainly was no Craftsmen wrench. It was magic. I figured I could use one of these here magic wands. So I fired a shot in the air, hoping that creepy mechanic would drop it and shuffle back into the ship with his buddies. Well, the four aliens stopped dead in their tracks for a minute then the fourth guy pointed that magic wand in our direction and shot a beam of bright light just to the side of us. Well, I wasn't going to wait for this alien to draw a bead on me so I raised my rifle but before I knew it Huey had shot and kilt the one with the magic wand and another one of the three. Jesus Christ, I couldn't believe it. Just like that, we had kilt two space aliens. I bet we is the first humans ever to kill some of these things. Well, the other two that was left picked up the third nearest them and hauled him into the ship. A few minutes later they come out and started toward the fourth one. But I shot my rifle in the air again and they got the message. We was going to keep that one. They turned and went back to their ship. The door closed and lickedty split, it zoomed off. We waited for a minute or two before we headed over to the dead alien and his magic wand. This guy was kind of giggling as we walked up to the spaceman. 'Looks kind of funny, don't he?' he said as we stood over him. 'Yup,' was all I could say. You could see where the bullet had gone through his chest but there was no blood. His eyes were closed and he looked like he was asleep. I picked up the magic wand and put it in my pocket. It felt nice and warm against my leg. I kind of nudged the alien with my foot, not sure whether he was dead or not. Huey jabbed him real hard with his rifle. He didn't move so we knew he was dead. I grabbed his ankles and Huey grabbed his wrists and we carried him back to my truck. We were both surprised at how light he was. He must have only weighed 70 pounds. As soon as we were loaded up we drove to my house where we carried him into my garage. We put him on my workbench and went inside to figure out what to do next.

'We got to tell Crawford,' Huey says. Crawford is the sheriff around these parts. 'No, if we tell Crawford, the govment will get involved and hush it up,' I said. I figured this stuff had been going on for some time but the govment had always hushed it up. I didn't want it to happen this time. So we didn't tell no one for quite some time. The strange thing was, as if this ain't all crazy enough already, is that Maurice, that's what we started calling the alien corpse, he didn't go rotten at all. You know, he didn't decompose. He didn't smell at all, neither. It's as if he had anti-freeze in his veins or something. He's perfectly preserved from the day we killed him. Three years and Maurice is still as ugly as the day he flew out of the sky. Course he's a little dirty what with trying to hide him from the authorities and such. I've had to bury him a few times in the garden and then dig him back up to show people. Yeah, I show it to people, the ones I like, that is. Except I don't show it to no kids. Damn straight. That's one rule I stick to. Kids don't need to see no alien. They got enough stuff going on in they lives without worrying about no aliens."

Jerry paused to take a drink from his coffee, which was probably cold by now considering he had been talking non-stop since Marva warmed it up.

"Finally I decided I needed some kind of body bag that I could put him in whenever I had to hide him in the ground. So I had Marlene, a friend of my sister's, sew me a canvas body bag though I didn't call it a body bag to her. I told her I wanted to have a deer bag for when I got deer hunting. You know something to put the deer in after I've dragged it back to the car. Course, there's no such thing but she don't know that. She don't know nothing about no hunting stuff. In fact, she once asked me why we don't go into the business of making these here deer bags. Can you believe that woman? Dumb as a post. Deer bag."

Huey chuckled lamely. I'm sure he thought the idea of making a deer bag was a good one but he was afraid to say so.

"So that's where I keep Maurice—in my deer bag. It zips right up and has handles in the middle so you can actually carry him around real easy."

I had finished my meal and wasn't sure what to do next. Part of me wanted to get as far away from Melba's as possible and the other part of me wanted to hear the rest of Jerry's tall tale. I yawned involuntarily.

"Well don't that beat all? Damn straight, I just told Graham here one of the most interestin', stories he'll ever hear and he's over there yawnin', like he's bored or sumptin," Jerry said shaking his head in disgust.

"Most people are down right entranced by my stories," he said rolling up the Weekly World News in one hand. He started to tap it softly on the countertop.

"Most people haven't driven all day before hearing it," I said, yawning again. "I'm sorry, it is interesting, it's just that I'm beat."

"Damn straight. I've got something that will wake you up," he said leaning forward. For a moment I thought his Frisbee-shaped hairpiece was going to drop in my lap. "Want to meet the alien?" he whispered, grinning as if he had just won the lottery.

"I don't know," I said hedging a bit, envisioning a long car trip out into the country with the yahoos listening to country music while drinking some gut-scalding white lightning concoction. "I'm really not into all that UFO business."

"Not into… I've never run into no human being who weren't a little bit curious about outer space. You are a phenomenon, you know that? I can't believe that you would not want to see a bona-fide, in-the-flesh space creature, perfectly preserved, no less," he said looking heartbroken.

"Maybe he's scared," Huey drawled, a crooked smile forming on his face.

"That's neither here nor there. If he don't want to take up this opportunity of a lifetime then that's his deal. Whatever. I just figured, Graham, that you'd want to see a real live, I mean dead, alien. Probably be your only chance unless they pick you to be one of they guinea pigs."

"I doubt I'd be that lucky," I said a bit too sarcastically.

"Hold on. Hold on for one cotton-pickin' minute," he said raising his voice again while he whacked the countertop hard with the rolled-up Weekly World News. "You mean I've been sitting here telling you all of this secretive stuff about our encounters with the aliens and you've been having it go in one ear and out the other. If that don't beat... this man thinks we done lyin' to him. This here damn Yankee thinks we full of shit." Jerry's face was a red as a beet.

"Damn," Huey responded so eloquently.

"Wait a second," I stammered. "I didn't say that, it's just that I...I..." I didn't know what to say. I did think they were full of shit but I didn't want to say it to their faces. For all I knew they would haul me out back and beat the tar out of me. And I was just too tired for that.

"Don't believe us, huh?" Jerry said reaching into his front pant pocket. "Then how do you explain this?" He said slamming a silver pen-like object on the countertop. "You know what that is? If you had been paying attention you'd know what that is. It's the magic wand that we copped from them there aliens."

"Yeah, we took it," Huey chimed in.

"That's proof ri'chere we had a run-in with them spacemen and if you weren't so lazy and anti-social we'd show you more proof. We'd show you the alien," he was just about shouting now. I quickly looked around the cafe and noticed that no one was paying any attention to us. They must have been accustomed to the troll's excitable behavior.

I poked at the wand with my finger like it was liable to bite me.

"Go ahead pick it up," he urged, grinning. Suddenly he was not angry anymore.

Slowly I wrapped my fingers around it and cradled it in my palm. It was warm as if it had been sitting in the sun for several minutes. "It's warm," I said quietly.

"I told you. And it ain't because it was in my pocket neither. It's always warm. I put it in my freezer once and came back an hour later. The damn thing was still warm."

"Wow," Huey said in awe as if he was hearing this, too, for the first time.

The pen felt like it was made of aluminum but was even lighter. On the narrow end it was concave just like a pen that you have to click to write with. Three-quarters of the way up there was as slight depression the size of your thumb print. Other than that, it appeared to be a solid piece of metal. No other marks, no way to open it up.

Although it didn't convince me of his story it did intrigue me, especially its warmth.

"Why don't you take this and Maurice to NASA or someplace like that?" I asked gently placing the pen back onto the countertop.

Before he could answer, his partner picked up the pen and started banging it loudly on the countertop. That got everybody's attention. "You don't have to be gentle with it, it's harder than goddamn nails," he slurred banging the pen.

Jerry thumped Huey on the chest with a fist and grabbed the pen away from him with his other hand. "Will you just shut up, you moron?

Damn straight, you vex me sometimes. You know that? You vex me." These two were a regular in-bred Laurel and Hardy.

"I'm sorry. He gets kind of excited sometimes when we talkin' about the spacemen. The reason we don't take him to NASA or anyone like that is because they would just take him away and we'd never see him again. They would just cover it all up. The authorities ain't too eager to spread the word that aliens do exist. As I told you already, they be hidin' it for years. And I ain't goin' to give up this magic wand because someday I'll figure out how it works and then I can use it to fix my cars and such stuff."

"Yeah, my four-wheeler done needs fixing," Huey said rubbing his chest where he had been thumped.

"And to be perfectly honest with you," Jerry continued. "I done grown kind of attached to Maurice. Before he came along everybody round here thought I was plum crazy. They still think I'm crazy but they listen to me now and they do come from miles around to see Maurice. Except for the kids. Kids don't need to see no alien. But the women. Especially the girls. 18, 19-year-old high school girls. They like to see him and they always giggle when they see he's naked as a jaybird. If I gave the alien away these people would have no reason to talk to me."

"Hmm, yeah, I see what you're saying," I said nodding. He was in love. He actually loved that alien or whatever he had killed in a bathtub gin-induced stupor. Maybe it was a bear or a hog or something but whatever he had killed he was convinced it was an alien.

I figured that this was probably as good a time as any to leave now that Jerry was in a somber mood. I threw $10 on to my empty plate and motioned to Marva to come clear my space.

"Well, Jerry, Huey, it was nice chatting with you but I should be moving along. I gotta get up and drive all day tomorrow," I said rising from my stool.

"See you later, Graham," Huey said as if he really expected to see me around here again. He blinked a couple times and headed back to his table.

"If you don't mind I'll walk out with you. I think I'm going to call it a night, too," Jerry said throwing a couple bucks on the counter. Standing next to me he reminded me of an alien himself. He was extremely short and his arms seemed long compared to the rest of his body. I've heard some people say that dog owners start looking like their pets after a while. Maybe he was starting to look like his pet Maurice.

As we stepped outside he looked left and then right as if he were making sure no one was around who could hear him. "You know, it's not like I'd have to dig him up or anything," he said quietly.

"What are you talking about," I said pulling the keys to the Caddy from my pocket.

"Maurice is here with me. He's in the trunk. All I'd have to do is open it up and you could get a quick look."

"Maybe next time I'm passing through. Right now, I just need to find a hotel room," I said as I picked up my pace leaving him behind.

"Well suit yourself. I just figured you'd want to see a real dead alien," he mumbled.

As I unlocked the Caddy and crawled inside I had a feeling of having done the right thing. Maybe there was an alien in his trunk. Maybe there wasn't. I had had too long of a day to care to find out. I had enough trouble dealing with the things on this Earth. If I were ever to make it to Florida I would have to recharge my batteries. I had to keep reminding myself that this was a job, that I was getting paid for this, that people were depending on me.

Jerry, Huey and Maurice would just have to go on without me.

Chapter Nine

I have always hated those movies in which the hero is facing certain annihilation at the hands of his enemy and you're thinking, 'Ah, this bites, the good guy is going to buy the farm' and then all of a sudden the hero wakes up from a dream, soaking in his own sweat, safe in bed.

It's a lame way to get the viewer's heart racing and yet it's used time and time again by tired, old directors who have about as much originality as vanilla ice cream.

So, I was pretty relieved when I woke up the next day without having dreamt about Nosferatu, or aliens for that matter. No scary monsters attacked me in my dreams. (I guess I saved them for my waking hours.) In fact, I don't remember dreaming about anything. I was so damn tired from the day before that I slept like a corpse.

It was 7 a.m., a time I'm not too familiar with, but I felt good. I had not had a single drink the night before and felt like a better man for it although I knew that this renewed vigor certainly wasn't going to lead to a life of abstinence.

For once, I had followed one of Tony's rules and stayed in an inexpensive hotel. I decided then and there that I was going to adhere to all of the other rules as well, at least for day two. No more speeding, no more hitchhikers, nothing but the task at hand.

As I gathered my things into my duffel, I kept reviewing the prior day's events in my mind. It seemed like I had watched it on television. I had actually taken on a homicidal maniac and escaped alive. And what was the deal with Jerry, Huey and Maurice?

I took an extremely long shower trying to wash the magnetic forces off my body that were attracting these nuts. Considering how weakly the water trickled out of the showerhead, I wondered if I had been successful.

I stepped out of the shower and struggled to wrap the paper-thin hotel towel around my waist. It barely went all the way around, and I'm not that big. I half expected to see the words "Charmin" on the piece of frail fabric.

I looked at myself in the mirror, dripping wet, looking like a stray mutt.

Was it something in my physiological make-up that attracted weird people? I'm not quite sure but it had been going on for some time. At college football games, I always got stuck sitting next to the drunken lout, who insisted on filling my shoes with vomit. This was after he spent three quarters trying to convince me that he used to play for the Hamilton Tiger Cats in the Canadian Football League.

Even back in high school, the nuts found me. At rock concerts, I always found myself having to deal with the space cadet who was high on glue or something. Inevitably, they would try to pick a fight with me because they thought I was breathing on them or smelling their hair.

I started thinking about taking up agoraphobia. It got to the point where I couldn't go out in public without running into someone who was determined to ruin my day. I was a target even waiting for the bus. One day when I was waiting to go downtown, a guy came up to me with a garter snake in his pocket. He said he was taking "Felix" for a walk. At first, I thought it was a rubber snake but then it tried to slither out of his grasp.

My mother would say these nuts were attracted to me because of how the stars were aligned when I was born.

Tony would say that it was my fault. If I would just tell these people to fuck off when they first approached I wouldn't be bothered. He would say I attract them because I'm too much of a sap, that these weirdoes can sense I am a loser the same way a cat can sense when someone doesn't like them.

Angela, on the other hand, would tell me that this nut attraction is a blessing in disguise. Take advantage of it, she would tell me, and help these tortured souls.

I think Tony would probably be the closest in this case. I mean why did Nosferatu pick me? Why did Jerry insist on talking to me?

I think I attract the lunatic fringe because I look like such a non-threatening person. I look like the kind of guy who would give you a break, a quarter for a cup of coffee, a dollar for a bottle of Thunderbird. The funny thing is that I'm not this kind of person at all. I attract this sort of people but I don't want anything to do with them. I wish I could be more like Tony (God did I just write that) and tell them all to fuck off. But I'm incapable. Instead, I just suffer through life, besieged by homicidal maniacs, alien imprisoners and Bible highlighters (I actually met a guy on a city bus who used to highlight his favorite Bible verses with a yellow pen).

"Picasso," I said to myself in the mirror. "Let's make today an uneventful one, all right?"

I must have listened to myself because day two was a breeze. Of course, any day compared to the day before would have been a snap. I cruised from Bowling Green through Nashville to Chattanooga, then Atlanta and down to southern Georgia with nary a story to tell. I even was able to stomach two hours of straight country and western music on the radio.

Every time I stopped to fill up the Caddy, which had an incredible thirst, I half-expected to find some nut sitting in the front seat. But the nuts stayed away. Apparently, in southern Georgia, they only come out at night.

By six o'clock, I had had enough driving for one day. I had put a lot of miles on and was easily within one day's drive of Miami. So I pulled off Interstate 75 and pulled into a bar called The Big Top for some dinner and a drink.

From the outside, The Big Top looked just like the name, only much scedier. Balloons had been painted here and there on the sides of the building and a rainbow-colored tent had been painted on top. A neon clown was pushing his head through the "O" in the word "Top." Part of the neon was broken, though, so the clown looked deformed. The parking lot was full of various beaters. I even saw a Vega.

In one corner of the parking lot there was an antique lion cage on wheels, the kind that was used in parades whenever the circus came to town. In another corner, there was a plastic statue of a ringmaster with both arms raised to the sky. He was standing on top of a platform, the kind the lion tamer would have his lions stand on as he whipped them into shape. The odd thing about the ringmaster is that his face and hands were painted brown. Whoever had painted it was obviously making a political statement about African-Americans, but all they had accomplished was making one of the largest lawn jockeys I had ever seen.

As I surveyed the scene, I began to think that maybe I should pass this bar by. I did not pull into the parking lot because I am a fan of the circus. In fact, I kind of hated the circus when I was a kid because the clowns scared the shit out of me.

Rather, I pulled in because I was tired and hungry and this place was close to the interstate.

As I locked up the Caddy and started toward the door, the skies opened up and started to rain. I ran toward the entrance and couldn't avoid noting the irony. Me, running toward a circus?

Not surprisingly, the bar was filled with circus performers or at least people who should be circus performers. A gaggle of dwarfs were playing pool, a bearded lady was throwing darts, and a group of tired old men, who looked like clowns sans the pancake, were nursing bottles of Bud Light as they stared at professional wrestling on the TV behind the bar.

The floor was covered with sawdust and I could make out the remnants of several circus props throughout the bar. They were few but I did see a couple people who looked like they had nothing to do whatsoever with the circus. They were sitting at the bar, my favorite spot, so I decided to sit next to them. Together, we would make our own little section of normal people in The Big Top.

"What's your poison?" a husky voice came from behind the bar, another dwarf. He had set up a series of benches behind the bar so he would be tall enough to serve the customers.

At first I had thought I just wanted a beer to quench my thirst. It had been a hot and humid day of driving. But then I spied a bottle of Bombay gin, my favorite, on the top row of bottles stacked up behind the bar. I decided a gin and tonic would go down nicely and it would be entertaining to see this little guy try to get that bottle.

"I'll have a G and T," I said smiling as I pulled a few bucks out of my pocket.

"Coming right up," the dwarf bartender said as he turned to grab a bottle of the bar's well gin.

"Ahh, make that with Bombay, if you don't mind," I said trying my hardest to hide my smirk. The bottle of Bombay seemed miles away from old Tiny. I might as well have said, 'Perform for me, dwarf. Let's see if you are really cut out to tend bar.'

He turned and moved down the bench a bit until he was standing right beneath the bottle of Bombay. He then hopped up from the bench to the back bar without disturbing a bottle. At this time I noticed that there was a series of thick ropes hanging from the ceiling about four feet apart. With a sudden burst of energy the bartender leaped up and grabbed a hold of the nearest rope. As able as a monkey he scurried up the rope, grabbed the bottle of Bombay and then slid back down the rope.

Amazed, I couldn't help but smile at his Herculean effort, all for an asshole like me. "Thank you very much," I said taking a drink of the G and T.

"No problem," the dwarf said nonchalantly. Several other times that night he performed the same trick whenever he had to retrieve a bottle from the top three shelves of the bar. No one went thirsty.

I was beginning to like this bar.

"Hans is one of the best bartenders we've ever had," said the light-skinned black woman sitting next to me. She turned to me and stuck out a hand. "Vereena Turnquist. I'm the owner of The Big Top," she said in a voice befitting a ringmaster.

"Hi, I'm Matthew." She looked too nice to lie to.

"Nice to meet you, Matthew," she said scooting her barstool closer to mine. She looked as if she had had a hard life, which didn't surprise me considering she owned a bar. She was attractive but her face had weathered quite a bit, like she had spent a lot of time in the sun. She was extremely thin and looked very fit.

"Is the food good here?" I asked opening up a tent-shaped menu.

"Pretty good if you like hot dogs, peanuts and popcorn," she said with a straight face and then broke into a gorgeous smile. "Actually, the food here if very good and it really has nothing to do with the circus."

"So what is the deal with the circus theme?" I asked as I finished off my drink and motioned Hans the dwarf bartender for another.

"Every one who works here either used to or still works for the circus part-time. Hans here," she motioned to the man handing me another drink, "was a clown. That big guy over there by the door is my bouncer, Erik, the strong man. The Bearded Lady over there playing darts is Zelda, another bartender. Much of the clientele is affiliated with the circus, or was," she added wistfully.

"Sounds like you are kind of upset about that."

"I am to tell you the truth," she said, reaching way behind the bar for a bottle of Bud Light. She had quite a reach. "We're kind of our own little 12-step group." She said opening the bottle with a small triangular opener that was dangling around her neck.

"So you were in the circus, too," I asked a little surprised because she didn't strike me as the circus type.

"Was, yeah. I am a contortionist. I can bend into about any shape you'd imagine. But don't ask me to prove it. I'm not in the mood," she said staring at the beer bottle in her hand. "I also was a ringmaster for a short time till the owner of the circus blamed the declining attendance on me. He said folks aren't ready for a black ringmaster, though he wasn't nice enough to even use the word black. I told him to fuck off and quit.

"His problems aren't with a racist audience, though," she continued, taking a swig from her beer. "The audience doesn't care what I look like. Christ, they pay to see Zelda, the bearded lady, and Ivan, a man with breasts. What would skin color matter to them? The man is just another racist. What else is new?"

I just shook my head in agreement.

"So after I quit in protest, accusing Mr. Beauchamp of racism, a bunch of the other minority performers quit, too."

I looked around the bar again and noticed that yes, that these performers were either black or Hispanic.

"We're all minorities here basically, even Hans," she said motioning toward the dwarf who was once again climbing a rope to retrieve a bottle of Glenfiddich. "He's got some Hopi Indian blood in him."

"How did you end up here of all places?" I asked.

"Well, there was a lot of us leaving Beauchamp and we didn't have a whole lot of money. Shit, we were broke. So we poured into the few cars that we owned and repaired a broken-down circus wagon that Beauchamp wouldn't notice missing. This is all the further we got in one day and decided to stop. We were all holed up down in central Florida. All the circus performers head down there during the winter. Some of us wanted to keep moving north but we weren't used to wintertime so we hung around here for a while and finally discovered this bar. It used to feature circus performances and was kind of a cabaret. The former owner just loved the circus. Several of us started to work here and we stayed. Last year, the owner died of a heart attack and he left the bar to me in his will. So now I run it with help from my friends."

"Wow, well it certainly is an interesting bar," I said looking at the sawdust on the floor and the various strange-looking occupants. "Do you still have performances?"

"Yeah, on the weekends. It's gets pretty crowded here. Some of the crowd is kind of rowdy though. On several occasions they have tossed Hans into the sawdust. He's tough but who wants to get tossed around by a bunch of drunks. And there's a group of truckers that are always chanting for me to take off my clothes. They kind of get a rise from seeing me contort my body. It always seems that on Saturday nights we end up with a fight between the truckers and the clowns. Frankly, it's getting pretty old. I long for the days when we have our own circus and don't have to put up with this bartending bullshit. I've decided that alcohol and circus performing don't mix."

"Hmm. Yeah, I think you've got a point there," I said, checking her out a little more closely. The thought of her folding her body into various positions kind of gave me a rise, too. There was something mysterious and exotic about Vereena, the contortionist. She was a little old for me but something about her gave off the aura of passionate sex. Maybe it was simply the fact that she could move her body unlike other woman. Maybe it was simply the fact that she was black and reminded me of Halle Berry.

I have often fantasized about making love to a black woman. As far as I knew, there was absolutely no difference between black, white, red or yellow women when it came to the bedroom but the thought of rubbing up against that dark skin gave me hot flashes. I motioned Hans for another drink and asked the exotic woman to continue.

"Our plan is to keep at this for a few more years, long enough to save up some money and then we'll hit the road with the first all-minority circus. We're still toying with the name. We kind of like the Royal Rainbow Circus so far. But that could change. We'll play before predominantly minority audiences, you know give some poor kids a few role models. Just think if kids joined the circus rather than joining a gang. They could earn a little money, see the world and stay out of trouble."

"You are assuming that all minorities are poor," I said, the smart-ass in me woke up for some reason.

"No, I'm not. But face it, we aren't the Rockefellers. White folk won't have any part of that."

My visions of having wild passionate sex with the contortionist started to fade. "I represent white folk," I said slowly, wiping the condensation off my glass with a bar napkin.

"I mean the white establishment," she said leaning toward me, touching my knee. "The power elite. You know, the politicians. They don't represent you or me but only their political interests. They are the ones keeping us down."

"Can we just change the subject?" I said, staring down at my drink. "I'm tired of race relations."

"Well, sure that's easy for you to say," she said, getting agitated. "You, as a white male, are the ones in power." Poof. There went my fantasy.

"I thought you just said it wasn't me. That it was the politicians."

"I meant that politicians are the ones keeping blacks from living their own lives. But race relations involve everyone and until white males take up the minorities' cause we will continue to struggle and go nowhere."

"If it's up to white males, then it's never going to happen. They won't willingly give up their power," I said, starting to rise. I wasn't in the mood to sit here and debate race relations.

"Hey, you don't have to leave," she said grabbing my arm. "Sit back down. We don't have to talk about race. I'm sorry. Please sit back down." She pulled me back onto the barstool giving me the sense that I had no choice. "Hans," she called out. "He drinks for free." Now those were sweet words to my ears. "I just get so worked up about the whole race card. I'm tired of race relations, too, but when you're black you can't just turn away from it. It's part of you every single hour of the day, every day of your life.

"But enough about race relations. Let's talk about us." She said batting her eyes in mock adoration. "What's your story, Matthew? How did you end up at the Big Top?"

One thing I had realized about being on the road—you had to tell your life story every other minute. And so far I wasn't very good at telling it succinctly. I would ramble and tell too much. I would leave out important details and put in innocuous ones. But it really didn't matter because I don't think the people that were listening really cared. They just listened politely waiting anxiously for their turn to spill their guts.

This one was different, though, so I told her everything. About my dad, my sister, Tony, my little errand to Florida. At first, I resisted bringing up Nosferatu but as Hans continued providing me with drinks and my hormones picked up speed I decided it was sound pretty damn macho to tell her of how I escaped the devil himself.

As I retold my little adventure with the hitchhiker I realized to myself that I didn't have to embellish it all to make it sound scarier than shit. She hung on my every word. A glow came over her and I had a sinking feeling that a certain organ of mine was going to get a workout that night.

As I gave the details of my escape we both drew closer together. She placed her hand on my thigh. I moved my left knee so it was between her legs. I could sense the heat coming off her body. This was going to make a great letter to Penthouse.

"And so I left him there on the side of the road, cursing and saying he was going to get me back some day."

She was breathless. "My God, that is so wild. And where did you leave this nut? Kentucky? Man, I would drive right around Kentucky on the way back. I don't care if he said he was going to go to New Orleans. Shit, I would change my name, get a different car, change my hair. Fuckers like that scare the shit out of me." With each swear word out of her mouth, I grew more and more excited.

"The sad thing is that they are everywhere. I don't know if it's because I've been in the circus half my life or what, but I swear half the world is nuts and the other half is just downright ornery."

I don't know if it was the alcohol or just an overdose of testosterone but what I said next was about as forward as I have ever gotten with a stranger. "I'm not nuts or ornery but I'm feeling like something that sounds like ornery," I said leering at her. Looking back now, I can't believe I had said something so lame.

Vereena, thankfully, did not laugh back in my face. "You're trying too hard to get into my pants. Just relax, babe. I'm a nympho," she said with such nonchalance that it almost caused me to spit out my drink. It was as if she had stuck her head out the window and simply observed, "It's raining."

"Excuse me," I said in a hushed tone.

"I'm a nymphomaniac. That's the technical term for it. I should just say I like to fuck." Again she showed no hesitation on her part to reveal such a bombshell.

"Whoa," I said quietly. "Let's not announce it to the entire bar."

"That's OK. All the people I work with know about it. It's not like I'm a slut or anything. I don't just sleep with any old stranger that wanders into the bar. I talk to them, get to know them, make sure they are not a weirdo. And if I don't meet anyone I like, I will go back to my place with Ivan or Hans."

"Hans," I said mouthing his name so he wouldn't hear.

"Yeah, he may be a dwarf but his penis is big enough and he knows how to use it. Actually he's just as big as Ivan."

"Ivan's the one with breasts?" I said trying to keep the freaks all straight.

"Yeah, I kind of feel like a dyke when I'm with him. He's so gentle. But I'm not a lesbian," she added with a laugh.

"I thought nymphomania was just an urban myth. You know something middle class teenagers conceived in their hormone-imbalanced minds."

"Hey, I'm here to tell you it's a reality. I have to have sex at least once a day or I get irritable," she said gathering her things into a red purse. "It's a medical condition. My doctor says it could last through menopause or go away any day."

"Doesn't having this, ahh, need, get in the way sometimes," I asked innocently enough. After all, even I don't think about sex all the time.

"I don't find it debilitating at all. You can always find someone who wants to fuck. I'm no dog after all."

"No, you're not," I replied quickly taking in a full-length look at her. "But what about diseases?"

"I'm clean," she said tersely.

"No, I'm mean with the guys you meet."

She laughed as if I had asked a stupid question. "Do you think I let them into the show without a ticket?"

Assuming she was talking about condoms, I laughed but only half-heartedly. I wasn't sure what to think about her admission. Isn't it every man's fantasy to do it with a black contortionist nymphomaniac? It's like handing a fat kid a $10 bill and giving him permission to buy all the candy he wants. "Go ahead, fatty, eat till you puke."

I was attracted to her, no doubt about that. She was exotic and all that. But knowing that I could get laid as long as I had a pulse and could get it up, well, it kind of defeated the purpose. Not that I'm a Casanova or something but with the 10 or so women I've slept with the pursuit was often more fun than the actual conquest. The sex was always fun, it's just that the anticipation leading up to the act seemed more enjoyable.

OK, let's back up a bit here. Ten or so women. Who am I kidding? I've slept with six different women and any guy who can't name all of the women he's had sex with is either a scumball or a rapist. My first was Jayne Kowalski back in high school. Her father owned a Chevrolet dealership in Bettendorf and I lost my virginity in the back of a two-tone brown van. Each weekend, Mr. Kowalski would bring home another lemon, which he was having a hard time selling, for his children to drive.

Then there was my senior prom date Ilsa Sorenson, the foreign exchange student from Sweden. She was a wild woman. All she wanted to do was get laid by American boys. I just happened to be with her on prom night. I found out soon enough that there was no emotional attachment to me whatsoever. She had made her way through half the football team when she decided to try some soccer players. That's where I came into the picture. I was captain of the soccer team. Rumor has it that she went back to Sweden pregnant and ending up having triplets, which she gave up for adoption at her parent's insistence. The fact that she had triplets doesn't surprise me considering she was so pumped full of sperm she'd sneeze out tadpoles whenever she had a cold.

Next up was a series of co-eds, evenly spread out between my sophomore, junior and senior years at college. I dated each for one semester. Cassie Lipnik was the sophomore fling. She liked drugs a little too much for my tastes. Christ, she was so stoned she never went to class. The sex, drug-induced and all, was pretty intense however. She later OD'ed.

My junior year, against my better judgment, I dated a sorority girl. By this age, most woman like to be referred to as a woman but not the gals at Delta Delta Delta. They were girls, dammit, and they just wanted to have fun.

There was a joke at school that if you couldn't get a date, try Delt. It was kind of funny in a sick way because it was true. I had had a bit of a drought with the ladies since Cassie so I let a friend fix me up on a blind date. Her name was Madonna Johnson and she tried to be like the original Madonna. But get a few drinks in her and she made the pop Madonna look like a virgin.

Why was I so strongly attracted to wild women? Psychologists say that you try to marry your mother. I wasn't intending to marry any of these women but isn't that why most people date—to find a mate? Well, these women were nothing like my mother. Or were they? There are some things you will never know, or want to know, about your mother like whether she is a freak in the bedroom.

Madonna was schizo. When she was sober she fought tooth and nail to maintain a facade of innocence, going so far as to get into slapping fights with other Tri Delts whenever they made remarks about her sex life. When she had a few drinks in her (she inhaled Fuzzy Navels) she fought tooth and nail to get your pants off. She believed foreplay was only necessary to get you hard and then she went down on you in bars, movie theaters, roller coaster cars. On more than one occasion we were discovered having sex in a public park or parking lot. I didn't care, I was getting laid.

Eventually, Madonna found God, literally. She claims he came to her one night and told her to stop drinking and carousing or she would end up in hell. I'm not sure if he directed her to the local mental institution but that's where she ended up.

Are you beginning to see a pattern here with the women I've slept with?

My senior year, my target of affection was Sally Sousa as in John Philips Sousa, the only composer of marches I've ever heard of. Sally claimed to be a descendent of the composer and, quite appropriately, played flute in the university's marching band. Sally broke my heart.

By this time, I was growing tired of all of these wild women. I wanted to settle down, fall in love. I did. She didn't. We met in a geology class. It was so romantic. I had fallen asleep during a lecture and Sally came over to me and gently woke me up after class. I made a joke about being eternally indebted to her for waking me before I fell out of my chair and broke my neck. She said she would settle for a cup of coffee.

We went out for two months before we slept together and when we did finally consummate the relationship, Sally decided to end it because she thought we were getting too serious.

Too serious? Of course we were getting too serious. Isn't that what love is about—commitment and a propensity toward seriousness? It didn't make any sense to me.

I didn't want to let her get away so I dragged it out for several weeks afterwards, trying in vain it turns out, to win her back. I couldn't understand how it felt so right for me but not for her. It just didn't register in my feeble mind.

Reality came crashing down when she had Rudy Wrigley, one of the band's sousaphone players, come by my apartment and persuade me to stop calling her and attending her band practice. I wasn't try to scare her but apparently Sally thought I was stalking her.

Now for those who don't know, a sousaphone is a rather large, unwieldy instrument made up of a ton or two of brass and another ton or two of fiberglass. It is a member of the tuba family and is made specifically for marching bands. It's an instrument that requires the player to be quite strong and virile like Rudy Wrigley, who did not only possess these characteristics but was also dumb as an ox. He may have been able to read music but I doubt I could say the same about him concerning the written word.

"Stop bugging Sally," Rudy grunted. "Or I will have to pound you."

"But…" I stammered as the brooding hulk towered over me with orange teeth. He must have had a bag of Cheetos on the way over to see me.

"No buts, Picasso, or I'll kick your's." He started poking my chest with his forefinger with such force that I swear he was going to break a rib.

I got the picture and Sally was out of it.

It didn't do much for my ego when a year later Sally married Rudy Wrigley. She broke up with me because I was getting too serious and yet a scant 12 months later she was serious enough to marry old orange teeth. Apparently, she just likes the strong, dumb type, which I certainly am not.

Sally was the last woman I was with until I slept with Trish, who I was sure was still leaving messages on my home answering machine. Trish ushered in a new phase for me, apparently. Gone were the long-term relationships, if you can call three months long-term. In were one-night stands because I had no intention whatsoever of going out with Trish again. She was a friend, my favorite bartender, but not girlfriend material.

One-night stand number two was getting up to leave.

"Do you want to come back to my place?" the black contortionist nymphomaniac said with a leer. She might as well have said, "Do you want to come back to my place to fuck?"

"Sure," I said rising, feeling the full effects of the alcohol that had taken residence in my brain, liver and bladder. I had to steady myself against the bar or I would have fallen over right there in front of Hans. "Right after I go to the bathroom."

As I made my way over to the men's room, a group of clowns, all of whom were smoking, watched me cross the room. They were out of costume but I could tell these guys made a living hitting each other with foam hammers and cream pies. I went into the john to do my business and when I came out was surrounded by a surly group of harlequins.

"Going home with Vereena?" sneered one with a 5 o'clock shadow and a trace of pancake under his left eye.

"Well," I stumbled, not sure how to respond.

The circle of clowns tightened around me. "So, Mr. Suave here thinks he's going to do it with the ringmaster?" said another clown with a large Afro.

"I wonder if he can even get it up," said yet another clown, this one's face scarred by pockmarks.

Great. I was going to be lynched by Black Bozo and his buddies. Ever since I was a kid I had hated clowns and this confrontation wasn't making me any fonder of them. A lot of smart-ass responses came to mind but, frankly, I was too damn scared to say anything. I could just picture this group of merry makers pounding the living shit out of me then piling into a VW Bug and driving off, honking various horns.

"What should we do with Mr. Suave, boys?" Five o'clock shadow said slowly as they continued to move closer and closer. My heart was pounding like the bass in a Public Enemy song.

"I think we… should… congratulate him," Mr. Pockmark said throwing his arm around my shoulder, giving me a big hug. The others erupted in laughter. Mr. Pockmark took a long drag off his cigarette with his right hand while he squeezed me close with his left arm. "Boys, let's welcome another member to the Vereena club." More laughter.

I pried myself away and made my way toward the door. Clowns. They don't fight fair with their fists so you can see a punch coming. No, they fight dirty with sarcasm and humiliation.

*   *   *

We drove the Caddy to her house, which was not too far from the Big Top. She had warned me that she had a couple of roommates but that they were really cool and I would like them if they were even around.

She couldn't keep her hands off of me, nearly making me lose control of the car several times during the short drive. I was still having some misgivings about this whole nymphomaniac thing. How many of those surly clowns back at the bar had slept with her?

I was getting a sick feeling in my stomach. Was it just nerves? Maybe that's why she plied me with so many drinks. She wanted to have sex with me and figured it was best to get my mind clouded with alcohol. For her, I would probably be a welcome change. I was certainly no chain-smoking, pot-bellied, washed-up clown. I could give her what she was aching for but did I really want to?

"Here we are," she said. With much relief, I turned off the car. As long as I wasn't stuck behind the wheel, I could escape. In the Caddy I was a captive audience.

Her house was not in the best of neighborhoods. If it hadn't been so late at night I imagine I would have seen quite a few folks sitting on their front porches, cleaning their shotguns. It must have been 10 years since any of the houses in this neighborhood had received a paint job. Tony could have made a killing here. Her house was gray or at least it looked gray. It was so dirty that it might have been white at one time. Did it rain dirt in Valdosta?

I didn't have much time to survey the house or the neighborhood for that matter as the ringmaster yanked my arm and dragged me inside. The inside of the house was just slightly cleaner than the outside. Maintaining a household was obviously down on the priority list for her. Old newspapers, paperbacks and People magazines were lying everywhere as if a tornado had ripped through a bookstore.

She led me over to couch that was only slightly less cluttered with Readers' Digests and TV Guides. With one hand she guided me by my belt while with the other she swept the crap off the couch. She then swung me around and threw me down. No sooner had I fallen on my back and she was undoing my belt, pulling my pants off. Subtlety was not her strong point.

I wasn't really acting or reacting. I was simply letting her do all of the work. I was obviously aroused enough to allow things to progress. She had completely pulled my pants off when I heard a shuffling on the other side of the room as if several pairs of feet were wading through the sea of newsprint on the floor.

In my erotica-induced stupor I kind of lost track of the sound for a minute but picked it up again as Vereena stood up to undress. Out of nowhere she pulled a condom and tossed it on my chest. "Here's your ticket," she said, slipping off her pants and underwear. She left her shirt on. I hate that. When I have sex I like both parties to be completely naked with as much exposed flesh touching as possible. It just adds to the sensation.

I don't think she was into the sensation, though, because as she got on top of me I tried to pull her shirt off and she slapped my hands kind of playfully but hard enough to discourage any further attempts at shirt removal. Her slap kind of brought me back to reality, too. I woke up from the cloud of ecstasy long enough to see two faces staring at us just feet from our heads.

Alarmed by this sight I pushed Vereena off onto the floor with a thud.

"What the fuck," she said, scowling, sitting on a stack of the Atlanta Journal-Constitution.

I jumped up from the couch taking my shirt with me to cover myself.

"Oh shit," she sighed as she saw the pantless Siamese twins standing at the other end of the couch. Suddenly it felt like all of the oxygen had been sucked from the room. I fell back down onto the couch, having trouble breathing.

"If I've told you guys once I've told you a million times, wait until the guy has entered me before you show your fucking faces," Vereena yelled. "Goddamn it. You guys fucking piss me off. Do you see what has happened? You've ruined the moment and now you don't get any pleasure out of it, either."

The twins stared at the floor. "We are to be sorry," they said in unison in thick Russian accents. Before me stood, to put it bluntly, a hideous sight. Siamese twins joined at the stomach. Two sets of arms, two heads, two sets of smallish breasts. The bottom half, though, was one person. One waist, one extremely hairy crotch and two unshaved legs. The twins were quite tall, standing nearly six feet, and looking rather malnourished. Although both faces looked the same, they did not share the same hair style. The woman on the left had extremely short hair, practically Marine length. The woman on the right had long, coarse hair like the hair they shared in the pubic area.

"It was Misha's fault," the head on the left said. "She said for us to be getting a closer look at this young man. She also said for us to depants ourselves now."

"This is not right, Natasha," snapped Misha. "We agreed to come forward to get better look. We are sorry if we spoil mood but you may proceed again now. We will be quiet."

I was dumbstruck. Russian voyeuristic Siamese Twins named Misha and Natasha. I looked at the nympho who was pantless, too. In fact, all three or four of us were naked below the waist. Vereena had an "ooops, can you forgive me?" look on her face.

"My roommates like to watch when I bring home men," she said sheepishly. "They've given up hope of ever finding someone who will want to share them so they've become world-class voyeurs. Living with a nymphomaniac, well, it gives them plenty to watch. It's really quite amazing to see them masturbate. They only have one snatch but they both experience the pleasure in completely different ways. Misha is very expressive and will thrash around while Natasha is quite reserved."

I looked at the twins again and shook my head. They looked so strange and uncomfortable standing there with two sets of arms. They wrapped their arms around each other's waist in an attempt to make themselves one.

I gathered up my pants, underwear and shoes. "I'm sorry but this isn't going to work. I'm not an exhibitionist."

She gave me a look like she understood and I realized that this wasn't the first time the twins had showed themselves too early and scared a "date" away. I'm sure my brother-in-law would have stuck around. Christ, he probably would have done the twins as well—but I'm not so automated.

Not that she wanted my sympathy but I felt sorry for Vereena. She had a problem that needed to be dealt with. Something was making her want to sleep with so many men and it wasn't a desire for sex or to procreate. Idealistically, I thought, maybe if she gets the Royal Rainbow Circus going it would fill that hole in her life. My or any other man's penis sure wouldn't fill it.

Chapter Ten

I had little desire to get out of bed on day three. Although the hotel in which I landed in outside of Valdosta was of the hourly-rate variety, the bed was horizontal and that's about all I needed to sleep. This errand for Tony had become quite a chore.

At this point, I had driven nearly 1,000 miles, almost been killed by a man who changed his name as often as his underwear, was offered a rare glimpse of an alien cadaver, had been accosted by a black nymphomaniac, who happened to be a contortionist on the side, and was spied on by pantless Russian Siamese twins.

As I looked at the glass, it was definitely half empty. I was thinking that this trip was destined to get stranger by the mile. Who needs acid? Just drive down to Florida with me.

As I have said earlier, I like to watch television. I'm not really a doer. I would have much rather enjoyed watching someone else meet Nosferatu, Jerry, Huey, Vereena and Natasha/Misha. You know, watch it for a couple hours then turn off the tube and go to bed. The problem here was that I kept waking up.

I should have spent that final day alone mentally preparing myself for the return trip. After all, Tony had warned me that Edgar and Gert were a little on the odd side. Instead, as I pulled the Caddy onto Interstate 75 once again, I decided it was time to figure out exactly what kind of job I was suited for when I did finally return to Davenport. It was a daunting task that helped me eat up the miles through the extremely long Sunshine State.

What can you do with a bachelor's degree? Well, just about anything you put your mind to. But what was I capably of doing realistically? I knew sales were out. Sure, I started in the minor, minor leagues of sales trying to hawk aluminum siding over the phone but I knew from that brief experience that I couldn't sell a drink to an alcoholic. I can bullshit people; I just can't do it for a profit.

Let me see, what else could I do:

Teaching—No. I don't want to baby-sit a bunch of hormone-addled pre-pubescents who are intrigued as much by their genitalia as they are with their boogers.

Journalism—No. I fulfill the cynicism requirement but I don't like the hours (all day, every day) nor do I like the physical results. Any good journalist worth his or her spit turns fat, myopic and generally irritable.

Public Relations—Yeah, right. Like I want to get on the phone with these fat, myopic irritants and try to get them to write about some stupid product that I say isn't stupid but really is.

Advertising—Nope. I just can't write a jingle for adult diapers or denture cream and be convincing. I'm afraid all of my ads would be reduced to first-class groveling. "Please, please, please buy this new style of liquid hand soap. It doubles as mouth wash and will help you get laid."

Lawyer—The only reason I would become an attorney would be to bring down the entire legal profession from the inside and I just don't have the stamina.

Doctor—Can't stand the blood and besides it would require additional schooling. While I enjoyed the social aspects of college, I hated the work.

Police Officer—I would love to be in charge of the world but I am morally opposed to the police and their fascist leanings so I would never be able to sleep at night. And sleep is too important to me.

Plumber—I don't have the ass for it.

Garbageman—Too smelly and I'm too weak.

Politician—Ah, now there's something I could do, which really means nothing. But where do I begin? How do I get involved in politics? I don't know the first thing about getting elected. But standing around flapping my gums, spending other people's money sounds like a terrific job.

So I drove on through the state of Florida trying to figure out an easy way to break into politics, hoping no thugs would mistake me for a foreign tourist.

Several times my thoughts turned to dad. Driving down Interstate 75 was the closest I'd been to him since he left the family, at least that I knew. He was down here somewhere in Florida, I just didn't know where exactly, though I assumed he was on one of the coasts. If you were going to be a nudist you'd probably want to stay near water. I'd suspect that they spend an awful lot of time washing crap off their skin. That's definitely one benefit of wearing clothes. Most of the time it's your clothes that get dirty not you. When you're munching on a hot dog the ketchup squirts on your tie or shirt not your nipple.

I spent a lot of time wondering what it would be like living in a nudist colony. Maybe it's just because I am so insecure but wouldn't it be embarrassing most of the time, at least for a young guy? I have a hard enough time keeping control of my erections seeing clothed women. What would it be like to see naked women all day long? I'm sure you would get desensitized to some extent after a while seeing everyone in the all-together and taking a gander at wrinkly old ladies and fat chicks. But I'm sure there are those occasions when you would run into some hot number and your penis would just take over. Then what do you do? Run away? Cover it with a palm frond? Just smile and say to the attractive woman, "Pardon my boner."

Maybe it's just accepted. After all, getting a hard-on is natural and these people are naturalists. Even if it is accepted, though, I'm sure people talk about it behind your back. "Did you see Jeffrey today? He got an erection when he walked passed Susan. How gauche."

And I'm sure there would be the inevitable references to each other's size. The boys would snicker around the water cooler. You can't tell me that that doesn't happen in a nudist colony. Maybe dad is well endowed and that's why he stays in charge. In the jungle I know it's the biggest animals that lead their respective genus. Because man is a little more advanced we resort to other measurements of who is in charge. In the Army, it depends on your uniform. Well, in a nudist colony you can't go by that yardstick.

These were the kind of thoughts I was reduced to on day three. Obviously, I needed to get some traveling companions or else I would go nuts. You can only spend so much time driving alone before you either start inventing friends or need to start chattering on a CB.

I wouldn't say I was looking forward to having the old couple in the car but at least I wouldn't be so damn bored.

For those who haven't driven it, Florida goes on forever. It is split in the middle by the new entertainment capital of the world—Orlando. Although I knew I couldn't stop, lest I be killed by Tony, I was awfully tempted to take a break at Disney World. It's not often I get down this way and maybe if I just got in and got out....

As I neared the first exit for Orlando, I thought I was going to stop. By the second I knew I was going to stop. At the third, I pulled off and drove to the nearest gas station. I really did have to get gas and hell, it wouldn't hurt to get the scoop on Mickey.

I figured anyone you bumped into in the general vicinity would know how to get to Disney World so I asked the female attendant for directions to the park. She was about 18 and hated life. She certainly could never get a job with Walt Disney. She had a bit of a mustache (and Walt doesn't allow any facial hair), a nose stud, and a buzz job that revealed a very pronounced widow's peak. The '90s female version of Eddie Munster, she was definitely one individual who should only come out at night.

"You don't want to go to that fucking fascist place, man," she opined as she walked around the Caddy, the chains wrapped around her black jeans jangling.

"Maybe I do," I said defiantly, not intimidated at all by the predominance of black in her wardrobe. I had known a lot of these depressing types back in college. The last thing they want is attention, yet they dress in a way that begs for you to glare at them.

"What the fuck are you looking at?" she barked, pulling the gas nozzle out of the Caddy after the tank was full. I had not pulled into the full-service bay, yet she was giving it to me anyway.

"I bet I'm looking at someone who thinks the No. 1 tourist destination in the entire world is run by Benito Mussolini," I said pulling the charge card out of my wallet.

"Hey, it's a goddam well-known fact. It's a fascist regime over there in La-La land. Think about it. It's so clean and all the employees have to dress alike and look alike. They don't allow for any individuality. If that's not fascist what is? And the funny thing is, Walt Disney would never have survived in a fascist environment himself, being a repressed homosexual and all."

All of a sudden it hit me. Spike here couldn't get a job at Disney World because of the way she dressed so she was stuck pumping gas at some Amoco off of Interstate 75, which is probably pretty dangerous at night. She probably resented the fact that she couldn't be herself, whoever or whatever that is, and work in the safe confines of the Magic Kingdom. Rather than change her appearance, she got angry.

"You know," I said, handing over my charge card to her. "You're probably right. I think I'll just skip Walt's world this time through Florida."

She narrowed her eyes, not quite sure what to make of my remark. "Come on, we need to ring this up inside," she said and led me inside the station. "Walt really was gay, man," she resumed her assault on Mr. Disney without prompting. "He really hated his mother. That's why all of his movies have evil woman in them. Snow White, Cinderella. He had a lot of hatred toward mom for some reason. I think those movies are poisonous to little girls. I'm surprised someone like Gloria Steinem hasn't done something about it by now."

I let her remarks slide. If Spike wanted to think that Disney was poisoning the minds of our youth, fine. Just as long as she didn't procreate. The last thing central Florida needed was a bunch of little Spikettes running around biting the ankles of tourists.

I got back into the Cadillac resigned to the fact that I couldn't afford to go to Disney World even if I wanted to. It cost more than $30 just to get in and that was about $25 more than I wanted to spend. I needed to complete this task so I set forth for Bal Harbour determined to drive straight through. Unfortunately, the Caddy had a different idea. About an hour after I had been schooled on the Walt Disney's sexual leanings, the Caddy got a flat tire, which was no big deal because there was a spare in the trunk but I am no mechanic and it took me nearly 90 minutes to get the spare on. In the process, I nearly broke my left hand when the tire iron slipped off the lug nuts and whacked me across the knuckles. I should have buried my hand in a bucket of ice but decided to drive on like a true macho man. Forget the pain, Tony's grandparents were waiting for me.

I drove the rest of the way with my right hand gripping the steering wheel while I cradled my throbbing left hand in my lap. I really would have been in trouble had the Caddy been a manual.

As a result of the flat tire and my sore hand, which caused me to pull off again to find some Advil, I was running at least two hours behind schedule. Then I got lost in their retirement complex for another hour, driving down countless cul-de-sacs with quaint names like Grandparents Avenue, Best Years of Our Lives Lane and Twilight Circle. By the time I arrived at their condo, on Sunset Boulevard Circle, it was 8 o'clock.

A crusty old pretzel of a man with a brown felt fedora, a navy cardigan and white polyester slacks was sitting in a fold-up patio chair on the sidewalk outside the townhouse condo. It had to be Edgar. As he saw the Caddy pull into the driveway, he slowly rose from the chair.

"Tony was never this late, dammit," he said, turning his back to me to fold up the chair. "The reservations were for 7 o'clock, sonny. I doubt they have held them for us. It's not McDonald's. You don't just come when you goddam please. Where the hell have you been? Christ, I've been out here for two hours waiting for you. I'm going to get skin cancer sitting out here in the goddam sun."

I looked around for the sun. Maybe it had been out two hours ago when I was expected but there was nothing but thick clouds in the sky now.

"I'm sorry, Edgar, but I hurt my hand and I got lost," I said holding my swollen hand into the air for proof.

"It's Mr. Vermicelli to you, boyo. I will be addressed as Mr. Vermicelli and Mrs. Vermicelli will be addressed as Mrs. Vermicelli from this point further. Not Gertrude. Not Gertie. Not Hey Lady. Not Ma'am. Got it? I hope so because if we are going to get through this trip all in one piece with our sanity or what's left of it intact we will be cordial and respectful. Understand?" With that, he waved his free hand in the air as if shooing off flies, and carried the chair into the house.

"No, Edgar, I don't understand, you old fucking geezer," I said to myself. Geez, I hate old people. I followed him inside without unloading the Caddy.

The inside was decorated on the cheap. They certainly left all of their good furniture in Davenport. The front room had an avocado-colored sofa that definitely was purchased during some furniture store's going-out-of-business sale. On either side of the sofa were two wooden TV trays that were serving as end tables. On each rested a lamp, one in the shape of a giant conch shell, the other as the wheel of a sailing ship. There were a couple more fold-up patio chairs in the room as well as a fold-up card table. The walls were adorned with several ocean scenes, of dolphins frolicking, of waves gently lapping against a beach, of a sailboat in a bay. The only picture that seemed to reveal anything about the Vermicellis was the oil painting of a young Frank Sinatra. Old Blue Eyes was right above the television, a place of obvious reverence.

The 26-inch television and VCR were the only objects in the entire townhome that were of any value. Furniture was simply comfortable enough, not fancy. The entire place looked like a warehouse for an upcoming unsuccessful garage sale.

I followed him through the living room, the dining room, and the kitchen into the back of the townhome where their bedroom was located. There, we found his wife shuffling back and forth getting ready to go out.

"Don't sleep in the subway, darling. Don't stand in the pouring rain. Da da da," she was singing to no one. After the first few lines of the song her voice trailed off and she hummed the rest.

"The kid is here," the old man barked as he barreled into the room. "Christ almighty, I hope Sylvester will still seat us and I bet they are all out of the prime rib now. Christ, what were you doing all day, sitting on your goddam thumb? I tell you, kids today don't have any respect for people's schedules. The only one they care about is their own."

Gert, in a sleeveless yellow polyester dress that went down to her knees, turned slowly. She resembled a pencil with arms. "What did you say, dear?" she said rather loudly holding a hand up to her ear.

"I said let's go," her husband barked as he removed his cardigan, threw it on the bed in a heap, put on a light blue blazer and shuffled past me out of the room.

"Hi, I'm Matthew. Sorry I'm late."

She said nothing, waving a hand in front of her face to indicate that the fact that I was over two hours late was nothing. She picked up the cardigan, picked a couple pieces of lint off the arm and hung it back in the closet.

As I headed out to the living room again, she was off on another tune: "Up up and away in my beautiful, my beautiful balloon. Da da da."

"Edgar, err, I mean Mr. Vermicelli, I'm sorry I'm late but I'm beat, my hand hurts and I really don't feel like going out to eat. I'd rather just get a good night's sleep so we can get an early start tomorrow."

"Nonsense," he said firmly. "Every year we come down to Florida for the winter. Every year Tony comes down and picks us up to go back to Davenport for the summer. When he arrives, he is tired too, but he always goes out to dinner with us as a farewell meal to Florida. It's tradition and some punk, who I am not even related to, who is nearly three hours late, who thinks the world revolves around him and doesn't care about a couple of old farts, isn't going to change tradition. You will respect me. You will respect my wife. And you will respect tradition. Got it?"

Edgar Vermicelli might have been a strapping lad at some time in his life. Maybe he was a boxer or a wrestler. Maybe he played linebacker for the Chicago Bears. But, right now, he was a little mole of a man resembling Quasimodo more than Dick Butkus. I could easily have had lifted him over my head and smashed him against the wall like a plate. I was tired. My hand ached. And I wasn't going to have some pint-sized drill sergeant, boss me around.

"You want my respect, Edgar, and I'm going to call you Edgar because I'm no child and I don't call anyone Mister anymore," I said evenly. "If you want me to give you respect, you'll have to respect me and stop bossing me around. I have just driven down from Iowa and let me tell you it's not a quick trip. If we are going to be cramped into that Cadillac for three days together we are going to have get along cause if we don't I might just have to accidentally lose you in some rest stop in Bumfuck, Georgia. To me this is just a job, a job I already regret taking. I have had a pretty shitty trip so far and I don't plan on it getting worse so shape up or ..."

The old woman shuffled into the room and seeing how frail and out of it she was we both curbed our anger.

"Let me get the Caddy cleaned up a little bit and then we can go," I said leaving without giving anyone a chance to respond.

*   *   *

It's amazing how much crap that gathers in every nook and cranny of a car on a trip. I was finding wrappers for things I don't even remember buying. I throw all of my stuff in the trunk and then started to gather all of the garbage. Fortunately, Edgar waited inside in the air-conditioning and didn't stand over my shoulder and tell me how to clean his car. As I was cleaning underneath the front seat my hand brushed up against

Nosferatu's gun. Just touching the cool, polished steel made me shiver. I decided to leave it where it was rather than put it in the trunk. It couldn't help me there, although I thought I could never bring myself to use it again. I slid it out a bit to get a closer look. I knew nothing about guns so I didn't know what caliber it was. All I could see was that it said Beretta on the side reminding me of the old cop show with Robert Blake and that white cockatoo. I wasn't old enough to watch it when it was first on but I have seen the re-runs. Carefully, I slid it back under the seat and finished cleaning up the car.

As I crawled out of the front seat, I saw that Edgar was on the prowl again.

"You don't have to detail the goddam car," he said walking toward me with a sense of purpose. His wife dawdled behind. "Let's go. I want to get some prime rib if they still have any. And there's some friends I need to say good-bye to before we go. Let's move it."

*   *   *

"Now, this is the only meal we are going to pay for the entire trip," Edgar said grabbing my right shoulder from the back seat, where both he and his wife sat against my wishes. I didn't like being a chauffeur but I guess that's all I was to them. Gert sat directly behind me and Edgar sat in the middle as if he was making room for a third passenger back there. I doubt it was because he wanted to be close to his wife of some 50 years. Through the rearview mirror I could see Gert. She was off in her own world, singing and humming songs from the '60s and '70s. She wasn't all there. It could have been the beginnings of Alzheimer's but I suspect it was that she had just decided a long time ago to tune her husband out. Maybe that was the secret of their marriage's longevity. If I were in her loafers, I would have certainly tuned him out.

At the restaurant, the old man worked the room like he had just bought it, greeting just about every male there. Mostly handshakes, but he did hug a few men who could manage to get to their feet without too much difficulty. He was pretty spry compared to the lot of them. Many had walkers or those motorized carts with a swivel seat.

Gert and I just sat there at our table in the back of the brightly lit, cavernous room. She didn't bother to pick up the menu. She must have already decided what she wanted for her last meal in Florida.

"Your husband is quite the schmoozer," I said surveying the menu for something that struck my fancy. I was amazed at the variety of food, everything from Matzo ball soup to chicken tacos. I was concerned that because of this great variety that the chef was unable to do anything well. I settled on a Rueben thinking that it would be hard to fuck up a sandwich.

"What?" she squawked.

"I said your husband is quite the schmoozer," I said increasing the decibels a few.

She gave me a concerned look and said: "Oh, I don't think so" and turned away to find him in the crowd of geriatrics.

Given her response I figured she either heard me say that her husband was quite the boozer or quite the loser. Either way, she wasn't happy with my comment.

This was going to be a long trip. Edgar and I got along about as good as the Arabs and the Israelis, and his wife was out to lunch even when we were out to dinner.

After several long, awkward minutes of silence, she began to sing in a shaky voice: "When the moon is in the seventh sky and Jupiter aligns with Mars…"

Edgar was finally nearing the table when a younger man with a black suit came up to our table. He kissed Gert lightly on the cheek, quietly saying, "Good evening, Gertrude." He turned to me and announced loudly with outstretched arms as if he expected me to get up and give him a hug: "Tony, you are looking younger than ever. You must be working out. My, you look marvelous."

"That's not Tony, Sylvester," Edgar said gruffly, finally taking a seat at our table.

"Not Tony? What do you mean that's not Tony? That's got to be Tony," he said scurrying over to Edgar's side to help him move in his chair. With a sweeping motion he picked up a menu and opened it for him. This Sylvester was working extra hard for a tip.

"I'm not Tony, thank God," I said under my breath.

"What the hell do you mean by that? Thank God." Edgar closed the menu and tossed it across the table at me. Apparently, his hearing was just fine. "What do you mean by that, you punk? Don't be talking cross about my grandson. I ought to come over there and slap the crap out of you. He is three times the man you'll ever be. He respects his elders. He treats his grandparents like kings and queens, not like some kind of American Tourister luggage. You could learn a thing or two from him."

"Like how to gouge seniors by selling them something they don't need?" I said crossly from behind my menu. I don't know where this comment came from. I didn't want to continue fighting with him but I was tired and there was something about him that just kind of pissed me off. I didn't respect him because he didn't respect me.

"You punk. You don't know Tony," Edgar shouted from across the table. Meanwhile, Sylvester stood there patiently in his black suit. "He is offering the seniors of Davenport a service. He is helping them protect their investment."

"Yeah, right. He sells them siding for a house that rarely needs it. Then they die and their children end up paying for the rest of the bill. He preys on their fears that if they don't buy his siding, the house will fall apart during the next tough winter."

The old man's face was getting so red I thought he was going to have a heart attack right then and there. "You son of a bitch. Sylvester, have this punk removed from the restaurant. Get him out of here."

Sylvester looked at me and shrugged his shoulders. He would have liked to kick me out but he knew he had no right to. I hadn't done anything wrong.

"Perhaps you'd like to order one of tonight's special," Sylvester said trying to defuse the tense situation at the table. "We have a wonderful rack of lamb or perhaps the prime rib? That's one of your favorites."

Edgar looked up at him like he should shut his fat trap but then the anger drained from his face. "I'm sorry. I shouldn't be arguing in front of you. You haven't done anything wrong. I will have the prime rib like usual and my lovely wife will have the Orange Roughy. For the rude punk across the table, you can get a peanut butter and jelly sandwich."

"I'll have some prime rib, too, if you don't mind. Rare. " I said quickly before he scampered away. I figured that because Edgar was popping for this and only this meal I should enjoy it, or at least try to.

"So, what time do you want to take off tomorrow? You must be excited to get back to Iowa?" I said trying to smooth the waters.

"Don't try to change the subject, you little bastard," Edgar scowled. "I'll tell you right from the start that I don't like that fact that you're not my grandson. We've been driving back and forth between Davenport and Bal Harbour since 1982. For the past seven years, it has always been Tony that has done the driving. I'm old and set in my ways. I don't like change. And I don't like some punk, who's not even related to me coming down here to treat me like dirt. If you will recall, I am the employer and you are the employee. If you don't treat me with respect I will fire you. Understand? I don't have to show you any respect."

"Whoa. Hold it there a second, big fella. This isn't slavery. I'm not doing this because anyone is holding a gun to my head. Yes, you can fire me but then how will you get back to Davenport. Seeing as you don't like to fly, that limits your options. I guess you can take a Greyhound. Boy, that would be a whole lot of fun. And yes, you do need to show me some respect because if you don't I will quit and that would kind of suck if we were in the middle of nowhere. How far can you walk nowadays, 200, 300 feet maybe?"

"I will walk over your grave, you little asshole," he seethed, throwing a pink package of sugar substitute across the table. The package missed its mark by several feet. It was such a pitiful excuse for a throw that I couldn't help but laugh. I had to keep reminding myself that this was a helpless old couple who needed me more than I needed them. I figured he was generally irritable because he was close to death and had to depend on just about everyone else for everything. It's a predicament that would tend to make anyone kind of surly.

"Is that what you would call your curveball?" I asked, once again trying to defuse a tense moment with comedy.

Gert, meanwhile, had her own way of easing the tension: "What goes up, must come down. Spinning wheel, da de da da…"

"You laugh now, punk, but I was quite a pitcher in my days," Edgar said, the scowl quickly melting off his face.

"Yeah, right. You throw like a girl and a particularly inept one at that."

"That's my unusual delivery, which was the scourge of batters in the major leagues during the '40s. They used to call me "Noodle Arm" Vermicelli. I would fling that old ball so fast it made their heads spin. In fact I once went three innings without allowing a batter to even hit the ball. Can you imagine that? Nine batters without a foul tip, hit or anything. Nine strike outs right in a row."

I didn't believe him for a second. If he had played professional sports, I'm sure Tony would have told me that the minute I met him. Tony was such a glory hound he wouldn't keep something like this a secret.

"Oh yeah, what team did you play for?" I asked in an attempt to trip him up, half expecting him to say something like the Minnesota Twins, a team that wasn't around in the 40s

"The Cleveland Indians. I played with them from 1942 until the damn war got over. Then all of the regular players came back and the owners thought they had to give them their jobs back. The bastards. And so, even though I was better than all of the returning pitchers, they let me go. I guess they were tired of winning games."

"I thought they didn't have baseball during the war. Didn't they just have women leagues?" I didn't really know. I just remember seeing a movie about it once.

"Women leagues. Bah. No, they had men leagues and I was there. I could have been in the Hall of Fame, I tell you. But that's ancient history," he said, stirring sugar into his coffee, another old man habit. I can't understand how these old geezers can drink coffee all day long. It's as if caffeine is the fuel that makes them go.

"I was a showgirl," a quiet voice said out of nowhere. Words, rather than lyrics, had finally passed Gert's lips. Edgar rolled his eyes and shook his head.

"Now, dear, don't go into that," Edgar said, giving his wife a patronizing pat on the hand.

"I was. In Vegas. It was before I met my husband," she continued. "It was during the '40s, too, while he was playing baseball," she said with a wink.

Again, their age was tripping me up. They had lived through the '40s and I had only read or seen movies about them so I was treading on shaky ground. But I forged ahead anyway. "I thought Las Vegas was more of a recent phenomenon, that it didn't really come about until the '50s. Didn't that gangster Bugsy Siegel start it up?"

"Oh heavens, no," she said closing her eyes as she shook her head. "No, Vegas has been around forever. I know. I was there entertaining the returning troops. It was quite rowdy, I assure you. Especially those Marines. Sometimes I feared for my life."

"Time out," Edgar said, unfolding his linen napkin with great flourish. Sylvester was scampering our way with our salads.

Gert, looking a bit annoyed, touched my hand. "He hates it when I tell this story. First of all, he always needs to be the center of attention and second, he doesn't like the fact that I showed off my body to the entire world. I was quite a looker at that time. Men would get in fights over me."

"I do not need to be the center of attention, goddamit," he barked as he poured on too much French dressing onto his mixed greens salad. "Dammit, now look what you made me do."

While Sylvester tried to convince Edgar that he could go get a new salad, one without a cup of dressing on it, the old woman continued her story, which Tony had forewarned me about. I was beginning to think that the only kind of stories these two knew how to tell were fabricated ones.

"Now, I wasn't a stripper even though I ended up completely nude by the end of the show. We would start off by doing some big production with all of this glitter covering our private parts. Then a comedian would come out and tell a few off-color jokes while we changed into a more risqué outfit. This next one would show off our breasts. I was pretty shapely back then. It seemed as if at every show some dapper young gentlemen would mouth the words to me: 'I love you' or 'Marry me.' A juggling or fire-eater act would follow as we took off more. By the end of the show the girls and me were completely naked. At first, I was kind of shy about it but then we never did any kind of suggestive dances or anything. We were just prancing around like show horses. And in a way, I kind of got a kick out how the men would hoot and holler just because they could see our breasts and pubic hair. Men are so juvenile."

She whispered "pubic hair" like she was talking about diarrhea in a television commercial.

"Are you quite through yet?" Edgar said, exasperated.

"Yes, I'm finished now. You may have the floor, dear," his wife said, focusing on her salad.

"Now what do you mean by that?" the old man roared from across the table.

"Nothing," she said quietly, gently stabbing pieces of lettuce. It appeared as if she knew how to push her husband's buttons.

"Women. They were put on this Earth for two reasons—to have children and to drive men nuts. Plain and simple." He pushed his salad away and throttled his drink like it was his wife's wrinkly little neck.

"I think they were put on Earth to save us men from killing ourselves," I chimed in. "Can you imagine a world without any reason? That's what you would have without women. Men would be so busy arguing about who's the boss or who's got the hairiest chest that we would be constantly slamming each over the head with clubs."

"You're full of it, shithead," the old man grumbled. "You know, that's what I think I'm going to call you the rest of the trip. Shithead. You are so full of crap. This younger generation just can't wait to mess everything up. We built this country into what it is today and now a bunch of restless, spoiled brats are going to bring it down."

"Well, I appreciate that vote of confidence. I'll keep that in mind tomorrow and the next day when I'm chauffeuring your ass across the country you so graciously built."

"See," Edgar said looking at his wife across the table. "That's what I mean. Absolutely no respect. The younger generation has no respect for its elders anymore. My father would have kicked my butt from her to Timbuktu if I talked to him like that. Tony never treated us like this, did he, Gert? Did he?"

His wife looked up blankly from her meal, blinked and went into song: "There's a kind of hush, all over the world tonight…"

Chapter Eleven

It's amazing what rotten dinner companionship can do to your appetite. It had been days since I had had a good, solid meal. My body ached to be stuffed. But my primal urges took a back seat to Edgar's unsavory behavior. I was frankly embarrassed to be sitting with him. And I was beginning to think that his wife's defense of singing pop songs to herself was a damn, good idea. Maybe I should start singing current songs.

I thought at the time that the old fart was just an asshole like the rest of his family but now I think it was just his fear of, or resentment of, getting old. The plumbing didn't work quite up to snuff, the hearing was shot, even the taste buds weren't all quite there. So he took it out on everyone.

"Sylvester, Sylvester," Edgar yelled after taking one taste of his prime rib. The waiter scampered in from the kitchen like a mutt hoping to be let out for the night.

"Yes, Mr. Vermicelli, what is the matter?" he said in between huffs and puffs. It appeared that exercise and Sylvester were not on speaking terms.

"This prime rib is overcooked," Edgar said, exasperated. "You know how I like it. Raw. Like it just fell off the cow."

"I realize that, sir, but all of the rare prime rib has been ordered. We only have so much and there was quite a run on it tonight."

I looked down at my prime rib and saw that it was slightly pinker than Edgar's. I don't really care how my meat is done as long as it tastes good so I decided to take one giant leap for diplomacy. "Uh, Edgar, my piece is a little more rare than yours. Do you want to trade? I've only had a couple bites."

Sylvester, on pins and needles, smiled half-ass and chirped: "That's a wonderful idea. What do you think, Edgar?"

The old man raised one eyebrow and scrutinized my meat. "Well, it does look a little pinker…" He then looked down at his plate, stabbed his meat with his fork and held it up for public display. "Yeah, it looks better than mine. OK," he said quickly and tossed his meat on my plate like he was throwing a scrap to a dog. He lunged over to my plate and stabbed my meat. "Sylvester, you should have given me this one in the first place. Christ, you know me better than him."

"Maybe he thinks I'm a better tipper," I said, cutting into my inherited piece of prime rib.

Sylvester winced. Edgar barked at me: "Keep it to yourself, shithead."

Not much was said after that. Edgar asked how the trip down was and I told him uneventful, the understatement of the century. He asked how the Cadillac was running and I told him fine. He asked me how my sister was and I told her still married, which he didn't find amusing. Apparently, Tony's side of the family was as sensitive about the marriage as we were except they were worried that Angela might some day leave him while our side of the family rallied around that distinct possibility.

Figuring that relations were over for the evening I turned on the car radio on the drive back to the couple's condo.

"What station is Jerome Paul on down here?" I asked, trying to find his show on the dial. My curiosity was needling me. Was Jerome Paul's head all in once piece still?

"That liberal fairy. What a piece of shit," Edgar grumbled. "He's on 1130."

"What's new pussycat? La la la la la la la," Gert hummed quietly to herself in the backseat.

I tuned it to 1130 just as a public service announcement calling for the banning of Joe Camel was finishing. An unfamiliar voice filled the cavernous Caddy. "Most of us were not born with silver spoons in our mouths. We fall upon hard times and there is no one there to give us a helping hand. We are estranged from our family or maybe don't even have a family. Should we be punished for this? No, the government should be there to help us out, to let us get back on our feet again, to get back into the work force. That was FDR's idea behind welfare and it was a good one. Tonight we discuss welfare. It will be a no holds barred discussion where I will take on liberal and conservative calls alike. But if you disagree with me and say we should abolish welfare you will be wrong and I will be right. Cleetus from Spirit Lake, Iowa, you're on the Joe Sweeney Show."

"Joe Sweeney," I said, feeling as if someone had thumped me on the chest. My God, Nosferatu had gotten to Jerome Paul. He had actually gone on with his plan.

"That's Paul's fill-in," Edgar said nonchalantly from the backseat. "He fills in all the time whenever Paul has one of his fairy obligations. Being King Queer keeps him pretty busy."

So the old man listened to him. Figures. I swear, more conservatives listen to Jerome Paul than liberals. They can't just calmly go about their private lives, counting their money, buying new safes, downsizing their corporations. No, instead they had to tune into some fat, bleeding heart liberal and have their blood pressure escalated. Maybe Nosferatu was right about people having to have enemies. Of course, everyone with a pulse was Edgar's enemy.

My heart rate returned to its usual nice, leisurely pace. It was just a fill-in. Jerome Paul's head was still intact.

As I lay down in my sleeping bag that night wondering if I would get any sleep on that rock hard floor in the condo, my thoughts quickly returned to Nosferatu. I was amazed at how quickly my heart rate jumped when I had thought Jerome Paul had been killed. The gravity of my life or death struggle with the madman kept me tossing and turning for several hours despite my overall fatigue. The longer I lay awake the more frustrated I became knowing that I needed all the sleep I could get to handle Edgar's surliness the next day. Eventually, I fell asleep, then....

"Up and at 'em," the old man yelled, kicking me in the right leg. "It's going to be a hot one today and I want to get the hell out of Jewville." I looked at my watch and saw that it was 4:30 in the morning. Christ, I must have only gotten four hours of sleep. We had never talked about a starting time but I just assumed that the Vermicellis would at least let me sleep until 6 o'clock.

"We didn't agree to get up at 4:30. Christ, the interstate isn't open at this hour."

"Bullshit, you pussy. Now up and at 'em," Edgar, the drill sergeant, barked. "If we leave under cover of darkness I won't have to worry about saying any more good-byes. Christ, these leeches down here can't stop saying good-bye. They're so afraid it will be the last time they ever see you. I wouldn't mind it at all if I didn't see half of these freaking idiots ever again."

"I'm sure you're too well loved down here either, Rasputin," I said under my breath as I crawled out of the bag. It was no use trying to go back to sleep now. Herr Edgar would goose-step in here every five minutes to make sure I was getting up. So I got up, brushed my teeth and started to throw my crap into the Caddy.

The old couple was packed and ready to go with their suitcases lined up by the front door. It was amazing to me how few suitcases they had to take back to Iowa. Between them they only had two large suitcases and a couple smaller ones. I know I couldn't live in Florida on this amount of clothes.

"Is this all you are going to take back?" I said as I lifted the two large suitcases, my arms nearly dislocating from my shoulders.

"What do you mean by that?" Edgar said defensively.

"I mean only this stuff right here? It doesn't seem like that much. Or are you shipping some of it back?"

"That's all we need. We're not as concerned about our clothes as you young people," Edgar said, walking back and forth around the condo, unplugging every appliance and light. "What else would you like us to bring back? The microwave or the refrigerator? Christ, I would think you'd be happy you don't have to carry more out to the car. Now get cracking, shithead."

"Hey, I'm not complaining. I just think you are probably forgetting something."

"What does that mean?" he said once again looking as if I had insulted him.

"Nothing, nothing at all," I said, sighing as I lugged the two suitcases to the trunk of the Caddy. After a couple of trips the car was packed up and ready to go. Gert had been pacing the living room floor, probably a bit paranoid thinking she might have forgotten something to pack. But when I returned from the car the last time, she moved passed me and took her place in the back seat of the car on the driver's side.

Edgar, who had supervised the loading of the car like the drill sergeant he was, was now nowhere to be found.

"Come on, it's time to go. I think the interstates are now open," I shouted so that wherever he was hiding in the condo he would hear me. The toilet flushed and out came Edgar a bit red in the face, clutching a small, bag that looked like the kind doctor's used to carry in old movies back when they actually made house calls. "Oh, did I forget one? I can take that," I said innocently enough putting a hand out to grab the black satchel.

He swatted my hand away. "I can carry it. I'm not helpless, you turd. That's what wrong with the younger generation—either you're not around to help or you try to help when you're not needed. Old people are not helpless you know."

"Chill out," I said not appreciating the lecture so early in the morning. "I'm just trying to help out. If you want to play Dr. Kildare and carry your little doctor's bag around, by all means, do it. I could give a crap. I didn't get up before the roosters to argue with you."

Christ, it was going to be a long day. That was obvious. Every time I tried to be nice, and believe me being nice for me is a stretch, the old man got surly. Every time I was not nice, he got rabid. It was a no-win situation.

He clutched the bag like a football as he roamed around the apartment one more time. I didn't bother to move him along because I would have done the exact same thing. My mother did it, too, when we were kids, especially when we left on a long weekend or for vacation. She would circle the house like a dog getting ready to take a nap. She'd check the burners on the stove even if she hadn't cooked something in three days. She'd check the back door to make sure it was locked, then she would go from window to window on the ground floor to make sure they were locked as well. Then when she was satisfied that everything would be OK for a week she would check the back door again. He was just doing what any God-fearing homeowner does.

"I don't know why I am so concerned about this place," he muttered as he locked the front door. "The damn landlord always lets his grandkids stay here. Oh, he thinks I don't know about it but I find the things he forgets to clean up. Like the schnapps in the liquor cabinet. I hate schnapps. It's like drinking candy. It's a baby's drink. I can't believe it's considered an alcoholic beverage. That sure in hell isn't my booze."

The mere mention of peppermint schnapps made my stomach lurch. Edgar was right on about it being a kid's drink. In high school, my friends and I would always drink schnapps before high school football games. By the opening kickoffs we were flying, confident that if any teachers or parents questioned our outrageous behavior and interrogated us our breath would not give us away. "We'll just tell them we're fond of hard candy," we would snicker as everything blurred around the edges and our insides grew warm and fuzzy. We continued this practice through our junior year until Rob Cantucci hurled on Heidi Holmberg's perfectly coifed head. Heidi's father, who was sitting an entire section away but apparently could smell trouble from a neighboring county, detected the reek of alcohol amongst the half-digested noodles and ground beef that was dripping down his daughter's hair. It was a cold night and the steam rose from Heidi's head like fresh urine in the snow.

Her father, Harold, a partner with Holmberg, Weiss, Sunholm, Francis, Scott and Key, threatened first to kick our drunken asses up and down the bleachers and then when cooler heads prevailed decided to sue us for the cost of Heidi's ticket, her outfit, and a visit to the hairdresser. Add punitive damages and the bill of $500 was to be split between me, Rob Cantucci and our other drinking buddy Steve Cash. Mr. Holmberg is still waiting for payment.

"I also find empty condom wrappers under the bed. It's a good thing I find them and she doesn't. She'd have a heart attack."

"Well, at least they're practicing safe sex," I quipped.

"The only people having sex in my bed is me," Edgar barked back. "Don't think that I can't remember being a teen-ager. I was an ordinary teen-ager with the ordinary desires and such but I never went around taking my pants off with every Jane or Betty I took to the movies. And damn it if they'd even let you if you wanted to. You kids today just want to run around naked all the time with your things doing all the thinking for you. Show a little restraint, will you? Christ, that's what's wrong with the world today. Too much copulating going on. Everything is sex, sex, sex. You can't watch a nice program on the television today without some nice little girlie talking like she drove a semi for a living. F-ing this, F-ing that. And the commercials, they're worse. You sit down with the wife to watch a little sitcom and if you're lucky you can get to the station break without hearing about someone *doing* someone else. And when the commercial comes on it equates everything with a sexual organ. Drink this beer and this bikini-clad bimbo will stop by your house with her nice car. Use this deodorant and the Norwegian Swim Team will come to your workplace to ride up and down the elevator with you while they rip your clothes off. Put on this perfume and some Charles Atlas lookalike will take you out for dinner and dancing. It's ridiculous. These commercial people are not creative. They're punks."

"Well, sex sells," I said, looking at the couple in the back seat through the rearview mirror. Gert averted her eyes when I said the word sex. "Give the people what they want."

"That's a bunch of crap. Do you hear me? Crap. Don't give them what they *want*, give them what they *need*," Edgar said settling in for the day's ride. He placed the doctor's bag between his legs on the floor of the Caddy and undid his belt to let his belly get some air. Gert remained rigid as a board in the seat behind me. "People have too many freedoms today."

"Uh, what was that?" I asked pulling the Caddy out of the driveway.

"I said people have too many freedoms today. What are you deaf? There's only three feet between my mouth and your ears."

"I heard you all right. I just can't believe you said that," I said clicking the radio off. The old man was beginning to sound more interesting than anything I would ever find on the radio.

"It's true. What's wrong with America is what's right with America. Am I going too fast for you, sonny? Because this may get complicated," Edgar said raising an eyebrow.

"Please proceed, oh wise one," I said, smiling.

"As Americans, in the land of the free, home of the brave, we like to tout our individual freedoms," he said, clearing his throat as if everyone in the Caddy was not paying attention. Gert was watching the landscape zoom by. Maybe she was saying good-bye to Florida in her own, spiritual way. Or maybe she was thinking of other pop songs she had heard through the years.

"Above all else, one inalienable right we have is our individual freedom. Damn it, I've got mine and don't mess with it. That's what everybody says nowadays. And we not only want people to leave our stuff alone we want them to leave our air space alone as well. Like all this crap that's been happening with smoking. As an individual I have the right to light one up here in my own car if I so please, but the minute I roll down the window and that smoke starts drifting into people's homes, or into their cars, damn it, throw me in jail. That's what they are saying. I would argue 'What's my smoke doing to you?' and they would argue that it's killing them. Waa, waa, waa. What a bunch of crybabies. Don't these people realize that anything in this life that's worth having, will probably kill us. If they don't, then it's time for them to grow up. *Don't smoke next to me*," he said in a whiny voice, obviously mimicking a Birkenstock-wearing, tree-hugging, Greenpeace member of the Church of What's Left. "Christ almighty. If you don't like it move. But would they ever think about moving? No, they cry, 'I don't have to move. I've got my rights to breathe clean air. Smokers should move. They are infringing on my personal freedom.' Bullshit. Get a life, you righteous hippies."

"But," I said, not really disagreeing with him but trying to probe him more. "What if I were to light up a stogie right here and kept the windows up and you two started hacking? I could argue that it's my right to be able to light one up. At the same time you could argue that it's your right not to have to suffer from it. So who's right and who's wrong?"

"I'm right because this is my damn car, you punk," he said, trying his best not to laugh. "And I say, give me one of those stogies because I'd like to smoke one in my car and for those other people on the interstate who don't like the smell of cigar smoke, they can kiss my hienie."

We both had a good laugh. Maybe we could find some common ground. We didn't have to have an Arab-Israeli relationship after all.

Although still early, the day was getting hot quickly. I could see why the snowbirds headed north for the summer months. I found it hard to believe, however, that the couple had not grown tired of driving back and forth. Sure, it was Tony, or me, who was doing the driving but when you're as old as the Vermicellis I would think you wouldn't to waste time seeing the same old scenery pass by.

"So what's the deal with you and flying?" I said after driving in silence for 20 minutes or so. I caught Edgar nodding off in the back. Gert had been sleeping for several miles by this point and apparently her husband decided to join her. I had other ideas.

"What? What did you say?" Edgar said opening his eyes.

"What are you deaf? There's only three feet between my mouth and your ears," I said, laughing.

"Shut up, shithead. I can hear just fine. I could hear a goddamn fart in a windstorm. My hearing is perfect. You just need to enunciate instead of that mumbling you're doing."

"I said what's the deal with you and flying?" stressing each word slowly. "Why don't you two just fly back and forth to Florida? The flight's only a couple of hours."

A pained expression filled Edgar's face. "Flying is not for us," he said looking at the floorboards in the back, then he turned to look out his window.

"We don't fly because, frankly, it scares the hell out of us, for good reason too," he said quickly, as if he had to screw up his courage to get the words out. "Back in 1975, we boarded a plane in Cedar Rapids to go to Cleveland to attend my mother's funeral. She had been dying of cancer for some time so we had driven back and forth a couple of times and didn't want to drive again. I had missed too much work as it was so we wanted to get to Cleveland as quickly as possible.

"Mother," he stopped a moment to look up at the roof of the car. "If you can hear me tell this story, I hope you're happy now."

He turned to me and continued: "It's not a long flight from Cedar Rapids to Cleveland. I would assume it was pretty routine but maybe we got an amateur pilot or he was so bored of flying such a routine flight that he had a drink or two before coming to work. Whatever the reason, we never found out. We had been up in the air for only a little when the pilot gets on the speaker and says everybody is to sit in their seats and buckle up. He says that we are coming up to some turbulence as if he were reading about it on some road sign. How the hell is he supposed to know? I swear he was slurring his words. Well, the plane starts to bounce around. I'd been through turbulence before but nothing like this. It was so rough that if you hadn't been buckled in you would have been thrown from your seat. This goes on for what seems like hours. Women and children are throwing up. The men are trying to put on a calm face but inside we are all praying. Gert is gripping my hand with such force I think that she is going to break my bones. Even the stewardesses, who are trained for such situations, are running around with fear in their eyes. Then all of a sudden the turbulence stops and everyone lets out a sigh of relief. For a brief second, there is complete silence, then comes the nervous talk about how scary it was but everything is fine now.

"We are just coming to our senses when the pilot gets on the speaker and says that we should remain seated because there could be more turbulence. More turbulence? Wasn't that enough already, we said quietly to each other. Everyone is looking at each other, probably thinking that these are the last people we will all see alive. I know we were thinking it. It wasn't the fact that the pilot said we were in for some more turbulence. It was how he said it. He was afraid and although he tried to mask it, it came through.

"Some loudmouth across the aisle from us unbuckled his seat belt saying he had flown hundreds of times and there was no big deal about turbulence. His wife, who apparently had not flown as many times as he, was almost in hysterics. She begged her big brute of a husband to sit back down and buckle up. But Mr. Macho said he was going to go to the john and no one was going to stop him. A frail stewardess unbuckled herself and came back to Mr. Macho to try to get him to sit down. He told her that she could go sit back down because she wasn't going to get him back in his seat until he wanted to get back in his seat.

"It was about this time that plane jolted again sending everyone into another panic. A mask of white fear replaced the smirk of confidence on the brute's face. He and the stewardess were vulnerable now, standing out in the aisle with nothing to hang onto.

"And that's when the plane went into a nosedive. The brute and the stewardess were thrown to the floor and both tumbled down the aisle like ragdolls. At first the passengers were stone silent, taking in the last few moments of their mortality but then the screams started. First it was the women and children, then the men joined in.

"Down, down, down the plane went dropping mile after mile. My ears felt like they were going to burst either from the screaming or the pressure from dropping so quickly. We squeezed each other's hand and prayed. I wasn't ready to die but at least we would go together.

"Then as sudden as we started to drop, the plane leveled off. Somehow the pilot had wrestled the plane out of its nosedive. For a few awkward moments, the passengers were quiet again, not sure whether to expect more turbulence or another free fall or that now they were truly out of danger.

"The pilot got on the speaker again and told everyone that he was going to land in Chicago immediately. He didn't go into detail but said that the plane had malfunctioned. He said he hoped everyone was all right. But everyone was not all right. The brute and the stewardess that had gone to get him to sit down were both moaning, tangled together like a pretzel on the floor. Later we would find out that he suffered a concussion and she had broken her left arm.

"Everyone else was just plain scared. I would not be surprised at all if everyone that was on that plane that afternoon never flew again in their lives. We never have and never will again. I know that the odds of something like that are very small but I don't want to take the chance. I saw it as a sign from God that we should stick to the ground."

If his story were true, I wouldn't blame him for being afraid of flying. I have never flown so I couldn't fully relate to the story. We never traveled much when we were younger and I couldn't afford to fly in college. Anyway, I never really had anything to fly to. All of our relatives lived within driving distance and dad never invited me down to Florida.

Exhausted from his dramatic tale, Edgar took a short nap, with his mouth ajar and his throat warbling. Gert, who had awoken during his story, simply stared out the window as we cruised along the coastal interstate.

Seeing Gert back there in her own little world, I decided to engage her in conversation—now that her husband was asleep. What was this woman about? All I knew is that she was once, supposedly, a dancer in Las Vegas. How did she meet her husband? How did she handle the news when a horny bear mauled her son, Vincente?

"Comfortable?" I said looking back over my shoulder.

She just stared at the Spanish moss-lined trees along the road.

"Need anything?"

No response.

"Hello," I snapped.

"Yes," she said, quietly.

"I said do you need anything?"

"What I need I should have asked for long ago so, no, I don't need anything."

I let that one lay there like a ticking bomb.

It struck me that what she needed was to be away from her husband. They hadn't said but a few words to each other since I arrived and I don't think it was because a stranger was in their presence. They were a couple that had run out of things to say to each other. As they grew old together, he got cranky and complained about everything and she retreated to some secret garden in her mind. Apparently, she was content to just dwell in that garden and wait for God to call her home. Maybe if Edgar died before her she would snap out of this funk and get back to enjoying her twilight years. She certainly was going to be like a swan, which dies from a broken heart when its mate passes on. No, she would probably start a new life without that anchor of hers.

So we drove on in silence, Gert dwelling among the hibiscus and magnolias of her mind's eye, Edgar ripping and snorting as he dreamed about God knows what, and me thinking about my long-gone father who was strolling along a beach somewhere in the Sunshine State, naked as the day he was born.

When I was younger, the other boys often teased me for not having a father. I would reply to their taunts by arguing that I did have a father, he just was somewhere else. They would then ask where he was. I had no reply to this. There were other kids at school who were being raised by just their mother but most of them did see their father from time to time whether it was in a visit to the local prison or around holidays when the loser would grow nostalgic for his kids.

I never knew where dear old dad was and I hated him for it. I fantasized a lot about where he was and what he was doing. Mom didn't offer up much information other than to say that he was still alive and asked about how Angela and I were doing. I would vacillate between wishing he were hanging from a tree, not quite dead but suffering greatly, and planning to run away from home to find him. This latter idea usually came to mind whenever my mother had exacted what I thought was an unfair punishment on me.

Christmastime was the worst. My mother did her best to fill both the female and male roles in the household but she couldn't put a bike together to save her life and she just couldn't get herself to buy me the kind of toys a father would—G.I. Joe or other types of action figures. As a result, I often got socks or pants or turtlenecks for gifts, which didn't make for very fun holidays.

The movies were the worst. Half of the movies made about the holidays seem to focus on the entire family being together or getting together. There would be some hardship that tore them asunder but by the time the credits rolled, dad or mom or sister was back home getting a big hug from everyone else. These movies hit me hard and after a couple years, I refused to watch any of those sappy Christmas movies.

For the Picassos, there would always be one empty seat at the Christmas table.

So here I was driving through Florida the closest that I had been to my father since I was a baby. He was out there somewhere but damned if I knew where to start looking.

"Where the hell are we?" a deep, confused voice said from the back seat. Edgar was up from his catnap. As he regained his consciousness, he quickly wiped away the drool that had been flowing down his chin. He frantically looked around the back seat, saw his wife sitting there quietly and me in the front and settled back into his seat.

"We're still in Florida. You can go back to sleep if you'd like."

"I wasn't sleeping," he shot back, blowing his nose into a white hankie he produced from one of his pockets. "I was just resting my eyes. I don't trust you with my car. I need to keep an eye on you."

"You know, you're quite the charmer. It doesn't take you long to go from complete unconsciousness to alert complaining, does it?"

"Shut up. Don't you ever have anything nice to say? You should show a little more respect. Maybe you'd be able to get a real job if you'd be a little more respectful. Bosses don't want some smart-ass kid working for them. They want someone who will kiss and fondle their ass if they ask for it."

"Maybe you have something there," I said, looking back at him through the rearview mirror. "I won't kiss anyone's butt. Maybe that's why I don't have a job. And, Christ, if that's the criteria for getting one I will never leave my mother's basement. I'll get married to some fat, welfare mama and never leave my subterranean fortress."

"You should be ashamed of yourself," the old man said, turning away to look out the window. "A man is measured by the work he does. You think you're being funny when you say you would hold up in your mother's basement but let me tell you there are some cultures that would practically force you to do just that. Not having a job is shameful in many societies and those without work are ostracized. You're lucky you live in a country full of deadbeats. Half of America would rather spend all day watching television and eating potato chips than going to work and earning a living. It gets back to what I was saying about too many freedoms. People think they have a God-given right to do nothing that the government owes them something because they are colored or a woman or a homo or because they were beaten by their father as a kid. I say bullshit. Get off your ass and get a job."

"I was a dancer...." Gert said quietly to herself.

We were silent for several more miles. I was beginning to understand Gert. Every time Edgar and I got into an argument, she would try to distract us by doing something that would make us think she was totally insane—singing a pop song or bringing up a topic that she had already mentioned. It was a defense mechanism and it worked on me because I felt sorry for her. I think it only pissed her husband off more because he would stew about it and start off on another rant.

"Why don't you go back to work for Tony?" he barked. "He's got a good business. You could go far there."

Aha, so Edgar did know who I was. Obviously, Tony had told him about our history. All this time, I had thought he only knew me as his grandson's brother-in-law.

"I don't have it in me to do phone sales and to work for Tony you gotta start in sales," I said matter of factly.

"Well, then what are you going to do? You drive pretty well, maybe you could be a chauffeur," he said, laughing to himself.

"Yeah, right, me a chauffeur. I told you, I don't kiss ass and kissing ass is all a chauffeur does except for know how to pick up prostitutes and score drugs for his boss.

"The long and the short of it, Edgar, is that I don't know what I want to do with my life. If I'm going to be working the rest of my life I want to enjoy it and so I feel I'm warranted in taking a long time to decide."

"Haven't you already taken some 20 years?"

"Yeah, right, like I spent my youth weighing my career options," I said, shaking my head. "Get real. I want to enjoy my job. I don't want to have to go to work each day and watch the clock until it's time to go home. I want a job in which I don't mind working extra hours because it's something I enjoy doing.

"Maybe I should just become a gigolo," I said joking, growing tired of job talk. I had heard enough of it from my mother and from everybody else in the adult world. I was beginning to think Michael Jackson was smart to hang around with kids. That way no serious topics would ever arise.

"You, a gigolo," Edgar echoed, clapping his hands together. "Yeah, like you know the first thing about pleasing a woman. You're nothing but a punk."

I looked back at Gert over my shoulder and noticed that she had nodded off. I figured that there must be a reason why Edgar felt it was all right to go into this subject matter.

"Oh, and you do, I suppose," I said to the man in the back seat who looked like he hadn't gotten a piece of ass since his last child was born.

"You're darn tootin', I do. I've got a lot more experience in it than you do. At your age you're so darn happy to be getting any, you only know one speed—pedal to the metal. But to really please the ladies you need to be able to go at all kinds of speeds. Sometimes the mood calls for slow, sometimes slow and fast, and sometimes just fast like a jackrabbit. The key is to interpret the mood."

"OK, Casanova, who died and made you the expert? You're lucky if you can still get it up," I said, laughing.

"Don't worry about me, sonny," he said, grinning in a sick sort of way. "My old soldier can still stand at attention. Christ, you could pound in nails with it. Why in my younger days, I was quite the stud. Before I was married I lived in Hollywood." As if that explained everything.

"Bullshit," I snapped, trying to nip this lie in the bud.

"It's true. You ask anyone in my family. I used to act in a lot of B movies, you know the movies that would not get the big budgets in Hollywood. Me and Dutch Reagan used to be pals."

"Wait a second, Dutch Reagan? As in Ronald Reagan," I asked incredulously.

"Yes, Ronald Reagan, as in the former president. What are you deaf? There's only three feet between my mouth and your ears."

"I don't believe you."

"Shut up, punk, and listen. As I was saying, Dutch Reagan and I would have these little contests for who would score at all of the Hollywood parties. Those were heady days, I tell ya. Rita Hayworth. Carole Lombard. Dorothy Lamour. Dutch never won. He would always chicken out at the last minute, right when he was about to bed the dame. I never chickened out, though. I've been in more Hollywood starlets than that geek, Warren Beatty. Of course, it helped that there was a rumor going around Hollywood that I was hung like Milton Bearle. Yes, I'm talking about the comedian. It was a well-known fact that his 'schtick,' as he called it, was no laughing matter..."

"Hold it, hold it," I said, nearly veering off the interstate. I had heard enough. I can take one or two little lies, but this was getting ridiculous.

Next he was going to tell me he was once president. "Wait a second, Edgar. You've going a little too far with this story. There is no way in hell that you were a professional baseball player and I'll be damned if you were a movie actor. And even if you were either of these, there is no way you would be shtupping those actresses. You look like a horse."

"Horse, eh? Hung like a horse maybe."

"Wake up, wake up back there, Edgar, you're dreaming. On behalf of all the other sane men in the world I have to call you on this one. You're short, you're ugly and you have the demeanor of an ape. A Hollywood starlet wouldn't waste her time to give you directions to Mann's Chinese Theater let alone let you hump her."

"You are so naive, punk," Edgar said, shaking his head. "Do you really think women are attracted to men because of their looks? You know nothing about natural selection, do you? A woman is attracted to a man because he's either rich or well endowed. It's a well-known fact. It's men who are attracted to women because they are good-looking. Your pea-size brain may not be able to comprehend this but we were put on this planet to procreate. That's our No. 1 job. That's why God programmed us with these hormones that make us horny nearly half the day. Women want a man who is rich so that her offspring are provided for and can grow up and procreate themselves. She wants her man to be well endowed so her son is well endowed so he can attract a mate. Man wants his mate to be good-looking so his daughter is good-looking so she can attract a mate. It's nothing we can control. It's all mapped out in our heads. It's purely instinctual. We're just animals."

Obviously, Edgar had spent a lot of time discussing this topic with other Cro-Magnon thinkers. I looked back at his wife who was still sleeping and wondered what his excuse was for picking her. She certainly was not going to win any beauty pageants. In fact, she was a little horse-like herself. I refrained from bringing up this line of reasoning with Edgar, however. I didn't want to offend Gert. She had done nothing wrong.

"Well maybe that's how things work in your family but we Picassos are a little more evolved than that. I'm going to marry someone who is intelligent and funny."

"Good luck. You'll probably end up with a couple of goofball kids, which wouldn't surprise me one bit."

"Go back to sleep, old man," I said to myself and popped a Butt Uglys tape into the tape player. As Snidley Whiplash, lead singer for the group, screamed that he was going to kill himself if he ever fell in love with a sorority girl again, I drove on with a smile. The Butt Uglys was one of those special English bands that can instantly give people over 30 a headache. Even people who like rock 'n roll can only take so much of them. I, myself, couldn't listen to more than four songs in a row without growing extremely irritable.

I knew the old fart would soon crumble and realize that I was indeed in power in the Caddy as long I was behind the wheel and control of the radio and tape deck.

"Suzie makes me want to cry, cry, cry. Why didn't she tell me she was in Delta Chi? Now I just want to die, die, die." Snidely sure had a way with lyrics.

"Will you shut this crap off," Edgar yelled at the top of his lungs. I turned it up a bit but then saw his wife starting to stir and turned it down. As long as she was in the car, I couldn't force myself to be cruel.

"How can you listen to that drivel? It's worse than that rap crap that Tony listens to every trip. With the swearing and the boom, boom, boom—it gives me such a migraine. And it scares her half to death. Whenever you hear that rap crap down in Florida, some nigger is driving by in some souped-up gangster car looking for someone to kill. The world would be a safer place if all of that rock and rap crap were outlawed. Just burn it all up."

"You just don't understand it. This music and rap are simply forms of expression from people you'd never begin to understand. You may not be able to decipher the lyrics because you're a confused old man but these musicians are really saying something about life."

I don't know why I even bothered to argue because it was a losing proposition. There was no argument I could win against this crustacean. He was right and I was wrong the minute I opened my mouth. Nonetheless, something deep down inside me wanted to chide him. I had unprocessed anger that I needed to vent and he was my target. Because he was old. Because he started criticizing me without even getting to know me first. And because he was there.

"They have nothing to say to me that would either educate or entertain me. They're all just worthless punks like you. Now pull over I've got to take a piss," the geezer said suddenly, his hand on the door handle as if he were going to open the door and step out while the Caddy was still zooming along the interstate.

By this time, we had made it half way up Florida. It had been a productive morning as far as driving was concerned. Having gotten on the road so damn early there wasn't much traffic. A bathroom break was actually a good idea. I just hoped that with the old couple's decrepit bladders that we wouldn't be stopping every 20 minutes.

We pulled off the interstate at an Amoco so I could top off the Caddy. Gert was still sleeping so Edgar leaned over to gently wake her. It was a sweet gesture on his part. He obviously still loved her deeply after all of these years. I know I would have lost patience long ago with someone as non-descript and seemingly senile as her. She opened her eyes slowly, taking in her surroundings bit by bit.

"Where are we?" she said in a birdlike voice.

"Some dump in northern Florida," Edgar said gruffly, grabbing his satchel off the floor of the Caddy. "Time for a potty break." He clutched the bag to his chest and headed toward the men's room. With snail-like swiftness, she gathered herself up out of the back seat and headed to the ladies' room.

As I watched the old man snap at the gas station attendant for the key to the men's room, I kept wondering what the hell was in that bag. It is must have been fairly important because he was guarding it with his life. It was too small to carry a nuclear warhead but it was certainly large enough to carry enough explosives to blow the Caddy to smithereens. Did he want to go out with a bang, literally? Maybe it was just an heirloom or a rare coin collection that he coveted. My mischievous side doubted it, though. He wouldn't take that to the bathroom with him.

Maybe he had a jones for smack and had to go shoot up in the john at the Amoco. Yeah, right. He could barely keep his hands from shaking long enough to feed himself. There was no way he would be able to chase the dragon without killing himself.

Maybe it was a cache of pornography, something so vile, he was embarrassed to show it to anyone. Maybe he was in that bathroom right now spanking over little boys doing headstands and jumping jacks. Although this sounded like a likely candidate I shook my head vigorously to get the thought out of my mind.

It was probably a bag full of pills—for his heart, high blood pressure, arthritis, etc. Old people pop so many pills it's a wonder they don't rattle when they walk. The more I thought about it the more it made sense. Maybe he was just embarrassed about the fact that he had to take so many pills.

As I finished pumping gas into the Caddy I figured I would quiz Gert about the mysterious satchel as soon as she came back to the car. Unfortunately, they finished at the same time.

I jogged inside to pay the bill, grab some Lifesavers and by the time I got behind the wheel both of them were in the back of the car ready to roll on, the black bag safely stowed between his legs on the floor. I let the mystery of the bag drift away as I clicked on the radio, no longer feeling the urge to argue with the Grump.

I surfed around the dial for several minutes trying to find something worth while but all I found was three country stations (I hate country music), a couple classical stations, about 50 oldies stations and some Bible-thumping programs.

"Stay on the classical music," Edgar said the times I wandered pass a station playing Mozart, Bach or one of those other old, dead guys. I didn't want to grant his wish because he was Edgar but I finally acquiesced when I couldn't find anything that caught my attention. So we listened to concertos while I nearly fell asleep at the wheel. In between tunes, some anemic pansy would get on the air and whisper the name of the concerto like he was announcing at the 18th green of the British Open. I realized that I hated classical music as much as country and western.

"Now that's music," the old man said, crossing his arms, waiting for me to make a smart-ass remark.

Background music, I thought to myself but kept silent. I was damn near falling asleep when it reached the top of the hour and Mr. Anemic came on to read the news. He mumbled something about continued tension in the Middle East and another former mistress of the president coming forward when I reached to turn the channel. I stopped short as Mr. Anemic mumbled: "Controversial talk show host and best-selling author Jerome Paul, whose ultra-liberal leanings have enraged conservative politicians for years, was found murdered late last night in an alley just blocks from the restaurant where he performed his nightly show. New Orleans Police are busy investigating the murder but concede that they have few clues at this point. They will only say that apparently Mr. Paul's head had been crushed by an automobile."

Crushed by an automobile. Jesus fucking Christ. I swerved into the right lane nearly forcing another car into the ditch, as I fought the urge to pee my pants. That other driver might have honked at me or flipped me off but I'm not sure. I felt lightheaded like I was going to pass out and suddenly I couldn't breathe. My heart pounding as the cavity around it tightened.

"What the hell are you doing? You're going to get us killed," Edgar yelled, pounding on the back of my seat.

His voice brought me back to the here and now. I shook my head vigorously and breathed in deeply gripping the wheel like a life preserver. I concentrated on the road and the task at hand.

Oh my God. Jerome Paul was dead. Nosferatu had actually gone on to New Orleans and killed him. Someone must have picked him up after I had escaped. What did he do to that person? Are they lying somewhere eviscerated on the side of the road? Shit, that could have been me. That could have been me.

"What the hell is wrong with you?" the old man yelled again. I looked at him in the rearview mirror and noticed that I was paler than Andy Warhol. "Don't tell me you're upset because some fat faggot was killed. Big deal. He deserved it. I'm surprised some nut case didn't do it a long time ago. He had pissed off so many people it was just a matter of time."

"No, it's not that," I lied. "I haven't eaten all morning. My blood sugar is down."

"Well, then pull over and have an Egg McMuffin already. I don't want to die just because you decided to go on a diet," the senior said, settling back into his seat.

I kept driving with the thought of pulling over at the next fast-food restaurant. I did need to get something to eat but with the knot that was now in my stomach I wasn't sure I would be able to keep anything down. Part of me wanted to tell Edgar about my confrontation with Jerome Paul's killer and part of me figured he wouldn't believe it or would simply come back with some story in which he faced something more perilous. The former professional ball player/Hollywood starlet boinker would never let me get the better of him in a story. Even if my story was true.

As if my time with Nosferatu and narrow escape from him was not enough to haunt me, this news about Jerome Paul made him grow into mythic proportions. He was real. And although he was hundreds of miles away physically, he lived inside my thoughts, growing more gruesome with each mile. He was no longer a scrawny drifter in my mind's eye. He was now a giant, sinewy monster, preying on my insecurities. As irritating as he was, at least Edgar wasn't going to kill me.

Chapter Twelve

"You'll never believe what happened," Angela said breathlessly as soon as she recognized my voice on the line. I hadn't even had a chance to say hello before she began rattling off the latest exploits of those merry pranksters, ARAT.

It was now day five of my trip. The day before had gone fairly smoothly even after hearing the news of Jerome Paul. Driving with the old man and his merciless bitching allowed me to shove the ghost of Nosferatu out of my mind. It's hard to keep thinking about something, anything, when you have a ripe bastard like Edgar Vermicelli constantly poking at you from the backseat.

For the rest of the day, he and I had argued about important stuff like why he thought Democrat was just another word for Communist and why golf was the greatest game ever invented. Meanwhile his wife just sat there, occasionally humming or singing the first few lines of a pop song. I never figured out why she was stuck in the '60 and '70s. Maybe that was the only time she had listened to the radio.

I had decided to call Angela late in the morning. We were near Chattanooga and I needed a lengthy break from Edgar who had been telling a particularly nutty story about how he had invented the Bismarck pastry treat but some German baker stole the recipe and named it after his great grandfather. He had planned on calling it the Magellan after the Italian explorer Fernidad Magellan, the first sailor to circumnavigate the globe. "See my cream-filled donut is round like the world. Get it?" he had said.

Having dealt now with Edgar's unique style of insanity for a day and a half I thought I was fully prepared for whatever Angela had to spew. But I had underestimated, once again, the imaginativeness of ARAT.

"I just can't believe it happened," she continued.

Ah excuse me, dear sister, but I've had an unbelievable few days myself, I wanted to say. I was just aching to tell someone about Nosferatu and how I was lucky to be alive. But Angela was hell-bent on telling me about her own run in with the devil—dairy farmer Clayton Dale Tuleen. In my dealings with half of the freaks in the free world, I had forgotten that she and her pals at ARAT had decided to do something really dumb.

"Are you all right?" I interrupted her as she rambled on about protests, guns and cattle.

"I'm just fine. Kind of keyed up. Tony is at work, I guess. I need to talk to someone. I'm so glad you called. We did it. We did it. I can't believe it. We took on Tuleen. And you were right. He has guns and he is not afraid to use them."

"Slow down, will you? What happened? Christ, it sounds like you are on speed or something."

"You know I would never take any drugs. I'm still running on adrenaline. Pick up a paper. I'm sure there's a story on us in there. You could probably read about it in any paper you pick up. Where are you by the way?"

"The middle of Tennessee, outside some diner." I said, surveying the surroundings. I saw several hounds trotting back and forth across the street. Apparently, there is no leash law in Chattanooga. "So tell me what happened."

"All right, all right. A group of about 20 of us headed out to Tuleen's farm south of the city. Someone got a school bus so we could all go down together. Jane Goodall was…"

"Wait a second."

"What?"

"You said Jane Goodall as in *the* Jane Goodall the woman who lived with and studied apes in Africa?"

"No, this woman's name is really Jane Green but she thought calling herself Jane Goodall would lend some credibility to ARAT."

"See. This is just what I'm talking about." I couldn't help myself. These ARAT fuckheads got to me every time. "There's no substance there. It's all image. They're deceiving you and they're deceiving the nation. Some nut calls herself Jane Goodall and someone hears it on the news and thinks it's *the* Jane Goodall and thinks this group must have some heavyweights behind it. But no you're just a bunch of posers."

"Do you want to hear the story or not, Matthew?" Angela said shrilly. She used to sound like this when we were kids and she was scolding me for something I had done. Something that she kept from mom. Something that would have gotten me in big trouble. "Do you want me to hang up here? This is quite traumatic for me and all you want to do is criticize. If it makes any difference to you I've quit ARAT. I'm done with it. Does that make you happy? Are you satisfied? I actually agree with you. They've gone too far. We're lucky someone wasn't killed out there. We're lucky Tuleen is getting old and isn't that good of a shot otherwise someone would have been killed and it might have been me. I was shot at, Matthew. He tried to kill me. Kill me simply because I think meat is murder. Simply for standing up for my beliefs..."

We were both silent for several seconds. I could see that the Vermicellis were asleep in the back seat of the Caddy. I had parked in the shade so that the car wouldn't heat up while I was on the phone. The couple must have thought it was the perfect spot for a catnap, which was fine with me. I had a feeling I would be on the phone with Angela for some time.

I had been nearly killed by a psychotic drifter. My sister had been nearly killed by a psychotic Nazi agrarian. It was quite a week for the Picassos.

"I'm sorry. I guess the stress of this errand for Tony is getting to me. I'll be quiet. Jane Goodall was doing what?"

"No, I'm sorry. I'm just kind of freaked out about this whole thing still. Are they driving you nuts?"

"Yes, but that story can wait. What happened with ARAT?"

She paused for a moment. "Jane Goodall was standing at the front of the bus buzzing instructions to us through a bull horn. I remember looking around at the other people on the bus and seeing fear in their eyes. Up until then I hadn't been nervous but when I looked and saw the concern in people's eyes I really got worried.

"With Jane leading, it had become a military maneuver not a protest. In the back of the bus a group was finishing up signs, writing slogans like

'Meat is murder no matter how you slice it' and "Cows are God's creatures, too.' Another group of women was helping each other apply different shades of green to their faces for camouflage. She was barking out orders left and right. I had thought that we were going to walk around with signs and chant a few slogans. But she had a different idea. She was saying how a group of women were going to surround Tuleen's house first. They were to take baseball bats for protection. If Tuleen resisted they were to knock him out. Another group of women was to take wire cutters and cut off all the electricity to the building where Tuleen and his workers had their milking machines. A third group of women was to take the heavy-duty wire cutters along a fence and cut a path of freedom for the cows. Clayton Dale Tuleen is a dangerous man,' Jane shouted at us. 'If he gets out of hand or comes out shooting we must be prepared to fight back. We can't back down easily.' As she was saying this I saw that my concern was shared by many of the other protesters on the bus. 'Fight back,' repeated one meek-looking woman next to me. 'I thought this was a non-violent group,' she went on. 'It is,' I told her. 'Just ignore Jane. She's mad with power.' Unfortunately, enough of the protesters were listening to her, especially the men in the group.

"We must be prepared to torch his house if worse comes to worse, Jane was saying up front. This remark got more of us looking around at each other. 'Damn it, this is war,' she said noticing that she was beginning to lose the troops. 'This man is a racist, sexist, homophobe. His crimes against cows and other defenseless animals are just the tip of the iceberg. He needs to be stopped. I have talked with his neighbors and they are all for this raid. They even went so far to say that they would be happy, and that the world would be a better place, if we just offed him. Well, you have got to draw the line somewhere but it just goes to show you that there is no love lost between Tuleen and his peers. It's time someone socked it to him and that group is going to be ARAT. Now, are we all together on this?' A meager show of support rumbled through the bus.

She pulled down the bullhorn from her mouth and adjusted the volume switch. 'Are we all together on this, I said?' she squawked with half of the bus holding their ears. She got a much better result this time probably because people knew that she was going to keep squawking with that darn bullhorn until we said yes as loud as we could.

"'All right, let's go then,' Jane said and then sat down. Her timing was terrible though. She had chosen the middle of the trip to give her little pep talk. Having finished we sat quietly for the rest of the trip. For 20 minutes we had time to think about what was ahead, why we should have gone shopping instead and why Jane Goodall was all of a sudden the leader of ARAT.

"It was a pretty somber group that arrived at Tuleen's farm. Certainly not the lean, mean fighting machine Goodall had hoped for. Like usual we had called ahead to make sure there would be TV cameras there and there certainly was this time. Everyone has heard of Tuleen and knew his reputation. The TV stations couldn't pass up on this opportunity. They were there waiting for us when we arrived, which in hindsight was pretty stupid. Because they had arrived early, Tuleen had had a chance to figure out what he was going to do to defend his property.

"As the bus turned up the long stretch of road that lead into his farm, Goodall told the bus driver to let off a group of protesters. The barb wire-cutting brigade would go to work out of the sight of the TV cameras. I figured she knew at this point that there was going to be trouble. That's why she wanted to make sure they fence was cut first off. Ten protesters scampered off the bus and immediately started clipping the barb wire fence that separated the cows from the road.

"'No matter what happens now,' she yelled to the bunch of dumbstruck, meek protesters sitting on the bus, 'at least a few of God's creatures will no longer have to live a life of slavery to Tuleen.' That is why we were there but given the circumstances it sure sounded silly.

"The bus rumbled up the gravel road sending a cloud of dust flying off across one of the fields. The cloud hid the fence cutters from the crowd that had gathered around the farmhouse. With their cameras rolling, she strolled off the bus followed by all but a few stragglers including me. I stayed back on the bus for a minute or two trying to screw up enough courage to join the sign brigade. I was supposed to carry a sign that read: 'Elsie doesn't work here anymore.' Get it, it's kind of play on the movie "Alice doesn't live here anymore."'

"Yeah, I get it," I said, looking over at my car companions to make sure they were all right.

"I stayed on the bus because I was trying to spot Tuleen. I kept on thinking about what you said about him having guns and being not afraid to use them. Through the grimy bus windows I could not make him out in the crowd. I didn't see anyone carrying any guns so I slowly got off the bus.

"It was a circus. TV trucks were scattered around the gravel compound. They had their huge antennas raised and pointed back to Davenport. It certainly was a media event. Reporters were already doing live remotes, setting themselves in the thick of the protesters and their signs. None of the reporters seemed to notice the fence cutters out by the road. Meanwhile there was no sign of Tuleen. I hoisted my sign in the air and joined the circle of other sign holders. A few of his farm-hands simply stood off to the side with their arms crossed, watching, waiting.

"The group that was supposed to surround his house tentatively took their position but didn't look like they could restrain a baby.

"This went on for 10 minutes or so. With each passing minute we all breathed a little easier. Maybe he wasn't even at home. While many of us were relieved, the TV crews seemed pissed off. We sensed that they wanted a confrontation and were not getting one. A couple crews started to pack up early. As the telescoping antennas on their vans started to descend, Goodall flew into a rage. 'You can't leave yet,' she screamed, spit flying from her mouth. 'You don't even have footage of our fence cutters.' The TV crews looked at each other quizzically. 'Fence cutters?' they asked. I'm not sure but I swear a few of them smiled. Here was their story. 'Where are these fence cutters?' 'Out there by the road,' she said, pointing off onto the horizon. 'Didn't you see the bus stop. We left off our fence cutters. They're now creating a path to freedom for these imprisoned cows. They have suffered long enough under that bastard Tuleen.' 'Wait a second,' said one perfectly coifed blonde bombshell, who I then recognized as Channel 6's Tiffany Shaw. 'Could you repeat exactly what you said. We didn't catch that on tape. That's great. Just say what you just said.' Goodall smiled and did exactly that.

"That witch. She was only in this to get on TV. It's obvious to me now. As she repeated the words 'bastard Tuleen' the old man stormed out of his house as if on cue. 'Get the fuck off my property you goddamn Commie bastards,' he shouted from his porch, firing his shotgun into the air. Everyone from our group froze. The TV crews immediately turned their backs on Goodall and rushed toward the house. The farmer fired another shot over the heads of the TV reporters freezing them in their tracks. 'And that goes for you, too. The only thing that I hate worse than fema-nazis is you journalist bastards. Everyone off my property before I start the blood bath.' He loaded a couple more shells into his gun as he was saying this and everyone knew he meant business. A majority of the ARAT people ran toward the bus in an orderly fashion. After all, they were just protesters not professionals.

Most of them weren't in the mood to get killed over their cause. I sure wasn't. And it was at this point that I realized that ARAT really wasn't for me. If I'm going to fight for something, something I really believe in I should be willing to get hurt if not killed for it. What is being done to animals in laboratories and on mink farms across the country is horrible but I'm not about to die for a mink or a beaver or a cow. That's just plain foolish.

"Goodall, apparently, wasn't worried about getting shot, though. She saw that the TV journalists were hesitating. They didn't want to leave but they didn't want to get shot either. They weren't sure if Tuleen was bluffing or not.

"'You can't get rid of us that easily,' Goodall said, moving toward him and the TV cameras. 'We came here today to force you to stop imprisoning your cows. To set them free. To send a message to cattle farmers across the country that what you are doing is wrong. Meat is murder, Mr. Tuleen. And you are a murderer.' The TV cameras were rolling again. She knew how to trip their triggers. The farmer set down his shotgun, opened his screen door, reached back into the house and pulled out a rifle. He raised it to his eye and pointed it right at Goodall.

"'You're fucking nuts, dyke' he spit out through tobacco-rotted teeth. I don't know if you've seen a good picture of Tuleen in the papers, Matthew. But he looks like an ornery Don Knotts. He'd be funny looking if he weren't so darn scary.

"Goodall didn't move an inch. Apparently she was ready to die for ARAT or as a star on the nightly news. Some of us on the bus were whispering that he would never shoot Jane in front of the TV cameras while others were saying that he would because he's insane.

"'I said get off of my property right now,' he yelled still pointing at Goodall. 'Set the cows free,' she said standing firm. The bullet whizzed past her head and hit the front of the bus busting out a light. The shot was close enough that we couldn't determine whether he missed on purpose or because he was just getting old. I think it was because he was old. You should have seen the hate in his eyes.

"She did a damn good job of pretending not to be scared. She turned to the TV cameras and said: 'We believe in non-violence. Obviously, those in the meat business do not.

"'I won't miss a second time,' Tuleen said raising the rifle again. But he did. This time he shot out the windshield of the bus. The bus driver, who we had simply rented for the day and who did not have one iota of sympathy to our cause hit the floor, saying something like: 'Jesus Christ you pet lovers are f-ing crazy.'

"All right, you've made your point,' Goodall said turning toward the old man on the porch. 'You obviously believe in violence. You believe in oppression and that might makes right. You're wrong but we don't have the means in which to stop you today. So we'll get off your property but you'll remember us the next time you milk your cows and we hope that some day you realize that what you're doing is wrong. God didn't put cows on this planet to serve us.'

"He lowered his rifle and spit a wad of tobacco off the porch. 'What did God put cows on this planet for then?' He shouted.

"Goodall ignored him and turned away. She asked the TV crews, 'Think you have enough?' One said yes and started packing up but Tiffany Shaw said, 'Aren't you going to answer him?' Goodall just blinked a few times and said quietly, 'I don't have to answer to a mad man.' With that she headed toward the bus and was followed by the rest of our group. The TV crews looked toward Tuleen as if to say, 'So what's your side of the story, Tuleen?' But he shouted before they got a chance to ask any questions, 'You, too, get the hell out of here. I still got plenty of ammunition left.' The TV crews didn't need to hear any more. They packed up and followed us out.

"We picked up the fence cutting crew as we left his property. The TV camera operators took some footage of the cut fence and of the cows roaming around, not realizing that they could escape if they wanted to. Then, a shot rang out from the farmhouse. The old farmer was still watching us from his front porch. The bullet fell short of its target but the TV crews got the point. The protest was over. Now it was up to the media to determine a winner. I figured Goodall would get the most press. She was the one taking on the crazy, old farmer. And the thing is, I don't even think she cares that much about animals. The rumor is that she still eats chicken and fish."

The misguided ARAT morons were lucky no one was killed. I had warned Angela about Clayton Dale Tuleen. He had been the scourge of state and local authorities for years. Growing up, the kids in my class used to tease one another that if they didn't do their homework or misbehaved that he would visit their room at night and slit their throats.

"I'm surprised no one was hurt by that nut," I said finally.

"Oh but some people were hurt," she said, perking up a bit. "I'm not done with the story."

"There's more? Did he come after the bus?"

"No. Our assault on Tuleen's farm happened two days ago. Well, either Tuleen didn't see that we had cut his fence or he didn't mend it right away because 16 cows did wander off eventually."

"Incredible."

"Yeah, they just kept walking. When he finally noticed that some of his cows were missing he went out looking for them and could only find a dozen of them. Four had vanished. Just like that. Well, one turned up. Apparently it was heading east and crossed over Highway 67 when a family of four came driving by in their Plymouth Horizon, you know, one of those itsy bitsy cars. The entire family was killed along with the cow."

"Jesus Christ."

"Is that bizarre or what? Here we are protesting Tuleen, he takes several shots at us and no one gets hurt. But a family of four just driving along the road is killed when they slam into a cow. It's a sign. I'm not blind. It's a sign from God that ARAT is just wrong. That's why I am done with them. I just feel horrible about this family. Apparently, they were heading to the Quad Cities up from Macomb to visit their grandma, who's dying of cancer. The TV news is going to really milk this one. The radio has already been reporting on it all morning. They talked to Jane Goodall for a comment and she actually said that she felt equally bad for the family, the cow and the cow's mother for the lost of her offspring. What a nut. Then she added that although she sympathizes for the family, in a war innocent people do get killed. And she considers ARAT's fight against cruelty to animals as a war. The radio report followed up with comments from the family's lawyer. Their grandma is going to sue everyone in Iowa and Illinois over this one. He said she was filing a suit against ARAT, Tuleen, Chrysler, because the car wasn't equipped with air bags, Lee Iacocca, because he was leading the car company when the vehicle was developed, and the American Dairy Association, because the cow was a milk provider, I guess. It's just ridiculous. I tell you, Matthew, I'm done with this group. This is just too crazy."

I was silent for a few seconds, glancing back to the car to make sure the old couple was still snoozing in the back seat. They were sleeping, weren't they? They didn't check out permanently while I was on the phone, did they? I decided I had better get back to them.

"It is crazy," I said. "You're doing the right thing to quit, though. There are plenty of other groups you can join that aren't going to get you killed and aren't filled with self-involved nuts. Why don't you just take a few days off from saving the world and relax. Go shopping with mom or something." As soon as I said this, I regretted it.

"Yeah, right. That's how all women relieve stress—by going shopping. Give me a break," she said reverting back to the old Angela I knew and not a stressed out fugitive from justice. "How's the trip going? Anything I need to tell Tony?"

"No. Everything's fine. We should be back tomorrow night. I will be glad to be back home. I'm tired of sleeping in hotel rooms, and they are kind of getting on my nerves."

"I bet. Did she tell you about her showgirl days?"

"Yup. And he has a million stories about his life and they're all big lies. I'll have a lot of stuff to tell you when I get home." I said now getting ancy to get back on the road.

"So do I," she said quietly.

"You mean more stuff about ARAT?"

"No, just other stuff that I don't want to go into right now. It can wait until you get home."

Once again, she was holding back crucial information. But I knew that if she didn't want to tell me, I wasn't going to get anything out of her. Especially over the phone.

"OK, we'll have a nice, long chat when I get back." I paused. "It doesn't have anything to do with mom, does it?"

"No, stop worrying. It's nothing earth-shattering. I'll just talk to you later. Just get back here safely."

"All right. I should get going." I said pausing again and then finished up by quickly saying, "I love you." I hung up before she could say anything. I don't usually say I love you to anyone, even my mother. But after all that had happened to me so far on this crazy trip I thought I should get it in. I don't believe in fate. I don't believe in omens. But I hate it whenever you hear of someone dying tragically and their father or brother or son says, "I didn't tell them I loved them enough." I didn't want to be one of those saps.

Not that I expected anything else to happen. Christ, just the trip down was enough to fill a book.

Edgar had awakened by the time I got back to the car.

"Did you plan on talking on the phone all day or are we going to do some driving? You know, we don't pay you to talk," he said, already back to his cranky old self.

"Good morning," I said cheerfully. "I was just talking to my sister. Wanted to see what the weather was like up in Davenport. Thought you might like to know."

"Is that the sister who's married to our Tony?"

"I only have one sister."

"She's a nice girl. Keeps Tony pretty happy. How is it that she's so nice and you're such a pain in the ass?" Edgar was leaning up toward the front so he could bark into my ear. I pulled back onto the interstate and headed north. I was hoping to get to Kentucky by the end of the day. "You know, you're kind of irritating when you shout into my ear. Could you ease up a bit and sit back down? We've still got a ways to go and I don't want to have you dump you by the side of the road."

"Oh, are you going to kick my ass or something, you punk? I'm a lot stronger than you'd think. I was a linebacker in college. Played for the Buckeyes. Finished third in balloting for the Heisman Trophy. The only reason I lost was because of politics. They'd never had a linebacker win. Instead they gave it to some fairy quarterback like they do every year. Christ, what a joke. I think they didn't want to give it to me because I'm Italian. With the war and all that business, there was a lot of Italian haters out there in college football land."

I didn't even bother to question this story. I was fed up with Edgar's lies. Professional baseball player. B Movie actor. Hollywood stud. Heisman Trophy candidate.

"You know you ought to write a book about your life," I said, searching through my duffel in the front seat trying to find a tape that struck my fancy.

"Why?" he said, leaning forward again.

"Because you've lead such an incredible life what with the baseball, football and acting. Sounds like quite a book to me." I kept on searching for a tape.

"Writing is for homos," he said abruptly and moved back into his seat.

Can't argue with logic like that. I finally found the tape I was looking for—The Vivid Details' "Swimming in Bullshit." I popped it in and cranked it up. Edgar withered in the backseat. His wife continued her journey in the Land of Nod.

"I'm up to my knees. I'm up to my neck," sang Deuce Dirtball, the leather-clad lead singer of The Vivid Details. "She opened her mouth, so I say what the heck. I dive right in and start to stroke. Coz when her lips are moving the truth has no hope. Swimming in bullshit. Swimming in bullshit. Whenever she talks, I'm swimming in bullshit...."

The words were lost on Edgar but they cheered me up.

Chapter Thirteen

"I almost had to kill a man once," Edgar said while leaning forward in the back seat to bug me for about the millionth time. It was day six and we were in southern Indiana. It was the final day and, frankly, I had grown so sick of his stories that I just nodded my head and focused my attention on the road or whatever was on the radio. I could no longer listen to my own music because whenever I would put in a tape the old geezer would start hopping up and down in the back seat like a monkey in a small cage. "Turn it off. Turn it off." He would scream, bouncing, waving his arms like a raving maniac.

Gert was either sleeping or staring out the window. Her songs were far and few between now. A radio that was low on batteries. By withdrawing into herself, she was simply coping with the confines of the car and the rantings of her whacked-out husband.

So when Edgar said that he almost had to kill a man once it fell upon deaf ears.

"Hey, punk, I said I almost had to kill a man once and I'll do it again if you don't listen to me," he said shaking my shoulder. This action had also been repeated many times. I'm surprised he hadn't caused me to drive into the ditch already. He had certainly caused me to veer into the other lane several times.

"Goddamn it, how many times do I have to tell you? Don't bother the driver. Do you want me to get into an accident? Don't you want to live to see 100?"

"Christ, I'm not that old, you little shit," he said poking my right shoulder with a bony digits. "I'm trying to tell a story here and you need to listen."

"I don't have to do shit except drive your wrinkly old ass back up to Iowa. Now, if you don't bother me we can do that before the sun goes down today. I don't know about you but I'd like to get there in one piece. So don't touch me."

He was persistent with this story, though. The past few he had told went in one ear and out the other with me. "All right, I'm just going to start talking and keep talking until you pay attention. You're working for me so you have to listen. God damn it all, I am going to slap that Tony when I see him. That shit should have never messed up his back. He better be back in shape by next spring when it's time to pick us up again."

For some reason this comment caught my ear. It took me a few seconds but it eventually sank in. "Wouldn't he have to be back in shape to drive you down in the fall?" I asked.

Edgar was stumped. I could actually see the gears in his head grinding for an answer. "Well, sure, he would," he said quickly then changed subjects.

Something wasn't right. Edgar had already proven that he was an excellent liar but not off the cuff. When he believed his stories he could lie with grace but when he didn't believe what he was saying it rang hollow.

"But you said you hoped he would be ready next spring not this fall. What's up with that?"

"Are you going to listen to my story or ask stupid questions? I misspoke. Big deal. So anyway," he said poking my shoulder again. He was going to tell me this story if it was the last thing he ever uttered. "The Mafia decided one Saturday morning that they were going to shake down our part of downtown. We had heard that they were in the neighborhood intimidating business owners into buying their insurance. Insurance my ass. It was extortion. I had had no beef with the Mafia. Being Italian I kind of sympathized with them. For many immigrants, you had to resort to crime in America if you were going to get ahead. Fortunately, I was able to run a successful, legitimate bakery.

"One of the guys I had seen around, Carmine 'Left Hand' Papatola, came in with two other goons. My customers got one look at this trio of intimidators and high-tailed it out the store. Carmine started off the conversation saying that he had heard a lot about my new pastry the Magellan and wanted to buy one for his pals here, Gus and Alfie. I knew that he hadn't come all this way just to buy three Magellans, as good as they were, but I just did as he had asked and wrapped up three of the biggest Magellans Gert had baked that morning. I thanked him for the business and started to walk away from the cash register. 'Say, Eddie,' Carmine said, figuring that I hated to be called Eddie because he knew full well that everyone always called me Edgar or Mr. Vermicelli. 'Say, Eddie, you don't actually think that me and the boys came all the way down here just to get some fucking donuts.'

"I played coy. 'Would you like some coffee to go with that, Mr. Papatola?' I said holding back a smile.

"'No, we don't want any fucking coffee. You know you're starting to, ah what's the word, irritate me. Now quit being cute and get your donuty ass down here so we can talk business. You know Gus and Alfie don't like it when they have to stand in one place too long. You know they start to get, kind of, what's the word, ancy.'

"Business? You want to talk business?' I said, getting irritated myself at this rude intrusion. Other shopkeepers downtown may have put up with this hood but I sure as hell wasn't going to. I walked back down behind the counter so that I was face to face with the three goons. 'We have nothing to talk about business-wise. Unless you want to start driving a truck for me. You see I've lost a couple of my drivers to the flu. So now my sons have to do deliveries for me when they should be studying in school. That's the only business we need to discuss and I highly doubt you want to drive a bakery truck for a living. Now if you want to talk about the Browns or the Indians, fine, we can do that. Or if you want to talk about the weather, we can do that, too. But business, there's nothing to talk about.'

"Oh, this got him really mad. His veins were popping out on his neck. Meanwhile, Gus and Alfie just smirked like two complete idiots, chomping on their gum. Carmine looked like he wanted to lunge at me over the glass counter but held himself back. He put his hands up on either side of him to signal his buddies to stay put.

"'Maybe you don't know why they call me Carmine 'Left Hand' Papatola. You know, I thought you did. I know how people talk in this neighborhood. But maybe you don't. So let me educate you. You see I have this, what's the word, propensity to uh, inflict great injury on dumbasses like you in the, uh, vicinity of their left hand. To put in plain English, I break people's left hand when they refuse to do business. Now all I'm asking you to do is pay me $100 a month for insurance. That's not too much. You know accidents happen. It would be a, uh, tragedy if something happened to your nice bakery here. You know, I especially, what's the word, admire your sign out front where it says 'Home of the Magellan' as if anyone knew what the hell you were talking about. Get a freaking clue and pay up. Or maybe you want to whack off with only your right hand in the future.

"Looking back now I think I must have been a little crazy to do what I did because, frankly, the thought of Carmine kind of scares me. He was crazy, crazy psycho but I was young and I didn't want to take no gruff from some two-bit hood. Yeah, I knew he was in the Mafia but I figured if you stood up to them they would back off and pick on someone who could be intimidated. What the hell did I know?

"So I said to him, 'Well, I appreciate your offer on the insurance, but I'm going to have to pass right now because I already have my place insured.' He cracked his knuckles and looked at his goons. His face broke into a broad grin. 'Did you hear that, boys, Mr. Eddie here says he will pass on our offer.' The two meatheads smiled, too, while Carmine leisurely took the glass cover off a display of donuts on top of the counter. He helped himself to one donut then one by one picked the others up and dropped them on the floor. The floor Gert had just finished mopping and sweeping.

"'Does your insurance cover it if someone comes in every morning and helps himself to one donut and then accidentally ruins the rest of your baked goods? I doubt it. How could you make any money if you have nothing to sell. And how will you wait on the customers with a broken hand.'"

"By this point I had had enough. We had slaved over this place. We weren't going to let the Mafia or anyone else take it away. I screwed up all my courage and turned on the testosterone to full tilt and looked Carmine right in the eye. 'Take your goons right now and get off of my property. I won't put up with your intimidation. I have friends on the police force,' I lied. 'They will fix you. They will fix you real good.'

"Carmine just laughed. Gus and Alfie followed his cue and started to laugh, too. Bits of donut were falling out of that pig's mouth. 'We've got friends on the force as well. And I can assure you they rank higher than your peon friends.'

"At this, I just lost it. I leaned over the counter and took him by his fat neck. I wrapped my fingers around his throat so tightly it felt like I was going to pop his head off like a cork in a champagne bottle. Pieces of donut continued to fall out of his mouth but the smile left his face. Surely he felt the strength in my fingers. Gus and Alfie were stunned. They had probably never seen any of the shopkeepers they had bullied fight back. My grip tightened. Carmine could only muster a wheezing sound.

"'Back off, you goons, or I will really strangle your boss here. You think I'm playing around. I don't play around. I told you I don't want any of your insurance and I said it in a kind way but if you people don't understand anything unless it is violent then violence is what I will give you. So back off or I will kill your boss. And I don't want you coming back or I will get out my gun and shoot you dead,' I lied. I didn't have a gun but they didn't have to know that. 'Now scram,' I yelled and let go of the nearly lifeless Carmine. He fell back nearly collapsing to the floor. I was only seconds from killing him, of that I am sure.

"Carmine spit and sputtered trying to gain back his senses. His goons just stood there like retarded bookends. 'You son of a bitch,' Carmine said rubbing his neck. 'You haven't heard the last of us. You don't fuck with me. You understand?' His voice was strained and I thought he was going to cry. Just like any other bully he didn't know what to do when he couldn't use violence to get his way. I had won this round and he was scared. He quickly left the bakery along with his goons and I'm proud to say that they never came back. I had truly won one for the little guy."

While Edgar had weaved this incredible tale he had been leaning over the front seat waving and gesturing nearly flicking me in the head several times. Gert had woken up and listened intently. I couldn't figure out why she was listening so closely. Was she reliving the event or was it the first time she had heard this crap? Having finished the story, the old man leaned back in his seat like the triumphant chess player who had just announced the words, "check mate."

I continued driving hoping that Edgar was satisfied in his telling of the tale and that he would leave it at that. Fat chance. "So what do you think of that? I took on the Mafia and won. They don't show that in those Hollywood movies, do they? You probably didn't realize the magnitude of the man you're driving around, did you?"

"Put a sock in it," I said quietly.

"What was that? Don't you believe me? What do you think, I'm just talking for my health? You stupid punk. You wouldn't know the truth if it came right up and bit you in the rear end. Everything I've told you is the God's honest truth. And if you don't believe me ask Gert. She'll vouch for me. She was in the back room when Carmine and his goons came into the bakery."

I glanced at the old woman over my shoulder, saw that she was still staring out her window and decided against trying to confirm his story with the space cadet.

"Do you expect me to sit here and except every one of your lies as the truth? Give me a fucking break. I don't believe for one second that you ever were a professional baseball player or a Hollywood actor or that you took on the Mafia single handedly and lived to brag about it. Christ, I don't even believe that you invented the fucking Bismarck or Magellan or whatever you want to call it. I'm beginning to wonder if you were even a baker."

Edgar sat there boiling, his fists clenched, grinding his teeth. When he opened his mouth to speak, I swear he was contemplating biting me in the neck: "I have put up with your condescending attitude for too many miles, you little punk. You disrespect me. You disrespect my wife. You disrespect my grandson, who is a fine upstanding young businessman. You. You are just some spoiled rotten punk who has never had to put in an honest's day of work in his life. And now you have the simple task of driving two, interesting senior citizens from Miami to Davenport, two people who have led incredibly fulfilling and intriguing lives, more than you could ever hope to live, and all you can do is sit up there with your smug attitude and insult us about this or that. Well, I've had it up to here with you. You don't believe me, eh? You don't believe that I took on the Mafia. Well, I'll prove it to you right here and now."

With that he lunged forward and grabbed me by the neck with both hands. As his fingers locked around my throat I realized that I had completely underestimated the old fucker. He wasn't as weak and frail as he had appeared. Maybe he wasn't 110 years old after all.

"This is the death grip I put Carmine in. The same one. Not so fake, is it?" In the rearview mirror I could see the madness in his eyes. He wasn't going to let go.

I tried to shout but that only allowed him to tighten his grip. I couldn't turn either to try to beat him off my back. I looked again in the mirror with pleading eyes but he was focused on killing me.

My anger quickly turned to panic as my lungs started to ache. It was all I could do to keep the car on the road. I braked suddenly but the car behind me honked and I had to accelerate again. Out of the side mirror I could see that there were several cars coming up on the left-hand side. In front, a large semi blocked my path. I was stuck in traffic with an octogenarian blocking my oxygen flow. Jesus Christ. Let go, you fucker. You're going to kill us all.

The pain was incredible. I'm sure he had bruised my throat with the initial wraparound. And not being able to breathe was anything but pleasant. Trying to keep the car on the road was preventing my mind from presenting my entire life in those short seconds. Here I was about to die and I was getting ripped off by not seeing my short, pitiful life flash before my eyes.

Edgar, meanwhile, was thoroughly enjoying this torture. "See. See. I told you I wasn't lying. This is exactly what I did to Carmine. Now you know why he never came back. It's a Python-like grip. I have fingers of steel."

Just as I started feeling lightheaded, the semi in front of us pulled off the road giving me room to move. I hit the accelerator and started to weave, hoping that he would get the point that if I died, he would go along with me. He got the point.

"There," he yelled as if to say 'I told you so,' releasing me from his death-grip. I frantically sucked in the stale oxygen left in the Caddy and vigorously rubbed my neck with my free hand as I sped to the next exit, with the plan to stop the car, yank him out of the backseat and then beat the living shit out of him for pulling such an incredibly stupid stunt.

"What the fuck do you think you're doing, you stupid piece of shit? You almost fucking got us all killed," I screamed. I didn't recognize the voice that was screaming, however, it was so raspy. He had done irreparable damage to my vocal chords. Surely, he would have to pay for this.

"I was proving a point. You didn't believe me so I showed you that I am not a liar," he replied smugly from the back seat. His arms were crossed and he stared out his window, looking like an 8-year-old muttering death wishes against his parents.

"Well, you proved your point all right," I croaked. "You proved you're a nut and that I shouldn't trust you in the back seat. When we stop again you're moving up front so I can keep a better eye on you. You're lucky I don't just leave you by the side of the road."

When things seemed like they couldn't get worse, they did. Just as I was getting ready to pull off the interstate to regroup I spied a state trooper in the rearview mirror coming up fast. He had probably seen me weaving back and forth while shit-for-brains tried to choke the life out of me.

"Looks like you've done it now."

"What?" Edgar leaned forward. I flinched. "What do you mean by that, punk?"

"Well, your childish antics have caught the attention of Johnny Law. There's a state trooper who is making his way up here through traffic. I'll probably get cited for reckless driving or something."

"Speed up," he stammered. "Speed up. We don't need a run-in with the law. He hasn't turned his lights on yet so just lose him in traffic. I used to do it all the time."

"I'm not going to speed up. You only can lose cops in the movies. Maybe I'll tell him about how you just tried to kill me."

"You're working for me, punk," he said, acting like an escaped con. "I said lose him, so lose him."

"And I said no. I'm just going to drive along here all nice and easy. If he pulls us over, he pulls us over."

"Goddamn it," he said, real agitated now. Every few seconds he would glance over his shoulder to check on the cop's progress. "We can't be pulled over."

"OK, what's going on here? Is this car stolen? Or let me guess—you killed a man," I added sarcastically. I just couldn't figure out his paranoia. What did a fossil like this have to be paranoid about?

"No, it's nothing like that. It's just that … It's just that… it's Gert," he shouted his wife's name all of sudden. I looked over my shoulder to see her reaction. She seemed as startled as me to be the reason why we had to avoid the state trooper at all costs. "She was once raped by a state trooper while she was driving in northern Wisconsin. He pulled her over, told her to get out of the car and then led her into the woods at gunpoint." He was now peeking out of the back window, crouched in the seat so the cop couldn't see him.

"Gert? Should we avoid this trooper?" She said nothing. Big surprise. Suddenly, Johnny Law turned on his lights and I put on the brakes.

Edgar turned forward again and sat quietly stewing about something he wasn't going to share with the rest of us. His face was white as a sheet and I could see a trace of sweat at the top of his forehead. He looked like he was about ready to crap in his adult diapers.

I pulled over to the side of the interstate, pulled out my license and started wracking my brain to come up with a good story on why I was weaving all over the place. He probably thought I was drunk. You know how college age kids and alcohol get along so famously.

I rolled down my window and waited for the trooper to walk up. He was taking his time, probably checking the license plates to make sure the car wasn't stolen. Considering all of the lies Edgar had been weaving I wouldn't be surprised to hear that it was indeed hot. Maybe he had stolen it from his Mafia friends, the ones he was able to intimidate with his two hands.

Johnny Law walked slowly up to the Caddy. Maybe they are always this cautious with cars with Iowa plates or maybe he was just another law enforcement asshole. I had had my run-ins with quite a few of those. His trooper hat was pulled down low over his forehead and he was wearing shades so he looked very much the bad-ass. I simply handed him my license and didn't say a word. I have found that with most cops it is speak only when you're spoken to.

"Picasso," he said in a thick Kentucky drawl even though we were now in Indiana. "Like the artist?"

"Yes, sir, no relation." I said trying to lighten the mood. Something was rammed up this guy's butt so far, he had to be in some serious pain.

"This car is not registered under your name."

"It's his, I said thumbing back toward Edgar, who was white as a ghost and cowering in the back seat. What the hell was he freaking out about? I did not believe his lie about Gert getting raped by a trooper for one minute.

I turned toward him in the backseat. I shot him a look that said: "Get your shit together, old man." But my lips said: "Can the trooper see your license, Mr. Vermicelli?"

Edgar, looking more frail by the second, fumbled for his wallet in his trousers. Finally, he handed me his entire wallet.

After several awkward seconds of fumbling through his various credit cards, family photos and 30-year-old business cards from flour and milk suppliers, I pulled out his license, glanced at the picture, chuckled quietly at his bug-eyed expression, then handed it over to the trooper.

"I'll be right back," he took both of our licenses and sauntered back to his car. Why didn't he ask for Gert's license? Talk about sexism. The old man and me could be outlaws but not the old lady? As far as the cop knew she was Ma Barker and we were just her cronies. I guess I couldn't blame him much, though. As I looked at her I couldn't help but see my grandmother, sitting there quietly as innocent as a newborn. How could anyone expect her of any wrongdoing?

"What's taking so long?" Edgar stammered after a minute had passed.

"He just has to call in to make sure we are not escaped lunatics, which means you're going to have to do a lot of explaining when he gets back."

He didn't respond. He was too busy looking left and right and then back at the cop. "Geez, it was just a joke. What the hell is your problem?"

"I told you. Gert was...."

"Bullshit. You know that's not true. Look at your wife, she's as cool as a cucumber. You're the one freaking out."

"I'm not freaking out. I just don't like the cops. Too much power. They have too much power."

"Well, you have nothing to worry about," I said smiling. "I'm the one who has to worry. I'm not sure that Jose dropped those charges against me. He said he was going to but you never know."

"What?" Edgar screamed almost bursting out of his skin. "What charges? What the hell are you talking about?"

"Chill out, old man. I'm just yanking your chain. My record is clean. Christ, you're going to have a cardiac arrest if you don't calm down."

The trooper was sashaying his way back up to the Caddy. No, officer we're not in a hurry. That's OK if you keep us here for another hour. Christ.

"All right, son," the trooper said as he took off his shades, slowly folded them and placed them into his breast pocket. "Can you explain why you were weaving all over the road?"

He didn't smell liquor on my breath. Otherwise, he probably would have yanked me out of the car. I had a feeling that we were going to get away with just a warning.

I took in a deep breath and tried to look as embarrassed as possible. "Well, you see, officer, it's kind of silly but I'm deathly afraid of bees and wasps. I was strung once by something once when I was pretty young and my hand swelled up like a football. My mother made a federal case about it and said I could die the next time a bee or wasp stung me. So now I avoid them like the plague. Well, to make a long story short, somehow a bee or wasp got in here and I started to freak out. The Vermicellis back there were trying to kill it. And in the process I guess I kind of took my mind off of driving. You see, I'm driving them to Iowa all the way from Miami. They're snowbirds and they are afraid of flying so they need to…"

"All right, I've heard enough, son," the trooper cut me off. I was talking a mile a minute. What an actor. Maybe I should go into the movies. I certainly could act better than half of the morons on the silver screen. "Did you kill it or are you going to start weaving down the road once you get going again?"

"I think he got it," I said quickly, keeping up the act of the stammering, bee-fearing freak. Edgar was able to manage a very lame smile in the back to acknowledge my lie. Inside, I'm sure he was screaming, "What bee?"

"You know, officer," I continued, "for all I know it could have just been a very loud horsefly. When I see a flying insect out of the corner of my eye. I just kind of panic. I'm sorry."

"OK, well just take it easy. And roll up the windows. We don't need you fighting off any other flying insects. You could kill someone with all of that weaving."

"Absolutely, officer. Thanks. I'm sorry. I won't let it happen again. I will roll up all of the windows. It will be air-conditioning only all the way."

I had done it. I had talked my way out of yet another ticket. Damn, I was a good liar. I certainly had a lot practice at it considering I spent my entire youth explaining to all of the other kids why I didn't have a dad. It was always another scenario. Never the truth.

As the cop sauntered back to his car, I rolled up my window which was the only window that had been open. Good thing, this trooper wasn't too bright. He should have noticed that my window was the only one down and that it wasn't too likely that a bee or wasp was going to fly into the window while I was going 60 miles per hour. Oh well, it just proved my brilliance at concocting stories that are so half-ass they are actually believable. Not stupid stories like playing professional baseball or fucking Hollywood starlets or fending off the mob. I, unlike the old man, knew how to weave a tale.

"Now that's smooth talking," I said to Edgar, who was still sweating bullets in the backseat. "You could learn a thing or two by listening to me."

"Just shut up and drive. We were lucky this time. It's a good thing you were pulled over by a moron. Christ almighty, a bee. What a lame excuse for an excuse."

I put the Caddy into drive and started to roll down the shoulder of the road, patiently waiting for the trucks and cars to let me merge. Behind the cop followed at a distance. Meanwhile, Paranoid Man continued to look out the back window at the patrol car.

The cop ended up following us for several miles. I was beginning to think that my bee story might not have been so convincing. Maybe he thought I was on drugs and wanted to keep an eye on me. I drove like my Driver's Ed instructor, Mr. Hamline, was in the car. My eyes darted from the side mirrors to the rearview mirror every few seconds just like you were taught back in high school. I kept the Caddy steady at 65 miles per hour and didn't veer an inch from the middle of my lane.

In the backseat, Edgar, who looked out of the back window nearly every 20 seconds, was so busy wringing his hands I thought he was going to rub his wrinkles right off. Gert, too, was beginning to look worried as well as she watched her husband fidget endlessly.

"Why is he still following us? Damn it."

"Would you stop looking out the back window? These troopers are trained to look for paranoid behavior and you can't get any more paranoid than the way you're acting. Just relax. Christ, you're getting so worked up you're going to have a heart attack. And you're scaring your wife."

"Shut up and drive. Don't tell me what to do. I've been around a helluva lot longer than you. Oh my God…"

"What?" But as soon as I opened my mouth I realized why he was freaking out again—the cop was moving up on us quickly. I remained cool under the pressure and just kept driving as if Mr. Hamline was sitting right next to me. I could still hear him smacking that Juicyfruit. It was his trademark. Most people who chew Juicyfruit will spit out the wad of gum whenever the flavor fails, which is usually shortly after you put it into your mouth. Mr. Hamline would just keep adding sticks of gum until he had an entire 7-stick pack in there. Fortunately, for Mr. Hamline he had a huge mouth. Unfortunately for his students, he tended to start smacking once his mouth contained more than three sticks. Have you ever tried to parallel park while someone smacked on a wad of Juicyfruit the size of a Buick? It's enough to make you ride a bike the rest of your life.

The cop was just about parallel with us and the labored breathing in the backseat was reaching a crescendo. I glanced in the rearview mirror just long enough to see that Edgar was still conscious. I seriously wondered if he was going to make it through this crisis.

As nonchalantly as possible, I meagerly smiled at the cop as he passed on the left-hand side. He wasn't even looking at us. As he passed us he started to accelerate and then turned on his siren, which just about made me crap my drawers. He was after someone else.

"He's gone, you can relax now," I said glancing in the rearview mirror. The old geezer's eyes were closed, his complexion ashen, his breath labored.

Oh my God, he was having a heart attack. "Oh shit, man, wake up, dammit. What's going on? Wake up." Suddenly his eyes popped open.

"What?" he said irritated.

"I thought you were having a heart attack," I stammered.

"Heart attack, ah, go on. There's nothing wrong with my ticker," he boasted, poking his chest with a bony finger.

Yet, I could still hear the labored breathing. Where was it coming from?

"Pull over, no don't pull over, get to a hospital. Gert, can you hear me, Gert?" Hell broke loose in the back seat. The old pop singer had collapsed against her husband. Her frail frame now took up two thirds of the back seat. Edgar was frantically clawing at the top of her blouse to loosen the collar. I could no longer hear her labored breathing, only the sobs of her husband. "Get to a hospital. Get to a hospital, you moron."

Now that I needed the state trooper he was nowhere to be found. I sped up to 70, 80 trying to catch up to him but he was long gone, hot in pursuit of a speeder. We were still several miles south of Indianapolis at this time, so I was thinking the chances of finding a hospital quickly were pretty small. Still, I sped along frantically reading every sign along the way, waiting to find one of those blue ones that would lead to a hospital. She had sure picked a bad spot to have her heart fail.

"No, no, no, don't leave me," Edgar cried in the back seat. He was out of control. He was sobbing so hysterically at this point, he was of no use what so ever to his wife.

"Try mouth to mouth," I yelled, trying to bring him back to his senses. "Try mouth to mouth."

He just sobbed uncontrollably as he hugged his wife's still body to his chest.

By the time we reached a small town and pulled off the interstate, 10 minutes had passed. I zoomed off the exit ramp and headed into town in search of a hospital. By this time, he had accepted the situation. "Stop the car. Stop the car, dammit. We're too late. We don't need a hospital anymore."

"Maybe she's still alive. Maybe they can bring her back," I said, though deep down, I knew she had probably died not long after she had slumped over in the back seat. "We should still find a hospital."

"No, I know what a dead person looks like, dammit," he yelled, tears streaming down his wrinkled cheeks.

We had ended up on a residential street in a town I still don't know the name of. It didn't matter. At least to me. I didn't need to remember this small town in Indiana as the marker of where this trip went dreadfully wrong. Christ, I shouldn't have been surprised. Considering all that had happened, a fatal heart attack was probably pre-ordained.

Poor Gert. Poor Edgar, I thought to myself as I snuck a look into the rearview mirror. I felt so awkward. Here, a man was saying good-bye to his wife of 55 years and I was a third wheel behind the wheel. I turned off the ignition and opened my door. "I'll let you alone for a while. I'm sorry."

I don't know whether he heard me at all. He was sobbing like a little child whose favorite toy had just been crushed. "Gert, don't leave me. Don't leave me." He kept repeating to his recently departed wife.

*   *   *

What a shitty trip, I thought to myself as I walked down the residential street, my hands stuffed deep into my pockets, my head down. The noonday sun was breaking through the clouds and was beating down on my neck. It was going to be a hot one. I figured I would have to keep my walk short because Edgar would get pretty hot sitting in the Caddy with the sun hitting the car.

What a goddamn shitty trip. To actually think that I had looked forward to getting out of town for a few days. If I had had even the slightest indication of what a wild ride this was going to be I would have stuck around Davenport forever. Why was I so eager to get out of town?

I could handle Trish. So I slept with her one night and now she's calling me. Fine, I can face the music. It's not like I got her pregnant or anything. At least, I doubt it. And the job search would work out. I couldn't possibly go on forever without finding a job. Yeah, I didn't know what I wanted to do but I figured I'd just start looking for a job and I'd eventually figure it out. Shit, people do it every day. I'm not that unique.

And Tony. I can deal with him. I've been dealing with him for years now. Of course, I've never had to explain away how I drove down to Florida, picked up his grandparents, argued with his grandfather the entire way, and then killed his grandmother. That was going to be tough. But then, how could I have prevented it? Shit. It wasn't my fault.

If it was anybody's fault, it was Edgar's. If he hadn't tried to strangle me I wouldn't have weaved all over the road and caught the trooper's attention. But then, I probably lead him to strangle me. I had been pretty tough on the old guy. I couldn't help it, though. He was old and he was such a liar. I hate liars, which is pretty hypocritical because I'm such a good one. But he did nothing but lie. I only lie to get out of jams, he made it an art form. Every time he opened his mouth, another tall tale rolled out.

Yeah, Tony was going to kill me. I would definitely need Angela to bail me out of this one as long as she wasn't in jail by the time I got home, which I had hoped would be later in the day. But with Gert dying, I wasn't sure when we'd pull into Davenport. We had to drive to a mortuary or at least a hospital or something and make arrangements to transport her to Iowa. Christ, I wasn't sure all we had to do. I've never been around a dead person. Come to think of it, I had never even been to a funeral. Isn't that odd? I had had sex with women I barely knew. I had fired a gun. I had outwitted a cold-blooded killer. I had been served a cocktail by a dwarf. I had met pantless Russian Siamese twins and a man who owned an alien corpse. But I had never seen a dead person until now. What a trip.

I started back toward the Caddy. It was time to face the music. The sun was getting really hot now and I was sure Edgar was baking in the car, not to mention his ex-wife.

I resolved to take it easy on the old guy the rest of the day. He needed support not some smart-ass punk. He was right where I had left him. Hugging his wife, balling like a baby. I slowly opened the driver's door and climbed into the spacious interior. I turned the key and adjusted the air conditioner to full-blast. The car was extremely hot. I could already feel the sweat forming on my brow as I shifted it into drive.

"Where to now? A hospital or a mortuary?"

"Home," he blubbered.

"Well, sure we're going to Davenport but we need to get her to a mortician or a doctor or something." I spoke in calming, quiet tones. I didn't want to set him off again.

"We need to get her home. She's my wife. I said let's take her to Davenport," he said, opening his eyes and directing his anger at me. Our little truce didn't last very long.

"Damn it. We are at least six hours away from Davenport. We can't drive all that way with a corp…. Gert in the back seat. We need to get her to the authorities. They can transport her home properly."

"She loved this car. She would rather be driven back in style. Not in some ambulance or hearse or whatever they would use. I was married to her for 60 years. Don't you think I know what she would want? Now go. I'm the boss here and I say let's go. Go. Go. Go. I want to get her home." As he said this he gently moved his dead wife over to her side of the seat and buckled her in. He propped her up so she would not fall over and folded her hands in her lap. She looked at peace as if she were simply sleeping again. I was convinced that we could actually drive back to Davenport with no problem but I didn't like the idea of having a dead person in the back seat. Frankly, it gave me the creeps.

"Be reasonable. What happens if we get pulled over? We could get in big trouble."

"Trouble for taking my wife home? Bullshit. We're going. Now move or I'll beat the shit out of you, you little bastard. This is all your fault. No one ever died when Tony drove us."

No one ever died when Tony drove us! Did he actually say this? Now I was really pissed. I don't care if this bastard's wife did just die. He had pushed me over the limit.

"Go to hell," I said turning to face the little widower in the back seat. "I can't believe you said that. It's not my fault. It's your goddam fault, you asshole. If you hadn't been choking me we wouldn't have been pulled over. You're fucking nuts. This whole trip has been one big fucking mistake after another. Christ, I'm lucky I haven't gone completely over the edge with all that has happened. You can't pay me enough to do this crap."

"If you would have showed me one ounce of respect and believed me when I told you about the mob I wouldn't have had to prove to you that I am someone to respect," he shot back, tears still wet on his face. "You have absolutely no respect for your elders. It's no wonder you can't find a job. All you care about is you, you, you. That's what's wrong with all of you young people today. All you ever think about is what will help you the most. You never think of others. That's what's wrong with America. You are all a bunch of selfish bastards. Now, for once in your goddamned life do something for someone else. Drive me and my wife to Davenport. Now!"

Imagining that the gear shifter was Edgar's scrawny little neck, I wrapped my right hand around it and gripped hard. I wanted to do a little choking of my own right now but I swallowed my anger and shifted it into drive. I was swallowing so much of my anger and frustration on this trip that I figured I could give up eating for a while.

No one ever died when Tony drove us. Jesus Christ. What did I ever do to deserve this? Sometimes I think God only punishes the good people and let's the fucking bastards have a hay day. Maybe God wasn't the one in charge. This trip certainly made me believe that the Devil was running the show now.

Chapter Fourteen

So we drove west through Indiana then Illinois with a dead octogenarian in the back seat. To be honest, the dead Gert wasn't that much different than the live model, seeing that she didn't add much to the conversation when she was breathing, just the occasional pop tune. Hell, the radio easily replaced her.

I did have to contend with Edgar's sobbing, though. He continued to cry for the next 100 miles or so. For the first 20 miles or so it made me sad as hell. This poor guy was really taking it hard. After 30 miles, I started to get irritated. Enough is enough. Yes, she died. But she was old. Everyone has to go sometime or another.

At 40 miles, I was getting pissed off. Will you just shut the fuck up, you blubbering old man? "Should I pull over and get you something to drink or take?" I suggested. "Would some aspirin help? Maybe a shot of bourbon?"

"Leave me alone, you bastard. Can't you see I'm mourning," he yelped hiding his face in his hands. I was beginning to think that he was doing this just to piss me off. He didn't treat her very well in the time that I had been around them and now he was crying like she was Mother Teresa or something.

After 70 miles or so I was ready to jump out of my skin. For the past 20 miles or so I had been incrementally turning the radio up more and more to drown out his cries. But he just sobbed louder.

So I preoccupied my thoughts with lists of things that required my full concentration. It was a game I had been playing in my mind for much of this trip whenever Edgar would get to be too much to bear. I would think of my top 10 favorite movies of all time. My top 10 favorite songs. My top 10 favorite TV shows. Inevitably, I would start thinking about old girlfriends. Girls that I slept with. Girls that I had wanted to sleep with. Girls that I can't believe I ever wanted to slept with. These insane thoughts were the only things that kept me sane while driving on Interstate 74 that day.

Finally after 90 minutes of crying, which now alternated between a simpering sob to all-out bawling, the old man had worn himself out. Like a baby who didn't get his way, Edgar had cried himself to sleep. It was an eerie scene in the back seat. A dead lady directly behind me, rigor mortis already working its way through her wrinkly body, and a half-dead body next to her. As I continued to glance in the rearview mirror, he looked more to me like the stiff. If he hadn't been snoring I would have thought he had cried himself to death.

What a clusterfuck, I thought. What a giant, humongous, incredible clusterfuck. What were we going to do when we pulled into Davenport? Drive directly to the neighborhood mortuary? Drive to the Vermicelli's house, so I could carry her in to the living room where she would wait for the mortician to come and take her away? Or would I drive to Tony's house, hand him over the keys and say, "You take care of the corpse, OK?"

I sure as hell didn't want to touch her. I was afraid her skin would come off in my hands or some of that old people smell would rub off.

I figured I might as well just plan to drive straight to the police station. I was sure driving across state lines with a dead body is a federal offense.

While I contemplated the magnitude of this clusterfuck, I realized that the Caddy was just about out of gas. So I pulled off the interstate to fill it up and escape the awkwardness of death that had enveloped the car. It was the middle of the afternoon and the gas station was buzzing with activity. Being in early June, kids were out of school for the summer and many vans were loaded down with crap as families headed off for vacation. Truckers went about their business filling up with diesel and gas station attendants were busy doing little else but raking in the cash. I made sure to pull into a self-serve stall far from the little booth where the cash register whirred away. Edgar was still asleep in the back seat, though not snoring anymore. I took my time, relieved to know that the trip would be over in a few hours. By my best guess, we were just over three hours away from Davenport barring any major road construction that had popped up in the past couple days since I had first driven through Illinois.

I filled up the Caddy for the last time and leisurely strolled up to the booth to pay the attendant. I decided to get a couple of candy bars so we didn't have to stop again for dinner. I just wanted to get home at this point. I was beginning to think that no one would notice Gert or at least the fact that she was dead. With Edgar back there snoring away any stranger who happened across the car would just figure they were two old geezers taking a nap. I bought several Twix bars for myself, a Snickers for Edgar and nothing for Gert.

Heading back to the Caddy with a bag full of sugar, I was feeling a little better. Sure, the old lady was dead and Tony would probably kill me but the trip was almost over and my life could soon go back to its normal, boring routine.

I had hoped that with all of this time to think I would have been able to come up with a game plan for the rest of my life but I wasn't any further along than when I had left Davenport. The only thing I was sure of now was that I was an excellent driver and that I could keep myself company even on the most mundane stretches of interstate in the country. Bring on Nebraska, dammit. I wasn't about to become a semi driver but maybe there was a life for me in transportation. I did enjoy seeing new places. I could become a pilot or get a job with Amtrak. I've always liked trains. Actually, that didn't sound half bad. See the world and I wouldn't have to be rich to do it. It would be part of my job. Maybe this trip had helped clear my head, after all.

Even before I got into the car I could sense that something had gone horribly wrong. An acrid stench was wafting out from the Caddy and it wasn't old person smell.

"Good afternoon, Faust. Do you mind if I join your little party?"

Oh, my fucking God. Where did he come from? How did he find me? Just when I was thinking that things couldn't get any worse, the homicidal, lip balm coveting, kaleidoscope wielding, talk show-host-squashing psychopath was back from hell. I'm dead. I'm goddam fucking dead.

"Sit down," he said patting the driver's seat gently with an open palm. "It appears that fate has brought us back together. Don't spoil it by trying to run away again." With a demented grin, he pulled an ever-ready stick of lip balm from his pants pocket and meticulously applied it to his lips. He had gotten a new suit. This one was brown and looked even older than the blue one. "Sit down and start the car. We're going for a ride."

"I can't fucking believe this," I stammered as the Caddy roared to life. Looking into the rearview mirror, I could see Edgar was still asleep. He was going to shit his Depends for sure when he woke up and found the Devil in the front seat. That's if he was still alive. I couldn't hear him breathing over the pounding of my own heart. Maybe he was already dead. Maybe Nosferatu had already killed him. How long had he been here? Did he sneak in right after I went up to pay? Could you kill someone that quickly? And how the hell did he find me here of all places?

"Oh, I do believe my luck has started to change." He pulled a knife out from underneath his jacket. The silvery long blade seemed to float above his lap. It looked sharp enough to slice rocks in half.

"But how..." My mind was clear as mud. Part of me told me to get out of the car and run. Fuck Edgar. He could be dead already for all I knew. The other part of me told me to do whatever Nosferatu wanted. I had escaped him once and he had found me. Maybe there was no escape from him. Maybe this was a test from some divine being with a sick sense of humor. A test to see if I could confront my own fears and by confronting them conquer them.

"Come on, let's move. Or the old man will be skewered like a pig. That is if he's even alive anymore. Since when do you drive around with two corpses in the back seat? Are you practicing to be a mortician? Have you finally found your calling? It's definitely a steady line of work. In fact, I'd go so far as to say it's a growth business with me around." He cackled and with that cackle became even scarier than the individual who had been haunting my dreams.

I put the Caddy into drive and pulled out of the gas station. I couldn't muster the courage for anything heroic at this point. I was beginning to think that maybe I wasn't destined to live past 24. Maybe I was meant to become famous by being the victim of some nut's killing spree. Without asking for directions from him I pulled onto the interstate as if we were just resuming our trip to Davenport, only this time we were taking Nosferatu home with us.

"You little shit," he hissed. "We weren't supposed to head west."

"You didn't tell me which direction to head in. You just said drive. I can't read your mind."

"It's a good thing you can't, otherwise you'd be crying like a little baby."

Somewhere along the line, he had lost his conversation skills. All of sudden he was melodramatic, which was fine if you were stuck in some stale TV movie, but this was reality.

"Cut the melodramatics, Harry." I said starting to regain my reckless disregard for everything. If I was going to die, skewered like a pig, I was going to do it talking back. Why change now? "How did you find me? Am I supposed to believe that you just happened to be hanging around that gas station? That crap only happens in the movies."

"No, actually I have been following you for some time, Faust," he said looking at me through his little fly's eye kaleidoscope. "But does it really matter? The point is I found you." He smiled. I wanted to jam that damn kaleidoscope into his eyeball.

"And now you're going to kill us," I said matter of factly. Thinking back, it's kind of weird to think I was brazen enough to actually utter those words. "Just like you killed Jerome Paul…"

"Jerome Paul deserved to die. I did the world a favor. I am not ashamed at all of the fact that I murdered the fairy. In fact, I'm quite proud of it. I think I will be heralded. I'll be up there with Lee Harvey Oswald and James Earl Ray. A political assassin. Forever etched in history."

"You're delusional."

"No," he said quietly. "Just psychotic.

"Now then, what have you been up to since we last talked? When you so rudely left me on the side of the road, in the middle of nowhere. You know I've been thinking a lot about you since that day. In fact, I was thinking about you when I cracked Jerome Paul's head open. I was thinking, 'Wouldn't it be nice to be able to do this with my good, old friend, Faust. The bastard who left me for dead.'"

Looking back now at this situation I can't believe that I didn't go completely ape-shit. Think about it. I was sitting next to a real-life Freddy Krueger who was counting the minutes until he crushed my skull like a ripe grape. Frankly, I'm surprised I didn't just open the door and jump out of the Caddy while we were speeding along at 65 miles per hour. At that point I had a better chance of surviving a long bounce down the interstate than the front-seat bloodletting that awaited me with Nosferatu.

Now the entire episode seems like a scene from the third sequel of a bad horror movie. The lunatic had become such a caricature of himself that I have a hard time taking him seriously. At the time, I was scared shitless. After all, he was planning to kill me and not only kill me but in a fashion that would be extremely cruel and gruesome. But for some reason I kept my wits about me. As if I knew that no matter what happened I would make it out alive.

"If you concentrate real hard, you can hear that sound. Like a clay pot filled with dirt, perhaps some marigolds too, falling to the hard concrete. It's not a sharp crack but a dull, muffled crack. And then there's the blood. After I had cracked his skull open I got out of the car and made sure he was dead. Blood got all over my boots. Do you know how long it took me to get the blood out of my boots? A very long time. But I didn't mind because as I labored over those boots I kept thinking of what a favor I had done for the world for killing that fat queer. The world owes me one huge pat on the back.

"And now I turn my attention toward you. Tell me, where have you been? I see that you've picked up some friends."

"Gert and Edgar Vermicelli," I said quietly, keeping my eyes on the frenetic interstate traffic. "She died earlier today. Had a heart attack. He is a heart attack waiting to happen. In fact, I think the minute he wakes up he will see you, shit his pants and then die. So really the only person you'll have to kill directly is me. That is if I don't outsmart you again." What the hell did I have to lose? I knew he wasn't joking when he said he planned to kill me so why not have some fun with him before he did it.

"Outsmart me. Ha." He turned toward me brandishing the knife. "I outsmarted myself. If I would have been carrying my gun rather than leaving it in my jacket you wouldn't have gotten away."

The gun. Jesus Christ. How could I have forgotten about the gun? It was still under the seat. Wasn't it? I hadn't moved it. Of course it was still there. It was just inches away. I wasn't going to die after all. All he had was a knife. I had a gun. Gun smashes knife, scissors cut paper. End of story. Of course, there was that tricky dilemma of when to pull the gun out before he turned me into a pin cushion.

If only I could surreptitiously check under the seat. Yeah, right. So I drove on with both hands on the wheel.

"What happened to the gun, Faust?" He said poking the knife into the air between us. Christ, could this guy read minds, too?

"I heaved it into the ocean," I lied. "I didn't want Edgar to find it. God knows what he would do with a gun."

"Oh, is this Edgar character a force to be reckoned with," he said, laughing. "He looks like a giant prune. Look at all of those wrinkles. And his ass crinkles when he moves."

"Those are his adult diapers. I think he has a problem with water retention or lack thereof."

"Well, he's slept long enough," he said leaning over his seat into the back. Here was my chance. While his back was turned I could grab the gun. But before I could make my move, the nut turned back around. He must have seen me start to move out of the corner of his eye.

"I think I'll refrain from turning my back on you. I don't trust you anymore. Wake up the old man yourself."

"Oh, I don't think you want him awake for any longer than necessary."

"I'll be judge of that. Now wake him up or I will wake him up with this," he said, jabbing the knife upward.

"Oh, Edgar, yoo hoo. Time to wake up from nappy-time," I sang in a falsetto. "I'd like you to meet our guest. What the hell was your real name again? Harry Jones or something?"

"Nosferatu."

"No, your real name."

"Nosferatu."

"Time to wake up and meet our guest, Mr. Nosferatu."

Slowly, as if he had been sleeping through the night and was just waking up at home safe in his own bed, Edgar came to. He first looked at his recently departed wife as if to convince himself that this was reality and that his dreaming was over. Yes, she was still dead. And now there was some drifter in the front seat. He took in the scene slowly, blinking his tired eyes. I had turned the rearview mirror so it was centered on the old man. I really didn't care about what was behind us anymore.

"Edgar, this is Mr. Nosferatu. He joined us while you were sleeping," I said in a soothing voice. I didn't need the geezer to start panicking immediately.

"Where are we?"

"We're in Illinois. It won't be long until we're home."

"What time is it?" He was really out of it.

"4:15."

"Why aren't we home yet? Damn you're a slow driver." Now he was getting back to his old self. "Who the hell are you?" he said leaning forward, roughly shaking our guest's shoulder.

"Some have said the Devil incarnate but I prefer to think of myself as just one of his legion." Nosferatu was back to his dramatics. New audience, I guess.

"What the hell does that mean?" the old man turned toward me. "Where the hell did this guy come from? I thought we had a strict rule about hitchhikers. Did you pick him up just to piss me off? Christ, isn't enough that you killed my wife and now you ask some nut to join us?"

"Faust, did you actually kill the old lady?" Nosferatu said, laughing. "How did you accomplish that? I didn't pick you as the murdering type. I thought you were more non-confrontational."

"Who the hell is Faust? Who is this guy? One of your stinking homo friends?"

Nosferatu had been mildly amused by the old man's surly disposition but when Edgar mentioned the word "homo" his smile melted away. Nosferatu nearly jumped into the backseat. "Don't you ever say that word around me or I will kill you. I hate faggots. I just killed the king of all faggots. Did you hear me, old man, I just killed a faggot and I will kill you if you make me mad."

The old man cowered in the back seat like a little child. Holy shit. If anything was going to give him cardiac arrest it was having a knife-wielding homicidal maniac in his wrinkled, suntanned face.

I was half-tempted to pursue this anti-homosexual line of conversation just to keep him off kilter. Sounded to me like he had a lot of denial built up. Angela has told me that psychologists argue that a lot of people with deep hatred toward homosexuals are just trying to suppress their own latent homosexual feelings. As fascinating at this topic was, I decided against pursuing the gay angle with Mr. Skull-crusher.

"Faust is the pet name our friend here has picked for me," I said. " Maybe we could come up with one for you, too. How about Cranky or Grumpy?"

Edgar looked generally hurt. "Sure, take this nut's side of things. You were just waiting to pick up someone so you would have someone on your side. Why did I ever agree to do this for Tony? Everything has gone wrong."

Do this for Tony? What did he mean by that?

"I think we should call him Stiff because that's what he will be soon enough," Nosferatu said looking at the old man through his fly's eye toy. "Stiff and six feet under. Or are they going to cremate you, Stiff?"

"I'll burn in hell along with you, numb-nuts."

"Well, well, well. Aren't we alive and kicking?" he said, laughing again. "You must be full of piss and vinegar since Faust killed your beloved. I never did hear how that happened." He turned toward me with a devilish smile. "Please, give me the details."

"Nothing to say. She had a heart attack earlier this morning and died. We're taking her home to Davenport to be buried."

"I don't claim to be a expert in law, or morals for that matter, but shouldn't you have taken her to the nearest hospital? She might have only appeared to be dead. She might have been saved. I think you've made a serious error in your judgment. The authorities might want to have a word with you when you pull into town.

"How about I do you a favor? Since you'll probably be in some trouble with the law I'll just kill you before you get to Iowa and then you won't have to go to jail or anything untoward like that."

Edgar sat stone silent in the back seat.

"How about you don't kill me and just say you did?" OK, I couldn't resist the smart-ass comment.

"Oh, you're practically dead in my mind already," he said as he applied more lip balm. "As for Stiff in the back seat, he, too, will soon join his wife in the hereafter. I'm kind of looking forward to the blood bath."

He turned his head to address the abnormally quiet Edgar in the backseat. "Do you think much about dying? When you're your age, I would imagine that you're constantly thinking about death. So many questions racing through the cobwebs up there. Did I get everything I wanted to get accomplished? Did I sleep with enough women? Did I follow the word of the Lord close enough? Was I good enough? Will I get to Heaven? Any of these questions going through your mind about now?"

The old man stewed quietly in the backseat. Here I had thought that I would make the time pass more quickly with him by being a smart-ass when actually the way to shut him up was to just threaten him. Stupid me.

"How about you, Faust?" Nosferatu turned toward me. With the knife in his left hand he started to carefully dig out the dirt that had settled under his fingernails. God knows where that came from. Was it the sweat-soaked dirt off the neck of some fat tourist he strangled before he stole his Buick? Or was it mud from some shallow grave he slowly dug for some other victim on his cross-county death spree?

As he worked the knife under his nails the light from the afternoon sun would occasionally reflect off the blade into my eyes. It was just another annoyance in our death ride.

"So what do you say? I would imagine that you don't think much at all about dying. You're young and invincible. You probably think even more so since you were able to get away from me the first time. I know that when I was your age I never thought about dying. Hell no. I could walk across four lanes of traffic high on dope and whiskey and never blink an eye. Cars would honk and swerve this way and that. I came out untouched. Why shouldn't I feel invincible? If my daddy and Everett couldn't kill me, then what could? Do you feel that way? Do you feel invincible? You probably think that you're going to get away from me again, don't you?

"I can tell you're scheming. You're thinking, 'How am I going to get away from this psycho?' Am I right or am I right?

"Meanwhile, Stiff back there is sweating bullets. He knows Death is just sitting there on the front porch in his favorite rocking chair, waiting for him to walk outside. He's creaking back and forth just biding his time while Stiff is busy asking himself, 'Have I done enough to get into Heaven? I don't want to go to hell. Please, Lord, have mercy on me. I promise to be good.'

"Isn't it funny how religious people get as they grow older? Walk into any church. The only young people you see there are morons. Your average young person is out sinning, drinking, sleeping with their neighbor's wife. I'd bet it's been years since you set foot in a church. But old Stiff probably goes every Sunday. As mortality becomes more inevitable, devotion increases. He probably pissed all over people when he was younger. He'd do anything to get ahead. Break the law. But now he expects the Lord to forgive all of those transgressions just because he goes to church.

"Well, you know what? I don't think God is so forgiving. I think he has a real good memory. You're lucky, Faust. You haven't been around long enough to piss God off. But, Stiff, old boy, you're screwed. I can imagine all the crap you've tried to get away with. Just the fact that you live down in Florida all winter is enough to piss him off. He's mad at you and he's waiting for you."

"Hey, shut the fuck up, will you?" I had had enough. If I was going to die, fine. But I didn't have to sit there and listen to all of this bullshit. Christ, I had been putting up with people's shit all my life. From Tony to Edgar to Nosferatu. I had had enough. Fuck Nosferatu. He can kiss my ass, I thought. What was he going to do stab me right here in the Caddy? I was driving. If I lost control at 65 miles per hour we would all die.

"So you have been listening? Good for you..."

"I've got to go to the bathroom," Edgar said in a tired, small voice.

Nosferatu turned toward the old man again, brandishing the knife in his face. "Go in your pants. We're not pulling over yet."

"But I have to go."

I had to come up with an escape plan and quick. I figured I had a couple of options. I could speed up and ram into another car or a tree and hope that I live through it or I could make a move to the gun. Both had major flaws in my mind. The tree plan was one of pure desperation. With my luck I'd only kill the old man and myself while Nosferatu escaped to kill again.

The gun plan was only a little better, though. I figured no matter how slick a move I put on the psychopath I would end up with a knife somewhere embedded in my body. The best case scenario here would be that he only gives me a flesh wound and I blow his head off. The worst case scenario is that he stabs me in the heart, grabs the gun away from me and then blows my head off. Of course, that wouldn't do him much good if I were speeding down the highway at the time. I couldn't stop or slow down if I was driving without my head.

So being behind the wheel was the only bright spot. But then, Nosferatu was such a crazy fuck that I think he would take the chance of dying if it meant that he'd get to add two more names to his body count. The more I thought about it, the more it looked as if the only way I was going to get out of this situation was in a pine box.

Then a third alternative presented itself. Up the interstate about a half a mile away I saw the back end of a state trooper's car. All I needed to do was speed up to the trooper and then ram him or break the law somehow so he was forced to pull us over. We are pulled over, I spill the beans on the fruitcake to my right and everyone goes home, or to prison, happy. Seemed like a good plan to me.

"Please, let me go to the bathroom. Can you give an old man a little dignity?" Edgar was almost in tears now.

"Shut the fuck up," Nosferatu spat at the old man. "I don't want to hear another word out of you. Understand?" In a huff, he turned around and instantly, as if he had radar attached to his forehead, saw the state trooper.

"Slow down, Faust. Don't try anything stupid." He moved the knife closer to me.

For a second I entertained the thought of denying that I had even noticed the cop but I quickly banished that idea. My options weren't numerous. This Chuck Manson wannabe was going to kill the old man and me. Or at least I had to believe that that was the case. So, I had no future. I had to try something. And the state trooper ahead was the only idea I had. I kept accelerating.

Nosferatu leaned closer and pressed the blade of the knife against my thigh.

"Slow down, kid," came a weak voice from the backseat. I glanced in the rearview mirror to see a ghost in the backseat. Edgar was still with us but his face was as white as a new snowfall. A ring of perspiration framed his wrinkled, tired face.

"Don't you see what's happening?" I said adjusting the rearview mirror so I could look him in the eyes. "This guy is going to kill us. That trooper is our only hope."

"This is my car. I'm paying you to drive us to Davenport…"

"We aren't going to get to Davenport. We're lucky if we get out of Illinois."

"Shut up, the both of you," Nosferatu hissed. "Slow down or I will cut you. Can't you see that the old man doesn't want to get blood on the upholstery? Now let the trooper just drive away."

"Let it go, Matthew," Edgar pleaded. "This man is not going to kill us. He's just playing a game. He's trying to scare you. He knows that if he killed us the cops would track him down right away. After all, didn't you tell Tony and your sister about the hitchhiker you picked up on the way down to Florida? Didn't you describe him and tell them his name?"

That crafty old coot. I hadn't told anyone about Nosferatu. Angela was too busy filling me in on the wacky exploits of ARAT and Clayton Dale Tuleen. No one knew about the lunatic and if I had told Angela about him, it's not like they had a chance in hell of finding him. He was just a drifter who went from one grisly homicide to the next. Like the police would actually be able to put an all-points-bulletin out on all fruitcakes using the name of an ancient German movie on vampires.

I appreciated Edgar's effort to get us out of the situation but his method wouldn't work. Our only hope of seeing the sunrise on yet another miserable day was that trooper.

"Listen to the old man," Nosferatu said applying pressure on my thigh. Any more and the blood would start flowing.

"I'm sorry but I'm hard of hearing," I said feeling like a true hero. If you're lucky in life, and you're a man, you only get a few chances to act really macho and get away with it. This was one of those times. I was willing to bet that as long as I was speeding along at 65 miles per hour, Nosferatu wouldn't cut me. He didn't want to die anymore than I did. I focused on the trooper. Soon, the trooper would have to notice this huge Caddy in his rearview mirror tearing down the highway like a big, old dinosaur.

"Stop, stop. I am begging you," Edgar cried. "We can't get pulled over, believe me we just can't." He was now sobbing uncontrollably in the backseat. "You've got to slow down. Please, I am begging you. We can't get pulled over."

A smile creeped back onto Nosferatu's face.

Goddamn it all. How was I going to get us out of this hairy situation if I didn't have some cooperation from the old man in the backseat? He was a lot more ready for death than me. He had lived a good, if not completely fictional, life. I, on the other hand, was just getting started. I hadn't met the woman of my dreams. I had never bought a house or even a car for that matter. I had never been to California. Christ, I had never held a real job yet. I was too young to die.

"Please, kid, I am begging you to slow down." The sobbing continued. I let off the gas and drifted back into the right lane. Nosferatu let out an almost imperceptible sigh of relief. The trooper grew smaller on the horizon.

"All right, old man, this better be good," I said through clenched teeth. "I'm not sure but I think your sobbing might have just killed us." Our guest was smiling big time now.

What the hell was he so freaked out about? So what if the cops found his wife dead in the backseat. Now they are going to find her and us dead in the car, or maybe in some soybean field in western Illinois. Nosferatu was a much scarier proposition to me than the police.

"I'm sorry, Gert, this is all my fault."

"What…"

"Shut up, Faust, and let the old man confess his sins."

"This is all my fault. We wouldn't have been in this mess if it wasn't for me," the old man said, looking at me with tired, drowning eyes through the rearview mirror. "We can't let the authorities pull us over because I've done a very bad thing."

"You mean with Gert…"

"No, it's not that. It's something we've done for quite some time now. I know we should have never agreed to it, but we couldn't get by on just social security. We didn't want to have to live in Davenport year-round. It's just that we have grown accustomed to our current lifestyle. We couldn't go back to the old ways. We had worked too hard. I had worked too hard."

"What the fuck are you talking about?" I shouted.

Slowly, his wrinkled hands produced the black satchel that he had coveted the entire trip. He sat it carefully on his lap and unlatched the top, revealing its contents. I knew what I saw but I still had a hard time believing it. Tony's grandparents were trafficking cocaine. And I was helping.

I immediately made a quick mental note to myself—if I got back to Iowa alive I would kill Tony. That fucker tricked me into this whole scam. That's why he had faked the back problem. He was probably getting too paranoid about the whole affair. He wanted to recruit some idiot that would do the job for him without knowing it. I fit the job description perfectly.

That explained why the Vermicellis refused to fly back. They weren't afraid of flying; they just couldn't get by security. It also explained why the old fucker wouldn't let the bag out of his sight. He knew that if I found out what was inside that I would never agree to drive them back to Davenport.

How long had Tony been using this connection? I had always thought he was a criminal and this proved it. God, I hated Tony more now than I had ever hated him.

"Well, isn't this just grand? Stiff is a coke dealer," Nosferatu said laughing as he pulled the knife away from my thigh. "Who would have thunk it? It's brilliant. I must commend you, Faust. Who would ever suspect an innocent old man like him? You could actually tell a cop that he was a dealer and the cop wouldn't be able to stop laughing. It's just brilliant."

"Fuck off, I had no idea the old man was carrying. Christ, I'm not that stupid. It's his grandson who's the brains behind this whole scam. I'm just a dupe."

"His grandson? Oh marvelous. I'd like to meet him. He's an enterprising fellow. Say Grandpa, could you smuggle a few kilos up from the Keys for me?" The nut was beside himself.

"You leave Tony out of this," the old man snapped. "He's a good boy. It's my fault. He didn't force me to do anything."

"Yeah right," I mumbled to myself as I looked for the trooper once more on the horizon. He was gone and with him were my chances of getting out of this alive.

Beside me, a mass murderer was busy laughing up a storm. In the back seat, a Geritol-swigging, coke dealer was nothing more than a wrung-out, old dishrag. He sat there, nearly as lifeless as his wife, whimpering like a child who no longer has any energy left to wail. His life was over. He didn't need Nosferatu to end it. He had killed himself.

I wasn't doing too well myself. I was nothing more than a lowly pawn, quickly sacrificed by a greedy king. Tony had tricked me. Edgar had tricked me. Christ, even Gert had tricked me. They all knew about the drug smuggling and all had successfully kept me out of the loop.

The weight of the consequences was weighing heavily on my mind and I started to get religious, which is a scary thought. Was sending Nosferatu to us God's way of punishing us for drug smuggling? But if that were the case, he wasn't being very fair? I didn't know about the drugs. Why should I have to suffer? Maybe God was punishing me for being so indecisive about finding a job? About not giving a shit about much of anything. I certainly wouldn't have been in the mess if I had stayed home to look for jobs in Davenport. Was God punishing me for being a slacker, a snot-nosed malcontent who didn't care about anything but himself and the almighty dollar?

But I had never put too much stock into God or at least the concept of him or her or whatever. I agreed with Nosferatu that half the people didn't go looking for God until they were expecting a visit from the Grim Reaper. The other half didn't embrace God until they had spent a long time sharing a jail cell with someone named Cuddles or narrowly escaped death. Like I had. So, maybe this was a test by God after all. He had sent me Lucifer himself in the first place as a test but I, being so self-centered, hadn't recognized it as such. So he sent him again. He must really like me, otherwise he wouldn't have given me another chance.

What the fuck was I thinking? This wasn't a test from God and even if it was I was flunking it. No, this was just good, old fashioned reality and it was biting me in the ass like an ill-tempered rottweiler. God wasn't going to get me out of this jam. I was. All I had to do was put the pedal to the metal and catch up with that trooper. Fuck Edgar and his cocaine. Fuck Nosferatu and his awfully sharp-looking knife. I wanted to live, dammit. I wanted to live.

I slammed my right foot down on the accelerator sending the Cadillac rocketing forward like a shark moving in for the kill. All four bodies in the car were thrown backwards as that American-built road hog roared down the pavement. Gert's inert body fell against her husband who was shaken out of his stupor. Nosferatu's smile melted from his face again as I shot him a "fuck you" sneer.

"What the hell are you doing?" he yelled, jabbing his knife into the dashboard upholstery. Like a steely, violent St. Christopher statue, it stood watch over the Caddy's contents. "Slow down. That trooper is long gone."

"We'll see about that, shithead. I don't care about you and I don't care about Edgar. You can both rot in jail for all I care. All I care about right now is Numero Uno." I smiled and let out an evil cackle. "So fuck you," I yelled jabbing a finger in his direction.

Nosferatu wasn't going to stand for my insolence. He grabbed the knife with both hands and yanked it off its perch. Seeing this, Edgar, too, went into action. From somewhere deep in his gut, he summoned up enough energy to save the day.

The mad man took the knife in his left hand and planted it deep into my right leg. Incredible pain, pain like I've never felt before, shot through my entire body. I gritted my teeth so hard I thought I was going to break them like pieces of hard candy. Despite the pain, my mind drifted off onto another plain. It was sink or swim time. That trooper was my only help. Or at least that's what I had thought until I saw the old man lurch forward from the backseat and grab Nosferatu by the throat. He moved with such quickness that the pscyhopath was caught in mid-breath. His eyes bulged as the old man's bony, liver-spotted hands clamped down on his windpipe.

Go, Edgar, go. I knew he had it in him to strangle a horse with that damn deathgrip. Christ, my throat still hurt as I remembered how he had demonstrated his strength on me just a day earlier.

In a panic, the killer frantically reached for his knife, which was still stuck in my right thigh. I beat him to the punch however and quickly pulled it out of my own leg and tossed it into the backseat. I don't know why I didn't try to stab him with it. I wish I would have. But I didn't. I simply tossed it somewhere where he wouldn't be able to get it without first going through Edgar. In just a matter of seconds, the geezer had gone from being the top dog on my shit list to my knight in leisurewear.

"Keep driving, I'll take care of this scumbag," he hissed as he moved back and forth, deftly avoiding the thrashing hands of the blue-faced drifter. The old man was getting close to turning out his lights. With each passing second, Nosferatu thrashed even more wildly. It was all I could do to keep the car centered on the road. He was trying his damnedest to break free but the old man would not let go despite the fact that the drifter was connecting with several punches to his tired, old face.

It was as if I was watching some Charlie Bronson movie on late-night TV. Real life violence right here next to me. Blood gushing out of my thigh, turning my Levi's in to red jeans. Edgar's torrid breath rushing in and out through flared nostrils. Nosferatu's violent thrashing death dance, spit flying, eyes bugging, greasy hair flying.

How much longer could this go on? Would Edgar be able to steal his very life away? Would Nosferatu be able to wrench his body free?

Suddenly, as the old man pulled back on his victim, almost pulling him into the back seat by the neck, Nosferatu's left foot swung over and kicked my right arm, sending the Caddy careening over into the left lane, which was already occupied by a semi. I quickly jerked the wheel to the right but with too much strength. We were suddenly on the shoulder of the road, gravel flying all over the place, hitting the bottom of the Caddy like popcorn. The car was moving too fast on the soft shoulder for me to keep control. Before I knew it we were in the ditch and I still had that damn pedal on the floor. It was if I was either in shock or the psychopath had severed a nerve in my leg with his knife. I couldn't move my foot to slow down. We were blazing through the ditch tearing through waist-high grass like a combine on nitrous. There was no way I was ever going to get back up on the road.

As I struggled with the Caddy, I glanced over to see that the old man still had the killer by the throat, only the demon in the front seat was no longer struggling. It appeared as if Edgar had prevailed, though it was hard to tell, giving the fact that I was driving 70 miles per hour over soft, green earth and the old man was still gripping flesh like it was a baseball bat.

What happened next is still hard for me to believe even though I have relived it every night for the past several months. In a way I guess I could blame it on Angela but I like to think Tony had something to do with it. After all, he was responsible for half the shit that had messed up my life, his grandparent's lives and my sister's life. I guess I have the power to rewrite history by chronicling all of this so I will say that Tony put that cow there in that ditch but deep down I know it was those lovely folks from ARAT who are to blame. Evidence? I don't need any. All I know is that a dairy cow was where it shouldn't have been.

That's right, one of the cows they had released from Clayton Dale Tuleen's dairy farm in western Illinois had wandered for nearly 60 miles, avoiding the authorities with the stealth of a convict on the run from the state penitentiary. Those nice folks had set this cow free but unfortunately, the cow was too stupid to make the most of its freedom.

It just wandered along until it came to this spot along Interstate 74 and now instead of living a life of servitude giving its milk so that young Midwesterners could grew up with strong bones, it was about to have all of its bones broken by the front of a luxury sedan.

By the time the car plowed into the cow I had managed to slam on the brakes with my left foot, my right foot still frozen on the gas. It helped a little. Instead of hitting that cow blasting away at 70 miles, we were only going about 50. But it was enough to make instant hamburger out of old Bessie and bring the careening Caddy to a bloody, violent, accordion halt.

The rest of the accident I had to piece together by talking with state troopers. My head went through the windshield, knocking me senseless. Gert, who was already dead but who had not been wearing her seat belt was found straddling what remained of the cow. One crude trooper joked that it looked as though she was trying to fuck it. They never did an autopsy on her because they figured she just died as a result of the car crash. I wasn't going to tell them anything different because there were no other survivors to call me a liar.

Nosferatu, who wasn't wearing his seat belt either, was found on the hood of the car. He would have flown farther but the old man's hands were still clenched around his neck.

This looked particularly odd to the authorities. They thought Edgar and Nosferatu had become entangled somehow during the crash. The first trooper at the scene thought it was the most bizarre thing he had ever seen and said as much to the reporter from the Quad City Times.

"If I didn't know any better I would have sworn that the old guy was strangling the tattooed guy," Trooper Willie Durbando told the press.

Because I was in a coma for several days I couldn't tell old Willie that he was right.

So Trooper Durbando had a story to tell his cronies around the water cooler the rest of his life and the paper had some of the most bizarre crime photos they would ever publish. I kind of wish I had gotten a copy of one of those photos. I could have looked at it every time I woke up in the middle of the night screaming my lungs out. Nosferatu still haunts me. He will always control a portion of my life. He'll forever be hitchhiking on whatever dream road I'm driving down. I could look at the photo and prove to myself that the Devil was indeed dead and could no longer torment me. Along with teaching me never to a) pick up hitchhikers and b) talk to strangers, the maniac has taught me to take better care of my lips. He also, though I'm sure it wasn't his intention, taught me to believe in God. I still struggle with it daily, but after escaping the devil incarnate twice and living through a car accident that killed two people (or three if you listen to the state troopers) I do believe.

Well, at least, I'm trying.

Chapter Fifteen

"Matthew, Matthew." A voice. A sweet voice. Was it the voice of God? It was a woman's voice. Was God a woman after all? I had always figured she was a he. After all, if you were God who would you give the burden of pregnancy to—your own type or the other sex?

"Matthew. Matthew." That voice again. It wasn't God. It was familiar. After floating in never, neverland for three days, I woke up in the hospital with Angela staring down at me, looking all the part of resident angel.

"Hey," I whispered. As my dreamlike state drifted away I gathered in the surroundings and began to recall what all had happened over the past week, that is up until we bulldozed into that bovine. A piercing pain shot through my temple and I tried to lift my arm to massage my aching head but my arms wouldn't move. My God, I was paralyzed.

She gripped my arm to reassure me that everything was going to be all right.

"Take it easy, you've been through quite an ordeal." Her eyes worked on my like a shot of morphine. She was in her element. Angela must have inherited Florence Nightingale's soul. "The doctor said you'd be pretty weak when you woke up. Thank God, you've finally come to. You've been out for three days. Your voice is hoarse because they had a tube down your throat. You had us pretty worried."

"Sorry," was all I managed to say before drifting off again.

Several hours later I woke up again. I could see through the venetian blinds that it was dark outside. My mom was sitting in a chair in the corner of the room reading the Times.

"Anything good in there," I said softly, wondering if my mom would even be able to hear me.

She jumped out of her chair like a rabbit, sending parts of the metro section fluttering across the room. "Oh goodness, I've been waiting for you to wake up. Angie had said you woke up briefly around 2." She rushed to my side and gripped my left hand. I must not be paralyzed I thought to myself because I could feel her firm grip. Her boyfriend's workouts were really turning her into a Jackie LaLanne.

"What time is it now?" My throat felt as if a plumber had used a metallic snake to clear away a giant hairball.

"It's just after midnight. I've been here waiting for you to wake up since 6. I knew you'd come around. I should have figured it would be around midnight. That's you're favorite time of the day, isn't it? The witching hour. Time to party." She laughed half-heartedly.

"Yeah, we'll I don't feel much like partying right now." I couldn't move without pain shooting through my body. So I wasn't paralyzed, but every bone in my body felt like it had been snapped in two. "Am I going to be all right, ma?"

"Yes," she said, wiping a tear from her eye with a tissue she must have been mauling for the past six hours. "The doctor said you suffered massive head trauma when your head hit the windshield. And both of your wrists were broken when the steering wheel broke off. It was a pretty serious accident. You're lucky to be alive."

"What happened to…"

"Everyone else is dead."

Mom looked like she wanted to ask me about the accident, about the trip, about the stranger in the front seat, but she held back.

She nodded gently. "There will be plenty of time to ask you questions later. In fact, the police will want to talk to you when you're up to it. But there's no rush, they said. Just as long as it's before you leave the hospital."

The cops. What did they want? I didn't do anything wrong. I was just surrounded by wrong-doers. Then it dawned on me that as far as they knew it was my satchel of cocaine in the backseat, my major-league knife in the back and my gun under the front seat. I could see why they wanted to talk to me. Maybe they were just waiting until I felt better and then they would drill me for information. Maybe they thought they had captured one of Davenport's major drug dealers.

Yeah, right. Even petty drug dealers could deal more coke taking a nap compared to the penny ante amount in Edgar's satchel. What the hell was Tony up to with this little Florida connection? Was it just for his family or did he just want to make a few grand on the side? Maybe it was for his gambling habit. Whatever he was up to, it was strictly bush league. It certainly wasn't worth losing your grandparents over.

I was tempted to tell my mom to send the cops in right now. I would set them straight about the entire crash and all of the contents of the Caddy. I was going to screw Tony to the wall so tight.

Then, speak of the devil, who should barge into the room but my brother-in-law. Mr. Big Time Drug Dealer. Mr. Follow the Rules or You Won't Get Paid. Mr. Exploit Your Own Grandparents. Mr. I've Already Screwed Up My Family Now It's Time to Screw Up My Wife's.

"Yo, yo, whassup, my man?" Yes, indeed, it was Mr. I'm Hopelessly White But Would Like to Think I Have an Ounce of Funk Left in Me From the '70s and he was here to make my night.

He slid into the room like he had grease on his shoes. After kissing my mom and giving her a fake hug of concern. He turned his insincerity toward me.

"Yo, moms, this is just terrible what happened to your son. Man he be messed up."

"I can talk," I said, wishing my wrists weren't broken so I could box his ears. It was, after all, his fault that I was lying here.

"Yo, thank God for small miracles. Well, that's a start, my man. Say," he said turning to mom. "Your son and me all need to have a man-to-man talk here."

"It's after midnight. He needs his rest."

"Yo, yo, yo I know but I be waiting to talk with him for so long about da trip and my g-parents and all that but I've been so busy down at the office I just couldn't break away until now."

Mom stared him down with a warning look. "Don't be too long. He has to get his rest."

"I dig it, moms. We won't be long."

As soon as mom left the room, the smile melted from Tony's face. He turned to me and flicked my forehead as hard as possible. I was so doped up I didn't feel it but winced anyway.

"What the fuck was that for?"

"Shut the fuck up," he said in forced whisper. "I should just fuck you up right here. You're lucky you're not on a respirator or nothing cause I would be pulling the plug on you right now, motherfucker. Damn, you fucked things up something awful…"

"I fucked things up?" I said trying to keep my voice down. "Your little errand just about got me killed."

"Well, ain't that too bad. You can't even get that right. Figures that you crash the Caddy, kill everyone in the car and a motherfucking cow but you live through it. You should have taken the manly way out and got killed."

"Well, excuse me for wearing my seatbelt."

"Yo, yo, yo that's exactly what I be talking about. Wearing seatbelts is for pussies. Only you would think of wearing a goddamn seatbelt."

"Hey, wasn't it one of your rules?"

"Hey, keep it down, moms will hear us."

"Will you shut up with the moms stuff already. You're not black. You're pasty white just like 90 percent of this goddamn city. I don't care if you drive a Caddy, wear Fila sneakers, listen to Kool Mo Dee or whoever you fucking listen to, you're not black. You're just a petty hood."

"Hey, for your information I don't listen to Kool Mo Dee, motherfucker. It's the goddamn '90s all right?"

"Just get the hell out of here. You're stupid drug errand just about put an end to my short life."

"Shh," he spit out savagely. "Will you shut the fuck up? I need to talk to you about dat. As much as I'd like to beat the shit out of you for wrecking the Caddy and getting my grands killed, you kind of got me over a barrel with that drug thing." He paused to look right, then left, as if there would actually be someone else in the hospital room at midnight. "You gotta keep quiet about that shit. I don't know what grandpa told you but I didn't know nothing about no coke."

"If you don't know nothing about no coke," I said mocking his bad grammar, "then why do you know that there was any coke?"

Tony stared into space, as if someone had just whacked him upside the head with a rolled-up comic book.

"OK, OK. I knew about the coke but it wasn't my idea," he said grabbing both of my shoulders. "You got to believe me."

"If it wasn't your idea, who's was it? Edgar's? Gert's? Give me a break."

"All right, I tell you everything but you have to promise me that you won't tell Angela. Man, if she found out I was dealing drugs she would leave me in a heartbeat. You got to promise me that you won't tell her. Come on, promise."

"All right, I promise I won't tell her."

"You mean it," he said as his eyes welled up with tears.

"Yes, I mean it." I was too weak to actually cross my fingers behind my back so I just drew myself a mental picture.

"It was my homeboy Super Blackness' idea."

"I'm sorry. Maybe it's the painkillers that they have in me but I didn't understand a word you just said."

"Quit 'ya jackin' around. You know Super Blackness. He's my boy, my homey."

"Your homo, what?" I knew what Tony was getting at. I just wanted to piss him off.

"Man, I should just kill you right now. I didn't say homo. I said homey. Super Blackness, you know, Lincoln Washington. You know, Link."
Now, Lincoln Washington was a name with which I was familiar. I had gone to high school with his younger brother, Jefferson. Their mother was fond of presidents. Apparently, she thought by naming her sons after presidents they would have a better chance at doing something important with their lives. She was wrong. Lincoln, Jefferson, Roosevelt and Hoover all ended up to be losers.

Jefferson was the oddest of the brothers. He headed up a gang of brothers back at South High School called the Exposers, whose mission was to see who could get the most shocked reaction from innocent bystanders when they exposed themselves. Old ladies, nuns, infants. It didn't matter. They did not discriminate. For every person they got to faint, they would add another tattoo to their left forearm like an officer would add chevrons. Jefferson had worked his way up to a Colonel by the time we had graduated from high school.

I heard while I was off at college that Jefferson finally reached the ultimate goal of every Exposer—he killed someone. Not with his bare hands, mind you, but with his pecker. She was a Russian emigrant named Oksana Stanislov Pestrovich. Legend has it that the old woman was making her way home from the local Denny's when Jefferson jumped out from behind a lilac bush with his schlong in his hand.

Oksana's heart screeched to a halt before she hit the ground. It was never determined whether she actually died from the sight of Jefferson's significant member, he was black after all, or whether it was just the fact that a young black man had jumped out in front of her from behind a bush. Jefferson was sentenced to two months for involuntary manslaughter and two years for indecent exposure.

And now my brother-in-law was hanging around with his older brother, Link, who although never ran with the Exposers had been acquitted of several rape charges over the years. Apparently, the Washingtons were incapable of keeping their penises inside their briefs.

"Yeah, I know Lincoln. How did he force you into drug dealing, threaten to whip you with his Johnson."

"What's up with this homo thing you got going?" He said, raising his hand up like he was about to flick my forehead again. "It was Link, I mean Super Blackness' idea to get a little money stashed away on the side because I keep buggin' about being an honorary brother. You know, man, so I can roll legit with his crew. Be one of the homeys."

"Will you make some sense? These drugs make it hard for me to concentrate."

"I was only dealing the drugs that we brought up from Florida to Super B and his boys. Nobody else. They had a connection down in Miami who would swing by with the goods every spring before I brought gramps and grams up here. I would have done it this year but I thought Angela was beginning to suspect so that's why I came up with the phony story about my back. I figured you could use the dead presidents as well."

"You mean money, right?"

"Man, you so white."

"Look in a mirror, knucklehead. You're white enough to be in the Ku Klux Klan and not have to use a sheet."

"Shut the fuck up. I'm talking at you." He looked left and right again to make sure mom was not within earshot. "So I'd bring up the coke from Miami and sell it to Super B, who would then distribute it. Each time I would make $10,000, tax free. Shit, I've got $60,000 stashed away right now. But now it's all over because you fucked up." Once again, he looked like he was about ready to flick me.

" I'd think twice about flicking me again," I said in a menacing tone. "I can't feel it but I don't like it anyway. And the way I see it, you need to be extra nice to me now because I could spill the beans to the cops or worse yet, Angela."

It was true, I had Tony by the balls. He was in no position to get me angry.

"Man, you said you wouldn't tell Angela. You're a man of your word, ain't you?"

"Yeah, but I didn't say I wouldn't tell the cops. They know about the coke. In fact, they are waiting to talk to me about it." And probably about Nosferatu's gun that they likely found under the front seat.

"Yeah, I figured as much but that's why I wanted to talk to you. You the man, right. I'll up your commission. One cool G. Consider it combat pay."

"You're going to have to do a little better than that to get me to shut up. Christ, my mom's going to have to pay a deductible on her insurance for my hospital stay. And my body is pretty messed up. I won't be able to work for quite a while now."

"OK, OK, you little shit. I'll make it five grand but that's it. You know if I told Super B about you he'd just come up here with a Glock and peel you cap back. Bang." He popped that last word out of his mouth like he was popping a balloon. I saw the back of mom's head stir in the hall. She must have nodded off out there waiting for her "black" son-in-law to talk to me about the last days of his grandparents' lives.

Tony would have to take off soon but something was still eating away at me. He made good money running the aluminum siding business and scamming the good people of Davenport out of their hard-earned cash. Why did he need all of that extra cash?

"Peel my cap back, eh? I'll keep quiet but you still haven't told me why you needed all of this extra cash."

After he was sure mom was going to stay at her post out in the hall, he swallowed hard and answered. "Super Blackness said the only way I could really be one of his homeys was to get him that coke. It was a test to see if I was down. Well, I'm down all right. He also said if I really wanted to be one of the brothers that I'd have to actually become a brother."

"What are you saying?"

At this point, Tony was looking awfully ill, as if he was about to hurl. It was a side I had never seen before. He was usually so full of swagger he seemed invincibly even though every one knew it was just an act. Now, he looked drawn, tired, and confessional. "What the hell," he said in his normal white as Iowa voice. "I might as well tell you. I've told you everything else already. Maybe I'm turning over a new leaf or something. Maybe I'm kind of freaked about all the shit that happened with grandpa and grandma and you. You're an asshole but you're still my brother-in-law. The reason I was saving up that money and hiding it from Angela was because I planned to have some operations, man. To make me more like a brother. Kind of what Michael Jackson has done but in reverse. You know, penis enlargement, but just a little bit. I mean, I'm already man enough down there. I figured Angela would like that part." Jesus Christ, that's my sister he was talking about. "And I was going to get some pigment injections so my skin would look darker. I was also thinking about getting some collagen injections in my lips, too, but I don't know about that yet. That's kind of freaky, doctors fucking with your lips.

"I definitely was going to get some rump injections, too. You know so I've got a fuller ass. I've got such a flat ass. And finally, I was going to roll out a new name when I got all of this shit done. I was going to call myself, The Original T. You know like Mr. T but I was the first even though I wasn't the first but he's such a lame motherfucker with all of that jewelry and that mohawk."

"And do you actually think my sister would put up with this?"

"That's why it was a secret, man," he said, changing his voice back to the black bravado that I had grown accustomed to. "I know she wouldn't be down with it so I was going to get it all done and just come home, you know, all improved and shit and then she wouldn't have no choice, man. But it's not like she wouldn't get anything out of it, you know. I mean, she's your sister and all but every white woman fantasizes about being with a black man. Now she could have the best of both worlds, you know. I would be white but have all the good qualities of being a nigga."

I couldn't believe he had actually thought this all out. And then again, I could. It was Tony after all. Part of me wanted to start laughing and part wanted to cry. This moron was actually married to my sister. He might actually be the father of my niece or nephew someday.

"Good night," I said quietly, wishing this whole visit from Tony would vanish from my memory.

"What's up with that?" he said looking a bit hurt. I could care less if he was upset. The confessional was closing. He was so full of bullshit that it was starting to interfere with the synapses in his brain. He wasn't thinking straight. He actually wanted to be a black man. As if he lame-ass attempts at having some soul and trying to be down with the brothers wasn't bad enough, now he actually wanted to go to a cosmetic surgeon and mess up his body. And these types of doctors would fall all over themselves to cut him open and shove jelly-filled bags in his lips and up his ass.

"I appreciate all of your honesty. But I've got to get some sleep. I need to be rested up for when the cops come in here tomorrow." I didn't know that the cops would be coming in the morning but it sounded like a good way to get him out of my room.

"All right, I'm leaving, but you gotta promise me again that you won't tell any of this to your sister or da cops. You do and you can not only kiss the five grand good-bye, you can kiss your life good-bye because I will tell Super Blackness and he will personally see to it that you will be taking a dirt nap. Dig?"

"I dig, Mr. Original T."

For good measure, he hauled off and flicked my head so hard it was sure to leave a welt. But, thank God for painkillers, I didn't feel a thing. I only wish those drugs could take away the pain of having a black wannabe brother-in-law.

"I mean it. You talk and you dead."

"I understand," I said, closing my eyes. On the way out, Mr. Original T hugged moms and told her that I was falling back to sleep and that I should be left alone for a while. When he was gone I called out for her and she shuffled in, humble as a servant.

"Mom," I said quietly, fighting off the exhaustion that was quickly pulling me under.

"Yes."

"Could you do me a favor?"

"Anything."

"I'm going to sleep for a while. But could you tell Angela to come in tomorrow morning. There's something I need to tell her. Something very important."

"Do you want me to just relay a message to her tonight."

"No, it can wait. It's something I need to talk to her about privately, if you don't mind."

"I don't mind at all. I'll call her first thing in the morning. Good night."

"Good night, mom," I said, then drifted off to sleep with a smile on my face.

*   *   *

After I was released from the hospital, I didn't stick around Davenport for too long. It was rumored that Super Blackness had a contract out on my head. Even if it wasn't true, I didn't want to take the chance of bumping into Tony or any member of his family for that matter. I figured, I would either have to change my name and grow a beard or else I would have to leave my hometown forever.

Angela filed for divorce not long after I told her everything about my trip and about her husband's plan to become a black man. My information only put her over the edge. Divorcing Tony was something she had been planning for some time now, she admitted. She had done a good job of hiding her unhappiness but apparently my accident made her think twice about her life and what was important to her. Now she spends more time looking after her own feelings and less about the down-trodden. I've always loved my sister for her altruistic ways but now I love her even more. She loves herself more, too.

Now that Angela is out of his life, I am assuming that Tony will go ahead with his operations. His only true friends now are Super Blackness and his crew.

As for myself, I'm now living in Florida. When I want to see my family I meet them in Chicago or some place in between. I've been down here for over a year but I still haven't found my father. I figured that maybe if I met him and spent some time with him I would be able to figure out what I was meant to do in this world. Right now, I'm driving a cab in Orlando. It's amazing how much money you can make driving old farts and Japanese tourists to and from the Magic Kingdom. I guess my errand for Tony taught me one thing—I kind of dig driving. And meeting up with the occasional harmless freak makes life interesting.

When I am not driving the cab as part of my job I am cruising up and down the east and west coasts of Florida in it looking for dad. I guess I could just break down and ask my mother for his address but I'm afraid of how she might react. She might view it as some kind of betrayal. So I'll just take my time searching the Sunshine State for proprietors of nudists colonies. When I started on this haphazard search, though, I didn't realize how many nudist colonies there were in this freaking state.

I know dad is out there. I'll find him eventually and when I do I hope he can shed some light on what us Picassos are made of. Maybe he'll have some answers for me, because I sure as hell don't have any.

6459

About the Author

A native of Davenport, Iowa, Daniel Hauser now resides with his wife and two children in Minnetonka, Minnesota. Hauser works full-time as managing director of a public relations agency in Plymouth, Minnesota. He wrote this book bit by bit, while the rest of his family slept.

6459